W9-CDV-518

BECOMING BONNIE

BECOMING BONNIE

JENNI L. WALSH

A TOM DOHERTY ASSOCIATES BOOK
NEW YORK

BECOMING BONNIE

A Forge Book
Published by Tom Doherty Associates
175 Fifth Avenue
New York, NY 10010

www.tor-forge.com

The Library of Congress Cataloging-in-Publication Data is available upon request.

ISBN 978-0-7653-9018-9 (hardcover)
ISBN 978-0-7653-9020-2 (e-book)

First Edition: May 2017

Printed in the United States of America

0 9 8 7 6 5 4 3 2 1

For my husband, Matt,
for putting my dreams before your own.

ACKNOWLEDGMENTS

So, that happened: my first book is published. Cue blurry eyes. Thinking back, the whole process feels like it went by in a snap, but the reality is that many years went into this moment and many fabulous people helped to bring this crazy dream to fruition.

To my agent, Stacey Glick: This wonderful craziness is happening because of you. Thank you for believing in me, advocating for me, and officially putting author in front of my name. Building a career as a writer doesn't simply mean the world to me, but to my whole family.

To my editor, Bess "Champion" Cozby: Where do I start? It's been a complete pleasure to transform and polish this story with you. You truly championed this book. I wish I could add emoticons to fully illustrate my appreciation for all you've done for Bonn and me.

To Forge and Linda Quinton, along with Desirae Friesen, Jessica Katz, Todd Manza, and the talented Seth Lerner: Having you all is like having my own Dumbledore's Army. I'm so fortunate and blessed.

I'm very blessed to exist within the most wonderful book world: the Fearless Five, Kick-Butt Kidlit, my Debutante Ball gals, fellow Pitch Wars mentors and '17 Scribes, Binders, Hazel Gaynor, Lauren Willig, Summer Wier, Lee Kelly, Lindsay Currie, Isabel Davis, Kelly Calabrese, Camryn Garrett, Sarah Van Goethem, Amy Rolland, Bethany Crandell, Rachael Dugas, and Kathy Coe. A world of thanks for lending your eyes, words, brains, positivity, well wishes, support, or all the above. Also, thank you to Carissa Katz McCutchen and Jeff Abelson for lending me your creative brains and artistic skills.

To my real-life friends and family who realized this "book thing" was a big stinking deal to me: Your inquiries, congratulations, and genuine interest mean so much to me. Sending you all ginormous thank-yous and hugs.

To my new readers: Thank you for debuting with me. I sincerely hope you enjoyed Bonnelyn's transformation to Bonnie as much as I enjoyed writing it, and hope you'll pick up the sequel, *Being Bonnie*, to see how Bonnie and Clyde finish their song.

To Carolyn Menke: You aren't merely a staple in my publishing day-to-day, but in my every day-to-day. A million thank-yous for being an amazing book bestie and friend.

To my dad: You once likened being published to making it as a pro athlete. As a child, we always joked about me playing in the Olympics. I'm going to go ahead and count this publication as my first appearance in the Book Olympics.

Truly, this book wouldn't be possible without my husband and without my mom. Thank you, Matt, for making my dreams your own and also, time and time again, for doubling your domestic duties from half to all so I can put words on a page. And thank you to my mom for packing an overnight bag every Tuesday night (for over three years and counting) so Wednesday could be my kid-free day of getting *all the things* done.

To my three-year-old and one-year-old kiddos, Kaylee and Devlin: Every single moment of this publishing journey has been for you.

Last but not least, to God: Thank you for giving me a hunger to write and create.

PART I

SAINT BONNELYN

1

BUT I, BEING POOR, HAVE ONLY MY DREAMS.

Hands in my hair, I look over the words I wrote on the Mason jar atop my bureau. I snigger, almost as if I'm antagonizing the sentiment. One day I won't be poor with dreams. I'll have money *and* dreams.

I drop my hair and swallow a growl, never able to get my stubborn curls quite right.

My little sister carefully sets her pillow down, tugs at the corner to give it shape, the final touch to making her bed. "Stop messing with it."

"Easy for you to say. The humidity ain't playing games with your hair."

And Little Billie's hair is down. Smooth and straight. Mine is pinned back into a low bun. Modest and practical.

Little Billie chuckles. "Well, I'm going before Mama hollers at me. Church starts in twenty minutes and you know she's got to watch everyone come in."

I shake my head; that woman always has her nose to the ground. Little Billie scoots out of our bedroom and I get back to taming my flyaways and scan my bureau for my favorite stud earrings, one of our few family heirlooms. Footsteps in the hall quicken my fingers. I slide in another hairpin, jabbing my skull. "I'm coming, Ma!"

A deep cough.

I turn to find my boyfriend taking up much of the doorway. He's got his broad shoulders and tall frame to thank for that.

I smile, saying, "Oh, it's only you."

Roy's own smile doesn't quite form. "Yes, it's only me."

I wave him off, a strand falling out of place. Roy being 'round ain't nothin' new, but on a Sunday morning . . . That gets my heart bumping with intrigue. "What ya doing here so early? The birds are barely chirpin'."

"It ain't so early. Got us less than twenty minutes 'til—"

"I know."

"Thought I could walk you to church," Roy says.

"Is that so?" My curiosity builds, 'specially with how this boy is shifting his weight from side to side. He's up to something. And I ain't one to be kept in the dark. Fingers busy with my hair, I motion with my elbow and arch a brow. "That for me?"

Roy glances down at an envelope in his hand, as if he forgot he was even holding it. He moves it behind his back. "It can wait. There's actually something else—"

I'm across the room in a heartbeat, tugging on his arm. "Oh no it can't."

On the envelope, "Final Notice" stares back at me in bold letters. The sender is our electric company. Any excitement is gone.

"I'm sorry, Bonnelyn," Roy says. "Caught my eye on it in the bushes out front."

My arms fall to my sides and I stare unblinking at the envelope, not sure how something so small, so light, could mean something so big, so heavy, for our family. "I didn't know my ma hadn't been paying this."

Roy pushes the envelope, facedown, onto my bureau. "I can help pay—"

"Thanks, but we'll figure it out." I sigh at my hair, at our unpaid bill, at the fact I'm watching my sister after church instead of putting in hours at the diner. Fortunately, my brother's pulling a double at the cement plant. Ma will be at the factory all afternoon. But will it be enough?

I move in front of the wall mirror to distract myself. Seeing my hand-me-down blouse ain't helping. I peek at Roy, hoping I don't find pity on his face. There he goes again, throwing his weight from foot to foot. And, sure, that boy is sweet as pie, but I know he ain't antsy thinkin' my lights are suddenly going to go off.

"Everything okay, Roy?"

"Yeah."

That *yeah* ain't so convincing.

"You almost done here?" he asks. Roy shifts the old Mason jar to the side, holds up the earring I'd been looking for.

I nod—to the earring, not to being done—and he brings it to me. Despite how this morning is turning out, I smile, liking that Roy knew what I was looking for without me having to tell him.

"Ready now?" he says.

I slide another pin into my hair. "Why's everyone rushing me?"

Roy swallows, and if I had five clams to bet, I'd bet he's nervous 'bout something. He edges closer to my bureau. He shakes the Mason jar, the pieces of paper rustling inside. "When did you write this on the outside?"

But I, being poor, have only my dreams.

I avert my eyes, being those words weren't meant for Roy's. "Not too long ago."

"Ya know, Bonnelyn, you won't always be poor. I'll make sure of that."

"I know I won't." I add a final pin to my hair. *I'll* make sure of that.

"So why'd you write it?"

"I didn't. William Butler Yeats did."

Roy shoves his hands in his pockets. "You know what I mean."

I shrug and stare at my reflection. "It inspires me, wanting to be more than that line. And I will. I'll put a white picket fence in front of my house to prove it."

"*Your* house?"

I turn away from the mirror to face him. His voice sounded off. Too high. But Roy ain't looking at me. He's staring at the wall above my head. "Our house," I correct, a pang of guilt stabbing me in the belly 'cause I didn't say *our* to begin with. "That jar is full of our dreams, after all."

Really, it's full of doodles, scribbled on whatever paper Roy had on hand. Napkins. Ripped corners of his textbook pages. The top flap of a cereal box. He shoved the first scrap of paper in my hand when we were only knee-high to a grasshopper: quick little drawings of me and him in front of the Eiffel Tower, riding horses with dogs running 'round our feet, holding hands by the Gulf's crashing waves.

Our dreams. Plenty of 'em. Big and small. Whimsical and sweet.

But this here is the twenties. Women can vote; women are equals, wanting to make a name for themselves. I'm no exception. Sure, I'll bring those doodles to life with Roy, but I would've added my own sketches to the jar if I could draw. Standing at the front of my very own classroom. At a bank counter, depositing my payroll checks. Shaking hands with a salesman, purchasing my first car.

Call it selfish, call it whatever ya like, but after struggling for money all my life, *my* dreams have always come before *ours*.

Still, I link our hands. "I'm ready to go."

• • •

"Hallelujah!"

The congregation mimics my pastor's booming voice. The women flick their fans faster with excitement. Pastor Frank shuffles to the right, then to the left, sixty-some eyes following his every movement. From the choir pews off to the side, I watch his mesmerized flock hang on his every word, myself included. My ma is amidst the familiar faces. She prefers to use Daddy's brown hat to cool herself, holding on to him even after he's been gone all these years. I can't say I blame her.

"Amen!" we chime.

Pastor Frank nods at me, and I move from the choir box to the piano. I bring my hands down and the first chords of "Onward, Christian Soldiers" roar to life. Every Sunday, I sit on this here bench, press my fingers into the keys, and let the Lord's words roll off my tongue. Ma says Daddy would be proud too. I sure hope that's true.

It's another reason why I'll make something of myself. In our small town or in a big city, it doesn't matter much, but Bonnelyn Parker is going to be somebody. Wherever life takes me, whatever final notice stands in my way, my daddy will look down on me and smile, knowing I ain't struggling, I'm thriving. I'm more than poor.

I push my voice louder, raise my chin, and sing the hymn's last note, letting it vibrate with the piano's final chord.

The congregation shouts praises to the Lord as Pastor Frank clasps his hands together and tells us all to, "Go and spread His word."

Voices break out, everyone beating their gums at once. I slip off the bench, weave through the crowd. A few people are always louder than the rest. Mrs. Davis is having a potluck lunch. Mr. Miller's best horse is sick. He spent his early morning hours in his barn, from the looks of his dirty overalls.

Ma's got more pride than a lion and makes certain we're dressed to the nines, even if our nine is really only a five. Still, my older brother's vest and slacks are his Sunday best. And even though we've got secondhand clothes, my sister's and my white blouses are neatly tucked into our skirts. We may be pretending to look the part, but our family always gets by. We find a way, just like we'll make sure that electric bill gets paid. Though I don't like how Ma let this bill get so late.

I rush through the church's double doors, sucking in fresh air, and shield my eyes from the sun. A laugh slips out. There's my brother, playing keep-away from my little sister with one of her once white shoes. Buster tosses the shoe to Roy. Roy fumbles it. No surprise there, but part of me wonders if his nerves from earlier are sticking 'round. On the way to church, he wouldn't let me get a word in, going on nonstop 'bout the weather. I reckon the summer of 1927 is hot, real hot, but not worth all his fuss.

"Little Billie, those boys picking on you?" I call, skipping down the church steps, keeping my eyes on Roy.

He takes immediate notice of me, missing my brother's next throw. "Say, Bonnelyn." Roy wipes his hairline. "I was hoping to do this before church, but you were having trouble with your . . ." He gestures toward his own hair, then stops, wisely thinkin' better of it. "I've a surprise for you."

"A surprise? Why didn't you tell me so? I could've hurried."

He also wisely doesn't comment on my earlier irritation at being hurried.

"Follow me?" Roy asks, his brown eyes hopeful.

"Not today, lover boy," Buster cuts in. "Bonn's watching Billie."

Billie hops toward me on one foot, her voice bouncing as she proclaims how she's eleven and doesn't need to be babysat no more. I bend to pick up her lost shoe, letting out a long sigh. Roy sighs too. But Roy also looks like a puppy that's been kicked.

"Will the surprise take long?" I ask him. "Buster doesn't need to be at work for another two hours."

"Actually an hour," my brother says. "But Roy here probably only needs a few minutes, tops." He winks, and Roy playfully charges him.

My cheeks flush, and not 'cause Roy and I have done *that*. Roy hasn't even looked at me in a way that would lead to *that*.

"Let's go." I bounce on my toes and push Roy down the dirt-packed street, then realize I don't know where I'm going and let Roy lead. Buster's laughter trails us.

We go over one block, passing my house, nestled between the cemetery and the library. An old picket fence that Ma's been harping on my brother to paint for ages stretches 'cross the front.

Cement City is barely more than an intersection, and there ain't much farther to go; just the cement plant, a few farms, and the river. Then there are the railroad tracks, separating us from Dallas.

I glance up at Roy, confused, when we stop at a home just past the library.

He motions toward the house, his sweaty hand taking mine with his. He swallows, his Adam's apple bobbing.

"What is it?" I ask him. "Why're we here?"

"My father said they are going to tear down this old shack."

With its crooked shutters, chipped paint, caved-in roof, I can understand why. No one's lived here for years, and Ma doesn't go a day without complaining 'bout its drab looks and how it's bad for our little town.

I nod in agreement.

"But," he says, "I've been squirreling away my pennies, and I've enough to save her."

A cool heat rushes me, but I'm not sure how that's possible. I wipe a strand of hair from my face. "You're buying this here house?"

"I am," he says, his Adam's apple bouncing again. "For you and me. *Our* house." Roy keeps talking before I can get a word—or thought—in. "Bonnelyn . . ." He trails off, digs into his pocket. "Here's another one for your jar."

My eyes light up, recognizing one of Roy's infamous black-and-white doodles.

It's our church.

It's Roy.

It's me, in a puffy dress.

I look up from the doodle. It's Roy no longer standing in front of me but down on one knee.

"Bonnelyn Elizabeth Parker," he says, "I'm fixin' to take you down the middle aisle."

I knit my brows. "Are you proposing?"

"Well I ain't down here to tie my shoe."

I'd laugh, but I'm stunned. Marriage? With Roy? I swallow, and stare at the drawing, his lovely, heartfelt drawing.

Sure, marrying Roy has always been in the cards. *But* . . . I'm not sure I'm ready yet. Some people wait 'til their twenties to get married, in today's day and age, giving 'em plenty of time to make their own mark.

Roy taps the underside of my chin, forcing my gaze away from his doodle and down to him.

"I . . . um . . . I'm flattered Roy. I am. But we're only seventeen—"

"Not now." He stands slowly and palms my cheek that's probably as flushed as his own. "We've got some growing up to do first. I know you got dreams for yourself."

I sigh, in a good way. Hearing him acknowledge my goals relaxes me. Those jitterbugs change a smidge to butterflies. "You really want to marry me?"

"I do, Bonn." Roy leans down, quite the feat to my five-foot-nothin' height, and presses his lips lightly to mine. "When we're good and ready. You tell me when, and that'll be it. We'll create a life together. How does that sound?"

I smile, even while my chest rises from a shaky breath. I curse my nerves for dulling my excitement. My boyfriend declaring he's ready to build a life with me shouldn't give me the heebie-jeebies. It doesn't, I decide.

"We'll finish school," Roy says.

I force my smile wider.

"I'll get a good-paying job as a reporter," he goes on. "You can become a teacher, like you've always wanted. You can lead the drama club, be onstage, do pageants with our little girls."

Now my grin is genuine. "We're going to have little girls?"

"Of course. A little fella, too. 'Til then, I'll fix this house up. She'll be spiffy when I'm done with her, white picket fence and everything."

"You think?"

"I know it." He dips to my eye level. "You're happy, right?"

Am I *happy*? I roll those five letters 'round my head. Yes, I've been stuck on Roy for ages. He made me happy when we were seven and he picked me dandelions, when we were ten and he stopped Buster from making me kiss a frog, when we were thirteen and he patched up my knee after I fell off my bike. The memories keep on coming, and I don't want that happiness to stop. His proposal caught me off guard, that's all. But, yes, we'll make something of ourselves, and we'll do it together.

I lean onto my tiptoes and peck his lips with a kiss. "Roy Thornton, I'd be honored to be your wife one day."

He hoots, swooping his arms under me. Before I know it, I'm cradled against his chest and we're swinging in a circle.

I scream, but it's playful. "You better not drop me, you clumsy fool."

He answers me with a kiss on the side of my head, and then another and another, as he carries me toward my ma's house.

Freeze, I think. I don't want the secure way he holds me, the way the air catches my skirt, the hope for what's to come, to stop, ever.

YESTERDAY THE EXCITEMENT OF ROY'S PROPOSAL FOLLOWED ME home, Little Billie wanting to know every last detail, and today the hullabaloo stays with me as I slip into my corner of the library, my little nook where I disappear into the pages of a book. I love them all: stories of war, where passion and desire still bloom; tales of wild inhibitions and reckless romances; and one of my favorites, a novel of how a sultan's daughter leaves her life behind in pursuit of true love, of her soul mate.

I hold the worn copy over my heart and stretch my numb legs out from under me. Between high rows of books, there's no better place to daydream—'bout Roy. I'm surprised I didn't think much 'bout being his wife before yesterday. Maybe 'cause things have always been comfortable, moving ahead one day at a time, never disturbed. I figured I'd get to being his wife at some point in time. That doodle sure did the trick to hurry it up. I smile, I do, 'cause this is a good thing, marrying someone I've known my whole life. No surprises. Safety. Always there for each other, like the time Roy got his first scar.

We were down by the river, Roy swinging on a rope. He shouldn't have been. Roy is as nimble as a bull. A branch sliced him, without him even knowing it at the time. When Roy surfaced, a trail of red ran over his jaw, down his neck. The water was cold that day and I refused to go in. But when I thought he was hurt, I splashed in, fully dressed.

No point marrying a man you wouldn't catch a cold for.

I peer through a gap in the bookcase at the wall clock and sigh, disappointed it's time for work but also anxious to get there. During the week, Mr. Banks normally lets me work a twelve, but not today. The diner being slow means he needs fewer girls on the floor, which means coming in late morning, and that's costing me tips. Money I could be putting toward our overdue electric bill.

I drag my feet as I make my way to the door and wave to Mrs. Davis, who's bent over her desk reading a book, her oversize eyeglasses low on her nose.

Next door to the library, my bike leans against our shabby fence. Fixing my ankle-length skirt, I settle on the seat. It's not even noon and heat is pooling on the dirt road. The sun beats down on my shoulders and the hot dust kicks up each time my feet go 'round.

After I get going, though, the breeze feels nice. I lean my head back, letting the air cool my neck, letting my thoughts drift here and there. At the old tracks, I'm careful to look both ways before I cross. A little girl was struck here, not more than a few years ago. She was from the other side, Dallas, so our little town didn't know her from Jane. It's still plenty sad though.

Dallas is a lot more bustling than Cement City, with a population three hundred times our own. It's got big ol' billboards, buildings more than two stories high, banks, clothing shops, a theater, and more.

But us, we've got a physician's office, general store, and telephone connections building. Though that last one doesn't do my family a lick of good since we can't afford a phone. But that's it. That's Cement City. We don't even have a school. We go into Dallas for that.

The diner comes into view and I raise a brow. My best friend loiters outside the diner's alley door, smoking a cigarette. That's a first—Blanche being 'round back, not her dirty habit of Lucky Strikes.

"Blanche. What ya doing here?" I ask her, amused that she's standing among the trash cans in her fancy knee-high dress.

"Waiting for you." She puffs from her cig before flicking it, then scans her surroundings with a wrinkled nose. "Been here a whole hour. I can practically smell that old dusty book on you. Bet that's why you're late."

"You cannot. Besides, I ain't late." I slide off my bike. "Mr. Banks cut down my hours."

Hand on hip, she says, "Should've told me."

I ignore her and pull open the door to the diner, knowing the ever-determined Blanche will be on my heels and that my boss won't care. Mr. Banks waves hello from one of the kitchen's sinks, his expression lighting up like it does every time Blanche comes in. Although expected, I narrow my eyes at him; he must've forgotten again 'bout his wife and three kids at home.

Grabbing my apron from a peg on the wall, I get right to work. Blanche follows me into the dining room like a lost puppy.

"Okay, Blanche, what's going on?" I ask as I scour the row of tables by the window, all mostly empty.

"I need your help," Blanche whispers. "My pa's demanding that I start paying my own way. Or find myself a man to do it for me."

Well, I got myself a man. My news 'bout Roy bubbles up inside of me.

"But," Blanche continues, her nose scrunched up like there's a skunk nearby, "I ain't 'bout to narrow down my list of suitors."

I nod, expecting her to say something like that, and keep my mouth closed 'bout Roy.

Blanche bumps my shoulder with hers. "So I got to figure something out. Or rather, *you'll* figure something out."

Oh, Blanche. Ma always says Blanche runs wild 'cause she doesn't have a ma of her own. Ma also says I should show her the ways of a woman, which is probably the only reason why we're allowed to be friends. And probably why Blanche has come to rely on me so much.

"So what do ya say, Bonn? You're the brains. What's the solution?"

"Get a job," I say in a rushed whisper. I turn my attention to a couple settling at a discolored booth. "What can I get y'all today?"

I jot down their order: two Cubans, a Coca-Cola, a lemonade, and a side of fries.

Blanche doesn't stop her yammering. "Don't think a job and I would get along." She looks 'round the diner, with its checkered floor and mismatched chairs, with a cringe.

I smile to the customers before I leave their table. "Fine, then," I say to Blanche as I—we—walk toward the kitchen, "find yourself a sugar daddy."

Really, it's meant as a joke. Using a man like that is wrong. But Blanche nods, taking me seriously. "Thought 'bout it. I did. More trouble than it's worth. In fact, I reckon it's more work than a real job."

I scan the tables to see if anyone is low on drinks. "How so?" I ask, sincerely curious.

"I'd have to go juggling 'em. Playing house with only one man is nothin' more than a death trap."

And that, right there, solidifies why I haven't told Blanche 'bout Roy and me. I should want to tell her, but I'm not sure she wants to hear it. I sigh. "So, how is having a few sugar daddies different than having a few fellas?"

"Plain and simple, a daddy pays my way, even if I don't have his ring on my finger. And if I got more than one boy, I got to keep 'em straight and away from each other. Don't want to find myself in a middle of a brawl, now do I? Besides, I don't fancy being called a gold digger. So let's hear how you're going to fix this for me."

A man at a far table raises his pointer finger to catch my attention.

"Bonnelyn, focus." Blanche steps in front of me, her eyes huge. "On me," she adds.

I can't help but laugh, shaking my head in disbelief. "That customer needs my help more."

She looks over her shoulder at the man, says to me, "Wait here."

Blanche saunters toward Mr. Banks at the register, flipping open the top button of her blouse. Then she goes and props her elbows on the counter, leaning forward so her bosoms show.

I roll my eyes before grabbing a coffeepot and heading toward the patron's table. I've just filled his cup when Blanche grabs the pot from my hand, puts it down with a bang.

"Got ya a five-minute break," she says.

"A break? I only got here."

Blanche grins, pulling me away from the table. And really, there's no use resisting. No matter what way it's spun, Blanche always wins, and time and time again I'm left thinkin', *Oh that's just Blanche. Blanche is going to be Blanche. There's nothin' to be done.*

I reach for the coffeepot and apologize to the man for Blanche's rudeness. She sits down at an empty booth, gesturing for me to do the same.

I hesitate. Mr. Banks is cashing someone out, so I slink down onto the bench, hoping he won't mind me taking my five in the dining room.

"So what do I do?" Blanche asks.

"Like I said, get a job. I could see if Mr. Banks needs another waitress."

"First, no. Second, he cut your hours. I reckon he ain't hiring. Third, this place is in the butt crack of Dallas. No wonder it's slow."

"Good point . . . points." I hate it when Blanche is right. "There's got to be a job more suitable for Blanche Caldwell."

Her lips narrow into a circle. "I've an idea! Let's go on the road, start our own act. You'll sing with that pretty li'l voice of yours. I'll dance with this fine body." She shimmies in her seat. "Money problem: solved."

"You can dance?"

She snarls.

I laugh, and I'm 'bout to crush her dreams 'bout skipping town, when a boy—a couple years older than us, nineteen or twenty maybe, figuring by his grown-up suit—tilts his chair toward us from his table, his voice low. "Hello there, lassie."

Between Blanche and me, furrowed brows and subtle headshakes say a mouthful.

You know him?

Nope. You?

Can't say I do.

Damn. He's a sheik.

The last nod toward his sex appeal comes from Blanche, punctuated by a raised eyebrow.

The boy leans a hairsbreadth closer to Blanche, spinning a pocket watch between his fingers. "You looking for work, baby?"

He's lucky God's gone and blessed him with good looks. Otherwise, Blanche would've whacked him on the kisser for calling her that. Not that *baby* is derogatory, but it's something ya call a girlfriend, and Blanche Caldwell doesn't belong to no one.

She bats her lashes. I avoid eye contact, not certain this character is a good one to talk to.

"Depends what type of work you're offering," Blanche says, her voice a purr.

"I may know of something for the right lass, or *lassies*," he says, his regard jumping to me at the end.

I frantically shake my head, wanting zero parts of a conversation with a fella who looks like he rubs elbows with the likes of Al Capone.

"Go on," Blanche says, not sharing the same conviction.

He gets up, slips into my booth. I scoot away, distancing myself.

Lowering his voice, he says, "A new juice joint opened 'cross town, ya know? Been getting busy and the owner is looking for more dolls to serve drinks and entertain."

"A juice joint?" I ask.

Blanche's eyes go wide. "Shh." She returns her focus to this unseemly fella. "Bonnelyn here lives under a rock. Rather, cement."

He moves closer, his breath warming my face. "A speakeasy."

I gasp, from the fact those places are illegal, from the slickness of his voice, but Blanche rolls her eyes. "Bonnelyn here also has the morality of a saint."

"Well," the boy says, scribbling onto a napkin, "if you and Saint Bonnelyn are interested, I'll be at this address tomorrow night. Come at 6:23, sharp. Ask for Buck."

"That your name?" Blanche asks.

"No." He stands, throws a handful of money onto his table. I can't help gawking at how much he overpays for an egg salad sandwich. "But," he continues, "it's what my friends call me."

With that, Buck walks away, each step confident, as he tosses his pocket watch into the air, snatching it again.

Blanche's hand shoots out, grabs the napkin. She kisses it. "That boy has just solved my problems, unlike you."

"You can't be serious," I say.

She looks up from ogling the address. "Jeepers creepers, I ain't joking. Why wouldn't I go?"

I can't believe she's even asking. The nation's ban on alcohol is in full effect, has been for years. I answer, despite the ridiculousness of her question. "You get caught and you get pinched. Then your daddy will be bailing you out of jail."

"He could get me off with his lawyer-y ways if he wanted to." She slides the napkin under her brassiere strap and claps once. "Oh, Bonn, this is like from a film, or that book you read by that Fitzherald man."

"Fitzgerald," I correct.

She waves me off. "It's 'bout time Dallas caught up to all the excitement of the big cities. We'll be flappers." Her eyes grow bigger. "We'll be vixens."

"No, we won't," I say. "'Cause, we ain't going."

"Six o'clock works, yeah? To pick you up?"

My ears must've quit working. I ignore her, the same way she ignored me. "Your five minutes are up." I start to stand from the booth.

She grabs my hands, holding me in place. "Bonnelyn, everything will be copacetic. Blanche promises."

"I ain't going. What part of 'illegal, underground establishment' do you reckon sounds like something I'd do?"

She's quiet a moment, and I wait for her to agree, to admit this is crazy. "How 'bout this?" A wicked smile spreads 'cross her face—the kind that makes my lungs ache for air. "I'm coming to your house tomorrow night. If you're there, great. If not, I may just see if Buster Boy wants to take a quick spin."

I rip my arm from her grasp. "You stay away from my brother. You hear? He ain't a toy."

She pats my cheek. "That spitfire can take care of himself. He finds fun well enough on his own. But it's 'bout time we found it together."

And she's right. I know Buster would happily be her plaything.

"Out," I say, pointing demonstratively to the door.

She backpedals. "Fine. But I'll be seeing you tomorrow, Bonn. You can count on that."

Blanche slips through the door, but not before blowing me a kiss.

3

WITH BLANCHE'S THREAT LOOMING OVER MY HEAD, TODAY'S been one of those days where everything goes wrong. I caught Ma pouring water into the milk jugs to make 'em last longer; it was Roy's turn to work a double at the cement plant, so I didn't get to see him; Mr. Banks sent me home early from work; and then, when all I wanted to do was read a gossip magazine I borrowed from Blanche, Billie's hound was barking incessantly, wanting to get out of the heat. I hollered at old Duke to be quiet; then, not even ten minutes later, I found the mutt in the bathtub, with my sister pouring cold water over him.

Now Ma finally rushes into the house, frenzied, her cheeks almost as red as her Ruby Lipstick lips, grumbling under her breath how the factory kept her late with no overtime pay and how the bus was running behind. I'm 'bout to offer to help her with supper, but she pins me with a *Why aren't you working?* look. So I sit right back down and pick up my magazine. Go figure, the ink is smeared from the dog shaking off excess water all 'round the house.

For once, Buster is home, not scheduled 'til tonight at the plant so he can get the extra midnight-shift money. Him and Billie are playing Checkered Game of Life, looking carefree. Not me. My foot is tapping a mile a minute while I stare at the front door—waiting for the dreadful sound of Big Bertha's engine, of Blanche's car. Blanche showing up is inevitable, but I ain't going inside that *place* with her. Not going to happen. Those places are illegal. I shiver. Hotbeds for raids.

Ma calls into the room for us to get washed up for supper. Not long after I shove a spoonful of lukewarm Van Camp's pork and beans in my mouth, Billie goes off, proclaiming how excited she is for Roy and me. She keeps doing that and, each time, she makes me smile. Billie has an infectious way 'bout her.

"Your daddy would like how that boy turned out," Ma says, much more pleasant than earlier.

Daddy's chair sits empty next to me. Always five seats 'round the table, never four.

"Is Roy a lot like Daddy was?" I ask her.

Ma smiles, a distant look in her tired eyes, as if she's remembering. "Your daddy had a lot of spunk. Always after bigger and better."

Billie giggles, and I can't help thinkin' that sounds a bit like me. "Daddy was a hooligan?" my sister asks.

"Now, I didn't say that." But Ma has a grin on her face, like she doesn't mind his once rebellious ways. I'm grinning too, liking that Daddy pushed the limits now and again, keeping Ma on her toes. "Your father was a good Christian man after he got the rest out of his system. The gentlest man who's ever gone and held a shotgun."

"When am I going to learn to hold one?" Billie whines, and not for the first time.

"Soon," Buster says.

"Daddy taught you when you were younger than me," she counters.

"I didn't learn 'til 'round your age, Billie," I say, smiling at Buster.

Ma pipes in. "You'll learn soon, baby girl. Your daddy would teach you himself if he could."

I love hearing 'bout my daddy. I glance at his seat, picturing him teasing Billie, the same way he razzed me, for getting more food on her face than in her mouth. Even now, I see Daddy in Buster's narrow eyes. It's as if he's always squinting, always tossing a million thoughts 'round his head. Probably a million ways he can get himself in trouble. And if I don't do as Blanche says, he'll be out on the town with my best friend. She could even take him to that juice joint in my place.

The sound of an engine breaks into my thoughts. Blanche is here. We all know it's her, immediately, even Duke Dog, considering most people in Cement City don't have a car. That type of prosperity hasn't reached this side of the tracks. One would think it would've, with concrete being so popular, but that's the problem: competitive plants have been popping up all over the West. And we're left not being able to afford luxuries like vacuum cleaners or dishwashers.

Duke's barking rumbles 'round my head, adding to the fear already rumbling through me. Billie rushes from her seat to the front door and Ma hollers how she hasn't been excused, but it's too late for that. Ma merely waves her hand, not bothering to discipline my little sister any further.

Seconds later, Blanche appears. My sister always pouts and says Blanche and I, with our blonde hair, look like sisters more so than she and I do. I just remind Billie how she's got Daddy's dark hair and it puts the smile back on her face. A smile rivaling the one she wears now, as she's wrapped 'round Blanche's waist like one of those life preservers, Duke Dog bouncing at their feet.

"Hello, Mrs. Parker," Blanche says. "I'm mighty sorry to interrupt your supper."

"Nonsense. Would you like a bite?"

"Oh no, I'm more than fine." Blanche turns to my brother. "Hi there, Buster Boy."

She's more snooty than seductive. That's for my ma, so she doesn't get any ideas that Blanche is crushing on Buster. The arrogant part is for me. If I deny her tonight, she'll make good on her threat and put her vixen claws all over my brother. And, with how Buster is staring at her like she's the second coming of our Lord Jesus, she knows she's got me by the throat.

Billie doesn't help matters. "Blanche, are you taking Bonnelyn out to celebrate? Roy is stuck at the plant tonight."

"I sure am!" she says, not missing a beat.

Her enthusiasm for something she knows zero 'bout still creates electricity in the room. Ma beams, Billie squeals, and Buster drools a bit more. Duke Dog even barks once for good measure.

Blanche turns to me, and I reckon I'm the only one who recognizes the hurt in her voice as she says, "I've been wanting to take Bonnelyn out ever since she told me the good news."

Guilt goes and jabs me in the gut. Yesterday I should've told her 'bout Roy and me, but ever since Blanche's ma left her daddy high and dry . . . well, I didn't want her stomping all over Roy wanting to make me his wife. She'd lecture me, sayin' how we should be luring boys, not settling down with 'em. I figured I'd tell her, eventually, but Billie let the cat half out of the bag.

"Sounds wonderful, dear." Ma hides a yawn behind her hand. "Where are you two headed?"

"Most likely Victor's," Blanche says.

Ma smiles approvingly; ain't much trouble Blanche could get me in at a soda shop.

And there it is. My fate is sealed. I rub the base of my neck; it ain't helping to soothe me one bit. Round one goes to Blanche, in record time, and in this case her winnings include my wary company, not at a soda shop but at a speakeasy. A *speakeasy* . . . with its scantily clad women doing scandalous things with wicked men.

"Let me get cleaned up." I push back from the table with shaky arms.

Blanche grabs me, releasing a squeal that rivals Billie's. But once I close the door to my bedroom, Blanche's deep voice is in my ear. "You got some explainin' to do."

"In the car," I whisper back.

That mollifies her, for now. Too much, I'd say, from how she doesn't nitpick my choice of attire or the modest way I repin my hair. Blanche is simply quiet, sort of. She hurries me along, insisting we can't be late. Some of her anger fades when I begrudgingly comply.

Ma is waiting for us in the living room. "Here," she says. "Put your lips together like this." She puckers and I copy her. Then she slides her best lipstick onto my lips for the first time. "A woman who's spoken for should look her best. Touch it up after you've finished your soda."

I rub my lips together and force a smile for my ma, wanting a do-over of this moment.

"Perfect," Ma says. "You girls have fun, but don't be home too late."

"Yes, ma'am," Blanche and I say in unison.

We ain't in the car for more than a second when Blanche says, "Spill the beans."

I pause, letting my head fall back, and stare through Big Bertha's open roof. "Do you believe in soul mates?" I rock my head toward my friend, expecting her to scoff at the term. But her expression ain't mocking; it's cocky.

"Honey," she says, and slides on her sunglasses, "Blanche don't believe in anything or anyone, 'cept maybe herself."

It's a typical Blanche response—one where she speaks 'bout herself as herself. Most would find it weird, but I find it sad—for me. I may sing at church and school, but I wish I had the Blanche-like confidence to put myself on display in normal life. Or the gumption to say exactly what's on my mind.

Blanche puts Big Bertha in gear, lets out an exaggerated sigh, and starts driving. "Please don't tell me you believe in soul mates, that you think Roy is yours. I heard what your ma said, how you're spoken for."

I raise my chin. "What if I do and what if I am? Roy is plenty sweet."

"So are candied yams." Behind her sunglasses, she takes her eyes off the empty road, looks me up and down, and I shrink deeper into my seat. "You're just chasing that silly 'American dream.' Though I don't see no handcuff on that ring finger of yours. Did he give you anything? A necklace even?"

For once, smugness clings to my voice, as I sit up straighter and say, "A house. Roy gave me a house for us to live in one day."

Golly, that shuts Blanche's fat mouth right up. She just sits there tapping her lip, 'til that finger is pointing at me. "What ya got to understand, Bonn, is that it's all in the eyes. Lust. Passion. You and Roy don't ogle each other."

I cross my arms, focusing on the stretch of farmland between my town and Dallas. "I love Roy. You're just sayin' all this 'cause you don't like Roy, never have."

Blanche shrugs. "Let me ask you this. Have ya made him your Roy Toy yet between the sheets?"

Her question *should* shock me. Instead, I rub my face, careful not to smear my lipstick. "Blanche, I ain't having a bull session with you. What Roy and I do—*that way*—ain't any of your beeswax."

And it's mostly 'cause we haven't done nothin' yet, it being wrong to do that before we're married. But that doesn't mean we're lacking passion. Maybe I define passion as something more long term, a love like my parents'. Nearly a decade may've passed since Daddy died, but Ma loves him all the same.

She clucks before saying, "Well, if you're insistent on marrying the fool, I suggest trying him out first."

"Blanche," I growl. It won't help telling her I've had years of trying him out—in other ways. I know he likes more peanut butter than jelly. Blue instead of black. Dogs, not cats. We've spent nights at the picture house, afternoons by the lake. We've got history. And, thinking of our doodles, we've got ourselves a future. Ogling or not, we've got something stable. Love *and* stability. Ain't those two things better than only having lust?

Blanche laughs at my growl. "One of these days you'll quit being a priggish Mrs. Grundy."

"Stop calling me that."

"Stop *acting* like one," she counters. "You're such a wet blanket I'm surprised you don't leave a trail of water behind you everywhere you go."

"*Really?*" I say. "I ain't that bad."

She chuckles. "Okay, that was a bit of an exaggeration. But don't go denying you ain't tight-laced."

Blanche slams on the car's brakes, inches before the train tracks into Dallas.

I exhale, looking left, right. "There ain't a train coming."

"Glad to see your eyes are working." Then she smiles, a devious Blanche-like grin, clearly no longer in a tizzy with me for withholding my news—probably 'cause she doesn't consider anything related to marriage *good* news. "We got to get ourselves ready."

Ready. For the speakeasy. Talking 'bout Roy distracted me from *that.* I lightly touch Blanche's arm. "Hey, how 'bout we go to Victor's, for real."

"We will," she says.

"I meant now."

"Oh, I know what you meant, but it ain't going to happen. This is important to me, Bonnelyn, and you said you'd help."

"You didn't give me much choice," I say between my teeth—which are seconds away from chattering, and considering how hot it is, it ain't from the weather.

Blanche lowers her sunglasses and looks at me over their frame. "What was that you just said?"

"Um," I start, hiding a cringe from her glare, "there has to be another way for you to make some money. This just seems dangerous and reckless."

"*Reckless* is my middle name." She pulls something from the backseat. "Here, put these on."

I take the bag she shoves at me and hesitantly peek inside. Clothing. It clicks. That's why Blanche didn't care what I was wearing. She brought a dress for me. Nothin' new there; been wearing the clothes she's outgrown for years, 'til her clothing became less modest. But this dress ain't old. I shake my head in annoyance, pulling it out and letting its full length show. "Oh, no, no, no. This here's 'bout six inches too short."

"Gasp." Blanche pulls her blouse over her head and shimmies off her skirt. A plunging red dress—that comes well above her knees—is all that's left.

My jaw drops open.

"What ya think?" she asks, reaching into the bag, fastening a headband over her loose curls. "I wanna ooze sex appeal."

"I can almost see your crotch!"

"I'm sitting. When I stand, the dress will be longer. Maybe." She shrugs and drapes pearls 'round my neck, pokes something into my pinned-up hair. "If you won't wear the dress, let's gussy you up."

I peek at Big Bertha's rearview mirror and my mouth drops open again. "You've gone and put a feather on my head."

Blanche takes one looksee at me and hoots with laughter. "I do suppose you look a bit like a peacock." She tugs at my hair, removing the feather and letting a few strands fall onto my neck. "At least let down your hair. You got 'em all wrapped up like it's the nineteen hundreds."

I swat her hand. "Leave me be."

She chuckles to herself and slides a cluster of bangles onto her wrist. "All ready."

A few minutes of my nervous foot tapping later, Blanche stops Big Bertha outside a row of buildings. I'm no stranger to Elm Street in the heart of Dallas. It's the way to school, where I run most of our errands, and Blanche and I have been to the picture house and soda shop here on many occasions, Blanche flirting and me blushing.

I scan the paved street. Nothin' is out of the ordinary. No illicit bars, no unusual crowds of rowdy people. Many people are carrying on with their business, but no one seems to be doing anything illegal.

Blanche yanks the napkin from Buck from her brassiere and examines the buildings. Her brows scrunch. "Well, this here is a physician's office."

I release a sigh of relief. "Yup. Looks like the address is phony."

Blanche pouts. "You think Buck lied to us?"

"Probably. He seems like the type."

"Rhatz." Blanche throws the napkin onto the dashboard.

The door to the physician's office is flung open, catching both our attention. A man—no, a boy—saunters onto the sidewalk amidst a handful of people and peers up and down the block. I don't like the looks of him, with his dark gray suit, bow tie and vest, and hair parted down the center. Too smooth.

I cringe, knowing who he is. And I was so close to getting myself out of this jam.

"Buck!" Blanche squeals. She practically lunges for the car door's handle.

I instinctively reach for her arm. "You're really going out there? Doing this?"

She's baffled, like she's solving an impossible mathematics problem in her head. "Ab-so-lute-ly. Now get your ass in gear."

I can't. Not when my imagination conjures police fabricating out of thin air and swarming the building. I lick my lips and shake my head. "Blanche, I'm sorry. I can't. I ain't going in with you."

She sulks, staring at me. I expect her to drag me out of Big Bertha, but instead she twists in her seat, toward Buck. "Suit yourself." The motion knocks my hand off her arm. "But I need this."

"Blanche . . ."

I can't help picturing her arms pinned behind her back, Blanche being forced into the back of a police car.

"Bonnelyn. Stop."

I grab her shoulder despite her warning, and she pierces me with her determined green eyes.

Blanche is going to be Blanche. I know she ain't going to listen to a word I say 'bout this being dangerous. Or how there's got to be another way to earn money to make her daddy happy. I pull my hand back. "I'll stay right here in Big Bertha. If I see any funny business, I'll come get you."

Even as I say it, I don't know how—or even if—I could help her, but Blanche's face warms, and telling the lie helps ease my guilt from staying behind.

"Thanks, Bonn. Now, how do I look?"

I sigh, still not happy with her, with this, with everything. But an idea pops into my head. From my pocket, I take the red lipstick my ma gave me and tell Blanche to pucker up.

She doesn't say thanks when I'm done, but she looks at me—really looks at me—how she does every time I mimic my ma and do something maternal, something Blanche's own ma would do, if she had one.

Blanche steps from the car.

"Be careful," I plead.

"Always." She winks before skipping off toward Buck, his fancy suit, and the physician's office, her heels clicking against the street.

I'm left in the passenger's seat, praying to our Lord God I haven't made a mistake by letting her go.

• • •

Day turns to night as I sit here in Blanche's soft-top breezer while God only knows what goes on inside that physician's office. At first, the three-story building 'cross the street casts a shadow over me. As time passes, the square of darkness creeps away, inch by inch, with the retreating sun. Streetlights flicker on above my head, and tiny spotlights line the sidewalks.

People wander the street, in and out of the lights. I scrutinize them, my eyes playing tricks on me. A belt buckle becomes a policeman's badge. In the shadows, umbrellas become guns. A shout becomes a threat of a raid. Each time, I grip the door handle. But I know, pathetically, that's as far as I'll go.

Fortunately, the only folks actually out and about are plain ol' men, and kids 'round my age.

A few people come and go from the physician's office—a group of men, a group of women. But never men and women together. Most women are at home, tending to their families. I reckon that'll be me, after I become Mrs. Roy Thornton.

I startle, that being the first time I've referred to myself that way. The title causes mixed feelings, as if I've put being a wife above all my other dreams. But that can't be true. Roy doesn't even know I'm here, can't know I even thought about coming here. He's ready to settle down, not saddle up to a bar, 'specially with his daddy's alcoholic ways. I got to imagine the idea of me being 'round giggle juice would leave a bad taste in his mouth.

I close the roof of the car, needing something to do to busy myself. For the seemingly millionth time, I wish I'd brought something to read—not that I'd even be able to read the darkened pages. But holding a book always puts me at ease, knowing a happy ending is in between my fingertips.

Movement catches my eye, and I hold my breath. Buck takes another step out of the physician's office. I slink down in my seat, afraid he'll spot me. He scans, sees me through the car's open window. There's a jump in his step as he approaches, lighting a ciggy by the time he gets here.

"Well now, Blanche said you'd be hiding out in . . . Big Bertha." He says "Big Bertha" as if it's a question. "She's just using the li'l girls' room. Figured I'd come see your bonny face in the meantime."

I swallow, not having much experience with boys who ain't Roy, and certainly not with boys with red lipstick staining their collars. I settle for a nervous nod, leaning away as much as the seat will allow.

"Harmless inside the office, ya know." He blows a puff of smoke.

"I'll take your word for that," I say, finding my voice, albeit an uncomfortable-sounding one.

He laughs, a mix of nicotine and booze on his breath. "You *are* reserved. And that friend of yours is a bearcat. How'd the likes of you become friends?"

I shrug, feeling like a naïve little girl in comparison to my bearcat friend. Not sure why that bothers me a smidge. Her wild ways with boys—and life in general—shouldn't be something that sparks even the slightest bit of curiosity within me.

As if Blanche's ears are ringing from my thoughts, she stumbles out from the physician's office. I'm relieved to see her, even if she can't walk straight.

"Your friend there," he says, pointing to Blanche, "had a bit of giggle water."

His voice sounds as if he whispered it into a megaphone, coming out dangerously loud. I gasp, peering up and down the remarkably empty and darkened street, expecting those police to materialize and apprehend her . . . us.

But Blanche falling into Buck's arms is all that happens. Scandalously, she wraps her leg 'round him. Buck grabs the bare skin of her upper thigh and nuzzles into her neck. A high-pitched yelp escapes from Blanche and she pushes him back. I avert my eyes but still hear her say, "Watch yourself now. Better not leave a mark or my pa will have your hide."

"Blanche." I stare at the dash, dim under the streetlight's glow. "I think it's time for us to go."

I feel for the handle, intending to help her into the car, when her face is suddenly next to mine, leaning into Big Bertha.

"Not yet," she whispers.

"Now," I say, and wait for her backlash.

For once, it doesn't come. She turns into Buck's chest. "Saint Bonnelyn is making me leave." I don't have to see her face to know a pout accompanies her words.

Buck winks at me, and an uncomfortable heat surges into my belly. "Hopefully I'll see both of you tomorrow."

I shake my head no, but he's too busy giving Blanche's rear end a pat to notice. She giggles, laying another kiss on him before opening the door.

"Scooch over."

"To the driver's seat? You know I've never driven before."

She rolls her eyes, all the answer I'm going to get. It ain't illegal, I don't need a license, so I move over, despite my lack of know-how, desperate to escape. I swallow down my nerves and lay my hands on a steering wheel for the first time.

Blanche's words slur as she climbs into Big Bertha, right on through the window, and drops the key in my lap. "Ishkabibble. It's easy. Just pull out the ring thingy, turn the crank, retard the spark, push up the throttle, *but*," she says loudly, "not all the way up. Then, crank again, advance the spark, push the hand lever, more throttle, stomp the clutch, and go." She yawns and mimics rocking the wheel back and forth. "Easy as pie."

"Helpful," I mumble, and survey the shadowed levers and pedals, trying to ignore the drip of sweat trickling down my back.

Blanche smiles, but her gaze misses me, and her "Mm-hmm" response is delayed.

I jump at Buck's amused voice next to me. "I'll handle the 'ring thingy' and the crank."

He strides to the front of the car, laughing, no doubt from my reaction to him, and I like him even less.

He bends out of my line of sight. I've seen this part done before and can picture him giving the handle three swift turns. Priming the engine, it's called.

Buck comes back to me. "Shall I walk you through the rest, Saint Bonnelyn?"

I steal a glance at an unconscious Blanche and nod briskly, despite the nickname, despite not wanting his help.

"All right. This lever goes up into the retard position," he says, reaching for the closest one. "And this . . ."

I bite my bottom lip. His arm stretches 'cross me, dangerously close to my chest.

"Is the throttle. We want it up, but not all the way—as Blanche here said."

I'm not sure it's possible to press any harder against my seat. When Buck's limbs aren't inappropriately positioned in my personal space any longer, I relax.

He points to the dash. "Key goes there."

That I know, but I keep my mouth shut.

"Turn it left," he adds.

I do, and Big Bertha's coil box starts buzzing. I hope the annoying sound will startle Blanche awake. No such luck.

"Back in a jiffy." Buck winks.

I hate that he winks.

With one hand on the front bumper, the rest of him disappears behind the front of the car to turn the crank again. *Always use your left hand, never your right. If the car backfires, and you're using your right, it'll go and break your wrist.* I remember Blanche sayin' this before, in her know-it-all voice. Buck's head bobs into view as he gives the crank a yank, and the sound of Big Bertha's engine roars to life.

I jolt from the sudden rumble. The car shakes as if it's fighting back. Beside me, Blanche stirs, her foggy eyes peering 'round. A smile stretches 'cross her face momentarily before she drifts back off. I confuse her smile as being for me, 'til I catch Buck from the corner of my eye. His hand is reaching into the car again. He pushes the left lever down, and Big Bertha's angry rumble smoothes to a soft purr.

"Good girl," Blanche says, awake again, and she strokes the dashboard.

Buck looks at her with—what is it? Lust? Intrigue?

Whatever it is, it's enough to make me blush. After a lifetime of looks from Roy, none has ever been as heated as what I just witnessed. But just 'cause Roy and I aren't throwing ourselves at each other, it doesn't mean we're lacking lust, right? I lust plenty, deep down inside.

I shake my head, clearing the thought. "What's next?" I grudgingly ask Buck.

He flicks on the headlights. "You drive."

While he shows me how to use the clutch, reverse, and work the brake pedals, I release a slow, controlled breath.

"You'll be fine," Buck says.

"Yes," Blanche agrees. "No crashing, though."

I glare at her before following Buck's directions. Big Bertha bumps forward and Blanche whoops, pressing her hands against the vinyl roof for support. "Bye-bye, *Buck, I want to fu—*"

"Blanche!" I scold, tightening my grip on the wheel. She giggles. Buck laughs more heartily outside the car, a few feet back.

I slide the right lever down and our speed accelerates, faster, faster. Big Bertha sputters, and stalls.

My pulse spikes, and I mentally go through the steps again, flying through the directions in my mind, afraid I'll be too slow and Buck will be at my window again.

Big Bertha lurches forward. Slow but steady, I get her moving. I risk a prolonged blink, relieved to be leaving Buck, his speakeasy, and the threat of a raid in the dust. *Never again*, I tell myself.

Double-checking my surroundings, my gaze flicks to the rearview mirror, and there stands Buck, waving.

"That was fast," I say under my breath, while I maneuver a right-hand turn.

"What was?" Blanche slurs.

"You hooking Buck. You're normally fast, but that boy—"

A car's horn erupts in front of us and I swerve, nearly clipping Big Bertha's side mirror.

Blanche slaps her hands against the dash. She screams. I scream. My heart pounds and I mix up my hands and feet, pulling and pushing anything I can find.

Big Bertha groans in protest. Then the car's quiet. Perfectly quiet. I've stalled again.

Blanche bursts into laughter. "Well, that was close," she says, and playfully slaps my arm. "Oh, Bonn, this adds to an already exciting night. Did you know Buck's been arrested before?"

My head snaps toward her. "What?"

"How scandalous and delicious."

"No, Blanche. Not scandalous or delicious. That's bad. He's bad."

"He's sexy. Oh, and you know what? He has a brother." She winks.

I shake my head. How dare she suggest such a thing mere hours after I told her 'bout Roy and me?

"The brother's been arrested too," Blanche says. "He could be as equally scandalous and delicious as Buck."

"Blanche, just stop."

She snickers, and then goes on rambling 'bout Buck and the juice joint. I half listen, trying to get the car started again, trying to will my erratic heartbeat to calm, trying not to get caught up in her excitement of the lights, the energy, the music, the—

"The music?" I parrot. The mere thought makes me want to touch the ivory of a piano.

The car's engine begins to purr. Blanche puckers her lips and wiggles her fingers, making short, chopped noises.

"What're you doing?"

"Well, I'm a trumpeter. Ain't it obvious?"

I chuckle, despite the stern response Blanche deserves for her drunken antics.

"Perhaps *this* is more obvious to understand." Blanche leans forward, shakes out the bust of her dress, each bill falling into her lap. She grabs a handful. "I made a lot of dough tonight."

My eyes lock on the fistful of green in her hand. "You made all that in a couple hours?"

Blanche nods proudly, though her head wobbles. "My pa problem is no more."

I shove Big Bertha into a lower gear, the car moaning. We're silent for a few seconds while my brain tosses 'round thoughts. Having that money could do a world of good, taking care of our electric bill and then some, but . . .

"What'd you have to do to get it?" I ask her.

Blanche whips toward me, no doubt to lash out at the implication. She straightens, going stiff. "Bonnelyn, you're going the wrong way."

"No, I'm not," I say firmly. "I'm taking you home. I'll walk to mine." I don't care it'll take me all night and end in nothing but blisters.

"Nope, my pa can't see me like this. We're going to yours." She grabs the wheel, and my heart skips a beat.

"Blanche!" I knock her hand away, righting the wheel. "What in God's name is wrong with you?"

Her eyes may be cloudy, but they hold venom. "Bonnelyn, I'm getting fed up with you and your Bible-thumping ways. All your life you've judged me. You know what? Sometimes part of growing up is doing what ya got to do to survive."

I shake my head, puzzled. "What does nearly driving us off the road have to do with God?"

"I don't know, but I'm sure you can twist it somehow to make it 'bout Him."

"You ain't even making sense. What'd you do in that club tonight, Blanche? What are you doing to *survive*?"

"Oh, get over yourself. All I did was mix a few drinks. Much better than marrying a man 'cause I got nothin' else and 'cause I'm desperate to be with someone like my daddy."

"Excuse me?"

"You heard me. You got a daddy complex."

"What's that sayin'"—my fingertips go white on the wheel—"'bout opinions being buttholes? Everyone has one, most of 'em stink, and no one wants to hear yours."

"Well, lookie here. I got Mrs. Grundy to say 'butthole.'"

I roll my eyes. "It's not even a real curse."

"Well ain't that big of you, finding a proper way to insult me."

Blanche, I start, rehearsing in my head how I'm going to respond, *you listen here. You listen good. There ain't nothin' wrong with marrying a Christian man and making a household together. And there ain't nothin' wrong with wanting someone like my daddy. You talk 'bout surviving? Well, this is how I want—no, need—to survive.*

I press my lips together, the words slipping away. All I ever do with Blanche is rehearse, never truly standing up to her. I turn onto my street, exactly as she'd instructed me to do, and let out a long, low growl, Blanche's snore eating it right up.

MORNING COMES. SO DOES THE DISTANT SOUND OF HEAVING, and the memories of last night. Buck's wink. Blanche's outburst. My lack of an outburst.

But also the money that came tumbling out of Blanche's bust. The allure of the music . . .

I roll over, trying to leave the thoughts behind, but don't go far. I open my eyes to slits and stroke my little sister's dark hair.

"Blanche kicked me out of my bed last night," Billie mumbles into my shoulder.

I vaguely remember Billie climbing into bed with me. But last I thought, Blanche agreed to sleep on the couch. I lift my head, seeing Billie's rumpled sheets but no Blanche.

She's too busy getting sick.

"Better get her before she wakes up Mama," Billie says.

I groan. She's right. For being so young, Billie's often right.

I'm relieved Ma's door is closed when I pad into the hall. I tiptoe into the washroom and roll my eyes. Blanche is hugging the John like they're going steady. No doubt the longest any John has kept her fancy.

She rocks her head up, her face seeming as if it's melting off, from her smeared makeup. "I wake you?"

Hand on my hip, I add sternness to my voice. "What do you think?"

She cringes, a hint of vulnerability in her eyes. "At least I feel better now, right?"

I rip a towel from the rack, but hand it to her more gently. "Get yourself cleaned up."

A voice seeps into the hall from the living room, stopping me from flopping back into bed.

"Buster?" I shield my eyes from the sunlight streaming in through our picture window. "What're you doing awake?"

My brother normally sleeps all day after working the night shift at the cement plant. But no, he's sitting on the couch, muttering to himself, a scowl on his face.

"Can't sleep." Buster shifts, wincing. The arm of the couch no longer blocks half his body. His arm is barely visible beneath a bag of ice.

I gasp. "What happened to you?"

"That dimwit Kenney Rogers happened, on my shift last night; could barely keep his eyes open." Buster's forehead creases in anger, or pain, or both. "End result was my hand stuck between two slabs of cement."

I bite my bottom lip. "How long do you think 'til you're back at work?"

Buster shakes his head. "Thanks for the concern, Bonn. I was on my way to manager."

"Sorry. I am concerned." But 'cause the bold red text from our electric bill flashes through my mind, not 'cause Buster's promotion will be delayed. I don't think bringing up our overdue bill will help matters, so I say, "But we need you bringing in money."

"No shit. But what can I do? Foreman says I'm no use to him 'til it heals. Won't promote me, either. Says I need more time under my belt on the floor first." Buster mutters a curse, shakes his head again. "Ma went into the factory early to see if they have any extra sewing for her. I could kill Rogers; she already works herself too thin."

We all do. But we'll barely be able to get by on just Ma's and my salaries, even if she works more, and 'specially if Mr. Banks keeps taking hours from me.

"I'm having my hand looked at tomorrow," Buster says. "Should know more then. Here, open this. I sure as hell can't." Buster tosses a pill bottle, the rattling sound stopping as I catch it. "At least Rogers was kind enough to give me these beauties after bashing me up." He rolls his eyes, his last comment obviously sarcastic.

I turn, go to the kitchen to get him water so he can take what

I assume is pain medicine. My voice cracks, and I'm relieved my back is to Buster to hide the fear on my face, when I say, "We'll be okay."

I lift the faucet handle and my mind rushes, like the water into the glass, 'bout how that may be nothin' more than wishful thinking. How long before the lights turn off? How long before the pantry's bone dry? Do we have a month, a week, a day?

I hand Buster the water and a pill and slump down on the sofa next to him. At least I'm due at the diner later, and I'll be sure to bring my best smile to get my tips up.

"Roy stopped by," Buster says, leaning his head back and closing his eyes.

I take the glass from him before it spills and raise an eyebrow at the fact Roy ain't sleeping either, after working all night. "How long ago?"

"Just a few minutes. He's down the street at that old house he bought. Said to tell you to also come down, after you woke up."

"What's he doing there?" He mentioned he was going to start fixin' up the house, but right away? We still got a couple more years of school.

Buster opens one eye. "I had other things on my mind, so you'll have to forgive me for not playing secretary." He smirks. "Go see for yourself. I'm good here."

"Where we going?" Blanche struts into the room in one of my nightgowns, way too short on her. She's got gams as long as an old tale. Somehow, she's also perky as ever. "Hey there, Buster Boy," she adds.

Both of Buster's eyes are now wide open. He nods hello like a cool cat.

Blanche's hand flies to her chest. "Oh my, Buster, are you oka—"

I shove her down the hallway, trying to keep the lingering scent of alcohol that wafts 'round her away from my brother. "Buster will be fine," I say, tired of her antics. "Now, I'm off to see my *fiancé*, and you're going home."

Blanche frowns, pouts, stops short of stomping her foot. But she eventually heads on back to Dallas, not bothering to apologize for last night.

I quickly clean myself up, irked by Blanche on many levels. The secret drinking, the way she wrapped herself 'round a boy she barely knew, the openly mean way she spoke to me. My poor face is nearly rubbed raw by the time I'm done fuming and ready to leave the house.

Roy is leaning against the rickety fence of our new home when I spot him down the tree-lined road, his face pensive. Simply seeing him washes away some of my Blanche-fueled anger.

"There you are, sleepyhead," he calls.

"Sorry. Blanche kept me out late."

"Yeah, figured. Saw her car out front. What were you two—"

"What're you still doing up?" I ask first, and cringe internally at the bowling ball–size heaviness in my stomach. He's already got suspicion in his eyes, and I'm sure he'd be surprised—and not so jazzed—by *where* Blanche took me last night, even though I stayed in Big Bertha.

"Wanted to start on the house," he says.

"So soon?"

"Once summer's over, we won't have as much time." He pauses. "Ain't getting cold feet already, are ya?"

I force a laugh. "With this weather? Don't think that's possible." I jog the last few steps to him, wrap my arms 'round his waist, and press my lips firmly against his, willing passion like Blanche and Buck had last night to create a charge between us, to overwhelm me.

He kisses me back, his hands framing my face. A tingle courses up my spine and I press harder into him. I smile, leaning back to gaze into his safe eyes.

"What was that for?" he asks, his thumb rubbing circles on my cheek.

"Just a hello." *Just validation.*

"Well, hello. And hey, how's Buster?"

"Drugged up."

Roy runs his hands down my arms, intertwines our fingers. "Before, when I said I could help you out, ya know, financially, I was serious."

"Thanks, Roy." I gesture toward our future house. "But I think you got your hands full here. She needs lots of work." And I can handle my family on my own.

He studies my face, finally saying, "Well, I'm not afraid of a little work if you ain't."

"Not one bit." But that's a white lie, the okay kind to tell. Really, the house needs more than a fresh coat of paint. Termites have attacked nearly every inch of her, causing the porch to slump. The windows are cracked, the shingles—and the roof itself—are missing in spots, and huge chunks of brick are gone, leaving holes in the chimney. It's no wonder Roy's so quick to get his hands on her.

I sigh, turning it into a yawn when Roy notices. "Shall we get to work?"

Roy takes my hand and we do just that: get to work, heading to the hardware store for supplies. I walk the aisles aimlessly, randomly picking up thingamajigs and gadgets. I tap a wrench, or maybe it's a screwdriver, against my palm while Roy adorably purses and twists and bites his lips while deliberating on what we'll need. His face becomes grimmer, and sadly less adorable, each time he checks a price tag.

"Should've saved a few more pennies," he says. "Maybe we can try our luck in the stock market."

I rest my head against his shoulder. "Well, I don't know a thing 'bout that, but I do know Mr. Miller has some of these tools down on his farm, and I bet ya we can borrow 'em."

Roy's chest rises slowly, giving away his concern, but he offers me a reassuring smile. "I bet you're right."

"You going to know what to do with these tools, once you got 'em?"

He gives me a pointed look.

"What?" I hold up my palms, smirk. "Remember that time you tried to make a birdhouse and—"

"The birds were fine."

But he laughs right along with me.

We end up getting a few inexpensive items—a scraper thingy, sandpaper, and paintbrushes—for repainting the porch, an easy enough project to start with.

Roy heads home after that to get some sleep before he's due back at the plant. I hurry home to change before hightailing it to the diner.

I'm off my bike before the brakes stop it fully, and toss it against the diner's wall. Out of breath, and a few minutes late, I skid into the kitchen and snatch an apron.

"Bonnelyn," Mr. Banks says from behind me.

I close my eyes, willing him to go easy on me for my tardiness.

"Bonnelyn, come and have a chat with me."

I plaster an optimistic expression on my face. The way Mr. Banks arches a brow from the doorway of his office, I reckon my big smile and wide eyes look more crazy than positive. "Yes, sir," I say, and he disappears inside.

I shake my head at myself as I follow him into the office and tentatively lower myself onto a simple wooden chair.

"Bonnelyn—"

"I'm sorry I'm late, sir." In my lap, I bunch my skirt. "I swear, it won't happen again."

He runs a palm over his bald head. "We're not sitting here 'cause of that. In the two years you've worked for me, I can count the number of times you've been late on one hand. The thing is, we're slow. We've *been* slow. People are more interested in buying stocks than steaks."

I nod, and that bowling ball in my gut seems like it's doubled in size.

"Look, Bonnelyn, I cut your hours, but it ain't helping my bottom line like it should, so"—he stops, starts—"it makes the most sense to let you go."

It takes a moment for his cheek-slapping words to register. "Okay," I finally say, even though it's not. It's not okay.

"Go on out and finish your shift. I won't rob you of that."

I stand, an instinct from being excused, and my legs shake underneath me.

Mr. Banks gives me a sorry look. "I always liked ya, kid. If things pick back up, I'll track ya down."

I offer him my thanks and stumble out into the kitchen, then the dining room. It's exactly as Mr. Banks said: slow. Only a few regulars sit at the counter, and a single table is occupied by the windows.

My shift drags on 'til I'm clearing my last table and counting the few coins I made in tips. When I hang up my apron for the last time, my hand lingers, but not 'cause I'll miss it here. It's 'cause, plain and simple, this is *necessary* income, and there's not enough time in the summer to find a new job. Plus, Mr. Banks always let me keep working a few hours here and there, even after the school year had begun. It's harder to get that leniency in the nicer parts of Dallas.

The air in the diner seems too thin. I rush for the door.

But, on the way home, my mind keeps trying to steer me in scary directions: my family and I not even affording canned beans; Billie getting picked on for wearing rags my ma's sewn countless times; Buster's hand keeping him out of work all month. Losing the house. I tighten my grip on the handlebars.

Exhaustion hovers over me stronger than the August sun by the time I cross the tracks back into my measly town. It's like God is taunting me with each run-down house I pass.

I get it, I want to yell. *We're poor. We'll always be poor.*

I round the corner, and Roy's and my run-down house comes into view. Looking at it, all I see are dollar signs. I turn away, but a pop of yellow on the grayed porch pulls my gaze back.

Flowers, I realize when I'm close. I should be happy. But I ain't. Roy's heart is too big. He must've recognized the sadness I hid in my eyes earlier and picked me flowers, like when we were seven. I grab the note, expecting the soft loops of his cursive.

Nope. I'd recognize Blanche's chicken-scratch handwriting anywhere.

I messed up, it says.

Ain't that the truth.

Getting herself skunked, painting some boy red with lipstick, passing out and leaving me alone with him, then having the nerve to tell me I'm high and mighty.

What I am is levelheaded, a girl with a plan. I drop my hand to my side, taking Blanche's note with it.

A plan that's on its way to hell, with all that's going on.

What am I supposed to do now? Find a real, low-paying, low-skilled, forty-hour-a-week job and not go back to school? I can say good-bye to my teaching dreams. It'll be the beginning of the end, everything unraveling from there, 'til I'm not thriving or surviving.

Could Blanche really be the one thriving, making more money in a single night than I made in a month at the diner?

I start to turn away from my disheveled one-day home. My eye catches on the public phone outside the library. I stop in my tracks, lick my lips. Could a month be all I need 'til Buster is all healed up?

I stare at the phone and finger the coins in my pocket. Doing nothin', letting my future go to hell, maybe that's more dangerous than going to the speakeasy with Blanche tonight, just this once. One night of recklessness to make a month's worth of dough to keep us afloat.

Before the smart side of my brain taps me on the shoulder and screams how I'm acting a fool, I slip two pennies into the phone.

A nasally woman connects me to Blanche's house.

"Hello," I hear, in her singsong voice.

I wipe my sweaty palm against my skirt and reposition the phone against my ear. Seconds pass.

"Hello?"

"It's me."

"Oh." More seconds pass. "I messed up," Blanche says, again.

"It's okay."

"Really?" Her voice is low and soft.

"Yes, really."

"The fact you never hold grudges is one of your best qualities."

"Yeah, well, sorry for judging you. That's one of my bad ones."

"Yes, Bonnelyn, not the Christian thing to do."

I bite my lip, knowing if I don't do this now, I never will, but the telephone's slick in my grasp as I think of the simple words I need to speak aloud. A big breath helps. "I'm going with you tonight to the 'physician's office.'"

Seconds pass.

"Hello?" I say.

"This is Bonnelyn Parker, right?" Blanche laughs before I can respond . . . or change my mind. "Well, attagirl. You won't regret it. I'll pick you up."

The line goes dead.

I simply stand here, listening to the silence, 'til the realization that I'm going to a speakeasy tonight—for real—swoops in and knocks me upside my noggin.

I rattle the phone into its holder. *This* thought and *that* thought bump into each other, colliding, fighting, 'til a single thought remains: *Forgive me, Father, for I'm 'bout to sin.*

I WIPE DOWN THE ICEBOX WITH BOILING WATER. THE FURNITURE is in need of dusting. And the porch, sweeping. At supper, I chew my chicken thirty times, the proper amount for optimal digestion, and then I help Ma wash and dry the silverware to prevent stains.

I don't allow myself to think, just do, happy to help Ma, who might as well be sleepwalking after working all day.

"Seeing Blanche again?" she asks.

I nod, not looking her in the eye, and escape to my bedroom to get dressed. My hand is shaky as I paint my lips red and slip from my housedress into an equally modest skirt and blouse.

The blouse caught Roy's fancy one time when we were down by the river. He said the blue brought out my eyes.

The sound of an engine starts slow, then grows, 'til it rumbles outside my front door. I nearly trip over Billie and Duke Dog to get out of the house. Buster narrows his eyes like he knows I'm up to no good.

As soon as my butt lands in Big Bertha, I want to claw my way out, 'cause I *am* up to no good. Buster's right. But Blanche ain't; she was surely mistaken when she said I wouldn't regret this here decision. I reach for the door handle.

"Oh no you don't." Blanche puts the car into gear. "This'll be good for you."

"How on earth is going to an illegal establishment *good* for me?"

"You're a blotter," Blanche says matter-of-factly.

"A what?" My fingers slip from the handle and find the safety of my other hand in my lap.

"A blotter."

"*Blanche,*" I say between my teeth.

She laughs, so easy and carefree. "I'm not trying to hurt your feelings by sayin' this, but you only ever go surface deep. Dab, dab, dab. That's how you approach life."

Dab, dab, dab.

"But sometimes," she says, "life needs some elbow grease, a good scrub to get the dirt out." She shrugs. "Yet you're a blotter. Tonight is the first step to recovery, Miss Parker."

I stare at my best friend blankly. With all the dabbing and scrubbing, I have no clue what this girl is sayin', but, still, I insist, "I ain't a blotter."

She shrugs again.

"Well, what do you reckon *you* are?" I ask her.

Blanche pauses, her one eye squinting. Finally, she says, "Blanche is a misbehaver."

"Anything beginning with *mis* ain't good."

"Come now, how 'bout *mis*understood?"

I open my mouth, close it, pondering that word. It ain't necessarily good to be misunderstood. It's only good if you're finally understood—but then only if it's a good understanding. I rub my forehead, confusing myself, and silence falls between us.

Blanche continues to drive, looking mighty satisfied with herself. She even hums. At least understanding the way Blanche acts is easy. Maybe it's myself I'm failing to understand. A blotter? She says I stop at the surface, but that can't be true—can't.

I love and dream and believe.

I'm sitting in this here car, putting myself, and my relationship with Roy, at risk so I can keep loving, dreaming, believing.

"So why'd you agree to come?" Blanche asks, as if she's creeping 'round in my head.

I wring my hands, nerves spiking from head to toe. "I'm doing what I need to do to survive."

She smiles. "I've an idea. Why don't you really let your hair down tonight?"

Keeping one eye on the road, Blanche plucks pins off my head. I paw at my hair. Even with it heavy on my shoulders and running down my back, I feel exposed.

"And," she adds, pulling up outside the physician's office and setting the parking brake, "you *could* be a bit more hotsy-totsy."

"What?"

"Here." Blanche opens Big Bertha's glove compartment. "A few embellishments, so you ain't any old Jane."

She slides a glistening thing with rhinestones onto my head and a bangle onto my wrist—the one she'd worn last night. Sucking air through her teeth, she wiggles her fingers midair, deliberating. The pit in my stomach grows, taking on a life of its own, crying out, *This is a mistake.*

Like a snake attack, her hand lurches toward me.

I don't even know what she's done 'til I look down. My chest's in plain view for the world to see, peeking out from a tear in my blouse. My mouth drops open. No words come out. I reckon this is what having a stroke is like. I lean away before she can somehow tear a few inches off my long skirt.

"Ready?" Blanche says with a sly smile.

Blanche climbs from the car in a short black dress with silk stockings rolled just below her knees.

I suck in a Texas-size gulp of air, my rear end glued to the seat.

"Bonn," Blanche calls, "did I just hear your electric being switched off?"

I groan. Blanche trots toward the physician's office. Reluctantly, I follow, feeling like Alice going down the rabbit hole. 'Cept, I know how that story goes. Alice is a foolish, foolish girl. And here I am, acting just like her. All I need is my own Cheshire cat.

Blanche grins at me, teeth and all, and I peer frantically over my shoulder, through the wide storefront window, at Big Bertha. The car practically opens its doors for me to hide inside. I could sit there, all night, like before. Again, a book would've been a good thing to bring.

"Not going to happen. Come on," Blanche says, and grabs my hand, pulling, prohibiting my dreams of escape.

"What?"

"Oh, don't play coy." She pauses, looking 'round the quiet room. "This way."

The corners of the waiting room are dark, the area behind the reception desk even darker. It feels criminal to creep 'cross the empty floor after hours. With the doctor living upstairs, as they normally do, I reckon he gets sick visitors at odd times. But it doesn't stop this scratchy rawness in my throat 'bout how I should proclaim this as wrong and how the police may be lurking behind this chair, that desk, or in the closet by the window. Officers could come bursting through the panes and restrain me any second.

Sad, they'd say. *So much promise and potential going right down the drain.*

"Buck!" Blanche's voice is an octave too high, and I shrink at the noise, going so far as to shield my head with my arms.

He's sitting on a stool at the end of a poorly lit hall. Everything 'bout Buck—his posture, his clothing, his confident smile—screams gangster.

My muscles tense, my jawline taking the brunt of it. Blanche drags me down the hallway, passing doors to rooms where a doctor would visit with patients.

We stop in front of Buck, and I hold my breath, as if removing the rise and fall of my chest will make me less noticeable.

With scruff hiding his otherwise baby face, it strikes me again how Buck looks older than us, even though it's only by a few years. Yet here I am, with the drooping neckline, pretending to be someone I'm not . . . for the money.

I slowly release the last little bit of air in my lungs.

Buck greets us each with a quick kiss—Blanche on her red lips and me on my cheek. I tense again, biting my own red lip and not knowing how to act, not wanting him to touch me.

"It's hopping tonight," he says, and grabs the handle of a door, revealing a staircase. He starts down it. Blanche pushes me forward, leaving me no choice but to do the same. I swallow, hard.

She stays on my heels, forcing me from one step to the next, yet time slows to a crawl. Above us, a row of lights hangs from the slanted ceiling.

On the walls on either side of the staircase, posters and clippings in an array of sizes date back nearly ten years.

JANUARY 16, 1919, A MOMENTOUS DAY IN WORLD'S HISTORY: U.S. IS VOTED DRY.

My hand slides down the railing to steady myself.

ALCOHOLISM MEANS DEATH TO THE NATION. PROTECT OUR COUNTRY.

My eyes jump from one print to the next.

EAST SIDE, WEST SIDE, ALL 'ROUND THE BLOCK, THE BOOTLEGGERS BE RUSHING BIZNESS AT ALL HOURS OF THE CLOCK.

KEEP OUR MEN PURE. VOTE AGAINST THE SALE OF LIQUOR.

The fact that both Prohibition and anti-Prohibition posters paper the walls makes me dizzy, as if the drinking regulation is one big joke. But I ain't laughing. I'm struggling to hold on, agonizing over what awaits me below.

"Are these stairs the only way out?" I manage to ask.

Buck's deep voice echoes up the stairs, "Yup."

Behind me, Blanche squeezes my shoulder before I have a chance to retreat. The squeeze turns into a nudge and I steady myself with an awkward and noisy step. That's when the quietness of this stairwell, the physician's office, dawns on me.

Most would find glamour in its secrecy and exclusivity. Not me. It only makes coming to the speakeasy feel more reckless and dangerous.

Buck faces us, but his focus is on me. "Ready?"

No. But I nod, slow.

"Just do as Mary says and you'll be fine. She's the big cheese 'round here."

"Mary," I repeat. My knees wobble at the idea of there already being somebody to impress.

Buck grins and swings the door open.

Energy crashes into me. Over the roar of music and voices, I manage to hear Blanche squeal. She grabs the hand that's covering my chest and pulls me into the juice joint.

My gaze sweeps the cloudy room, and, at first, the details are lost on me. Cigarette smoke hangs in the hot air, stinging my eyes. I cough and wave my hand, straining to see a blur of faces and tables, a dance floor.

Chaotic motion catches my eye before a hue of red lights, beaming onto a stage, steals my attention. Three girls wearing mini top hats and equally mini silver dresses sing, the hypnotic music everywhere.

I spot the long bar as we come to it, as if it materializes from thin air.

"Here we are," Buck says, leaning too close to my ear. "I got to get back upstairs. Blanche, show her the ropes?"

Blanche swings a fake rope, her hip moving with the motion. On anyone else, it'd look embarrassingly pathetic. On Blanche, it's sexy. Buck eats it right up, whistling.

My head swirls as Buck returns to the door. I'm still not sure how I got from there to here.

"Isn't this the bee's knees?" Blanche asks.

"The bee's knees . . ." I repeat, fully knowing and understanding the expression, but too befuddled to do anything but repeat the sayin'.

"Hey!"

I jolt toward the sound. A girl with dark, short hair mans the bar. She drops below it, straightens again, holding a deep green bottle in one hand and a cigarette in the other.

"You here to work? Or gawk?"

"Work!" Blanche trots toward her, lifting a partition in the bar's tabletop, which stands in her way.

I pass through, grab it from her, holding my breath and closing my burning eyes as I slowly lower the partition. What am I doing here?

I open my eyes and am met with a sly, cool smile from the other side of the bar. It belongs to a boy with slicked-back hair, wearing suspenders over a light-blue shirt that brings out his eyes. Not high school age, but he can't be much older, by the looks of him. Handsome.

He smirks. "Say—"

I flee, not allowing myself to fall victim to what he says next, and rush to Blanche's side.

"Like you did last night," the dark-haired girl says, midsentence, to Blanche. "And you . . ." She surveys me, taking a puff from her cig. "You're no better than furniture right now. Why don't you start by clearing the tables?"

I stare at her like she has multiple heads.

"You go out there." She points with her cigarette-wielding hand to the cluster of four or five tables. "You bring the glasses back here. Think you can handle that?"

I nod.

"Good," she says, gently patting my cheek, the red tip of her cig coming dangerously close to my face.

"What's your name?" I blurt out, already knowing the answer. But it's like when I have a bruise. Sometimes I press it to make sure it's still there.

"Mary," she says, and I swallow again, already doing a poor job of impressing the boss. "Can you go get those glasses now . . ." She gestures toward me.

I say, "Bonnelyn."

"Ain't that cute. Now, go."

Mary is gone before I can say okay.

I exhale, trying to regain my composure. It helps that the boy with the confident smile is nowhere to be seen. I duck beneath the bar's partition, then hesitate outside of it. The room is more than a bit intimidating.

A grand chandelier hovers over the dance floor. It casts winks of light onto the wooden bar. I hold my hands out, turning 'em front and back, examining how shimmers of color dance over my skin. The red neon sign, spelling out DOC'S, acts as a backdrop for the stage. There, a man sits at a piano, his hands banging into the ivory.

The sudden high notes of a trumpet erupt in the room. A dark-skinned man breathes into the instrument, bending at the waist, a mirror image of another man with a saxophone. Front and center, the three girls croon into microphones, each swaying to the beat. For a second, I forget where I am and how the police could come barging through the door at any time. I softly rock from foot to foot. What a thrill it'd be to be onstage, creating the sounds that fill this room. Extraordinary, breathtaking. Sensuous.

My cheeks blush.

The dancing, if that's what it can be called, reddens my cheeks further and stops my feet from swaying. In front of me, arms and legs flail wildly. And no, it doesn't matter I'm not partaking; the act of watching feels sinful enough. Suffice it to say, there are certain places better fit for such half-dressed movements, and the government closed those houses down along with the bars.

The sweaty smell of sex—or how I'd imagine nookie would smell—wafts over me. I blow the thick air from my nose, but the perfumed, musky scent goes nowhere.

Me, on the other hand . . . I could escape upstairs. I'll run home, crawl under my covers, pretend this night never happened. Tomorrow, Roy will hold me, tell me the paint color he prefers for our walls, and I'll push away any thoughts of the betrayal in coming here.

Over my shoulder, I search for Blanche's familiar face behind the illicit bar. Only Mary's wide eyes stare back. She signals with those eyes and a quick tilt of her head toward the tables. Her simple command to get the glasses shouldn't be so scary. For years, I've been clearing tables at the diner—a job I no longer have.

Income I no longer have.

In time with the saxophone's roar, I shuffle forward, keeping to the outskirts of the room. A woman nearly knocks into me and I risk glancing at her. She flings her head back and her partner buries his face into her neck, kissing her.

I steady myself against the wall. The brick is cool to the touch, and I want nothin' more than to press my face against it, letting the coldness seep into me and numb the guilt swarming my insides.

But I keep moving forward, doing as I'm told. With each step, laughter and booming voices and music swirl together in the room, surrounding me.

I stop at the first table I come to, hesitating before I reach for a glass. A man drapes himself over the table, arms folding 'round a pile of poker chips. I'm sure they clink together as he drags 'em toward himself, but the room swallows the sound. Only his smug laugh and the other men's boisterous groans cut through the noise.

Quickly gathering glasses, I fill my arms and scurry to the bar.

Back and forth I go, in barely more than a daze, the hours ticking by. And 'cause I'm technically not the one mixing or serving the drinks, I try to convince myself being here ain't wrong. It helps I don't see that boy again, the one who smirked at me when I first arrived, part of me wondering what he was 'bout to say.

Each time I return to the bar, Blanche flicks her attention to me, beaming widely. This time she fills a glass, slamming the now empty bottle hard against the table. The men lined up at the bar raise their glasses and cheer.

The man Blanche serves next is a gross type—slick and gross. Wearing a fancy three-piece suit don't make you fancy—or at least that's what Ma says.

He reaches up, wraps a wisp of Blanche's blonde hair 'round his finger, but Blanche is acting cool as a cat, giggling and leaning closer. It's the tapping of her foot that broadcasts, to me, that she's unhappy with how he fondles her.

I avert my eyes, too uncomfortable to watch.

When I turn back, Blanche is pouring a shot of liquor. One is already filled, in front of me.

She nudges me with her elbow. "This here gentleman bought us some drinks." The shake of my head is automatic, and Blanche might as well be speaking French when she whispers, "Stop staring at it like I've gone and poured you poison."

A hand shoots out, grabbing the small glass.

Mary slams it down, empty. She puffs from her cigarette, scrutinizing me, blowing the smoke toward my face. "Take them glasses into the kitchen to wash 'em."

I oblige, going quickly, without another glance at Blanche or the disgusting man.

The back room is quieter and I release a breath. It's easy to lose myself in the simple motion of cleaning and rinsing the glasses, and I don't realize 'til a few minutes later that my hands move to the beat of the muted music, my fingers tapping against the glass as if against the piano's keys. My shoulders, though—they stay rigid.

"What are you doing here?" a sultry voice says.

I whip toward her, suds dripping onto the floor.

Mary steps closer, slipping her cigarette between her lips. The way she moves somehow seems seductive. Her clothing, her bobbed hairstyle, the tilt of her hip—everything suggests she has *it*.

Sex appeal.

Self-consciously, I brush aside my hair with my wrist, leaving soap on my cheek. I lift my shoulder to dab away the residue, feeling like a child.

"Cat got your tongue?" she asks me.

"I, um, Blanche brought me."

"Yes, but *why* are you here?"

I think of our unpaid bills. But I can't help thinkin' further off, picturing a life that'd make my daddy proud. I think of Roy's doodles and the need to support my ma. This here could pad my way, but now that I'm hiding out in the back room, thankful to be washing dishes . . .

"I . . ." I stumble over my words, not sure how to answer, not sure those reasons are enough to keep me here.

"In over your head," Mary says, reading me perfectly.

I nod, and honesty slips out. "I'm not sure this is the right place for me."

Mary releases a slow stream of smoke. "But it's right for me?"

"That's not what I meant."

"So you didn't mean to judge me?"

Judge her. The conversation is moving too fast, my mind too slow. I squeeze the slick glass tighter.

Mary leans against a table, locking her gaze on me. "So what's so wrong with being here?"

Now my mind races and I try to figure out whether or not the question is a trick. My voice shakes and I fall back on familiar words, reciting, "God says not to—"

"Let me stop you there. Instead of thinkin' 'bout what God says *not* to do, I reckon it makes more sense to focus on what he says to *do*. Ya know, like forgive and forget when naïve girls insult you."

I don't know what's wrong with me. I should stop now. I'm that naïve girl, flinging insults, but I keep babbling. "Well, God says to follow the laws of the land. Being that this place is illegal, you certainly ain't doing that."

She stares at me blankly, as if disinterested.

And my mouth goes on moving. "For there is no authority 'cept from God, and those that exist have been instituted by God. And therefore . . ."

I can't remember the *therefore*. This place, this girl, has me all shook up. My nervous ranting comes to a close. I stand here awkwardly, still squeezing the wet glass.

"I ain't much for authority." Mary shrugs, yawns, takes a drag from her cigarette. "Besides, you seem to be picking and choosing what you follow, too." She pushes off the table, sashays toward me, stopping inches from my face. "For tonight," she says, and slams a handful of bills onto the counter beside me. "But let me be clear. We don't need you. Plenty of pretty girls out there. I get the sense you need us, though. Let me know what the Man Upstairs says 'bout that."

Then she's gone, the volume of the music growing louder as she slips through the door.

I OPEN MY HAND, WHERE A FEW COINS AND A CRUMPLED BILL are left in my palm. In front of me, in all its pathetic glory, is my one-day home. At my feet, two paint cans sit unopened, ready to nice up our porch and fence. A few houses down, our pantry's stocked a mile high and a lamp shines in Ma's picture window—and will keep shining, for this month at least, now that our electric's been paid.

But what 'bout next month?

Taking a deep breath, I slump down, using the paint buckets as an uncomfortable seat.

Perhaps that's why uncomfortable thoughts—rather, Mary's voice from last night—gather like ants on a crumb. She's right 'bout me. I mixed right and wrong together 'til I found a comfy spot in the middle.

I lied to my ma, to Roy. I spent last night at the juice joint, telling myself it was fine 'cause I wasn't the one serving drinks, dancing, or letting men fondle my hair. I scratch my neck and along my collarbone. Then, today, I had no problem sneaking 'round while Ma's at the factory and Roy's sleeping off work, spending the money I made from an illicit juice joint, and now—I'll admit—I wish there was more of it.

No matter how bad Buster's hand turns out to be, I imagine what working another night, two nights, or more could do for us.

I could buy Little Billie new clothes so she doesn't get picked on.

I could ensure the lamp in our picture window stays on.

I won't have to drop out of school.

Only two days ago I asked Blanche, *What part of "illegal, underground establishment" do you reckon sounds like something I'd do?*

The answer to that question is suddenly a bit fuzzy, even if the idea of Doc's and of getting locked up behind bars still gives me the shakes.

With an unsteady hand, I pick two pennies out of my hand. Next door, at the library, I slip 'em into the public phone. There's that same nasally voice, that same hello from Blanche.

No sooner have I hung up the phone, it seems, than Big Bertha sits idle at my curb, and then I'm back in front of the physician's office, acting like Duke Dog chasing his tail. *What am I doing? What am I doing?* That same question circles in my mind, always coming back to how Mary was right 'bout something else: I do need Doc's.

"Don't be having a panic attack on me." Blanche inhales, blows out a puff of smoke. "I'll give you two more minutes."

'Til we go inside.

Blanche filled me in on how staff can enter at any time through a special door—the entrance for the apartments upstairs. For everyone else, there're rules.

Men and women can never enter together.

Never in groups more than two.

Only two groups at a time.

Only between the hours of five and eleven, unless you work at Doc's, then being there before five is preferred.

Men on the thirteens and fifty-threes.

Women on the twenty-threes and forty-threes.

That's a selective total of ninety-six people a night, not counting us staff. *Us staff.* I shake my head, not believing I've gone and referred to myself that way, yet hoping it can stay that way and Mary won't make me leave.

"God, Bonnelyn," Blanche says, with humor in her eyes. "Don't look so guilty, like we're 'bout to rob a bank."

Not looking guilty: an unspoken rule I keep breaking.

"Okay, let's go," she all but sings. "You've delayed enough, and I want to get inside before the next group arrives."

She takes a final drag from her cig. My wristwatch says 5:12.

If it weren't for the rules, and for Blanche, I'd hesitate. But she's already upset it's after five. I don't want to make us later or disrupt this well-oiled machine called Doc's. A layer of uneasiness already lines my stomach at the thought of seeing Mary again.

Of course, it had to be not only the boss but also the doctor's niece who I insulted last night with my high-hat morals. Something Blanche hooted 'bout on the car ride here. "High-hat" was her word, not mine. I'm going to have to do some major butt kissing tonight to get back into Mary's good graces and prove to her my worth.

For once, I welcome Blanche's vise grip on my hand, 'cause I'm not too sure I'd be able to move on my own. She yanks me toward Doc's. With the week halfway gone, throngs of adults crowd the sidewalk, looking to reenergize. And with summer dwindling down, normal kids—the ones not sneaking into a speakeasy—hover outside the soda shop, wanting to enjoy every last minute of freedom. One of those normal kids calls Blanche's name.

Blanche looks over her shoulder, waving wildly back. "Hi there, darling! Sorry, running late! Save me a soda."

Those few seconds are all Blanche spends on a girl named Hazel I ain't too fond of, from school. Two men pull open the door to the physician's office. We slip through the adjacent apartment door.

"Do you know where you're going?" I ask Blanche, eyeing the staircase leading to the second floor, and, off to the side, a single door.

"There're three or four apartments upstairs. But this door"—she knocks—"is a back entrance into the office."

The door creaks open and a boy's face stares back. It takes everything not to gawk at the huge mole on his forehead.

"Buck's girl?" he asks Blanche.

Considering I only see the back of her head, I miss her expression, but I'd say this fella should be counting his blessings that Blanche lets his greeting slide.

"And Saint Bonnelyn," the boy says, noticing me.

I want to shrink away. Nothin' in his voice is hard, but he comes off as a rough-and-tough bimbo. Even though he doesn't make me as nervous as Buck, his tone is enough for me to nod and not show any distaste toward the spreading nickname.

"I'm Raymond," he says, opening the door wider. "Ah, hold on."

He turns his attention to the two men we saw outside, positioning himself so he's blocking them from the basement door to Doc's. Blanche pulls me from the hall into the physician's office, and I press myself against the wallpapered wall.

"Here to see the doctor?" Raymond asks the men. Two more walk up behind 'em; 5:13's four-man quota has been met.

"Think we may have colds," one with graying temples remarks.

"The doc does honest work," Raymond says. "I assume you plan to be honest, too?"

The other man steps forward, keeping his voice soft. "We ain't pigs, if that's what you're asking."

Raymond stares at him, his face unflinching. His lips curl into a grin and he slaps the man's shoulder. "First ones here. Got the place to yourselves. Go on down."

After Raymond opens the basement door, the men gesture for Blanche and me to go first.

My second trip down the stairs is a different experience than the first. I smooth my already-tucked hair behind my ears and take a step down on my own accord. Last time, coming here could be rationalized away as a one-and-done thing. Now I'm choosing to go back. *Choosing.*

I open the door, and music hits me. I wouldn't be surprised if the upbeat tempo and rhythm blows back my hair. Being that Blanche convinced me to take out all my hairpins, it'd be a whirlwind of blonde strands.

I ain't more than a single step into the room, with its empty bar, its empty tables, and its empty dance floor, before Blanche chuckles next to me, bumping my shoulder. "Well, this ought to be your theme song."

"Why?" I ask, noting how the stage certainly ain't empty. I'm told the performers vary from night to night—one singer, two, sometimes three. Tonight is a single girl: dark skin, dark hair, dark dress, draped in pearls. She raises a gloved hand to say hello.

Blanche laughs again and swings her bent arms dramatically. "It's called 'When the Saints Go Marching In.'"

"You slay me," I say sarcastically. But then I turn more serious. "What's this type of music called?"

"Dixieland. New Orleans jazz. Hot jazz. It goes by many— Well, ain't he looking yummy tonight."

Blanche picks up speed. Buck is her destination, in his pin-striped suit. I suck in a breath; Mary is right behind him, coming out from the bar's back room. Having nowhere else to go, I follow Blanche. It feels like the four men from upstairs are following me, too, but that's only 'cause they're on their way to the bar.

Buck breaks his kiss from Blanche to greet me, his smooth hello somehow making me feel uncomfortable and two feet tall. Behind him, Mary shakes her head in amusement. When our eyes connect, her smile fades. She saunters over to the bar in her dress shoes and swishing dress without sayin' a word.

I wring my hands at Mary's snub and avert my gaze, which lands on my own satin pumps with ridiculously decorated heels.

"Looking good, Saint Bonnelyn," Buck says, upping my level of discomfort. "Wasn't sure I'd see your face again."

"My protégé," Blanche says, saving me from having to respond, and wraps her arm 'round my waist, pulling me against her like a doll.

My black pantsuit was a compromise. I didn't want to wear a shorter hemline and Blanche didn't want me to wear a long skirt again. Apparently, women's trousers are popping up here and there. Enough, anyway, for Blanche to allow me to wear 'em. She conveniently had a pair that she'd purchased the other day, in my smaller size, waiting for me in Big Bertha.

Not like she'd wear 'em even if they fit. Her sleeveless dress has layer upon layer of a fabric that moves with every motion she makes. "The right kind of glad rags for a night out on the town," she insisted on the drive here.

"You lassies okay working the bar and keeping the glasses clean?" Buck asks us. "We just made an alcohol run, so you should have more than enough for the night."

We both nod, Blanche a bit more enthusiastically.

"If you need me, I'll be back at the tables, keeping the games going. Mary will be 'round, too."

After that, we all get to work. By the end of each hour, eight more people have filed in. Before I know it, Doc's is at full capacity. Even though we stop letting people in at eleven, I've no doubt the party will be hopping 'til the wee hours of the morning, my deadline to impress Mary.

I clear the tables at lightning speed. I gather drink-mixing ingredients for Blanche as quickly as possible. I wipe down the bar top without being asked. And when my butt is squeezed and I jump, catching Mary's attention, I convince myself it's only a bump of an elbow—that can somehow grip.

On edge, I keep my head down, focus on the work.

That is, 'til a boy steps up to the bar—the boy from the other night, with the lopsided grin, who looked like he had so much to say.

"Gin Rickey, please," he says now, ignoring Blanche, his eyes narrowing in on me.

Gin, lime, sugar, soda.

Loudly, I set them out for Blanche to do the mixing, annoyed with myself when my hand shakes from the intensity of his gaze.

"No," he says to me with a cocky smirk. "I'd like *you* to fix my drink."

If Blanche wasn't so amused, I think she'd be mad at his brush-off. But no, she pushes the small of my back 'til my stomach bumps the bar. "Go on," she whispers into my ear.

I know how to make the drink, been watching Blanche do it all night, but I'm only seeing black spots where *Pour gin and lime juice over ice, top with club soda* should be.

There might as well be a spotlight over my head, the way they both stare at me, but I only have eyes for Blanche.

I don't want to do this, my eyes say.

Why, I swear she says back.

I widen my eyes farther, shocked she ain't seeing how this boy is gawking at me like he could eat me right up, and how that attention is wrong, coming from a non-Roy.

"Is there a problem here?"

Mary's voice. I swallow, my mouth too dry.

I tighten my hand 'round the bottle's neck, turning to her. "Not at all," I say, barely looking at her. "Going to fix this man a drink."

"Good," she replies, and disappears into the back room.

The nameless boy whistles from 'cross the bar. Arrogant. Self-satisfied.

Amused. Frustratingly attractive. If I were one to cuss, now'd be the time for it. I've spent the night trying unsuccessfully to meet Mary's unreadable expressions with a *Forgive my insults* smile, while working my rear off.

This boy ain't going to ruin it for me.

Swallowing a growl, I prepare his drink, pushing it toward him through the spillage when I'm done. Taking his money feels dirty, with how he licks his lips. His "Keep the change" feels even dirtier.

Then he goes and opens his mouth again.

"Excuse me," I say to him, to Blanche, to anyone in earshot, before he can speak.

With an empty glass in each hand and one tucked under my arm, I escape to the back room and close the door behind me, leaning against it. The subdued noise of the back room is a godsend. I don't want to think 'bout how that boy looked at me, in a way even Roy doesn't do—and this non-Roy has no right.

A voice distracts me, Buck's voice, coming through the crack of the office door. "So what are we going to do?"

"How much attention are we getting?" another man asks.

"Enough. My brother's heard of Doc's," Buck says, "and he hasn't been back in town long."

"Doesn't mean the police got wind of us," a girl responds.

It's Mary. I should leave. I want to leave. But the last thing I need is her hearing me and thinkin' I'm eavesdropping.

I don't dare to step farther into the back room, nor do I dare backpedal into the main room and let the noise seep in again. I'm stuck.

Buck comes into view through the slit in the door. "Look, all I'm sayin' is, when I picked up last night's order, I felt like I had eyes on me, ya know?"

"Is there any way to be more discreet?" the man asks.

I hear a clucking noise, and then, "What if I do the pickup?" Mary. "No one would suspect a woman to pick up bootlegs."

Buck laughs. A hand slaps him. The glasses are sweaty in my grip.

"It's not a bad idea," the man says.

"Not one bit, Dr. Peterson. But Mary ain't exactly known 'round town as the Virgin Mary. No offense."

"I'll do it."

It takes a beat of my heart to realize who just spoke. I'm not sure I truly believe it, 'til Buck's head whips in my direction. "Well, hot damn, Saint Bonnelyn."

But nothin' 'bout me is hot. I'm cold, right down to the bone. Denial hits me. I *volunteered*. And worse, I did so for the sole purpose of winning over Mary. All so I can keep an illegal job and spend its dirty money.

I take a tiny step back, my heels bumping the door, and one of the glasses slips loose from my hand. It shatters, and the office door swings wider. Mary stands there, mouth dropped open, before her lips curl into a smile.

Beside her is a man I recognize from a photograph upstairs: Dr. Peterson.

"Welcome to Doc's," he says. "Glad to have you on board."

Regret and worry shoot goose bumps down my arms. "God help me," I mutter.

7

THAT BOOTLEG RUN IS COMING SOON? WHO KNOWS WHEN Mary will tap me on the shoulder? For the past few days, I've been trying to keep myself distracted, falling into a routine: work at Doc's, work on the house, work at Doc's, work on the house. In between, *worry* wedges itself in.

Right now, it's work on the house, and I dip my paintbrush into the bucket, stroke the white paint down the sanded-down fence.

"Bonn? You all right? I think you got that part of the fence just fine."

I startle at Roy's words and turn, craning my head back to see the roof through the late-August sun.

Roy smiles. But it's not a lopsided grin. It's not a smirk. It's not laced with desire followed by a demand that I, and only I, make him a drink. I shake my head, clearing away the memory of Non-Roy from the other night, and glance again at the fence, where I've painted the same board multiple times.

It's a peculiar thing, worry. It can morph into paranoia or disguise itself as guiltiness, sometimes even creates doubt.

"Sorry. Got a lot on my mind." I pause and think of the update my brother gave me yesterday. "Buster saw a doctor."

"Yeah, he told me."

Broken in three places, a hand that's no good to the foreman—for months—'til it heals.

"Bonnelyn, I'll say it a third time. I can help—"

"We're making it work." I hurry my next words so he can't ask how. Ma already questioned me 'bout the pantry full of food, and I ain't sure she believed I had a gangbuster couple of days at the diner. With her working 'round the clock, she's none the wiser. "How's it going up there?"

Roy motions with his hammer to the roof. "So far, so good. This part is finally all patched up, and I only hit my thumb once."

"An improvement over yesterday."

He narrows his eyes at me, but in a playful way. Then he slides down the roof. I hold my breath, keep holding it while he not so gracefully scurries down the ladder.

"How we doing on paint?" he asks.

"Should be enough."

The porch is already shiny as new, and the fence is just 'bout done.

"Oh, good. I reckon Old Man Willard doesn't have too much to spare."

I scrunch my brows. Old Man Willard. Right. I lied, again, sayin' I got the paint from him in exchange for helping his daughter with her English homework.

"But we do need some things from the hardware store," Roy says. "You want to come?"

"She can't," Blanche says.

Blanche? I look over my shoulder, and there she is. Big Bertha is parked down the road at my ma's house.

Roy narrows his eyes again, but this time there's nothin' playful 'bout it. He and Blanche don't see eye to eye, haven't since she convinced me to pocket money from the offering plate for candy when we were seven. "And why can't Bonnelyn come?"

"Wouldn't you like to know," Blanche says.

"Blanche," I say, between my teeth. I touch Roy's arm. "I got to work soon." I conveniently leave out where. "Thought you did too?"

"So why is *she* here?" Roy nods his head toward my best friend.

My mouth opens, but no words come out. So I do something that could bite me in the butt. I redirect Roy's question, putting the much-deserved heat on Blanche. "I don't know. Why ya here, Blanche?"

There's amusement in her eyes, and it only makes me more annoyed.

"I know you've got work later and I got a hankering for some cheese grits. Figured I'd give you a ride into Dallas."

"How sweet. Could've taken my bike, though, like I normally do," I say. Roy doesn't look convinced, probably 'cause I forced the words out.

"What are friends for? I see you ain't quite done yet, though," she says. "And I ain't one to get my hands dirty, even for grits. Is Buster Boy home? I'm sure he can keep me company while I wait."

Roy rolls his eyes, then reaches for my paintbrush. "I'll clean up here. You go ahead."

"You sure?" I ask him.

"If you got to work, you got to work."

"I do," I say.

It's the truth, nothin' but the truth, but somehow it still feels like a lie. And there's that worry, that guilt again, jabbing me in the belly.

"Oh, and Blanche," he says. "You may want to lay off the cheese grits."

Blanche slaps her hip. "Boys don't have a problem with our curves. Ain't that right, Bonn?"

"Hey, you leave me out of this," I say to her. To Roy: "Don't listen to her."

"Never do," Roy says, but I don't think I'm the only one flinging lies.

I lean up onto my toes, peck his stiff lips. "I'll see you at church tomorrow?"

Roy nods and kisses the top of my head, his good-bye.

Blanche is already skipping away, having won. I follow, glaring at her back, but stopping for a second to watch Roy put the lid back on the paint can. Roy's good to me—too good. And I won't do anything to mess that up.

• • •

"I'm through with flirtin'," I sing along softly, lyrics that are constantly ingrained in my head, and grab a rag to wipe down the bar at Doc's. *"It's you that I'm thinkin' of. Ain't misbehavin'. I'm savin' my love for you."*

I set my gaze longingly on the stage. Sometimes I wonder what it'd be like if I ever had the nerve to stand up there, letting words pour from my mouth. To me, singing is the purest form of feeling free. My daddy said it's 'cause those words, those melodies, come from deep within.

Same with our hopes and dreams, he believed. Daddy talked big, always wanting the best. It's why he simply had to have our ma. I scrunch the rag in my fist, hoping my daddy wouldn't disapprove of where I've been spending my nights.

Blanche flits up beside me, bumping me with her hip. "Why the long face? You ain't still mad 'bout earlier, are ya?"

"Don't know why you had to open your big mouth with Roy."

She shrugs. "He's easy to get worked up. Couldn't help myself. Besides, I'm sure he suspects nothin'."

I scratch my hairline, not convinced. "He better not. Lying to him is making me all itchy."

"Please. I'm the one suffering. Can't get those cheese grits out of my head." She laughs, clearly dismissing her earlier actions. "Listen, I'm staying here tonight." Blanche points toward the ceiling, bouncing on her toes, barely able to contain her excitement. "Buck's got one of the apartments upstairs." I raise an eyebrow at her news. "So take Big Bertha to get home. I'll get her in the morning."

"Okay," I say.

"That's it?" Blanche fires back. "No condemning me to hell for staying overnight with a boy?"

"I've got enough on my mind without worrying 'bout the fate of your soul." And, really, she's been sleeping on my couch every night this week. A night off from Blanche duty would be nice.

"Fine by me." She drops her car keys on the bar, slaps my butt. I yelp. She laughs. "Hey, if Roy won't, I will."

I sigh and get back to wiping down the bar.

Not long later, I fitfully drive away from Doc's and pull the parking brake into place outside my ma's house. The lights are off, the night is quiet, the promise of a new day is only a few hours away. A day I hope doesn't include that tap from Mary. I wiggle out of my pantsuit, shove it under my seat, pull a more age-appropriate dress over my corselet, and take a long breath. The weight of keeping one foot in both worlds is exhausting.

Creeping into my house at two or three a.m. is part of the reason why. I slip inside, press the door closed, and step forward, then to the right, avoiding a noisy floorboard.

"Bonnelyn Elizabeth Parker."

I jolt. A light flicks on behind me.

I turn slowly, knowing the expression that waits for me: disappointment.

But *why* is what's important.

"Yes, Ma," I say, surveying the glimpse of her face in the lamp's glow. Dark circles hug her eyes. Eyes that are sad, as if she's been crying. She puffs on a cigarette, a dirty habit she picked up after Daddy died, as a way to comfort herself.

I lower my head, wring my hands.

"Where have you been?"

"I was working—at the diner."

"It's nearly dawn, so I know that's not true," Ma says from her chair, blowing out a puff of smoke. I try to respond, but she cuts me off. "Were you with Blanche again?"

"Yeah." I droop my head even lower. "We went to Victor's after."

"You've been spending a lot of time with her. More than usual. She's been here nearly every night this week." Ma narrows her eyes. "Are you girls staying out of trouble?"

"Yes, ma'am," I say, and hope to God her cigarette smoke covers up any lingering scent on me from Doc's.

She presses her lips tightly together, like she knows I'm up to something but is trying to hold the words inside. "With school starting soon, that behavior can't last much longer. You hear?"

I nod, my mind now spinning 'bout how I'm going to justify staying out late once summer is over. Ma knows the diner closes after the dinner rush, and we can't give up the money from Doc's, not with Buster in a cast up to his elbow.

"Is everything all right with Roy?"

That question rips Doc's from my thoughts.

"Yes, ma'am," I say again. "Blanche is just, um, having some problems with her daddy, so I've been with her a lot. Roy understands." Ma purses her lips before her face softens, and I subtly release a breath before yawning to fill the void. "I'm sorry I kept you up."

She waves her hand in dismissal, then grinds her cigarette into an ashtray. "I couldn't sleep anyhow." She meets my eyes again. "I suppose you'll be fixing up your house all day tomorrow? 'Bout time someone cleans up the neighborhood."

I nod, and Ma nods, her expression unreadable. Worry creeps in again, surfacing this time as paranoia, while I fiddle with a loose thread on my dress. I can't help but think she knows. She knows I work with Roy on the house every day to escape, to feel better 'bout sneaking 'round at night while he's slaving away at the plant.

I wonder if she'd accept my rationale: the world we live in today gives me little choice but to mix up right and wrong, doing what I got to do to get by.

I shift toward the hall, wanting to get away from the speculation I fabricate in my ma's eyes. "Well, good night," I whisper.

"He stopped by, Roy did," my ma says, and I pause with my back to her, my hands clenching my dress.

"Why? I saw him earlier today. What'd he want?"

"He went by the diner, looking for you. You weren't there, so he came here."

I face my ma, hoping my expression doesn't give away that I'm a big, fat liar. "Oh, he must've just missed me."

Ma pushes up from her chair. Her arms quiver and I leap forward, reaching for her. She waves her hand again to dismiss me. "I'm fine. Just been sitting here awhile."

I help her anyway, leading her to her room.

"Don't forget to say your prayers," she says, and tucks a strand of hair behind my ears. "And get some sleep. You look like you've been working yourself too hard."

She kisses my forehead before slipping into her bedroom. I creep into my own, careful not to wake Little Billie. In bed, I pull the covers to my chin, despite the stuffiness of the room. I *am* working too hard, trying to stifle all this damn, relentless worry. It's enough to make a girl do crazy things, so help me God.

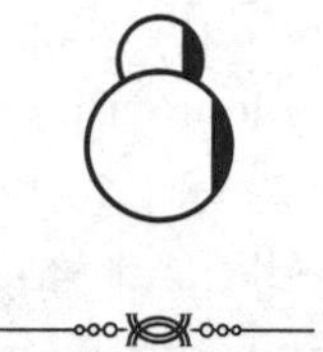

"*FORGIVENESS COMES IN ALL FORMS,*" I SING AT CHURCH IN THE morning, trying to make eye contact with no one and everyone in the boisterous congregation. Between verses, so many breathe in at once that it's hard to believe any hot air is left in the chapel.

Or maybe this doomy feeling of suffocation is left over from last night, from this whole week.

My voice falters. I look down at my hymnbook to find my spot, happy it's not my turn at the piano, then look back up, singing more loudly. My eyes fall on Roy, his parents, and my family, in the same pews as always. Ma's tired. Probably 'cause of me. Roy's face is complacent, like I don't know if he's happy or unhappy. 'Cause of me?

"*Repent, and set yourself free,*" I sing in an uneven voice. Old Woman Myers glances at me from the corner of her eye. I ignore her, my practiced gaze returning to my family.

This time, Roy's attention is on me. Heat travels down my neck, like I've been caught doing something bad, like I got caught *not* being at the diner. Between breaths, I force a smile, willing him not to be upset with me. He tugs on his collar, looks away.

I sing louder, staring at the clefs and notes on the page. I belt out the last word, forcing my voice stronger. When the hymn comes to an end, I sink into my seat, welcoming the reprieve from the feeling like I'm standing in a trial box instead of a choir box.

Pastor Frank offers the congregation his parting words, signaling the service's close.

Right now, I know a few things 'bout this afternoon: Ma is working. Buster is hunting ducks with friends, though I can't understand how he can do *that* but not work. Billie is going to a friend's. Roy is off to the plant. None of them are expecting to see me after church.

I look over my shoulder toward the chapel's back door, knowing something else: the line at the front door will be a mile long. That line could mean bumping into Roy and having to lie—in a church—'bout why I wasn't at the diner last night. All thanks to Blanche and her big mouth.

I frantically weave through the crowd, toward the back exit, knocking into people and muttering apologies as I go. I'm relieved that the town's largest oak tree stretches over the church, when I burst outside into its comforting shade. I quickly slip from one tree's cover to the next, hugging the edges of properties to stay out of sight. I nearly roll my eyes at my own dramatics.

You've lost it, I tell myself. *Doggone crazy for escaping like that today.*

I shake my head, 'cause really I'm doggone crazy for escaping every day this week. Doesn't matter who it's from—my ma, Little Billie, Buster, my nagging thoughts—I'm acting like a loon. The destination is always the same: Roy's and my one-day home.

Being that Roy's normally at my side, he's the only person I can't escape. I stop, hand on the doorknob of our house. 'Til this here very moment, I never allowed myself to think it . . . that Roy is someone I've wanted to escape, too.

Shame escorts me inside the four walls.

My hand flies to my chest. "Roy, what're you doing here?"

"I'm here every day," he says coolly, his expression unreadable.

"But . . . I thought you had to work?"

"Yeah, well, I thought you had to work last night."

I choose my words carefully. "And that's nothin' but the truth. I was just done at the diner by the time you came by."

Roy crosses his arms and I fight the urge to tug at my neckline.

"Look, Blanche has had a rough go of it lately with her daddy." I pick up a brush from a bucket and mindlessly rub my hand over the bristles.

"She's been sleeping on my couch all week. Guess my ma didn't tell you that part."

His headshake is subtle, but his annoyance is not. "I don't like you spending so much time with that girl."

Blanche. I groan internally and squeeze the brush's handle. Her shenanigans yesterday certainly ain't helping me now. "She's harmless, you know that."

"Do I?"

"Roy, come on." I soften my voice. "You ain't mad, are you?" I promptly bite my bottom lip.

He stares into the bucket as if he's searching for something to say. But I count my blessings when he only says, "I'll get you some water."

Off he goes with the bucket, the type of boy whose actions are stronger than his words. Chances are, he's still running things through his head as he brings back the bucket and heads to work, but at least I ain't in his crosshairs while he's doing it. Bet ya Blanche is.

Can't blame him. As I'm scrubbing the floor, I keep grumbling her name, too.

Blanche, who put me in the position of having to sneak 'round and lie to my ma in the first place. Blanche, who not only makes me question my passion for—and really, my whole relationship with—Roy, but also puts me in situations where I have to keep secrets from him. Secrets she almost blabs, making Roy feel the need to stop by the diner, to do what? Check on me? Then here he was, minutes ago, ambushing me for answers. Blanche, who uses stupid words like *blotter* and *dab, dab, dab.*

Her big, nonsensical mouth once proclaimed how I *blot*, only going surface deep.

Life needs some elbow grease, a good scrub to get the dirt out, she said.

Well, lookie here, Blanche, I'm going to speakeasies. Speakeasies! And here I am now, literally on my hands and knees, practically rubbing the grain out of Roy's and my hardwood floor. I scrub harder, proving it.

From all my recent acts of escape, our fence: perfectly white, picketed and everything. The porch: looks good as new. The old wallpaper: stripped clean. Would a blotter be able to do all that, in a week?

And, and, would a blotter agree—*no,* volunteer—to do an illegal pickup for an illegal establishment? I don't think so.

Okay, maybe my brown-nosing words slipped out before I could stop them, to get on Mary's good side and keep my job, because my moron brother got himself hurt. And maybe I'm dreading going on that alcohol run. I throw my brush into the dirtied, soapy water, sending suds everywhere.

If all of that ain't the definition of going more than surface deep, then I don't know what is. With the back of my arm, I wipe my wet face. So there, *Blanche*. I nod curtly, *not* feeling a single bit foolish for my one-sided, disorganized, slightly irrational, grumbly rant.

I drop my head into my hands. I'm losing my mind. I blame stress. And Blanche. I blame Blanche, clearly.

But that's stupid, and I roll my eyes at myself, letting out a slow, calming breath. I examine my one-day living room. This helps, staring at the barren walls and empty room, imagining the possibilities, reminding myself why I went to Doc's in the first place. So I can line my pockets with money. So I can live in a house with elegant wallpaper, polished floors, crown molding, and elaborate, ritzy draperies. It's for Roy and me, sitting in matching armchairs, getting off our feet after successful days of teaching and reporting, reminiscing 'bout being young and stupid. It'll be perfect.

Even Blanche will admit how perfect it is.

That's when I allow foolishness to set in. Blanche's words, even her made-up ones, have too much power over me. Blanche does, in general. Sure, I'm doing this house stuff for us, Roy and me, but part of me also wants to clean this house up nice and good to stick it to my best friend for razzing me 'bout wanting the "American Dream."

I lean back on my heels, an idea coming to me, and push to my feet—leaving my brush, bucket, and mess behind—and hurry past the library to my ma's house. Straight I go to the washroom, not allowing myself time to think further.

The coldness of the metal shears gives me pause, but I refocus, pulling my hair into a low ponytail. And I cut. I scrunch my face, squeezing the blades, again and again, 'til the last blonde curl drops to the floor.

In the mirror, a defiant girl with straight hair to her jawline peers back. I press my hands against my outer thighs, stopping myself from tugging on the ends of each strand. Being self-conscious would defeat the purpose. Bobbing one's hair is usually an assertion of independence against older folk—the ones who say girls should be in long dresses and pinned hair.

My bob is for Blanche; each cut helps ease some of my resentment, as if I'm taking back control from her. Really, my bob is for me. So is my choice of attire. If I'm going to dress like a flapper, I want to be the one doing it. I ain't Blanche's doll. I slit the neckline of my pantsuit deeper and steal sequins from Blanche's headband she left at my house. Using my ma's old, beat-up sewing kit, I stitch each sparkle along the hemline. After I stain my lips red, noisily popping 'em, I'm ready for Doc's.

Soon after, Big Bertha's rumbling starts quiet, growing 'til I know Blanche is outside. I take a steadying breath before scurrying to the front door, nearly barreling into my sister.

"Lynny," she screeches. "*What* did you do to your hair?"

I should ask her what she's doing here and not at her friend Sally's, but I stand here like I've never before heard the English language.

Little Billie's eyes narrow. "And that don't look like anything you've ever worn to the diner before."

"I, um," I stutter.

"You ain't going to the diner, are you?" she asks, hand on her hip.

Feeling like our roles have reversed and I'm the younger one, I simply shake my head.

Little Billie's eyes grow larger. "Can I come, Lynny? We can cut my hair, too."

And I laugh. For the first time all week, I feel lighter. Pulling my sister against me, I kiss the side of her head. "You don't even know where I'm headed."

"Don't matter. I'll go anywhere. You've been gone so much lately."

"I know. I'm sorry. But you can't come with me. You're a bit too young."

She squirms, creating distance to see me better, slightly worried this time. "Would it make Ma mad to know where you're going, dressed like that?"

"Probably. So let's keep this our little secret, like that time you broke Ma's heirloom china and I said Duke Dog did it."

"Okay," she whispers, putting her head back down and mumbling into me, "'cause something is wrong with Ma. She's always tired, but she's extra tired, like something ain't right."

I think of last night and how Ma struggled to get out of her chair, how she had bags under her eyes, the way she seemed distracted, sad. And suddenly that lightness Little Billie brought me only a moment ago is gone, replaced by this gnawing feeling that my sister is right and that something could be wrong with our ma. Maybe she's worrying 'bout our financial situation more than she's let on. She has been working herself nonstop.

I kiss the side of Billie's head again, pressing my lips against her hair longer than normal to comfort us both, and whisper back, "Everything will be okay, but I got to go. Did you eat at Sally's?"

"Yes."

"Good. Buster will be home soon."

I slip outside before my brain can catch up and feel bad for leaving Billie alone, before I can scrutinize what Billie said, *twice*, 'bout our ma looking different.

The late sun blinds me and I cup my hand over my eyes. Like myself, Blanche is already dressed, her bright red dress and feather popping out from Big Bertha.

"There you are!" Blanche calls over Big Bertha's idle purr. "I was just 'bout to beep and—" She tilts her head, mouth hanging open. "Your hair . . ."

My little sister caught me so off guard that I forgot to strut out of the house confidently, ruining my big *ta-da*.

Blanche holds up her hand, and I add some pep to my step. "You are *not* getting in Big Bertha 'til you explain to me what you did to your hair."

I bounce the ends of my new bob against my palm. "Oh, just something new I thought I'd try out."

"Are you on the rag, Bonnelyn? All week you've been a killjoy like it's your time of the month." Her eyes narrow. "Why?"

"*That* is none of your beeswax."

"You spend all day working at that house," she continues, ignoring me. "Then you're all doom and gloom at Doc's. Now you go and do this? I reckon blood loss is making you screwy."

I overlook her grossness. "You're just jealous you didn't think of cutting your hair first," I say.

Her head whips toward me. "Oh, trust me, honey. Blanche has no reason to be jealous of you."

But we both know, this one time, she is. I smugly crease my forehead, begging her to deny it again.

"Wipe that look off your face, Bonnelyn. And stop blaming me for everything. I know you think all your angst 'bout the bootlegging and Roy and your stubbed toe is all my fault."

"What? I haven't stubbed my toe."

"Yet," she says. "But you probably will, and the blame will *somehow* be on me. Admit it, you don't hate Doc's. And that's why you're drowning in that angst. You *actually* like it. You *enjoy* it there."

"No." The tone of my response comes out a bit too defensive. Hearing her say it makes my rant seem even more foolish.

She rolls her eyes. "Phonus balonus. Forget your stubbed toe; next you're going to blame me for defiling your innocent hair."

"I didn't stub . . . I happen to like my hair. A lot."

She releases her death grip on Big Bertha's wheel. She inhales, exhales. Finally, Blanche says, "It does look nice. Great, even."

"Really?" I say, hating that her approval melts some of my resentment.

"Of course. Now strut that too-skinny butt of yours inside the house," Blanche continues, "and don't come back without scissors." She checks her lipstick in the rearview mirror. "I can't have you stealing the show without me."

She smiles, and somehow Blanche has demanded her way back into my good graces, the same way she always does.

Fortunately, I'm able to sneak in and out of the house without seeing Billie. Blanche sits perfectly still, for once keeping her mouth closed, while I bob her hair, leaving blonde strands right there on Cemetery Road.

When we walk into Doc's, arm in arm, it's the best I've felt in days. Sometimes a gal needs an irrational rant, an assertion of independence, and a moment of acceptance—all jam-packed into an afternoon.

If only it didn't leave these *Ma looks different* and *Roy is on to me* fears that have wedged themselves in the back of my brain. But Buck's and Raymond's jaws nearly hitting the floor at our appearances somehow pushes those thoughts away. Not that I want their mouths wide enough to catch flies, but it's still nice to have others thinkin' you look nice, even if they are gangster-type boys that you wouldn't dare bring home to your mama.

"That boy of yours is brave to let ya out of the house like that," Buck says, coming up to me and bumping my shoulder. I flinch at his touch and concentrate on steadying the glasses I nearly knocked over.

Blanche hoots. "Roy don't even know she's here."

I laugh deceptively, guiltily, along with the others, all the while giving Blanche a *Better stay that way* look.

She laughs harder, and we disperse before opening our doors to the first group of thirsty patrons.

Before long, drinks are flowing, some even by my own hand.

I think 'bout what Blanche said earlier, 'bout me liking it here. And it may be on the verge of being true. I reckon my daddy would be okay with that. After all, Ma did say he pushed the limits now and then with his rebellious ways.

A man I've come to recognize, someone I've coined Mr. Champagne Cocktail, sidles up to the bar, slides his reading glasses into the inner pocket of his suit jacket.

Blanche makes him his drink of choice, then turns to me. "Mary says I can take my break, so I'm headed up to Buck's apartment." She's got a gleam in her eyes. "We're going to use every second of our fifteen minutes, if you know what I mean."

Unfortunately, I do. Though it's strange . . . "You've been spending lots of time with him."

Blanche laughs. "Here and there, but it ain't like we're married. I'm free to sample him or"—she scans the dance floor—"anyone else who catches my eye. But for the time being, Buck is a mighty fine sampler."

I let out an exasperated breath. "Go."

She laughs again, skipping toward the bar's partition.

I fall into a conversation with Mr. Champagne Cocktail, 'bout the stock market boom. I don't know a dang thing 'bout it, and it's mostly me bobbing my head in response, between mixing drinks for other patrons. Though his story of how a maid made a killing on stocks has me leaning closer to hear him better.

Raised voices rumble through the crowd like a wave. I stop listening, my gaze jumping 'round the room. Chairs are knocked over. The music abruptly stops.

"What's going on?" I ask Mr. Champagne Cocktail.

"I don't know," he mumbles, and shifts off his bar stool. With his hand on the bar for support, his head jolts left, right, left again. The dance floor is a frenzy of people pushing, shoving. A woman falls to the floor. Mr. Champagne Cocktail turns back, rigid. "Police!" he hollers, his voice barely carrying above the other voices in the room.

"Police?" I parrot, and clutch his hand.

"A raid!" he calls, tearing himself free from my grasp. Then he's gone, already moving toward the stairs, like nearly everyone else in the room.

Behind me, Mary's voice rings in my ear, but my mind can't piece together her words. *Raid* pounds in my head. Any other sliver of brainpower is consumed by the chaotic, frantic screams and yells on the other side of the bar.

"Bonnelyn!" she says, and seizes my arm, her fingers digging into my skin. "Hide!"

Hide. I remember Buck's words from the first time I came to Doc's, his casual "Yup" in response to me asking him if that staircase is the only way out.

"Now!" Mary screams.

I stumble through the door to the back room, but not of my own accord. Mary drags me. The door closes at our backs and mutes the screaming and banging noises coming from the other room.

Mary grabs a handle to a small closet, yanks it open. She slips inside, her face serious, pale. "Hide," she says again, and slams the door.

I turn on my heels, my arms wrapped 'cross my torso like I need 'em there to hold myself together, and search the back room: office, sink, cabinets, a table. Wrapped beneath the table, there's a curtain.

I fling back the curtain and crawl under the table, my knees scraping against the cement floor. My head bumps the table's underside and I yelp, quickly clasping my hand over my mouth. An abrupt noise fills the room, someone coming through the door, and I frantically reach for the curtain to hide myself.

"Wait," a male voice says, and I stop, hand frozen on the fabric. I've been found already.

Black shoes cross the room toward me, each footstep pounding in my head as I envision my future slipping away. I press back against the wall, praying they'll go easy on me. Won't make me go to jail.

The shoes stop in front of me and I clench my eyes shut.

There's a light touch on my arm.

I peek between my lids.

Staring back at me is a lopsided smile laced with concern. I almost call out "Non-Roy," but catch myself.

Then he's beside me in the cramped space. He twists, sliding the table's skirt back into place to hide us, and faces me again.

"Hi," Non-Roy whispers through the near-darkness, looking completely uncomfortable with his knees too high.

I wipe away the moisture beneath my eyes. "Hi." My voice is weak, my heart sputtering—and for more than one reason.

He laughs low, quiet, and lightly touches my arm again. Goose bumps erupt over my skin. "I saw you come back here. I wanted to make sure you were okay. Are you, Bonnelyn?"

"You know my name?"

He laughs. "Of course I do. I found that out the first night I saw you here. But this . . . This is new." Non-Roy reaches out and touches my shorter hair. "A nice new."

"Ow."

I feel stupid as soon as the irrational response leaves my mouth.

My discomfort adds fuel to Non-Roy's fire, his smile growing, his eyes hungry. "Do I make you nervous?"

"No," I say, too fast. "Why are you here? You could get caught."

"I could, but like I said, I wanted to make sure you're safe."

I meet his eyes, quickly lower my gaze. "I, um, I have a Roy."

"A what?"

Looking at him, finding a smirk on his face, only flusters me more. "I have a boyfriend, a fiancé."

"You have a boyfriend and a fiancé?"

"No, I mean—"

He chuckles, and I hate that it sounds nice, contagious even. I hate that I sneak a peek at his empty ring finger and that his hypnotic laugh steals the rest of my thought.

"Well, I don't see a Roy here, unless there's another table he's hiding under." He feigns peeking out of the curtain.

"No—"

"Good. We'll ride out the raid together then, without Roy." He pauses, looking years younger than his early twenties as he finds a more comfortable position. "Sorry. Am I coming on too strong? I don't think I've made the best impression so far. You make me nervous."

"*I* do?" His vulnerability catches me off guard, although it's a welcome change from his self-assuredness.

"Yes." He smiles, revealing a crooked tooth I didn't notice before beneath his cocky grins. Somehow, that imperfection puts me more at ease. "Word of Saint Bonnelyn and her flirty sidekick have gotten 'round."

"You think Blanche is my sidekick?" I ask, keeping my voice low.

"Oh, is that her name? I only cared 'bout finding out yours."

The back of my neck prickles with heat. Non-Roy nudges my chin up. Hotter. "Would you like to know my name?" he asks, his voice teasing.

I want to say no. He's Non-Roy. Not someone with a real name. Not someone who could or should go beyond the boy with that hungry look in his eye. My body betrays me. I nod again, and a burn creeps into my cheeks, no doubt turning my skin red. I study a piece of lint on my pantsuit.

"Henry," he says.

The sound of *Henry* pulls my attention back to Non-Roy in a heartbeat. "That was my daddy's name."

He smiles, showing that perfect, imperfect tooth. "Did you know it means 'ruler of the home'?"

"No," I whisper. I think of my daddy and how providing for us was all he focused on.

"I'd make a great king," Henry says, his confidence seeming playful instead of arrogant.

"Why is that?"

"Well, there're my dashing good looks. But I'm also fair and honest and swell. Maybe you'll give me the chance to show you."

I take a deep breath, finding it hard to meet his eyes. Finally, I do, and even in the darkness, they sparkle. "Maybe."

• • •

From our hiding spot beneath the table, we wait, left with only questions and prayers.

A door is opened and closed, and I can't help inching closer to Henry. My head cocks when I think I hear my name. But I can't be sure. I ain't 'bout to check, to answer. Henry holds a finger to his mouth—as if I need a reminder not to give us away.

Eventually, all is quiet. I let out a breath, even lightly chuckle at the absurdity of the situation, but the rapid beating of my heart continues long after. Henry's gaze is equally unsettling.

Though he unravels my unease as the night lingers on, as we fill it with soft-voiced questions, responses, and muted laughter, 'specially 'bout how he lost all his clothes in a poker game.

I fall asleep on the hard floor, tiredness and the unknown state of Doc's keeping me here. When I wake, my breath catches in my lungs, stays there. My back is pressed against Henry's hard chest; his arm is slung carelessly over me. With a hand pressed to my forehead, I curse myself for being here with him, like this. I untangle from his arm and practically dive out from under the table, throwing caution to the wind.

Standing in the quiet back room of Doc's, I rub my face, a flurry of unknowns hitting me at once—ones 'bout the raid and what this means for Doc's, 'bout Blanche and if she's safe, 'bout Roy and if . . . if it's truly possible I let another boy capture my attention all night long. And why? 'Cause he put himself at risk for me? 'Cause he looked at me in a way that made me feel wanted? In a way that boys only ever gawk at Blanche? In a way that Roy hasn't yet?

A sliver of Henry shows beyond the curtain, and I groan, knowing the answer to all those questions is a pathetic yes.

Busying myself, I study the back room, the door into the main room, the office, the sink, the cabinets, the closet where Mary hid. I tiptoe toward it, whispering her name. Laughter whips my attention toward the exit. The door is flung open.

"There you are!" Mary comes in from the main room, her voice loud. Raymond is on her heels.

Guiltily, instinctively, protectively—I don't know which—I glance at my hiding spot, at the blue of Henry's shirt, slightly visible. I step to my left, blocking Mary's and Raymond's views of him, and paw at my sleep-ridden hair.

"Is everything okay?" I ask, confused by their lightheartedness.

Mary waves a hand. "Yup."

"The raid?" I ask.

"Never happened," she says flippantly.

I raise a brow.

"False alarm. Buck's brother came by, said how he heard talk of the police. One of the patrons overheard and started yapping." She sounds exasperated by the end of her explanation.

"Damn drunk started a stampede," Raymond adds. "Caused quite the scene out on Elm Street, but nothin' came of it. Thank God."

"Where's Blanche?" I ask, my mind still trying to catch up.

"She went back to bed," Raymond says with a smooth smile.

Typical.

"So everything is fine?"

"Eh," Mary says, "my uncle wants to shut down for a few nights, to be sure. Timing is good, though. We need to make that alcohol run. So get yourself ready."

My stomach grows hot. I knew this day was coming.

"Mary . . ." Raymond says, a warning in his voice.

"What?"

He talks more softly, as if that helps, with me standing only a few feet away. "Your uncle said *not* to involve Bonnelyn."

She rolls her eyes, and part of me wonders why Dr. Peterson said this. Before, he was happy to have me make the run.

"Saint Bonnelyn will be fine," Mary says.

"But he said—"

"She'll be *fine*," Mary says, her voice stern. Raymond opens his mouth again and she cuts him off. "We need her."

"Don't you think Blanche would be better at it?" I suggest.

Mary shakes her head sharply. "No. We need your virginal look, as not to attract attention. Even with this shorter bob of yours. But hey, if you're going to look like a flapper, perhaps you should start acting like one." She steps closer, pats my cheek. "So we're good here, right?"

"Mary, I—"

Behind me, there's rustling.

Henry.

"I can do it," I say urgently, even as I regret the words. I walk toward them, coaxing 'em out of the back room. "When do we leave?"

"Not *we*," Mary corrects. "You and Buck are going. Tonight."

"Buck?"

We enter the main room, my eyes widening. Chairs are overturned; glass covers the floor; tables lie on their sides.

Mary doesn't look pleased, with the room, with me, with anything. "Is there a problem, Bonnelyn?"

I swallow. "No."

"Good. I already got enough on my plate. This is going to take all day to clean up."

Raymond kicks a bottle. "First, food. Want to come?" he asks me.

"Um, thanks, but I should get home and face my ma."

Mary shrugs. "Suit yourself."

With each step toward the exit, my mind races and my mouth becomes drier. All I can think 'bout is Henry under that table and how I'm going to get him out unnoticed.

"Oh, shoot," I say, slapping my hands against my legs. "I . . . forgot something."

I fidget, but Mary and Raymond don't seem to notice. Mary acknowledges me, barely, and is more than satisfied to keep on going without me.

The door closes behind them and I retrace my steps to the back room, coming to an instant stop. Henry is sitting on the table, legs swinging.

"I was wondering if you were coming back for me." A crooked smile stretches 'cross his face and my stomach muscles tighten. "Let me guess . . . You want to hear more 'bout that time I walked out of the poker game in nothin' but my birthday suit?"

I laugh before I can stop myself. "Should've had a better poker face," I tease.

He hops down from the table, crossing the room in a matter of steps. "I assure you, my poker face is top notch." Then his hand is on my cheek. "We should do this again sometime."

"What? Hide together?"

Stop, I tell myself. I don't know why I'm engaging in banter with him, letting him touch me like this.

"I like hiding," he says, and pulls his hand away, my cheek cold without his fingers there. "But I should go."

Henry's abruptness has me taking a tiny step to balance myself. "Um, yes, me too."

We leave the back room, Henry whistling at the mess in Doc's before we climb the stairs. On the main floor, I push him through the door leading to the apartments and casually walk through the reception area of the physician's office, completely out of place in my flapper dress. Two Ma-aged women wait in wooden chairs, both reading *Time*. The older of the two peers over her magazine at me, apparently not pleased with my progressive attire. I exit, coughing to feign sickness.

Elm Street's sun is blinding when I step out. I squint, finding Henry tying his shoe. He stands, walks by me, grazing my skin. In a soft voice, he says, "Thanks for the bedtime stories. See you soon, Bonnelyn."

I shiver at his slight touch, unable to think of anything as simple as the words *Okay* or *Bye* before he's gone, confidently striding down the street.

I'm left standing alone, relieved that my night with Henry has gone unnoticed.

My skin still tingles.

BILLIE BOUNCES BESIDE ME, TAKING THREE STEPS TO MY ONE AS we walk toward our bikes. The girl won't stop yammering 'bout how excited she is to be going shopping for clothes.

It'll be the first year the Parker girls will strut into class in non-hand-me-downs. I can't think of a more satisfying way to take a step closer to my dreams.

Shopping is also a good distraction from last night with Henry and tonight's illegal escapades with Buck.

"Hey," Billie says, beaming. She points at my one-day home. Behind a long piece of wood is my one-day husband, struggling to carry it toward the house. "There's Roy. Let's go say hi."

She's leading me by the arm before I can react. I scratch the back of my neck and pull my fingers through my shorter hair. This is the first I'll see Roy since he ambushed me, the first I'll see him with my new bob.

"Roy!" Billie calls, releasing my hand to run toward him. He bobbles the board, resting one side of it against the grass, and squints against the sun. "Lynny is taking me shopping."

"Is that so?" he says to her. The question is obvious in his voice. Bet he's wondering how it's something we can afford. Bet he's also wondering why I didn't tell him my plans, since I'm normally at the house with him each afternoon. Henry's the answer to that one. Guilt kept me away from Roy, had me making a beeline for my bike instead.

His gaze rises to me, a few steps behind Billie. His head cocks to the side, his lips part. I reckon those original questions are gone. My heart pounds one, two, three times. I can't help feeling like I've been on shaky ground with Roy, and I don't want something as silly as a haircut to cause him to crack.

I shift my weight. "Do you like it?"

Roy doesn't answer right away, but I recognize intrigue in his eyes, the same look I got from Henry last night. Then Roy's eyes flicker to my sister, and he only smirks.

I smile. "Something new I thought I'd try out."

His face falls, as if his head catches up to his initial delight. "'Cause of Blanche? That girl seems to be your answer for everything lately."

"I cut mine first," I say quickly, then force a laugh. "Of course, she had to bob hers too."

"Well, that ain't surprising." He regrips the piece of wood. "Looks like a hairstyle that could get the two of you in trouble."

I swallow. "Don't be silly."

• • •

It's just me who could get in trouble tonight, not Blanche. I'm the one sitting next to Buck, a convicted felon, in his slick Model T, staring out the window into Dallas's dusk, not just pretending to be a flapper, but acting like one, too.

I breathe deeply.

Everyone has a defining moment in life. At least that's what Ma says. For Blanche, hers came early. Her ma left. No warning, no explanation. Just gone. Blanche's daddy nearly fell apart, but Blanche stayed strong, even if *marriage* did become a dirty word.

I reckon I would've done things differently, taking on a maternal role, but Blanche didn't. Blanche put Blanche first, doing whatever she had to do to survive, to be wanted, to feel whole.

For a long time, I judged her for that, always wanting to fix her and show her "the way." Now I wonder . . . is Blanche the one who's been leading me? No one put a gun to my head. But somehow I'm on my way to help the illegal Doc's get illegal alcohol. I could've found another way to earn my keep. But I didn't. Instead, I made the choice to move forty miles per hour toward the unknown. So what if I'm as far away from Buck as the bench seat will allow?

"Uh-oh," Buck says, glancing at me. "Penny for your thoughts?"

Despite my uneasiness with being 'round him, one side of my mouth curls into a smile 'cause of his very un-gangster-like question. "I'm not sure they'd make sense."

"I've spent a lot of time lately with Blanche, ya know. She rambles 'bout a lot of things that don't add up."

I laugh. It surprises me, and it feels good.

"She called me a 'stripe' the other day," he says, his voice booming—for whatever reason, Buck's voice always seems like it's booming—and he regrips the wheel to veer right. "Had this elaborate explanation for it. I still have no clue what the word means."

"She confuses me all the time, too. Did a stripe sound like something you'd want to be, at least?"

He shrugs, but he grins too. "Ya want a butt?" Buck pulls a second cigarette from his jacket's breast pocket.

I hesitate, not sure why I'm making the acceptance of a cig yet another defining moment. Society no longer frowns on women smoking. Even got fancy ones just for us ladies. "Sure."

One-handed, he fumbles with the tip of his cigarette to light mine, passes it to me. I take a small drag, willing myself not to cough. I cough. The act of smoking is calming, though. I peer out the window, no longer recognizing the street names or this area of Dallas.

"Nervous?" Buck asks me.

"Yeah," I admit, still staring.

"This kind of thing does that to ya. Makes ya nervous. I've made a few trips, and it still gets me jumpy, ya know? Want to walk through the plan again?"

I turn my head back toward Buck, blow out a slow stream of smoke, for once seeing him as a normal person and not some scary bimbo. "No, that's okay."

It's not as if my part will be difficult.

I fluff my Sunday best dress over my legs, feeling more comfortable in its longer length. While finalizing details 'bout our alcohol run, Blanche complained how she could wear a dress just as well as I could, but Mary countered with how innocence was the proper look. She needed a doll, not a moll. And Blanche didn't fit the bill.

I bob my knee anxiously as we drive, Buck announcing we're only a few minutes away from the restaurant. For the umpteenth time, he looks in the rearview mirror.

"Everything okay?" I ask, not sure I want to know the answer.

"Yup. My brother is tailing us."

"Your brother?" I twist to peer over the seat. Two pinpricks of light stare back.

"Yep, the one and only Clyde Champion Barrow," Buck says with a wink. He takes another puff of his cig. "He'll flash his lights if he spots any po-lice taking notice of us on the way."

"Why'd they care 'bout us now? We don't got the bootlegs yet."

"Well," Buck says, and licks his lips, "this here car is hot."

I jolt straight up in my seat. "What?"

Buck chuckles. "Can't expect me to use my own car. Don't even have one."

Panic seizes me. Going on the run to begin with is one thing. A big thing. Going on this run in a stolen car is a whole other shebang. "I want out. I want out this very second."

"Sorry, Saint Bonnelyn, not going to happen. If we don't show up where we said we would, when we said we would, these jokers are going to come looking for us. And trust me, we don't want that happening."

"Trust you? Why would I ever go and do a thing like that? You all lied to me." My voice rattles 'round the car, hurting my own ears. "My God, did Blanche know?"

"She's the one who suggested not telling you."

"No," I say, rubbing my forehead, needing for that not to be true.

"She said to give ya a few minutes and you'd come 'round."

I drop my hand to my lap, clutch it with my other hand. My nails dig into my skin, but I almost relish in the pain, something I can control when everything else is moving too fast.

"Look, it's safer this way." Buck pats the steering wheel. "No one will know she's gone for a few hours. But if I were to take the doctor's car and things go south, the car will track back to him, and most likely to us. Can't have that, can we?"

I feverishly shake my head, but it's not only to answer Buck's question. It's also out of disbelief that I haven't thrown open the passenger-side door.

"I know why you're here, Saint Bonnelyn. Blanche told me how money is tight at home."

And that, right there, is why I'm still here. I stare out the window, the betrayal I feel from Blanche growing. But she ain't wrong. I wish things were different for my family.

"Want to know why *I'm* here?" I turn toward Buck, and he takes that as a yes as he says, "My brother got real sick a while back. Doc Peterson kept him alive. So if he asks something of me, I'm going to do it."

"Why does he even do this?" I let out a slow breath, trying to regain my composure. "Why'd he open Doc's?"

"Doc Peterson uses whiskey to treat patients. It's allowed, ya know, medicinally." I nod, although I didn't fully realize that. "And the pharmacies were having a hard time filling his alcohol scripts 'cause of low production. The government controls all that. Doc Peterson took matters into his own hands."

"For his patients?"

"Yup. Patients like Clyde got the ball rollin'. Then him and a few of his buddies started playing poker in his basement, which eventually led to the full-blown Doc's."

My lower back is moist from all this talk, but my head ain't spinning anymore, even if nerves still jump 'round my stomach. "Has this been going on for a while?"

"Which part? Bootlegging?"

I scratch my nose, my chin. That word makes me uncomfortable. "Yes. No. I guess everything."

"The doctor covers his tracks, if that's what you're after. He's been bootlegging for medicinal purposes for years and years. The poker playing—not as long. Maybe three or four years. I ain't too sure. Doc's is still a baby, just a few months old. Took years to discreetly get everything set up downstairs. And I can assure you he was discreet. That's why that raid was nothin' but a false alarm."

I also don't like the sound of *that* word. It would've spelled bad news for my family and me if it'd been real. But it wasn't. I'm okay. We're okay.

Better than okay, maybe. Makes me wonder though . . . "How come Doc's is so busy?"

"What ya mean?"

"Many places are doing great after the war. But Dallas ain't spreading its wealth too well."

He nods a few times, like he's familiar. "For those pinching pennies, I suppose they like pretending. Ya know, it ain't illegal to drink."

"It's not?" I scour my memory. My parents weren't big drinkers. But Roy's daddy was, alcoholism running in his family and all. His ma was plenty happy when Prohibition was passed.

"Nope. Anyone is free to drink the stuff," Buck says, turning his head left and right. He crosses a small intersection. "The government just wants ya to think you can't. But the law says ya can do it in your home. You just can't make, sell, or distribute it."

I narrow my eyes, thinking. "But how do you get it to drink it?"

Buck slaps the wheel and I jump, my nerves already on edge. "Attagirl, Saint Bonnelyn. He's corrupt, ain't he?"

"Who?"

"The government. There's so much poor going on and he's focusing on what? Booze? Ridiculous. I ain't surprised people take matters into their own hands," he says, half paying attention, peering through the windshield. His voice lowers, as if talking only to himself. "Here we are."

I get a chill. On our left, we pass MacGregor's Restaurant, and Buck releases an audible breath. That ain't helping my nerves. When we make a left turn into its alleyway, his fingers tap against the wheel, the noise pounding in my head.

Buck pulls the brake lever, silences the engine, cuts the lights. I shift again to see over the seat. Clyde's car passes in the streetlight's glow.

"All right," Buck says. "This will be easy-peasy."

I snort at his vocabulary, as if Little Billie said it and not some bimbo in a suit.

He hops from the car. Before I know it, my door is opening. Buck stands there, backlit, making it hard to see his face.

He offers me his hand. I hesitate.

"It's okay," he says. "I know you ain't crazy 'bout any of this, but I'm okay." I'm barely able to distinguish his facial features, but I can still tell my hesitation hurts his feelings. "Ya know I was arrested, don't ya? Is that why you're squirrely 'round me?"

My expression must betray my desire not to admit it. His outstretched hand drops to his side.

"What I did wasn't so bad." Buck flicks his cigarette into the dirt and twists it into the cracked pavement with his shoe. "I got caught with stolen goods last year—me and Clyde did. Funny story, really."

"I'm not sure I'd agree that spending time in jail is funny."

"We stole turkeys."

"Turkeys?" I scrunch my brows.

He chuckles. "Clyde wanted to make the holidays special for our ma and—"

"That's sweet."

"That's Clyde for ya. He planned this big ol' dinner we couldn't afford. Reckon it's my fault we got pinched, though. I had this bright idea we could make some clams by selling turkeys—at a premium, of course, but still less than the store was asking, those crooks."

"So you stole turkeys?" I reckon that ain't too bad.

"And sold 'em. The po-lice only locked us up to scare us straight. We were out in no time, even though that bullheaded Clyde put up a fight, always does. They almost kept him longer for resisting arrest. But they ended up just keeping us a night in the box. We were home in plenty of time to carve that bird for our ma."

"So you're sayin' you're like a modern-day Robin Hood?"

Buck slaps his leg, letting out a hoot of laughter. "Saint Bonnelyn, I like that spin, I gotta tell ya."

His story settles between us. The back of my head itches, but I don't move to scratch it. Right and wrong has been so muddy lately that my thoughts also stay still, not sure which way to go.

"Look," Buck continues, his voice barely more than a whisper, "we can't be futzing 'round out here. They'll be here soon, and I can't keep them waiting. You and I are a team now, right? You got to trust me."

He offers his hand again, and this time I slowly place mine in his. After he helps me from the car, he pulls my hand through the crook of his arm. I take another quick puff of my cigarette then stomp it into the ground.

Together, we walk down the alley toward the street, Buck navigating the many potholes.

"Okay," he says. We round the corner onto the sidewalk, the buildings high around us. A car passes. The storefronts have people here and there but ain't overly crowded, it being suppertime. "Pretend I said something funny."

I take a quick breath and think of what Clara Bow would do in her film *It*. I lean into Buck and laugh.

An older couple passes us, the woman smiling at me in a grandmotherly way.

"You're a regular actress," Buck whispers. I smile at that.

He pulls open the door to MacGregor's Restaurant, and I go in first.

A hostess greets us, not a single wrinkle on her dress. Buck responds, with the words *anniversary*, *girlfriend*, and *celebration* louder than the rest. I almost shush him, this seeming like the kind of place where you can't speak more than a whisper. The tables are covered in white, the utensils sparkling, the lights dim, the music low.

We're seated, Buck pushing in my chair, and I don't think anyone has taken special notice of us. But really, why should they? They don't know we're here to bootleg alcohol. We're here for a nice supper. Probably the nicest supper I've ever had.

I peruse the menu. Despite my own pep talk, my hands tremble. My eye catches on Crown Roast of Pork. When I put the menu down, Buck lays his hand over mine, offering me a reassuring smile.

"Aren't you two adorable?" the waitress remarks, suddenly at our table. "Would you like to hear our specials?"

"I think we're all set," Buck says, glancing at me for my agreement. I nod and take a sip of water to busy myself.

With our order placed, the waitress gone, and Buck and I alone again, he leans 'cross the table. Any nosy bystanders would think he was whispering sweet nothings to me, something Roy would do.

"All right," Buck says, "I'll be right back. Just need to use the li'l boys' room." He winks.

What he really means is: *All right, I'll sneak into the alley, meet the distributor, quickly load the car with alcohol, then be back for the main course. You stay here, my perfect-looking fake girlfriend, so that no one thinks it's odd that I've left.*

"Hurry back," I say, covering the nervous inflection of my voice with a flirtatious undertone.

Buck kisses my hand before walking toward the back of the restaurant. My gaze follows him 'cross the room, my heart thumping in my chest. I close my eyes, tell myself that there's nothin' to worry 'bout. I just sit here. Sit here and wait. That's it. And he'll be back in a few minutes.

So what if last time Buck made an alcohol run he thought he had police watching him? This time is different. There were no flashing headlights from Clyde. That's got to mean no one knows we have a stolen car. Not yet, at least. And, so far, no one's acting strange in the restaurant. The waitress thought we were a real couple, even. We're being nothin' but discreet.

My heartbeat slows and I open my eyes.

Staring back at me from 'cross the room is Hazel Griffin, Southwest Dallas High School's most notorious chatterbox and lead writer of our school's gossip column. Next to her is Jimmy . . . whatever his last name is. All my brain can comprehend is how Hazel pins me with a *That wasn't Roy* expression. She studies Buck's empty chair and her lips twist.

I instinctively stand, my chair scraping against the floor. My napkin falls from my lap.

"Hazel," I whisper, as if sayin' her name louder will make this situation worse.

She sashays toward me, Jimmy trailing behind like he always does. "I underestimated you, Bonnelyn Parker. He's a Casanova," Hazel says. "And you? Two-timing Roy Thornton? Just like Ethel Bowens did to Harold Monroe. Wow. Haven't you two been together since you were pups? Didn't Roy buy you a house?"

"No," I say, and madly shake my head. "I mean, yes. He bought me a house, but—"

"And your hair? Now that's scandalous. It really makes me wonder what you've been up to this summer. I got to believe Blanche Caldwell has been involved in some way or another."

"Hazel—"

She steps closer, presses her finger to my lips. "Shh. Don't you worry. After I figure out all your secrets, I'll be sure to keep 'em to myself." She laughs. "See you at school, Bonnelyn. Can you believe it's starting so soon?"

Hazel brushes past me, my mouth doing nothin' but catching flies. Jimmy follows, lowering his head.

"Hazel," I say, louder, and turn to also follow, to tell her that she's got it wrong. She doesn't stop. My God, Hazel Griffin never keeps a secret.

I picture my world coming down 'round me, starting with Roy unraveling all of my lies.

All I can do is stand here. For a minute? Five minutes? Time also stands still, 'til I hear a scream, easily swallowing the soft din of the restaurant.

A deep scream.

A man's scream.

My hand flies to my chest, the earlier pounding now seeming like child's play.

The deal's gone bad. I know it.

10

ALL THOUGHTS OF HAZEL GRIFFIN AND HER BIG MOUTH ARE gone, vanished, unimportant.

That scream . . .

Buck? *No,* I tell myself, hands on my chest. *It's not Buck.*

Something's gone wrong, but Buck is fine.

He'll come waltzing into the dining room any second now. But the seconds pass and I'm left standing here by myself, gripping the back of my chair, easing some of my weight against it.

Some patrons are frozen, forks in midair. Others are on their feet, looking 'round with questioning, panicked expressions. The volume of MacGregor's spikes, creating the type of commotion reserved for tragedies.

One voice rises above the rest, screaming into a phone. "Get me the police."

The police.

I blink, holding my lids closed, and pray that, when I open them, Buck will finally be coming this way. We'll leave. We'll count our blessings.

The soft light crashes into me when I open my eyes. But no Buck.

I turn on my heel, racing for the door, for the alley.

A handful of people have gathered on the street, the same puzzled looks on their faces. By the grace of God, none belong to Hazel.

For a second, I think of fleeing, running in the opposite direction. But I find myself kicking off my heels and plunging into the alleyway.

The car's interior light leaks from the open back door, softly illuminating a carload of crates and Buck's body propped against the car, his head tilting to the side, a black circle spreading on his stomach. His hands lie limply on either side, inches from a bloody knife.

He's quiet, his eyes fluttering open and closed.

Only feet away from Buck, two men grapple. Their footsteps are heavy, their struggle throwing them left and right 'cross the small space. I stumble side to side. A gleam of light catches the object they are fighting over. A pistol. A completely terrifying pistol. More terrifying than our shotgun. A shotgun is bigger, and I can see it coming. But a pistol is small, discreet, and can come out of nowhere. And this one is pointing all over the place—at me, the wall, the ground, the sky, Buck—too fast to fully register.

I feel the weight of the crowd forming behind me, but I'm afraid to turn to see how many. I'm afraid for them to see *my* face. Even worse, the police could join them any second.

And here I am, feet away from a brawl. A stolen car with a backseat full of giggle juice. A man with a knife wound to his stomach. My insides tremble, my hands tremble, it feels as if even the alley's walls tremble, as if they're inching closer with every breath I take.

I can only speculate 'bout what went wrong, fearing that my earlier hesitation made Buck late. But I know I must do something, anything.

"Stop!" I scream at the two men—the first word that comes to mind.

They jolt, and the gun slips free. It clatters against the pavement. Close. Too close. And I squeak like a child.

"Get it!" the smaller man yells—to me. His face is hidden in the shadows, but there's something in his voice that makes me want to obey. A punch connects with his jaw and he grunts, cutting off his next plea.

They scuffle; the shorter man throws his own right hook. The other man staggers backwards, his heel bumping into Buck's foot. Buck doesn't react.

My eyes dart to the gun, back to the men. The smaller man—no, a fella my age—looks up, the light from the car now illuminating his face. Our eyes connect. And those eyes—they reflect his pain and fear as if he's put them into words.

I breathe out, slow, controlled.

"The gun—" he calls, the rest of his words swallowed as he dodges a punch. He finds me with his eyes again. "You can do it."

This time, there's more I see in him: a reassurance. It sparks this unexplainable urge to prove him right. And, in that moment, my heart rate slows and the franticness of my brain clears.

The gun's warm against my fingertips, even warmer in my palm. I stand, fumbling with it, not sure where to place my nonfiring hand, without a shotgun stock to grip. I wrap my left over my right, squeezing the pistol's handle tightly. With my thumb, I struggle to cock the gun. It clicks into place.

I don't aim. I don't know how, when the gun's not on my shoulder. I don't know how, when my target is a person and not a bird.

Twisting, I fire off a shot at the base of the brick wall.

The recoil snaps my hands back and the gun drops. I stumble away from it, shaking out my wrists and arms. My insides tremble again from the echoing sound, which mixes with the screams behind me. I refocus before the walls seemingly get any closer. The taller man, who must've been thrown off guard, is now knocked out cold. The boy who spoke to me hovers over him, his chest heaving in and out from their fight.

He lifts his head, the blackness hiding his features. "Help me get my brother in the car."

Brother.

Another slow, controlled breath. I know who he is.

Clyde.

The one and only Clyde Champion Barrow.

Following his lead, I slip my hand under Buck's armpit and pull. Buck stirs and moans, the blood spot on his stomach growing. Clyde reacts, moving faster, and I match his pace. Together, we slide Buck, limb by limb, into the passenger side of the car.

Clyde slams the door. "Go," he says to me, the light catching a glint in his hazel eyes. "Get Buck to Doc Peterson."

I run to the driver's side, jump into the seat. Clyde reaches in, flicks on the car. Unlike Blanche's car, there's no crank, this one having an electric start, saving us precious seconds as the engine roars to life.

Staring at the three pedals, I try to remember which one reverses the car.

"The middle one," Clyde calls, as if reading my mind. He's already backpedaling in the opposite direction, his shoes scuffing against the cracked cement. "Go! Doc Peterson! Now!"

The darkness hides the intensity of Clyde's eyes, but I can feel his urgency in his demands. I slam my foot on the middle pedal, barely able to see beyond the crates, and the car lurches backwards. I pull the throttle, increasing the speed, silently pleading with anyone behind me to get out of the way. I blindly swerve left and right, thumping over potholes, scraping the alley walls.

Skidding into the street, I duck my head, trying to hide my face, and switch my foot to the other pedal. Without my heels, the slickness of my stockings makes my foot slide off. I curse, stomping down again.

"Move!" I scream hysterically, avoiding eye contact with the innocent, curious bystanders crowding the street. "Move, move, move!"

Buck stirs beside me.

"Buck!" His eyelids flutter, and I shake him. "Buck, wake up. You're okay. You're going to be okay."

He touches his stomach, his hand coming away glistening. "Shit," he mumbles. "Damn guy . . ." He sucks in a shaky breath. "He got me with a shiv then ran away. Other fella took my gun. Clyde—"

"He's fine," I say. "You're fine. Put pressure on your stomach." I grab his hand to cover the blood. Too much blood. He groans but doesn't resist. I take a deep breath. "Keep talking to me, Buck. I need you to help me. How do I get us back to—"

A car rushes toward us, its headlights growing too fast for a normal person to be driving.

Buck curses under his breath. "Just stay calm, Saint Bonnelyn. Slow 'er down. We'll be okay."

I fight my urge to shrink in my seat. The determination in Buck's voice is all that keeps my hands firmly in place on the wheel and my foot steady. We both know that Buck doesn't have time for us to be stopped, questioned—'specially with a backseat full of giggle juice.

"Okay, okay," I say to myself, letting up on the throttle.

The car approaches. Closer. Closer.

It whizzes past and, as suspected, I catch a glimpse of the word *Police* plastered 'cross the car's side.

I flick my attention to the rearview mirror, seeing red lights peek through a space between the crates. The taillights keep going.

"Thank God," I say between my teeth, and I press my wrist against my chest to stop the line of sweat creeping down my neckline.

"Ya did it." Exhaustion pours from Buck's voice. He wheezes, coughs.

Instinctively, I reach for him, forgetting that he ever made me uncomfortable. The paleness of his skin can only mean one thing: he's running out of time. "Buck, I need you to help get me to Doc Peterson."

He looks at me, but his gaze is adrift.

"Buck," I say firmly, even though I'm on the verge of crumbling. "We're a team now, right? Which way do I turn?" I risk shaking his arm.

He stirs and peers out the window, sweat falling on either side of his droopy eyes. "Go right."

Hand over hand, I make a brisk turn. And the ones that follow.

"Talk to me, Buck. Keep talking to me. What happened back there?"

"They got spooked," he manages to say. "Took too long." His eyes begin to roll back in his head. I shake him, his head rocking forward, and I thank the Lord Jesus when Doc's comes into view.

Blanche is out front with Raymond, both casually yet tensely leaning against the brick exterior. She sees us and her hand grips Raymond's wrist.

I slam on the brakes in front of Doc's, jump from the car. Blanche and Raymond are already at the passenger side, helping Buck.

"What took you so long?" she seethes.

Her attack surprises me. My mouth falls open.

"Stop it, Blanche. She got him here, didn't she?" Raymond says. He hoists Buck over his shoulder. Buck cries out in pain.

Blanche is frantic—her eyes, her speech, everything. "Clyde was here minutes ago. Minutes!"

"Just help me," Raymond demands.

I race for the door, holding it open for him and Blanche to carry Buck through. Blood covers my hands.

Trailing behind, Mary and a handful of nurses scatter like ants. Noticeably missing is Clyde—the boy in the shadows, with the captivating eyes, who fought off an attack, helped me get Buck in the car, raced here to warn everyone we were coming, but is now nowhere to be seen.

Doc Peterson ushers us into a sterile-looking room. Raymond carefully places Buck on a table, looks up at the doctor expectantly. But Doc Peterson is staring at me and doesn't seem pleased. "Out," he demands, already reaching for the door.

11

TREMBLING, I SNEAK INTO THE HOUSE AND FEVERISHLY SCRUB the blood from my hands under a slow trickle of water, as not to stir my family. I force myself to sleep, each dream soaked in red. I wake with a metallic scent somehow stuck in my nose.

At the breakfast table, Ma hasn't asked me a single question 'bout why I'm only stirring my oatmeal 'round and 'round. She simply watches me as she folds laundry, creating a stack of neat clothes beside me on the table.

Buster rushes into the kitchen, and I clutch at my heart. Part of me thought he was the police, coming to take me away. In the midst of folding a shirt, Ma reaches for the chair he's knocked, but she's too slow to catch it and it cracks against the ground. I watched it falling, the entire time, but still I jump from the gunshot-sounding bang.

"Shh," Ma chastises. "Your little sister is still asleep."

Buster drops into another chair at the table and, with his good hand, unfolds a newspaper, painfully slow to lessen the noise. He grins mischievously, like I bet my daddy would've done. I wasn't double-digits yet when Daddy passed away during surgery in the Great War, so the resemblance could be all in my head.

I hope my sky-high nerves from last night are also all in my head.

"Can I see a page or two of that paper?" I ask my brother.

"Bonnelyn, this here newspaper is fact, not one of your fairy tales."

"Buster." Ma slumps down into her own chair. "Give your sister the paper."

He sighs, removing the sports section, and pushes the remaining pages 'cross our small table.

I discreetly tap my foot and flip from page to page, only fake-reading the headlines. That is, 'til I come to the one that has my fingers crinkling the thin paper: an article proclaiming how hooligans caused a disturbance in Dallas last night.

The gory details—'bout the blood, the screams, the chaos, the gunshot, the speculation of bootlegging alcohol—are all there. What's not written in black and white is a solid idea of the hooligans' identities. There are varying accounts of our appearances. I steady my foot, feeling relief. For me, at least. This here newspaper can't tell me a thing 'bout how Buck's doing, and all I want to do is hide away in my fairy tales.

I step outside. The mercifully cooler air greets me before I escape to a familiar corner of the library, book in hand, with the musty smell of a story written long ago. I tuck my legs under me and breathe out a slow breath, eager to lose myself in the calamities of Jane Eyre's life instead of my own.

It ain't long before I hear footsteps. I fear it's Roy, but he's still sleeping. Like usual, I'll see him at the house in the afternoon, after I've had time to get my nerves in check. No, the fast-paced gait coming toward me is Blanche's. I quickly lower my head, puff out my cheeks, not sure what to expect from her.

"Bonnelyn."

I narrow my eyes, concentrating harder on my page.

"Bonnelyn," she repeats, far louder than the whisper she's supposed to use in here, and this time she crouches down to my level.

My shoulders rise, fall. "What do you want, Blanche?"

"So, last night . . ."

"Yes?" I snap my book closed, the sound echoing throughout the library.

"I shouldn't have been so hard on you. I was just worried 'bout . . ."

Finally, I look at her. There may not be tears in her eyes, but there's moisture there. And . . . sincerity.

"I was worried 'bout Buck," Blanche finishes. She lowers herself from a crouch to a cross-legged position and takes my hands. "I ought to thank you, though. Buck says he probably wouldn't have made it without you there. He was babbling 'bout how you two are a team. You ain't moving in on my man, are ya?"

I scrunch my brows. "Your man?"

She smiles coyly. "Thought I could sneak that in without you noticing. That dope may mean more to me than"—she scratches her head, drops her gaze—"maybe Blanche has let on."

"Blanche Caldwell is goofy 'bout somebody? Never thought I'd live to see the day."

She playfully slaps my knee. "Don't go making a big deal 'bout it."

"I'm glad your *boyfriend* is okay, Blanche."

"He will be," she says confidently. "Doc Peterson almost had to take him to the hospital. But he finally got the bleeding to stop and stitched him up good as new."

"Good as new." I finally loosen my grip on my book and let my shoulders relax. Buck is fine. I'm fine. Last night is over.

"He's all loopy on painkillers, though. Looser in the mouth. I almost got him to tell me his real name. It ain't Buck, ya know. 'Cept he wouldn't tell me."

"Bothers you, huh?"

Blanche sighs. "Don't you know it." I see the moment she moves on, humor filling her eyes. "So," she says, drawing out the word, "I heard you almost shot someone, Bonn. Didn't anyone ever tell you that thou shall not kill?"

I hide my smile. "I fired at the wall. On purpose."

"Uh-huh," Blanch teases. "You're turning into quite the moll."

"Thanks to you." I roll my eyes, lower my voice. "I can't believe you didn't tell me that car was hot."

She cringes. "I did it for you, ya know. I didn't want you backing out. I know you need Doc's."

I nod my head, both of us knowing it's true and that, despite last night, it'll continue to be true. It has to be. Ma hasn't mentioned my late-night outings again, even with school starting the day after tomorrow. For lack of a better plan, I'm going to keep doing what I'm doing, then work extra hard to bring home good grades. Though, lately, with Ma going to bed right after supper, I ain't sure she'll even notice I'm gone.

"Besides," Blanche continues, "I didn't tell ya 'cause I knew you'd be in good hands with Buck and his brother."

Clyde.

Casually, I flip through the pages of *Jane Eyre*, then pop my head up, as if a question *just* came to me. "What's the deal with Buck's brother, anyway?"

"Ooh." Blanche clasps her hands together. "You interested in Clyde? Could you imagine: me with Buck, you with Clyde? How grand would that be?"

I move to the shelf and say, "No." I add a shake of my head, thankful my back is to her. "No, Blanche." Though, if I'm being honest with myself, if she didn't make that leap, I may've tried to learn more 'bout the mysterious boy. But no, of course Blanche went there, and now I bite my lip, thinking of a follow-up to my question. "I mean, why did Clyde warn you that I was on my way with Buck and then leave? I thought he'd stay to make sure his brother was okay."

"I asked Buck the same thing. They have this rule. They call it their 'heat rule.'"

"Which means . . ." I ask, facing her again.

"Let me finish." She feigns exasperation in her own headshake. "If they ever get in a situation where things get a little hot, they separate. Even in life-or-death situations. That way, if someone gets caught, it won't be both of 'em."

I nod. There was a time that the idea of being in a life-or-death situation and getting pinched by the police would be outside the realm of possibilities. That time has passed.

Over the next couple of nights, that thought becomes even more apparent, 'specially after four large bathtubs are rolled into the back room of Doc's so we can brew our own hooch. No more alcohol runs for us.

That makes me happy. At the bar, I look down at my hands and notice how the cherries, other garnishes, and bottles are now all lined up in the way I've come to prefer it. After spending so much time here, and after putting my life—Buck's life—on the line for this place, Doc's has become familiar. It's become mine.

My eyes wander the room. Rosie is fidgeting with the height of her microphone, getting ready to sing her first song. Mary is skirting 'round the room, doing last-minute preparations. Blanche is double-checking she has everything she needs. Raymond is pulling out a seat at one of the poker tables, ready to carouse with the men who join him.

And me, I don't feel like I'm pretending anymore to be somebody I'm not.

The first group of patrons will walk through the door any minute now. Rosie or whatever band is playing always catches their attention first. People peer through the smoky room, shoulders already starting to shimmy, trying to find the source of the music. Or perhaps that's only how I enter.

I wonder how Roy would enter. He's home tonight, having a rare night off. Maybe I could slip out, finally bring him here—to my place. Shouldn't I be sharing this with him?

"Bonnelyn," Blanche says, and smacks her hands against the bar top. "I've a feeling tonight is going to be epic."

I smile. "Is that so?"

"Uh-huh. Doesn't hurt I'm going to end the night playing nurse to Buck. I even got myself a li'l outfit to look the part."

"Of course you did."

"Ya always got to leave 'em wanting more."

She winks, I shake my head, then our night begins. Four men flow into the room, none of which are Henry. I reckon that's good. Four women are next. The cycle continues—men then women, men then women—'til the roar of Doc's curls my lips into a smile. I lose track of what time it is, but I know hours must've passed, by the amount of people who now dance, giggle, tease, sling back drinks, and gamble their money away. I wipe the back of my arm 'cross my forehead, trying to keep up, and realize I never did put any more thought into sharing my world with Roy.

Blanche nods toward Mr. Champagne Cocktail. I've his drink made even before he can tear his eyes away from Blanche to ask me for it.

"First one's free," she says, with a smile that rivals a film star's. Then Blanche takes a sip of her own drink.

I watch her a moment. Like so many times before, I envy Blanche's easiness at being herself, free. Perhaps part of that is 'cause she goes with the flow, accepting life with open arms. That could be me.

There's a lull in the music, and I look at the stage, all the while twisting a dishrag, 'cause I can't stop thinkin', *I wish it were me up there.*

And then I'm opening my arms and throwing down the rag. I leave the bar. My eyes arc trained to the left of Rosie, on a vacant microphone.

The dance floor may as well be the Red Sea, with how people separate to form a path. Rosie smiles, her black dress shimmering in the light. I wonder if she's seen the way I've longingly set my eyes on the stage, watching her sing. I wonder if she knew it was only a matter of time before I found myself under the lights. Rosie gestures, extending a hand to the microphone beside her. She lowers it to my level, as if sayin', *Join me.*

A high-pitch piano note begins the song, and my step falters. I twist, trying to see Blanche, but hands are on my back, my shoulders, pushing me forward again. I swear I hear someone say, "Sing, Saint Bonnelyn."

I refocus on the stage, fingering the pearls around my neck. The way the spotlight lands on Rosie, it's like little pieces of confetti dance behind her. She taps a tambourine against her leg, in perfect harmony with the piano's melody—a cluster of twinkling stars that fall one at a time before tumbling all at once.

Rosie motions again, more urgently this time, giving me the encouragement I need to step onto the stage. The trumpet's sudden deep notes fill the room, making it feel as if that moment was made for me, welcoming me.

And then Rosie's singing, "*No one to talk with . . .* "

I step up to the second microphone, fingers tightly interlocked, not yet touching it.

"*All by myself,*" she croons.

I stand there, the words I've sung to myself so many times stuck in my throat.

A deep breath settles me. I lick my lips, clear my throat, and stare at the many feet on the dance floor.

She sings another line. I subtly bob my knee to the beat, waiting for the chorus, a place to make my entrance. This feeling of anticipation is the most alive I've felt in days, weeks, maybe even years. It rumbles through me, and I lean 'til my lips touch the cool metal of the microphone.

I swallow. Then I'm singing, "*Ain't misbehavin'* . . . " I pause, and the piano carries me to the next note. "*I'm savin' my love for you.*" I stretch the last word, my voice strengthening, deepening to become sultrier. The way the song is intended.

This earns me hoots and hollers from the people on the dance floor and from those sitting at the tables, but I don't dare look up from their feet. I unclench my fingers, lace 'em 'round the microphone stand.

Rosie bumps me with her hip, my body falling into a natural sway. I count down the beats 'til the next verse. Three, two, one. "*I know for certain the one I love,*" I purr, enjoying the silkiness of my voice. "*I'm through with flirtin'. It's you that I'm thinkin' of. Ain't misbehavin'. I'm savin' my love for you.*"

The lyrics pour out of me, ones I've heard here at Doc's, ones I've secretly heard at home on our radio, ones I've hummed in the time in between. Line after line, I sing, my voice melding with the song's rhythm 'til the drums pick up, like rain pinging on a roof. The piano matches it, and then a cowbell, and finally trumpets, the instrumental solo creating a frenzy of feet on the dance floor.

Mary Janes and men's dress shoes move at lightning speed, hopping, skipping, tapping. Men swirl the women 'cross the dance floor. My eyes trail up the bodies to hands that join and unjoin. People are thrown smoothly from side to side, between legs, into arms.

Their faces: enthralled and without a care in the world.

I smile, relaxing my shoulders and loosening my grip on the microphone stand. Rosie glances at me, shimmying her shoulders to the beat. I match her movements, reveling in how free I feel.

The instrumental solo is beats away from ending, and anticipation courses through me again. I feel the words bubbling from deep within me before they slip out, aligning 'em with a dip of my hip. "*I don't stay out late, got no place to go. I'm home 'bout eight, just me and my radio. Ain't misbehavin'. I'm savin' my love for you.*"

I repeat the line, the chorus, leading to the song's end.

"*Savin' my love for you . . . for you, for you*"—my gaze bounces playfully 'round the room, from face to face—"*for you.*" I let the word hang with the remaining few beats.

It's as if my curtain of inhibitions falls with that last note and is swept away by the boisterous crowd.

Freeze.

I close my mouth, lick my lips, brush aside a strand of hair. This moment is one I'll forever relish. The cheering crowd. The sound of clapping. The way I feel alive.

Gulping in a breath of air, I hold it in my lungs—a last-ditch effort to savor this moment—then slowly blow out. Blanche clutches a glass behind the bar, her head shaking back and forth ever so slowly. But her face . . . her face looks proud. Astonished, even. With a playful tilt of her head, she lips, *A-ma-zing.*

"Thank you," I whisper back. And I mean it. Not just as the appropriate response to her compliment, but—I'll admit—for bringing me here, the place where this moment happened.

"Bonnelyn," Rosie says. "Sing with me anytime."

I nod, but the response feels inadequate. I step closer, but she's already turning to the pianist, preparing for the next song.

I sigh. An enormous part of me wishes my feet could grow roots in front of this microphone. Another glance toward Blanche, swarmed by patrons at the bar and visibly in need of a second set of hands, tells me another tune will have to wait.

The pianist starts a new song, and I reluctantly step from the stage. I take those few beats with me, humming to myself while I blindly navigate toward the bar.

Someone moves in front of me.

I sidestep. "Excuse me."

The body shifts again, blocking my way.

I look up into a confident face that instantly quickens my heartbeat.

"I'm flattered," Henry says.

"Why?"

"It's sweet of you to save all your love for me."

"What?" His words catch me off guard. I swallow. It was Roy I thought of while I sang. Not Non-Roy. But, if I level with myself, I've been hoping yet dreading to see Henry again after our all-night hideout. Thinkin' maybe he'll look at me in that same hungry way.

The way he's watching me now.

The trumpet roars to life and he leans closer.

I lean back, instinctively, 'cause this is wrong. Wrong. But curiosity gets the best of me when I notice the darker skin beneath his eye. "What happened to your face?"

He rubs his swollen cheekbone. "It was difficult to get into Doc's tonight. But it sure as hell was worth it. I needed to see you."

I think of the rules: only four men per hour.

"You fought someone for his spot?" I ask incredulously, trying to push the *I needed to see you* out of my head.

"Of course. It was a gamble. I wasn't sure you'd be working tonight. But here you are. And may I say, *Wow*. That performance . . ." His hand cups my cheek before I can stop him, and my knees buckle. "How is it that you make me so crazy, Bonnelyn?"

I stumble away without answering, only my feet moving. My name coming from his lips sounds too familiar, and I need to get away. I need to see the boy I've *really* been saving all my love for. I weave 'cross the dance floor, and the entire time Henry's gaze is heavy, oh so heavy.

"I have to go," I shout to Blanche as I rush past the bar.

"What? Where?"

But I'm already pushing through the crowd, my eyes locked on the exit.

12

I'VE NEVER RIDDEN THROUGH THE STREETS OF DALLAS AT MIDnight before, my legs moving so fast that my feet slip from the bike's pedals. I've also never had this overwhelming desire to see Roy before, ever.

I fly 'cross the tracks, violently shaking with each bump, continuing to thump as the road turns to dirt. The air is cool, twisting my short hair 'round my face. It's invigorating. And Blanche was right: tonight's been epic. And I don't want it to be over yet. Not 'til I've seen Roy.

My breath comes out ragged. I leave my bike and my sparkly shoes in his front yard, tiptoeing toward Roy's first-floor window. Light from a neighboring porch guides my way.

I don't allow myself to stop or think. I ping my knuckles against his dusty window and wait, smoothing my windblown hair. A whole second passes before I cup my palms against the window to peer in. In the shadows of his room, his handsome face peeks out from beneath a disheveled white sheet.

I knock harder. He stirs. I tap again, 'til his head twists toward the window.

"Roy," I call, and recognition appears on his face.

His tall frame lumbers 'cross the dark room, and I wiggle my toes in the damp grass. My lips curl into a timid smile.

"Bonn?" he croaks. He tugs open the window. "What are you doing here?"

"Why was your window closed?"

"Bugs," he whispers simply. "Is everything okay?"

"It is now. I needed to see you," I say, mimicking Henry's words to me.

A smirk appears on Roy's face, but his eyes are narrow. "You've become quite the night owl, haven't you?"

"Well, tonight it's all 'bout you." I reach through the open window, shaking my hand for him to take. "Unless you'd rather I leave." I begin to withdraw my arm.

Roy pulls me into his room.

My feet touch the ground and I advance, both hands against his chest, not giving him a chance to question me further, pushing him toward his bed. We tumble onto it, amidst his rumpled sheets.

His perplexed expression only makes this moment more important. My mind flashes to the other week, how Buck looked at Blanche with instant desire. Instant. Yet Roy has never lusted over me quite the same way. I think of Henry. My mind drifts to the intenseness I felt from Clyde's eyes. I stop any further thoughts. I need to. I'm here for Roy. I crush my lips to his, needing to feel that spark, needing Roy to be more than the safe small-town boy I've known my whole life.

Roy kisses me back. I slip my tongue into his mouth and fumble with his shirt.

"Bonn?" he mumbles against my lips.

I shake my head, his head moving with my motion, the two still linked together.

Deepening the kiss, I sink into him, feeling him, knowing my surprise visit is exciting him as much as me. I smile, pulling back to see his face.

His eyes are still narrow, but that smirk is gone. Desire stares back at me as he licks his lips. "Is this how girls with short hair act?"

My stomach flutters. "It's how I act."

He runs his hand 'cross his forehead. "Guess that makes me a lucky man."

I laugh, music to my ears. A new thought springs to mind. "Would you ever fight someone for me?"

This time Roy laughs. No doubt I've caught him off guard again. "Are you forgetting James Tucker?"

"James Tucker," I repeat. That's right. Roy whopped him good, a few years back, for razzing me 'bout having a tear in my hand-me-down skirt.

Through the darkness, I drag a fingertip down Roy's mouth, pulling his lower lip, imagining the cut James left behind. And I want more, more. This night is like diesel fuel.

"Touch me," I say, on top of him. My tone is low, seductive, the voice I used when I sang. I grab Roy's hand, moving it to the small of my back, then lower, squeezing his hand so his fingers dig into me.

And then I'm on my back, Roy looking down at me, kissing me. The rhythm of his breathing pulses into me, matching the erratic beat of my heart.

"I want you," I murmur into his mouth, followed by a moan. The sound is unfamiliar yet intoxicating, like something out of a Jane Austen book. "Do you want me?"

"Where is this all coming from?" Roy asks, each word slipping out between kisses.

"Would you rather I stop—"

"No."

Self-satisfaction swells in me.

I was done saving my love. I wanted to show it, experience it, prove it. And Roy's being receptive.

It only strengthens my desire to share Doc's with Roy. Maybe he'll want to swing me 'round the dance floor. Or play a round of cards at the tables. He's a good cardplayer—one time he didn't have to do his chores for a week, after he beat his pa in a game. And just 'cause his daddy had problems with alcohol, it doesn't mean Roy will. Soon. Yes, soon I'll tell him. But tonight . . . I want tonight to be 'bout us.

A sense of power courses through me, driven by Roy's desire, forming another thought in my head: *I can leave him wanting more. He'll want more.*

Just as I pushed him onto the bed, I push him off of me. The shadows of his room once again coat his face in confusion.

I backpedal toward his window.

"Wait. Where are you going?"

I slip one leg into the night, straddling the windowsill. "I'll see you at school, Roy."

"Why not tomorrow? I'll be at our house."

"Busy," I say flippantly.

"But . . ." The light flicks on next to his bed. Roy's eyes are big, his lips swollen, his cheeks flushed. He points down at himself, clearly happy I'd decided to stop by. "You're leaving me like this?"

I chuckle—I've awoken a beast, one that's been sleeping our entire relationship—and climb through the window.

Running 'cross Roy's yard, flinging myself onto my bike, I'm giddy.

I've never ridden through the streets of Cement City after midnight before, my adrenaline moving my legs so fast that my feet slip from the bike's pedals. I've also never had this overwhelming feeling of power before, ever.

13

AFTER LAST NIGHT'S FORAY INTO SINGING AND HEATED FOREplay with Roy, my current mood is "craving attention." I grudgingly step off the stage at Doc's, a place Mary has encouraged me to go whenever the mood strikes me. I've been innocently flirting with the crowd through the sway of my hips and my sultry tone all night.

When I get back to the bar, Blanche is grinning at me like a goon. "Keep doin' what you're doing, Bonn. Tips go up, way up, when you're prancing 'round under those lights."

I laugh. An upstanding English teacher who moonlights as a seductive speakeasy singer. Wouldn't that be rich?

"But it also means I'm going through these bottles faster," she adds. "Mind getting me a new one?"

I turn on my heels, a pep in my step.

"Hold up!" Blanche says, and I face her. "I got so caught up in playing nurse last night that I forgot to ask you where you ran off to. Is there any other reason why you're glowing?"

"Maybe." I draw out the word.

"Bonn!" She grabs my shoulders. "Stop being such a closed book."

"Fine," I say, but I hesitate, partly 'cause I enjoy watching Blanche squirm, and also 'cause I want to keep my Roy-related excitement to myself a bit longer. Blanche has shared her conquests with me many, many times. But Roy ain't a conquest, even if last night did feel like a victory.

"Bonn . . ." She grips my chin, holding my face steady.

"I went to Roy's—"

Blanche's eyes go wide, her fingers tightening on my cheeks. "In the middle of the night . . . you did not."

"Uh-huh."

"And did you make him your Roy Toy?"

"Blanche, no, we ain't married."

Her hand falls away, thumping against her leg. She holds up a finger to a man at the bar who is trying to get her attention. "Okay, well I'm half impressed. 'Bout time you two kicked it up a notch."

I smile to myself. In that moment with Roy, the idea of freezing time didn't cross my mind. I wanted more. More touching, more kissing, more pleasure. Heck, I still want more.

"You're grinning all goofy," Blanche says, smiling too.

"I think I may've created a monster. Roy didn't want me to leave."

She laughs. "I take it back. I'm fully impressed. Maybe *I've* created a monster. Ya know, it's not too late for me to introduce ya to Buck's bro—"

"Blanche . . ."

She laughs. "Fine. In that case, I'm done with this conversation. So how 'bout you"—she turns me toward the back room, slaps my butt—"grab me some whiskey. I feel some very thirsty eyes on me."

Over my shoulder, I smile—the expression stuck on my face—and give a quick wave to Buck, who is ever so slowly settling onto a bar stool, his hand gripping his injured stomach.

In the back room, I pull open the closet door, flicking on the dim light inside. Wooden crates are lined on shelves, and I peek through the cracks for a green bottle.

Found it.

Bottle in hand, I turn to leave, running straight into a crooked smile.

My free hand flies to my chest. "Henry, you scared me."

He smiles and steps closer.

I look left, right, not sure what I'm expecting to find other than bottles. "What're you doing back here?"

"You ran out on me so fast last night. I wanted to see you. Really see you."

I bite my lip. "You did?"

He nods, confident. "And you want to see me, too."

I push out a hip, meeting his confidence, and create a subtle curve to my body. "Think so, do ya?"

"I know so."

Now I swallow and bring that hip back in. "How did you get back here, anyway?"

"Your sidekick was distracted with that boy of hers. Slipped right on back." He steps even closer, runs the back of his hand down my cheek. "I hear you already sang tonight. I wanted a private show."

Just like that, my insides are engulfed in flames. I tighten the grasp on the bottle's neck, feeling as if the dark glass could shatter any moment from knowing this is wrong. Or maybe my grip's so tight from the way the tips of our shoes touch, the way he made our shoes touch, coming back here for me. I can't help myself; I tease, "Those don't come cheap."

"How 'bout this for payment?"

Henry cups my face with both hands and my eyes betray me, falling on his lips before finding those hungry eyes. He tilts his head forward 'til our foreheads touch. I should pull back. But the way he breathes me in . . .

A second passes, and another.

My arms hang limp at my sides. The bottle slips from my grasp. I vaguely hear the breaking of glass, hardly notice the wetness that splashes my legs.

He crashes his mouth onto mine, just like I'd done to Roy last night.

Roy.

Our life together.

I pull away, gasping for air. "I'm sorry. I need to go." The broken glass gleams in the dim light, and I stumble backwards. "I shouldn't be doing this."

Brushing past Henry, I rush back into the main room of Doc's.

"No way," Blanche is saying to Buck. "Bonn will kill me if I miss the first day of school."

My erratic movement catches Blanche's eye.

"Bonn? Bonnelyn? What's wrong?" Her eyebrows rise. "Who's that, Bonn?"

"He followed me back," I say lamely.

Buck still sits at the bar. The pocket watch he tossed plunks against the bar, forgotten. Henry steps forward with an outstretched hand and introduces himself. I stare straight ahead, not making eye contact with anyone, too in denial 'bout what just happened.

"Hello, Henry," Blanche says, not accepting his handshake. "Taken an interest in my girl?"

"You could say that."

He's grinning. I know it without seeing his face.

"Are you okay with that, Bonn?" she asks me.

I don't answer.

"Bonn?"

"I . . ." I struggle for words. "I dropped a bottle. Broken glass," I stammer, and weakly point behind me.

Blanche steps forward, takes my hand. "I'll take care of it. Say, I was 'bout to go get some clean bandages for Buck. Why don't you go grab that for me? They're in the closet upstairs." She turns to Henry. "And why don't I get you some drinks to take back to your friends?"

I'm happy to leave, quickly zigzagging 'cross the dance floor and clacking against each stair.

Doc Peterson's office is dark, quiet, and a bit eerie. I hurry toward the reception area, slowing my pace to soften the noise of my heels, and enter an all-purpose room full of supplies, patient records, and a small dinette area. The far wall is nothin' but closets, with three separate doors.

I proceed to the first, pull open the door, find random office equipment. I go to the second, pull open the door, find a plethora of files marked with patient names.

I step to the right, hand on the third door's knob. I stop. The name Parker catches my eye. The name Parker, Emma.

My ma.

My family doesn't see Doc Peterson. We go to Dr. Monroe in Cement City—our local physician for the trivial illnesses and injuries that have popped up over the years.

With a shaky hand, I reach for my ma's file. I hesitate before opening it, convincing myself that this pounding sensation in my head is an overreaction to what I'll find to be another trivial sickness—a bad cough that Ma just can't shake.

But my ma hasn't been coughing. She's been overly tired, she's seemed weaker, she's seemed distracted.

Opening the file, I start reading, and sink to the floor.

14

BLANCHE FINDS ME SLUMPED ON THE COLD FLOOR, STARING AT my ma's health records. She takes me home, puts me in bed, gives me a sleeping pill she snagged from Doc Peterson's stash, whispers that she'll see me at school tomorrow. She pauses in the dark before she leaves, and I imagine her sad expression, mirroring my own.

I lie there, unmoving, knowing only a wall separates me from Ma—who is sick. She's sick, and not from a cough or a common cold. I think 'bout getting up, curling in bed beside her, but I don't. I ain't ready to talk 'bout it yet. Talking means it's real.

And phrases like "possible mammary ductal carcinoma" don't exist in my world. My world is already too full and confusing, and that unknown phrase sounds too damning.

When morning comes, I wring my hands and fight through the residual grogginess from last night's sleeping pill. The clock ticks closer to the library's opening, and I linger on our front step, debating if I should miss the first day of school and bury my nose in a thick medical book. Skipping class wouldn't be the worst thing I've done lately. Wouldn't even come close. But do I *want* to know what "possible mammary ductal carcinoma" means?

No, I don't. I'm not ready to know. I step out onto our porch, hugging my book bag to my chest.

"I know I said I'd see you at school . . ."

I look up to find Blanche. I was too caught up in my own thoughts to hear Big Bertha's rumble.

"But I wanted to make sure you're okay."

I bury myself in her arms. "Thank you, Blanche."

"So are you? Okay?"

I step back, rub my forehead. "Yeah."

She dips her knees, leveling her eyes with mine. "You ain't. But I read those confusing medical records, too. So here's the deal: today is Bonn Day. We can do whatever you want. We can go talk to Dr. Peterson and demand he tell us everything. We can go see a show. Or we can get in Big Bertha and drive. Just drive, anywhere you want. The Gulf?"

"The Gulf? Blanche, the Gulf is five hours away."

"Or," she says, twisting her lips, "we can—"

"Go to school," I finish for her. School is part of my plan, and I don't want to mess that up.

Blanche slings her arm over my shoulder and leads me toward her car. "I was afraid you'd say that. But I guess that's okay. I'm kind of jazzed for my first photography class."

I tilt my head. "Really?"

"Um, should my feelings be hurt that you're so surprised?"

"You've just never expressed an interest before."

"Well," she says pointedly, "I just did. Now let's go have the best Bonn Day ever!"

• • •

Together, we trek up the three-tiered steps to Southwest Dallas High School. Self-consciously, I keep my head down and pull at the waistband of my new stockings, their tightness confining me. The sweater I bought with Billie feels too heavy for the early fall weather, yet I still wanted to wear it.

I'm supposed to be strutting. I'm supposed to welcome school starting again, be ridiculously excited, 'specially now, when I ain't feeling so poor. The problem is, I'm feeling guilty—from that kiss with Henry—and afraid—'cause of my ma's health records—and scrutinized—from the weight of my classmates' eyes on me. I've no doubt those sideways glances I'm receiving have Hazel Griffin's name written all over them.

And all that leaves me slumped over, studying my shoes, which are also new.

Blanche twists left and right beside me, her school bag knocking me in the arm, as if she's trying to absorb as much of the attention as possible. "I reckon they're jealous of our hair," she says. "Guaranteed, everyone will bob their hair by the end of the week."

I force a laugh—'cause really, bobbed hair has been popular for years in the big, big cities—and yank open the heavy door.

"Doesn't this feel surreal?" I ask, surveying the hallway lined with lockers, groups of students in their knee-high skirts and dresses lingering here and there. The walls are already littered with posters for an upcoming bonfire or to sign up for the yearbook staff, the debate team, the glee club, the prom committee. What? No mixology group?

"What's surreal?" Blanche asks, and dodges one of our classmates.

"Going to school after the summer we've had at *you know where*."

"Oh, *that*. Yeah, I'm just here for my pa. That man is always raggin' on me 'bout something. I reckon I won't last long, though."

I stop, giving Blanche no choice but to do the same. "Please don't tell me you're thinkin' of dropping out of school?"

"I'm older than the legal dropout age. Why wouldn't I?"

I sigh. "I don't know, Blanche . . . to get a diploma and have a career?"

"Those are merely fancy words. Besides, that's your dream, Bonn. Not mine."

"So, what . . . You're going to leave me here all alone?"

A girl bumps my shoulder, shouts a friend's name.

"Hey!" Blanche yells disapprovingly at the girl, but her voice is swallowed by a slew of our excitable classmates reuniting after the long break from school. She turns back to me, her expression no longer annoyed but sultry. "Your Roy Toy is coming this way. I best skedaddle."

"No," I say, too quickly, and pull her in the opposite direction of him.

She raises an eyebrow. "Anything you want to tell me, Bonn?"

Only that I've double-crossed my boyfriend 'cause I'm a despicable human being.

"Nope."

I'm too ashamed to admit, even to a best friend who'd shrug it off as nothin', that I got swept up in being wanted—right into another man's arms.

The bell rings, and I straighten, telling Blanche we can't be late for class.

She shouts something at my back—probably how that don't matter—but I'm already gone.

The rest of my day is spent in a state of fleeing, rushing through the halls between classes to avoid just 'bout everyone: Blanche, Roy, my curious classmates. Of course, Blanche tracks me down, telling funny stories or pointing out how Mrs. Anderson resembles a walrus, but I only chuckle to make her feel like she's succeeding in helping me have a good Bonn Day.

Finally, one period of the day remains. World history. I slump down in a chair, exhausted, and drop my head onto my folded arms.

I welcome the steady drone of our teacher's voice going through this semester's syllabus. What I don't welcome is the "Psst" and "Bonnelyn" I hear behind me, a few minutes before my not-so-good Bonn Day is finally over. Nor am I happy, when I lift my head and find Hazel's face, smoothed over with faux innocence.

"How are things with your boyfriend?" she whispers. A few girls 'round her softly titter.

I try to keep my expression blank, and turn away from her, much preferring to watch the clock at the front of the room slowly *tick, tick, tick*.

Hazel's hand clamps onto my shoulder, recapturing my attention. "I hope I haven't said anything wrong."

I could growl at her sarcasm. "I don't see how it's any of your business, but Roy and I are fine," I whisper pointedly.

"Roy?" she asks, her voice rising with the question. "I meant your *other* boyfriend."

She pauses and I panic, my body temperature seemingly rising to dangerous levels. She can't possibly know that Henry kissed me.

Hazel scrunches her brow. "Maybe it was the lighting in that restaurant, but that didn't look like Roy Thornton's hand you were holding."

Buck. She's referring to that night with Buck.

Hazel rocks her head left and right, no doubt enjoying the amused responses on either side. Our teacher makes a shushing noise, barely lifting her head from the syllabus.

"I knew you were into theatrics, Bonnelyn Parker, but that looked like real life to me."

I lean closer, hoping the redness of my cheeks don't betray the sternness of my voice. "What exactly is it that you're trying to accomplish here, Hazel?"

"Oh no, I've upset you."

"No," I say.

"Aw, sweetie. There are tears in your eyes. I'm only looking out for you. I've seen Blanche Caldwell 'round town with that *same* boy, doing more than holding hands." Her friends all nod their heads in confirmation, some covering their mouths as they tee-hee. "I wouldn't want to double-cross Blanche Caldwell. Besides, I thought she was your best friend."

"She is."

Hazel tilts her head like a lap dog. "Well why would you do that to her then?"

"I'm not." I bang my fist on my desk. A few chairs scrape against the floor or groan with the shifting of weight. Our teacher clears her throat, peering over the frames of her glasses. I wait for her to continue reading, then pin Hazel with a glare, saying, "Enough. Stop trying to make something out of nothin'."

"Maybe I'll just have to talk to Roy again, see what he has to say 'bout all of this."

"Again?"

"Why yes, Bonnelyn. Roy and I are going to the soda shop together after school."

She smiles. I jump to my feet, my own chair making an ugly scraping noise. Once I'm standing, I've no clue what to do next. Throttle her neck? Slap her? Demand she stay away from Roy? My options bounce through my head while twenty pairs of eyes stare at me, while our teacher insists that I sit down.

"Bonnelyn"—Hazel sucks air through her teeth—"you're making a scene."

My brain kicks into gear. I flee.

The final bell chimes at the same time I yank open the classroom door.

I have one blissful second of aloneness in the hall before my classmates swarm, pouring out of doorways.

People must think I'm crazed, the way I storm toward the exit, sobbing, zigzagging, plowing into shoulders.

The cooler air is a godsend. I step out onto our school's empty promenade and take a deep, calming breath before I continue my escape, walking at a near-jog toward Blanche's car on the street.

I yank Big Bertha's door, but it's locked.

I kick the tire and curse, pleading that Blanche won't be long.

"Bonnelyn?" I hear behind me.

No. Please no. Not now.

"Bonn?"

My bottom lip quivers and I hold back more tears.

"Hi, Roy," I say softly, and face him.

He takes a step closer, running a hand through his hair. So many boys today grease their hair, but not Roy. Roy doesn't get caught up in that stuff. Never has.

"What's going on?" he says gently. "I haven't seen you all day."

"What are you doing with Hazel Griffin?"

Immediately, I'm annoyed with myself. There's so much I could say, and I say *that*.

Roy's brows scrunch. "Hazel?"

"Yes, Hazel. Apparently you two are going out after school?"

"Sure, but with Ruth and Shirley, too."

"You are going out with three girls?" I ask, even more annoyed with how my voice sounds shrill.

Roy laughs, actually laughs. "We're all on the paper together. Hazel is fanatical 'bout our first edition and wants to brainstorm."

I bite my lip. "Right."

Roy shoves his hands in his pockets, rolls back on his heels. As he rolls forward, he says, "Now that that's cleared up, want to tell me why you've been avoiding me?"

I open my mouth, close it, afraid of the lies that'll come pouring out. I desperately want to tell him 'bout my ma. I want his arms 'round me. But I don't feel like I deserve his comfort.

"This Bonn," Roy continues, "and the Bonn that snuck in my bedroom window are two very different girls."

I look away, embarrassed, not by how I acted then or now but by the Bonn in between.

He nudges my chin, focusing my attention on him again. "Do you regret it? Us, together that way?"

"No," I say, and mean it. I touch his arm, needing to feel that contact, even if I'm undeserving. What I regret is Henry. Every single moment I've ever spent with Henry.

"Good." Roy takes my hand. "I was kind of hoping that'd happen again."

I laugh, needing to laugh. But behind Roy's lighthearted comment is a tense jaw. My laugh trails off and we're left with an awkward silence.

"Roy," I say quietly, noting the other students 'round us. "I don't know if you've heard the rumors—"

"I have."

"Oh." I moisten my lips. "What Hazel's sayin' 'bout me ain't true."

"So you weren't with someone else?"

My cheeks flush. Henry's silhouette from the darkened closet and the sound of breaking glass crashes into my mind.

"Bonn?" Roy presses.

"I was with someone, but I was with Buck."

He repeats the name, as if it's a dirty four-letter word, and I quickly clarify. "Blanche's boyfriend."

He sighs. "Now that's the first thing that's sounding like a lie."

"I swear it. Blanche really does have a boyfriend." I put so much conviction into that statement 'cause it's the truth. And lately, for me, the truth has been hard to come by.

"'Tis true," Blanche says, all but skipping toward us. "I'm spoken for."

Roy's hand tightens on mine, and it's obvious he ain't happy to see her.

"Somehow I find that hard to believe," he says to her.

"That ain't my problem. Look, Roy, I get you're annoyed Bonnelyn has been spending so much time with me, but I've needed her. In fact, I'm going to need her all night. You can have her back tomorrow."

Judging by the slow rise of Roy's chest, he ain't a fan of Blanche telling him what to do.

I give his hand a squeeze. "You really should go, Roy," I say.

His forehead creases, probably not a fan I told him to leave, either. But it's for the best. I've got work. I've got Blanche. And I don't want her opening her mouth again and making Roy's jaw any tighter.

I watch him go. Blanche is already climbing in and out of Big Bertha to get her started, yapping 'bout something. I'm too distracted to listen. Hazel has tramped down the school's stairs and is now throwing her arms 'round my boyfriend. Roy does nothin' to stop her, like how I'd done nothin' to stop Henry, and Hazel grins all vamp-like in my direction.

"Bonn!" Blanche calls. "Get in."

I slam the door behind me, harder than necessary.

"You mad? I know I shouldn't get him riled up. But, like I told you before, he makes it so easy. Once I get going—"

"It's fine." I keep my eyes trained ahead, refusing to look in Hazel's direction again and add to her self-satisfaction.

Blanche is quiet a few beats, then says, "Okay, good. 'Cause we've got bigger problems."

"What?"

"Those rumors 'bout you and Buck."

I sigh. "Roy doesn't believe 'em. Everything is jake."

Blanche purses her lips, puts Big Bertha into gear. "Whatever you say."

"What's that supposed to mean?"

"Roy's hot and cold."

"He's only cold with you, Blanche."

She snorts. "Maybe. But you know Hazel is hoping he gets hot with *her*. She's been pining for him for years."

"She's with Jimmy."

"Uh-huh . . ."

I shake my head. "You ain't helping me have a good Bonn Day one bit."

"You're right. I'm done. But I reckon Roy's not done thinkin' it all over."

"Maybe you shouldn't have interrupted us, then." I cross my arms. Dallas passes outside my window. "Why's it even matter to you, Blanche?"

"What? You and Roy? Besides the fact you're my best friend?" She smiles sweetly at me.

I give her a *Be serious* look. We both know that Blanche's main concern is Blanche.

"Fine. I'm 'bout to admit something to you, Bonn, *but* you can't do that thing where you purse your lips. Deal?"

"I don't make deals with the devil."

"Fair enough," she says, with a strangely shy smirk. "I'm envious."

I sit up straighter. "Of me?"

"Of you and Roy . . ."

She pauses, as if waiting for me to react, but I don't. Externally, at least. Inside, I love that Blanche is jealous of something I have, 'specially something she's never taken seriously.

"It's just that . . ." she continues, navigating Big Bertha 'round a bend. "Well, Buck is amazing. I've been fighting it, but I could see us one day getting . . . hitched." She forces the word out, sheepishly glancing at me.

Blanche Caldwell has my full attention.

"Stop that," she says.

"Stop what?" I ask.

"Looking at me like you've just seen a unicorn." She takes a deep breath. "Anyway, like I said, I'm envious 'cause I wish me and Buck was like you and Roy. I wish Buck was my first and only boyfriend. Kind of like a tooth."

"Excuse me?"

"You've got the same teeth your whole life."

"Huh?"

We bounce over the tracks into Cement City.

"We're not sharks, Bonn, that loses one and grows another."

She says it as if the concept is obvious, which it ain't. It never is with Blanche.

"What 'bout baby teeth?" I ask.

"I reckon I forgot those existed." She laughs, then her face lights up. "Aha! All those other boys were simply my baby teeth. So they don't count. Buck is my adult tooth."

"But we have like thirty-some adult teeth."

Blanche growls and slows Big Bertha as we approach my house. "Stop poking holes in my tooth analogy, will ya? I'm all balled up now."

I laugh. "So what you're sayin' is that Buck is important to you and the rumors are takin' away from that?"

"We ain't sharing him."

Blanche's voice is so serious I almost raise my hands defensively. "Everything will be okay. I promise."

"I think you should tell Roy 'bout Doc's." She glances over at me, as if she wants to make sure I'm listening. "It's only a matter of time before he finds out for himself, and it'd be best if it came from you. Besides, I could see him liking it there."

"I don't know," I say, and I mean it. Before, I was ready to share that world with him, also believing he might enjoy Doc's. But now there's this Henry-sized fear standing in the way.

"Think 'bout it. In the meantime—and I can't believe I'm sayin' this—don't do anything stupid to mess things up with Roy. The gossip mill would love that."

I mumble some type of reassurance as I get out of Big Bertha, then race inside my house, as if it's a safe haven, as if I'm running away from the memory of Henry's body pressed against mine, the shelves digging into my back, the feel of his lips on mine.

15

AS THE DAYS GO BY, THE GOSSIP ESCALATES. BOTH ROY'S SKEPTICISM and Blanche's annoyance escalate right alongside it. But, being Blanche is louder, her worries are front and center, and she's hounding me on a daily basis 'bout finally telling Roy 'bout my flapper alter ego.

Tonight's the first night all week that she hasn't uttered a word 'bout it. I'd almost rather she would. Her yammering serves one good: it keeps my mind off my ma.

Blanche pours a drink, slides it to Mr. Champagne Cocktail, looking quite pleased with herself. Nothin' new there.

"Hey," she says, her voice seeming hesitant, "ain't that the boy who followed you out of the back room? Haven't seen him since then."

Henry and I lock eyes, and a blast of heat courses through my body. He smiles wickedly at me.

"I think so."

He turns away, strides 'cross the room, shaking hands, patting shoulders, throwing back his head in laughter.

"Bonn," Blanche says, "you never told me why he was back there with you."

I bite my lip and drop beneath the bar to get a new bottle of whiskey. When I stand, I come clean to Blanche as fast as possible. "I made a mistake, let him kiss me."

"You let him?"

"Well, I sure as hell didn't stop him."

Blanche shakes her head. "And now," she says, slowly, "we're in this predicament."

"It's fine. Henry is fine. It's no big deal he's here."

"Yeah," she says, drawing out the word. "Why don't I have Raymond ask him to leave?"

"God, no. That's so embarrassing. It's fine." I give Blanche a pointed look when she opens her mouth, and say, "Really."

Blanche doesn't look convinced, and I ain't too sure, either. I discreetly watch Henry as the night wears on, hating that I do. Eventually, he swaggers toward the bar, as if he doesn't have a care in the world.

"I'm okay," I whisper to Blanche.

She taps her fingers against a bottle, as if she's deliberating, but eventually she curses and turns to Mr. Champagne Cocktail to see if he'd like another drink.

"Hi, Bonnelyn." Henry casually slings his jacket atop the bar. "Miss me?"

"It's been a while," I say, and wipe down a spot on the bar that ain't even wet.

He smiles. "I'll take a drink. And, another kiss."

I reach for a glass and steel my nerves at seeing him again. "I can get you that drink, but I'm afraid there won't be another kiss."

"Aw, Bonnelyn, I do recall you kissing me back." He flashes a smile. "Don't punish me for being away for so long."

"I'm not. Just don't think it's a good idea."

"'Cause of your boyfriend fiancé?"

Hearing Henry acknowledge Roy turns my stomach.

"I won't tell if you won't," Henry adds.

And that comment toughens my resolve. "Sorry, Henry, bank's closed."

"You're kidding, right?" His demeanor shifts, hardens. "You're going to tell *me* no?"

His name may be Henry but his narrowed eyes are nothin' like my daddy's. My daddy's eyes were never cruel.

"Sweetie," he goes on, his voice patronizing, "girls like you are a dime a dozen."

I clench the glass. "I reckon it's time you're on your way then. Like I said, you ain't going to get another kiss from me."

Henry turns, leaves, goes straight for the door.

I let out a breath and put Henry's empty glass back, my hand not quite steady.

Blanche is immediately at my side. "Real glad to see he's gone."

"Yeah." I exhale.

"Don't worry 'bout him. Henry's on his way out. Things with Roy and you are good. Buck and I are good. All is good. Who knows, maybe things are 'bout to get even better."

"Yeah?" I drop my hand to the bar, right atop Henry's jacket. "Ah, shoot. He forgot his coat."

Blanche rips it from my hands. "I can take care of that for ya."

"I'd feel better returning it now." I move to take the jacket from Blanche, but she holds on. "I know what I'm doing, Blanche. This way, he doesn't have a reason to come back."

I yank the coat free.

"Bonn—"

I'm ducking under the bar's partition before Blanche can say another word.

This chapter of my life, I just want it to end. No loose ends, or jackets.

I hurry out of the room, up the stairs, and give Raymond a quick wave. He shouts something at me, but I don't hear him, either. I'm already slipping into the apartment side of the building, and then outside.

Sidewalk traffic is calm this late in the night. I easily spot Henry's back and a puff of smoke. I call his name and hold out his coat. He turns, a conceited expression appearing on his face.

"Couldn't stay away, could ya?" He closes the distance between us in three giant steps. "I knew you'd be back for more."

His smoky breath hits my face, and I hold my own. He reaches to stroke my cheek. My fingers tighten 'round his jacket. I take a small step back.

"No, Henry."

At the same time, someone else shouts, "Henry!" but this voice is shriller, angrier.

Down the sidewalk is another woman, older, draped in a dark fur coat, her arm wrapped protectively 'round her belly.

"Who is this?" the woman demands, pointing at me, her whole body rocking with the motion. Her fedora shifts and she fixes it. "I've been wandering the streets, worried sick that you're late, and you've been with her?"

"No." Henry takes a step away from me. "I got stuck late at work, that's all."

"Liar!" she screams, and storms toward us.

"Gertrude," Henry calls. "Don't make a scene."

"Who are you?" She comes so close she nearly bumps me with her belly. "Why do you have my husband's jacket?" She rips it from my grasp.

Husband. Husband?

"I didn't know he was married," I say weakly, too stunned to say anything more intelligent. This poor woman saw me inches from her husband, with Henry 'bout to stroke my face.

"You didn't know?" she screeches, her voice cracking. "How could you not have known he was married? He's wearing a goddamn wedding ring."

Henry steps closer to his wife, his hand closing 'round the woman's arm, displaying a wedding ring that wasn't there before. "Calm down," he says to her. "Gertrude, this isn't good for the baby."

"Don't touch me!" She rips her arm free and throws the coat in his face. He doesn't bother to catch it, lets it fall to the sidewalk. "I knew it. I knew you were cheating. I bet you were with her that night you never came home."

"Gertrude, honey," Henry says, softening his voice. "We've already talked 'bout that. You're confused and it's late. Let's go home."

She ignores her husband, turns back to me. "Who do you think you are, you little wench? Henry is married. Henry has a baby on the way. You think 'cause you're young and beautiful that you can have any man you want?"

"No." I wildly shake my head, my thoughts frantic and unfocused. "I'm not like that. I didn't know. I'm sorry. I didn't know."

The woman starts weeping, her face falling into her hands.

I want to reach for her, comfort her.

Henry does, and she shakes him off. "Don't touch me!"

For the first time, Henry looks at me. His expression shocks me, as if he's mad at me, as if all of this is my fault. His crooked tooth shows within his snarl, and there's nothin' endearing 'bout it.

"Tell her!" I scream at him. "Tell her the truth!"

"Honey, this girl was only returning my jacket." He bends to pick up his coat and puts it over his wife's shoulders. "I'll take you home."

"No." She lowers her hands, exposing red, angry eyes. "No, I'm going to my sister's." She pins me with another menacing glare. "You can have him."

"Please, Gertrude," I say, hoping the use of her name will sound more sincere. "Listen to me. It's not like that. We're not together, I swear."

"Then why were you close enough to kiss my husband?" She stares at me, waiting for a response.

I—I can't form words to answer that question. My head's too balled up to know what to say.

Part of me is relieved when she flees, running down the sidewalk with one hand under her belly, her hat flying off.

Henry takes a puff of his cigarette, blowing the smoke into my face. "You were a mistake. A mistake from the minute I laid eyes on you."

He jogs after his wife, calling Gertrude's name and swooping her hat off the sidewalk.

I stand there, fury and disbelief and shame radiating through me. I press my fingers into the corners of my eyes to keep tears from falling.

Taking a deep breath, I hold the air in my lungs, my chest quivering.

I exhale, trying to breathe out every essence and memory of Henry. My breath hitches, and I know it's from the way his wife's hand shook as she protectively clutched her belly. I turn back toward the apartment building's door, certain that visual will stay with me for months to come.

Out of the corner of my eye, I catch a subtle movement.

My stomach plummets before my mind fully registers who's standing only a few feet away.

Roy.

16

ROY AND I STARE AT EACH OTHER, BOTH AT A LOSS FOR WORDS.

He simply stands there, his clothes seeming baggy, his face seeming droopy. His hand hangs limply at his side, holding a piece of paper.

"Roy," I say shakily, and step closer. "How much of that did you hear?"

He makes me wait for what feels like an hour for his stern response: "Enough."

That single word is packed with so much anger. I wring my hands. "I can explain."

"Of course you can. I can't believe how stupid I've been."

"No, no," I say. "You're not stupid. I am."

"That may be the only thing we can agree on right now."

His words push me back a step. I struggle to meet his gaze. "I deserve that. But Henry is nobody."

"Henry?" Roy's eyes get bigger. "You're on a first-name basis?" He looks away, back. Roy gestures behind me, to the spot where Henry and I argued, the brownness of his irises seeming darker. "I guess you would be. Who is he, Bonnelyn? Is that the guy Hazel caught you with?"

"No," I say quickly.

"Go figure. Even Blanche has too much self-respect to be with a fella like that."

His words sting, but I deserve it. I deserve getting caught, getting yelled at. Still, I take a step forward, trying to make our conversation more intimate, and give Roy what he deserves: the truth.

"I ain't at the diner anymore. I'm a bar-back at a speakeasy. It's called Doc's." I wait for Roy's face to change at the admission of my secrets, but it doesn't. "And that guy, he comes in. But he's nobody. I told him today to leave me be."

"And before *today*?"

I swallow, searching for the right words. "He was just someone at Doc's. I didn't know he has a wife, I swear."

"Him having a wife is a different matter. Who *is* he to you? He's obviously more than *someone*."

I blink my eyes closed, hold 'em that way while I collect my thoughts. A tear slips out. Normally Roy would leap forward and wipe that tear away. Not today. I do it myself, and say, "We flirted a little. I liked the attention he gave me. I did. I'm sorry. I'm so sorry Roy. I love *you*."

"What kind of attention?" Roy asks, his voice dangerously low.

"I don't know. He said nice things to me."

Everything 'bout that sounds lame, downplayed. Roy's face mimics my sentiment. "So what did you do *with* him?"

I reach for Roy, but he twists, avoiding my hand, and I insist, "He's nothin'—"

"Stop sayin' he's *nothin'*. Obviously he's *something*, if I caught you arguing with him and his poor, pregnant wife. What did you do with him, Bonnelyn?"

I reluctantly respond, barely more than a whisper, "He kissed me once. I shouldn't have let it happen. I'm so sorry."

"He kissed you?"

I nod.

"And you just stood there? An innocent bystander?"

My chest quivers. "No."

Roy runs his hand through his hair. He's silent, thinking.

I pick at a bead on my dress. "I'm so sorry 'bout the past few months and for lying to cover everything up. I was afraid if I told you the truth, you'd be upset. And I needed the money—it was always 'bout the money." I unsuccessfully reach for him again. I end up hugging myself, trying to rid myself of the chill I feel, from both the air and Roy. "I did this for us, 'cause I wanted to create a better life for you and me."

He steps backwards, shaking his head. "No, don't you dare do that.

Don't say we're standing here 'cause of your feelings for me. It's the opposite, Bonnelyn."

"I'll apologize a million times if I have to. Please forgive me. We can get past this."

"You lied, Bonnelyn. You kissed someone else. How could you have done that if you truly wanted to be with me?"

"I—"

"I don't know if I can get past that. I've been a fool, trying to convince myself that you running off with Blanche was nothin', your new look and how you've been acting was nothin', the rumors were nothin'." He looks beyond me, down the sidewalk, as if he's picturing poor, pregnant Gertrude. "Hell, this is worse than the rumors. But I just kept telling myself, 'This is Bonnelyn, the Bonnelyn you've wanted to marry since you were a boy.' "

"That doesn't have to change. Please, don't let that change." But even as I say it, I know I'm not that Bonnelyn anymore, and I so desperately want Roy to get to know the Bonnelyn I've become.

"It's too late," Roy says.

"No, it's not. It's not too late."

"God, it's been so easy for you, hasn't it?"

I shake my head. This hasn't been easy. Not at all. "Roy—"

"I go to work all night, you come here." He lets out a long, controlled breath. "This whole time, I'm none the wiser."

"I wanted to tell you. Come inside with me. I'll show you everything. I'll—"

"Here's the thing I don't get, Bonn. Why did you even ask me to come tonight, if that jerk also comes here?"

"What?"

Roy waves his hand dismissively. "Don't even bother answering. It doesn't matter. None of this matters anymore. I shouldn't have come. You shouldn't have written this." He holds up the piece of paper I forgot he was holding.

I stare blankly at him, my mind desperately trying to catch up, to understand, to fully digest that Roy catching me wasn't by chance.

Roy's patience seems to have run out. He tosses the paper flippantly in the air, frowns, then turns on his heel.

I'm frozen in place. Tears stream down my face. My legs give out, and I slump to the ground. Through blurry eyes, I watch him walk away from me.

A tortured sound bubbles out of me and I lower my head, noticing the paper he's left behind. I crawl to it, fumbling to pick it up. I start reading, and my breath catches.

Roy, I want to share something with you that I've been afraid to tell you. 34 Elm Street. Saturday night. 11:03, on the dot. Ask for me at the door.

No, no, no.

I would recognize that chicken scratch a mile away.

"God damn it, Blanche." I wipe away my tears.

I don't realize I've stormed from outside to downstairs 'til I slam the note atop the bar, a splotch of wetness seeping through and smudging Blanche's words.

"How dare you?" I scream at her.

With knowing eyes, she looks up from the drink she's preparing and cringes.

"Blanche!"

A few patrons turn to stare.

Mary rushes over, grabs my arm. "Not here. I don't give a rat's ass if y'all fight. But don't do it here."

I stand there, fury too overwhelming for me to be the next one to move or talk.

"We can go in the back room," Blanche says quietly.

I follow her back.

I shake with anger.

I cross my arms.

I wait for her to speak, pinning her with a glare.

Blanche chews on her bottom lip, finally saying, "What happened?"

"What happened? I'll tell you what happened! Roy caught me outside with Henry and it's all your fault."

"Mine?" Her face wrinkles like she smells something sour. "Nope. None of this is my fault. You should've told me 'bout kissing Henry before tonight, Bonnelyn. Frankly, I'm hurt that ya didn't."

"Let's not make this 'bout you, Blanche."

"Me? All I've been doing is thinkin' 'bout you. Blanche wrote that note for *you*."

My hands ball into fists. "Enlighten me. How on earth was inviting Roy here supposed to help me?"

She sighs, but her voice is testy when she begins. "You kept dragging your dogs, not telling Roy 'bout your 'other' life. So he comes, he sees. Done. You're both happy."

"You've never liked Roy. Why the hell do you care if we're happy or not?"

It dawns on me, remembering our conversation from the other day. This ain't 'bout me and Roy; it's 'bout her and Buck. It's always 'bout Blanche. She opens her mouth and I hold up my hand to stop her.

"It all makes sense now," I say, and narrow my eyes, stepping closer, talking slower. "You *really* invited Roy here to reveal my secret to Roy to help stop some stupid gossip? All 'cause you're insecure?"

"I am not—"

"I am *not* done. You didn't stop to think that I wanted to figure out how to share all of this with Roy? In my own way? Or," I say, even louder, "that maybe I'm afraid that Henry will be here and cause some scene. Oh wait, *that* happened."

"You were living a lie, Bonnelyn. It was bound to catch up with you. Hell, I bet you only liked Henry 'cause he has your daddy's name and he looked at you in a way that Roy never bothered to do."

I ignore the last part—Blanche nailing the truth—and focus on the blame she slings at me. "That's your response? That this is *my* fault?"

She shrugs again, looking smug. "You're the pushover who was easily seduced by Henry, not me."

I throw my hands up. "You are unbelievable. How I've put up with you all my life is beyond me. But not anymore."

Blanche's mouth falls open. I storm out. Mary doesn't question me when I inform her I'm going home.

Telling myself I can't let Blanche win, I fight back tears. But when I collapse into the comfort of my bed, I fall apart.

I bury my face in my pillow.

I beat my thin mattress with my fists.

I cry.

A light touch lands on my arm.

"What's wrong, Lynny?"

"I'm okay," I say to my sister, the pillow muffling my words. "I'm sorry I woke you. Go back to bed."

Little Billie squeezes my hand. "You can talk to me. I'm not so little."

I roll onto my side. A soft glow lights up her sleepy, doe-like eyes.

My door creaks open, and I see our ma standing there. I curse myself, hating that I woke her.

"Billie, honey," she says. "Why don't you sleep in my bed tonight?"

It's not a question, but Little Billie hesitates, as if she's searching for an answer. I cup her chin, putting a fake smile on my face. "Thank you for checking on me."

She takes a deep breath before her bare feet pound 'cross the room. Somehow, Little Billie is overtaking Ma in height, and quickly outgrowing her nickname. She scampers by Ma and out the door, our ma patting her butt as she goes.

In the dark, Ma takes careful steps. I scoot toward the wall, giving her room to sit on my bed.

"You've been going through a lot lately, haven't you, dear?"

Like with Billie, this sounds more like a statement. I nod, my bottom lip starting to quiver.

"I reckon that's part of growing up. Why don't you start by telling me 'bout that speakeasy you work at?"

I shoot into a sitting position. "What?"

Ma smiles. "Now what kind of mama would I be if I didn't know where my daughter slipped off to nearly every night?"

After the past few hours, I think my head may explode. "Are you mad?"

"I was. Had your daddy's belt in my hand, ready to whop you good."

I cringe. "But you ain't mad anymore?"

Ma sighs. "Sometimes, Bonnelyn, being a mama is hard. Knowing what's right and wrong can be even harder."

"How did you find out?" I ask.

"It's not as if you girls covered your tracks real well. When I was leaving for work one morning, I saw that napkin with the address on it, smack dab on the dash of Blanche's car."

"Blanche is a moron."

Ma's eyebrows rise. "So those tears are 'cause of her?"

Not all of 'em. But I can't bear to tell my ma what I've done. "Blanche invited Roy to the speakeasy tonight without me knowing," I say. "He got mad at me, and I don't know what's going to happen between us."

"He's a good boy. I'm sure he'll come 'round."

I rub my tired eyes, hoping the pressure keeps any tears from falling. "I'm not sure he will." *Not sure he'll forgive me for kissing someone else,* I finish in my head.

And damn it, Blanche is right. This is my fault, and I am plumb out of ideas 'bout how to fix it. "Did you and Daddy ever have rough patches?"

"Of course we did, sweet girl. No relationship is ever perfect, but you work at it. And in the end, you find each other again."

"Like the first time Daddy found you?" Ma tilts her head, and I explain, "The first time you met."

She chuckles. "Your father was a determined lad, that's for sure."

I laugh, too, already having heard this story a million times, and each time a sense of giddiness settles over me.

"There we were," Ma continues, "at a school dance. Your daddy was the new boy in town, which already gave him an air of mystery. Well, he saw me from a ways away, dancing with another boy, no less. Our eyes met, and it's like he spoke to me from 'cross the room. Of course, I did the proper thing and focused on my date."

"But Daddy had other intentions."

"Yes, he did. He marched right over to where I was dancing and tapped my date on the shoulder to cut in." She smiles, a hint of sadness lurking in the way her chest rises. "Once your father had me, he refused to give me back. But"—she taps my nose—"it doesn't mean I didn't try to push him away now and then when he got my blood pumping. Didn't stick though. It never stuck. . . ."

I frown. My parents were torn apart by death, not by choice. But Roy is choosing to push me away. Shoving, actually. Though, really, I may've been the one pushing him first, ever since he proposed, ever since that first fear of being nothin' more than Mrs. Roy Thornton.

"Do you think Roy and I can find each other again?"

"If that's what you want. He may just need a li'l prodding from you. Remind him that there's something worth fighting for."

I sigh, not knowing what to do.

"Come here, darling." Ma stretches out her arm, and I slide closer to her, lay my head on her bony shoulder. I almost pick my head back up in surprise. She's always been thin, but never like this. My stomach grows hot 'cause of what I'm 'bout to say, what I'm 'bout to face. I'm still not sure I'm ready to hear the truth, 'specially when my stomach is already raw from how things are with Roy. I count to three, working up courage, then I whisper, "I know you may have mammary ductal carcinoma."

She stiffens.

"Ma?"

She hesitates further before stroking my hair. "You aren't the only one with secrets lately."

I lift my head to see her face, swearing she has more wrinkles than yesterday.

Ma sighs. "Dr. Peterson agreed not to tell you."

"He didn't. I saw your file by mistake."

She nods, the simple action seeming to exhaust her. "Do you know what that fancy term means?"

When I shake my head, she continues in a somehow even voice, "Breast cancer."

"No." I repeat the word 'til Ma pulls me into her arms.

"I'm sorry, sweetie," she says into my hair. "I should really thank you. If you weren't being a devious young adult, I wouldn't have ever found out."

"What do you mean?"

"After I copied the address, I went there. I made an appointment, when I saw it was a doctor's office, to try to figure out what you were up to and if you girls were okay. Dr. Peterson did a physical on me. I should've had one long ago, but life was too busy to stop and think 'bout myself."

"Maybe he's wrong and you don't have cancer," I say desperately, once again leaning back so I can see her face in the darkness.

"Maybe. He found a lump. Look, honey, you don't need to worry over the details. Dr. Peterson and I are trying to fix it."

"How? What are you doing?"

She frowns at my persistence. "It's taking a bit of time to save up for it, but I'm having surgery in a few weeks."

"What?" My mind falters, triggering a memory of my daddy and his surgery and him dying. "And you weren't going to tell me?"

"I guess you could say I was working up the courage." She pauses, patting my hand. "But that's not the only way I've been selfish."

My ma and I never spoke like this before—like adults, like equals. I hate the *why* behind us doing so, but I like that she feels she finally can. If only I could be fully honest back.

"Right away," Ma says, "Dr. Peterson asked me if you were my daughter. So much happened from there. He reluctantly explained to me his *other* business. Said he'd ask you to leave, if I didn't want you working there." Ma scratches her head, casting an eerie shadow on the wall while she formulates her next thought. "At first I was appalled, and he assured me he'd let you go, but then we started to discuss payment for my doctor visits and the surgery. The amount"—she blows out a long breath—"the amount is a lot. So Dr. Peterson agreed to keep a careful eye on you. He also agreed to skim a little from your tips to put toward my medical bills."

"Ma, it's okay."

"No, it's not. I'm so sorry, Bonnelyn. It was selfish of me, and careless. That place is dangerous, and you shouldn't be working there. Every day, I've hoped you'd stop going. But with Buster still out of work, I'm scared, so scared. I can't die and leave you, your brother, and sister without any parents. So I've been taking your money for myself."

"I don't care," I say quickly. "I have more money. I started a bank account. You can have it. All of it."

"No, I've already taken too much from you. You're not mad, Bonnelyn?"

"Of course not. I want you to be better. I'll do whatever I need to do to make sure you get better."

Anything, I think to myself, and hug her. It's the God's honest truth.

17

SUNDAY MORNING I GO TO CHURCH WITH MY FAMILY, SOMEthing I still do every week. So does Roy—or at least I hope he'll be here today. From the choir box, I wring my hands and study every face that walks through the chapel's arched entrance.

Then there he is: his golden hair, his handsome face, coming in behind his parents.

Roy's eyes dance everywhere in the room, 'cept for on me.

I go through the motions of the service, standing when I'm supposed to stand, singing when I'm supposed to sing, pressing my hands together when I'm supposed to pray. All the while, I try to gauge what it means when Roy shifts from foot to foot, when he continually runs his fingers through his hair. Or, more importantly, why he's wearing the flight jacket I got him.

He knows I saved months and months for it. He knows I bought it 'cause it reminds me of my daddy's, which Ma still keeps in her closet. Why would Roy wear it if he were truly and fully done with me? Or do boys not think the same way as girls? What if his wearing it means nothin', if he put it on this morning 'cause there was a chill in the air?

Remind him, my ma said.

I bite my lip, pretending to listen to Pastor Frank's sermon, and rack my brain on how to fix things with Roy. An apology seems inadequate. But a promise, that could work. A reminder of the life Roy doodled for us.

A buzz runs through me. I open my hymnbook, flip from page to page 'til I find one that's mostly white. Old Woman Myers shushes me. I tear the page out, and she gasps.

Because I'm determined, it's easy to ignore her as I grab a pen from the pew. It's crude, my drawing skills leave much to be desired, but Roy's and my house takes form on the page, and then a sun. Birds speckle the sky. On the porch, we sit in rocking chairs, holding hands, smiling. I angle the paper away from Old Woman Myers, the next part too private for her prying eyes. Coming from my stick figure's head, I sketch a thought bubble: *Grow old with me.*

I neatly fold the drawing, hold it between my palms, and pray I won't lose my nerve. As soon as Pastor Frank is done with the closing prayer, I'm on my feet, out of the choir box, rushing down a less-crowded side aisle, the sanctuary resembling a hive of bees.

There's a line at the door by the time I get there, Roy three people ahead of me.

I tap my foot, urging everyone to shake our pastor's hand faster, to stop their mindless small talk.

Pastor Frank smiles when he sees me. I give his hand a firm shake and flutter past him. The late morning sun is blinding, and I shield my eyes, finding Roy halfway down the stairs.

My heart pounds. My legs feel like rubber as I follow him.

"Roy."

I swallow, nearly losing my nerve as he turns, not quite looking at me, but past me.

Like a schoolgirl, I shove the drawing at him. "This is for you."

• • •

Over the next few hours, every time I think of something better I could have said in that note, I rub my eyes, my forehead, my lips.

Like a caged animal, I pace my bedroom. Each lap, my eye catches on my Mason jar. Part of me wants to fling it against the wall. The other half of me is still hopeful Roy will accept my apology and we'll add the doodle to the rest.

Little Billie stays on her side of the room, like she's expecting I could have a breakdown any moment.

It's possible.

And I need out. I need to be somewhere that I feel free. Within minutes, I'm dressed and out the door, heading toward Dallas. In my haste, I nearly stumble down the stairs to Doc's.

Empty . . . so different than at night. My gaze lands on the piano. I walk toward it as if it's calling my name. I settle onto the bench, my feet barely touching the pedals, fluff out my skirt, and straighten my back. There's something 'bout sitting before a piano that requires being proper.

I start slow, my fingers lazily hitting each key. Graceful, even. But this type of piano playing is a lie. Blanche's words and accusatory glare replay in my head. I press more firmly on the keys. The cowardly way I shoved a note into Roy's hand slams into me like one of those new wrecking balls. Not knowing if he'll read it, if he'll forgive me, hits me on the backswing. I move my hands left, away from the high-pitched keys, needing the lower, bass-filled sounds. Hazel's smug expression hits me again, pulling me deeper into my own gloom. The visual of Ma struggling to stand from her chair adds to it all, another blow.

I close my eyes and let my fingers bring my feelings—so raw, so real—to life against the keys. My face becomes lax. I'm letting the music move me, but my arms remain stiff and in control.

"Whoa."

I rip my hands from the piano. The melody abruptly cuts off. Mary stands by the door.

"That's some dark stuff," she adds. "But don't let me stop you."

"No," I say, not even sure if that's an appropriate response. I rub the back of my neck, trying to bring myself out of a moment that was meant to be private, personal, intimate. "No," I repeat, and avert my eyes. "I'm done."

"Perfect," Mary says, looking a bit uncomfortable, too. "You can help me stock the bar."

So I do.

And I wait, and wait, for Blanche to strut in with her chin raised.

Only, she doesn't.

Mr. Champagne Cocktail and his friends come waltzing in first. I check the door repeatedly, wondering why Blanche hasn't paraded through. The minutes tick by, and I shred a napkin to pieces. Another hour mark nears, and I grab a sturdier dishrag instead, becoming more irked at Blanche for making me wait to face her.

"Careful," Mary says, snagging a bottle. "You're destroying this place. You've already left two piles of glass in the back room. And at the rate you're going, you'll scrub right through the bar."

"Sorry," I mutter.

Mary starts to turn, then stops. For once, her detached and unruffled facade is softer. "I heard 'bout what happened with that fella, with your boy—"

"What?" I ask, my nostrils flaring. I *know* it's Blanche's big mouth that blabbed, probably to make herself look better.

"It ain't like things stay a secret 'round here. Honestly, I'm surprised you lasted weeks without your boy finding out 'bout all your dirty little secrets."

"Yeah," I mumble, scrubbing the bar top even harder. I don't need Mary's voice to add to the one already in my head, 'bout how Roy's and my ailing relationship was never really Blanche's fault.

Mary shrugs. Over her shoulder, the door to Doc's slowly opens. Four men walk in, and I gasp. I know them well. Charles, George, and Edward, from the cement plant. The final man: none other than my brother.

"Buster," I say under my breath. Someone else who's 'bout to unravel my secret. I brush past Mary, pushing the dishrag into her stomach.

I know I could hide from him, but I won't, and I fight my way 'cross the dance floor, carelessly knocking into people. The entire time, my mind races 'bout what I'll say to my brother. The moment he sees me, recognition lights up his narrow eyes.

His friends flank him on either side, his group lingering inside the door as if they don't know which direction to go next.

"So this is where you go every night?" Buster shouts over the noise. Not even a hello.

I examine his face, but I don't know if he's angry or not. "Yeah, guess it was only a matter of time before you found out." I scan the familiar room. "It's a good place."

Buster's expression is impossible to read as he says, "It was hell getting in. Bouncer only agreed 'cause I told him that you're my sister."

I raise my brows at how he knew I'd be here.

"Roy told me."

His name is a punch to my gut.

"Wow, Bonnelyn," George says. "This place is amazing."

"Thank you?" I reply, not sure if that's the right answer. Doesn't matter; a girl on the dance floor has already stolen Buster's friends' attention.

I roll onto my tiptoes to talk into my brother's ear. "Ma knows 'bout this place, Buster. So don't go thinkin' you're going to tattle on me. She's already got enough going on."

He studies me before he says, "She's sick." When I don't act surprised, he goes on, "Having surgery soon."

"So she told you?"

He nods.

"Does Little Billie know too?"

He shakes his head. "Not yet."

Good.

"This place pays well?"

I raise a brow. "Yeah."

He bobs his head. "Ma told me she's got to stop working to get her strength up. She's been 'fraid to tell you. Says she's doesn't want to put any more pressure on you."

I swallow, already feeling the weight of being the family's only breadwinner, and turn toward Rosie onstage. Our conversation feels too heavy for Doc's. I come here to feel free, but my real life keeps tailing me.

Buster's eyes follow my line of sight to Rosie. She motions for me to join her. "You get up there and sing?" he asks.

I smile. "Yeah. It makes me happy."

"I reckon if it makes you happy, this place can't be all that bad."

"So you ain't going to hog-tie me and carry me out of here?"

"Nah. We need the money. Besides, that'd be hard with only one hand," he says. "But I don't need two hands to have myself a drink."

I should've known Buster and his wild ways would like Doc's. His friends certainly do, having already disappeared onto the dance floor. I smile, and pride that Doc's is mine flows through me. "Follow me."

Mary snickers at me when I return behind the bar, Buster grabbing a seat on the other side. "Sheesh, Saint Bonnelyn, how many men do you have? You're going to need a new nickname."

"Funny," I say dryly. Then I turn to my brother. "She's only razzing me."

He gives me a *Better be* expression.

"Mary," I continue, "this is Buster—my *brother*."

She accepts his handshake but addresses me. "I reckon that look in your eye means he's off-limits."

I nod, and Buster laughs.

"Just as well," Mary says, and points to Raymond at a poker table. "I've got that buffoon over there. He's enough work as it is. Now, how 'bout some brown."

Mary grabs a bottle of whiskey and sets out two small glasses, fills 'em, pushes one to Buster, keeps one for herself. "Shall I pour another?" she asks me.

Buster hoots. "You're telling me that you've been here all these weeks, Bonn, and you haven't had any?"

Mary rocks her head back and forth, answering for me, and I shoot her a glare. My brother beams proudly at me, then he gets this flicker in his eyes. It's a tiny ache in my heart, with how much it resembles our daddy's mischievousness.

"Well then, let's add some hair to your chest," he says.

A third glass is set in front of me, and I blow out a breath.

"Bottoms up." Mary slings back her brown. Buster drinks his, grimaces.

I hesitate. "Oh, what the hell," I say, figuring the alcohol may ease my Blanche-related anxiety.

I grab the glass, spilling some. I take a mouthful, swallow it down, cough, my throat feeling as if it's on fire. I open my mouth, hoping some of the heat will escape, and cough again.

"Tickles, doesn't it?" Mary says, smiling.

I breathe out, hoping no one realizes there's still a little whiskey left in my glass. "Something like that." My torso and limbs feel warm.

Buster asks me if I want another, and I feverishly decline. I fix him another drink, though, along with the other men and women who stumble up to the bar. It's nice, spending time with my brother. In between patrons, we talk. I actually laugh. He doesn't utter Roy's name, and I'm thankful for that. Neither of us mentions our ma or our money situation again. I don't think he wants to face it, either.

"How 'bout one more?" Buster asks.

"Mary ain't going to like I'm giving away all her juice." But I've already got the gin in the glass and I'm working on adding the soda.

Buster grins, turning in his seat and propping his elbows against the bar. Leaned back, that boy doesn't look like he's got a care in the world. Or maybe he's just got himself a real good buzz, this being his third drink in less than an hour.

"Bonn." With his back to me, he turns his head. "Bonn," he says again.

I drop beneath the bar to grab a new bottle. "Yeah?"

When I stand, Buster is facing me again, his shoulders no longer relaxed. "Who's that guy?"

"Which guy?" I ask, and imagine Mr. Champagne Cocktail doing something stupid again. Just last week he used his pants like a cape on the dance floor.

But, no, Buster is acting every part of a protective big brother, the way he's shifting his chair farther to the right, blocking where I stand.

"I don't like the way he's looking at you," he says.

I lean to the side and heat stabs me in the stomach.

Mary comes up beside me. "No way. Never thought I'd see him again."

Me either.

"Why? Who is he?" Buster says, his tone sounding dangerous.

Henry strides toward the poker tables, smirking at me every few steps. It's hard to fully describe the raw fury I feel toward him. He acted like he was something he wasn't. He played with my emotions. He tempted me, made me fail. He's the real liar, the real cheater. Nothin' more than a despicable excuse for a husband and future father. How is it that men like him exist, when my daddy—a kind, decent, loving, faithful Henry—no longer does?

I take a slow, controlled breath. Henry may have lured me, but never again will I let a boy bend my will. "He's nothin'."

Mary examines me. "If you're going to implode, please don't do it here."

"What's going on?" Buster says, louder.

"Honestly, Buster. Let it go."

He shakes his head. "If that's the fella Roy was telling me—"

"Buster," I say firmly, more firmly than I intended, ashamed my brother knows I cheated on Roy. "He's just some jerk who ain't worth either of our time."

My brother sips from his drink, and I notice the deliberation behind his eyes. "Fine," he says eventually. "Unless that creep comes any closer."

"Thank you," I say.

But I don't follow my own advice. I search the crowd again, looking beyond the chaotic dancing, needing to know where Henry is.

The first face I see is Raymond's. It's hard to miss him, when he's the only one unmoving, the only one staring at me, hoping to catch my attention. He nods toward Henry at the next table.

"I know," I lip.

Raymond opens his mouth, but my eyes jump to a new movement: Henry's.

Midlaugh, he turns his head toward me. The anger from the other night is gone from his expression. His residual cockiness is back, but there's something more in his pinning gaze and smirk. Defiance. It's as if he thinks he's untouchable.

He's not.

The tempo of the music increases, fueling something inside of me. I lock my eyes with Henry's, fighting the urge to shrink away. My next gesture ain't for Henry. It's for Raymond. But I want Henry to realize that this is *my* doing. I nod confidently toward the exit, silently demanding, *Raymond, get this sorry excuse for a man out of here.*

Two hands land on Henry's shoulders. Raymond yanks him out of his chair. Henry shouts, but the noise of Doc's swallows his protests. He tries to shake Raymond off, so desperate and childlike. I watch Henry, wholeheartedly enjoying the power I've wielded, as Raymond escorts him away.

The door opens as they approach it. Blanche enters, Buck coming in next. Blanche's features instantly morph from hesitance to anger, her lips pursing. Her hand winds back, flies forward, smacking Henry 'cross his face. Raymond's shoulders bounce in amusement. Blanche steps aside, and Buck slams his shoulder into Henry's as Raymond gives him the bum's rush. Blanche kicks the door closed.

She takes a moment before she turns, Buck's hand on her lower back to guide her. Blanche instantly searches behind the bar, for me.

A slow smile appears on her face.

I realize that a smile is already on mine. I straighten my lips and ask Buster if he wants another drink.

"I'd rather you tell me what the hell's going on."

"Later," I lie, and I get to fixin' him another Gin Rickey. "I've got to deal with *her* first."

Buck pulls Blanche 'cross the room, toward the bar. I'm ready for her, adrenaline still coursing through my veins.

"Y'all need to talk," Buck says to me, his arm stretching fully behind him, with Blanche hanging on as if he's a lifeline. He yanks her and she stumbles forward. "Now."

I push the drink toward Buster, then fold my arms over my chest.

No one says a word, my brother looking back and forth between Blanche and me with scrunched brows.

Buck shakes his head. He grabs my hand, pulling Blanche and me toward the back room. The voices and music ring in my head when the door closes behind us.

"Blanche will go first," he says.

She glares at him, and he smiles sweetly before leaving the two of us alone.

"Fine," she mutters. "I'm an ass. I should never have written that note."

Her sort-of apology catches me off guard. I'd been mentally preparing myself to go toe to toe with her. "Do you understand why?" I ask condescendingly.

"It was selfish. I did it more for me than for you. But part of it really was for you. I swear to that God of yours." When I don't answer right away, she continues, "Bonn, I really am sorry. You *know* Blanche never apologizes."

"You really messed up, Blanche."

"I know. I won't do anything like that ever again. Please forgive me? I slapped that jerk good and hard for you."

I sigh, the fight in me diminishing, 'specially since I know I messed up, too. "Okay, but—"

"No buts. I'm already a big enough ass."

I scrunch my brows.

"I know that didn't make sense," she says, "but at least you don't look like you're going to slaughter me anymore." I roll my eyes, and Blanche bites her lip. "How 'bout this . . . That Halloween bonfire thing is in a few weeks. I'm sure Roy will be there. Everyone will be having fun, be more relaxed. We can woo him."

"Weeks?" I ask, and rub my forehead.

"Time heals all wounds, Bonn."

"I don't know. I think I messed up too badly."

Buck pops his head into the room, bringing a wave of noise with him. His shoulders relax.

"We've all been there," Blanche says with a half-smile.

"Maybe. But I let that two-faced jerk affect me too much." I motion with my hand, slowly, steadily to the right. "It's like my life was moving on this good path with Roy. Then Henry smiled at me and *wham*"—I stop, start moving my hand sharply to the left—"that path started going the wrong way."

Blanche grabs my hand. "I can fix this, and your, um, path. Let me try. How did you leave things with Roy? Did he say it was over?"

"I don't know. He told me how he wasn't sure if he could get past me kissing Henry. He just walked away. Then today"—I let out a slow breath—"I gave him a doodle."

"You gave him a doodle?"

"Yeah, like one of those drawings—"

"Oh, I know what ya mean. I reckon you could've thought a bit bigger, though, Bonn." She claps her hands once. "But I can work with this; it's all promising. There's still a chance."

Considering Roy couldn't so much as look at me at church, I ain't so sure I agree, and now I'm doubting my apology even more. Bigger? I should've gone bigger. But how?

Buck steps forward. "Please let her try to help."

I smirk at his desperate tone. I can only imagine the earful Blanche has given him since our fight.

But I think 'bout being at that bonfire. I ain't convinced it's a good idea. Though I'm not convinced it's a bad one either.

Blanche stomps her foot, like an honest-to-goodness two-year-old, and brings her hands together as if she's praying. But she wouldn't actually ever do that.

My chest rises. "Fine." I exhale. "I'll go."

Blanche squeals.

I MOAN.

"Smile." Blanche taps her foot. "Come on, Bonn."

Buck—or should I say, Buck the Court Jester—leans closer and whispers to me, "Let's just get this over with. I feel ridiculous too."

I force a grin, showing too much teeth. Blanche rolls her eyes and snaps a photo. "Thanks," she says sarcastically. "Okay, now one of me and Buck."

He groans, and I catch the camera she shoves at me, knowing *one* picture really means ten. Poor Buck is a human prop while Blanche poses with him, on him. I take the photos, glancing at the clock in Buck's apartment. The bonfire started over an hour ago.

Over the past few weeks, when I'm not at Doc's, I've been at home, washing, scrubbing, trying to get the house as spotless as possible before my ma's surgery. Where I'm not at is school—excused 'cause of my special circumstances—while Buster, Billie, and I take shifts caring for our ma, not letting her out of her favorite chair, so she can get her strength up. Blanche brings me my schoolwork so I don't get behind. I've done enough damage to my love life; losing that hold on my teaching dreams would be too much to bear.

It's bad enough I spend my days exhausted, stretched too thin, but also hoping that Roy didn't simply toss my doodle aside. I'm endlessly questioning our passion, if our love is anything like my parents': long-lasting and enduring.

It's that thought that led me to doing something bold, something permanent, to show Roy my commitment.

A few days ago, Blanche skipped behind me, giddy with excitement, yapping 'bout how this was exactly the "bigger" she meant before.

The initial prick of the needle felt like nothin' more than a cat's scratch. From there, a bee sting, a careless swipe of my razor. Then it worsened: a hot needle being dragged over my tender skin, again and again.

Blanche held my hand and tapped my cheek whenever my eyes began to roll back in my head.

But I've done it.

Roy's name will forever be inked on the delicate flesh of my inner thigh, a spot only he will see.

If he forgives me today—and frankly, I'm worried. I stopped going to school, just like that, and Roy hasn't come knocking. I kept thinkin' I'll look up and see his tall frame taking up my bedroom doorway. But no, nothin'. And I told Blanche to leave him be; didn't think her pestering him would win me any points.

"Ready!" Blanche wipes her lipstick from Buck's face. "Bonn?"

I moan again.

"There you go," Blanche teases. "That sounded sort of pirate-like."

I look down at my black-and-white dress, the red scarf tied 'round my waist. "Nifty," I say sarcastically.

A few minutes later, the football field comes into view, and I hesitantly get out and shut Big Bertha's door. A huge bonfire blazes beyond the field's end zone. A bunch of my classmates dance 'round it, skipping and shouting our school fight song in tune with the marching band.

I scan for Roy but, from this distance, the costumes and setting sun make it hard to distinguish who is who. "So how do I do this? What am I supposed to do? Do I—"

"Go and talk to him," Blanche offers, and starts down the path toward the stadium, hand in hand with Buck.

"*That's* your master plan?" I ask.

"My master plan is constantly evolving. But, he's bound to forgive you, eventually. He bought you a house, which he's paying on every month. It'd be in his best interest to patch things up so he ain't out all that money."

I frown. "Good rationale, Blanche. Very romantic."

She shrugs. "If it were me, I'd have slapped ya and been done with ya. But Roy didn't do that. Is that rationale any better?"

Buck chuckles and pulls a flask from beneath his vest. He takes a swig, passes it to Blanche. "Baby, where're these violent tendencies coming from?"

She smiles, midsip.

"Let's see if we can get through the night without any fights," Buck says, pointing to his stomach. "I'm not at the top of my game right now."

"Still hurts?" I ask him.

"Yeah, a knife wound will do that to ya." But then he smiles. "Man, I don't think I've been in a fight in years. Clyde and I threw some punches this one time over the stupidest thing." He pauses, thinking. "These two fellas said Mickey Walker should've won this boxing match. But we thought Harry Greb won it fair and square. I'll tell ya what . . . Clyde may be small, but he's mighty."

I picture Clyde in the alley, an image I'm ashamed to admit slips into my head now and again.

"Well," Blanche says, "there will be no brawls tonight. Just good, clean fun, and hopefully some make-up necking between Blanche and her Roy Toy behind the bleachers."

"Yes." I curtly nod, Clyde Champion Barrow now a distant thought, 'cause he needs to be. I already allowed one man to distract me.

Blanche says, "Okay, let's mingle. Bonn, act like you're having oodles of fun. Roy will notice that. Guaranteed."

"But I don't want him to think that I don't think what I did was wrong."

"You're overthinking," she says simply.

Buck nods. "It'll probably work."

Blanche looks pleased. "Come on." She nuzzles under Buck's arm 'til she's wearing him like a scarf. I cross my arms. I want there to be *no* confusion 'bout who Buck's girl is.

We're not even two steps onto the field when people start noticing Blanche.

There's squealing, excitement, and, to my surprise, one of our classmates leans in close and whispers, "Do you still work at that secret bar?"

I gasp, yet Blanche whirls her tail. "I guess that cat's out of the bag."

Our classmate Shirley Johnson laughs, then grows more serious. "You have to get me in. Some of us tried to go the other day, but we got turned away."

"Sorry, it ain't up to me." Blanche shrugs casually. Though, inside, I know she loves the attention, 'specially with Buck's arm possessively draped 'round her.

Shirley pouts, but turns to me. "And you, Bonnelyn . . . People are sayin' you went into hiding after your showdown with Roy on the street. Either that, or you ran off and joined the circus. Is that why you ain't coming to school no more?"

"You've got to be kidding," I say.

"Sheesh," Buck says, drawing the attention to him. "Y'all are brutal. Leave Bonnelyn alone." He passes me his flask. Shirley's wide eyes follow the movement.

I take a long swig and decide that Shirley ain't worth any more of my time. "Let's dance."

I grab Blanche's hand. She latches on to Buck, dragging him along with us.

"Toodles, Shirley!" she calls as we skip away. Blanche playfully elbows me in the side. "Are you keeping stuff from me again, Bonn? How dare you not tell me you joined the circus? I know you like being onstage, but that's a bit severe."

"If that ain't the definition of horsefeathers, then I don't know what is." I shake my head, putting that ridiculous rumor out of mind. "Doesn't it feel ironic that everyone knows our secret 'bout Doc's, but *now* we're wearing masks?"

"Technically, that ain't a mask, Bonn," she says of the patch that covers my eye. "But if you want, we can rip 'em off"—she lifts her cat eye mask—"and be our true, renegade selves."

"Renegade? Let's not add any more fuel to the gossip fire."

"Outlaws?" she offers instead.

Buck laughs.

"God, Blanche. That's even worse. We're not fugitives."

"Stop squashing my fun."

"Meow," Buck says. "Blanche has her claws out tonight."

She paws at him, hissing.

I drop my head into my hands, the handkerchief Blanche tied 'round my head shifting. "Dance," I say. "I want to dance."

The type of dancing at Southwest Dallas High School's bonfire is a bit tamer than at Doc's, at first. Apparently, we ain't the only ones who snuck in alcohol. I hear Hazel—the sorriest excuse for a princess—bragging to someone 'bout how her older brother is in a fraternity and can get her liquor anytime she wants.

The night progresses and our teachers spend most of their time separating boys and girls. But not me and Roy. With every swirl, twist, movement I make, I search for him among the clowns, knights, and pumpkin-themed costumes dancing 'round the blazing fire.

My enthusiasm for dancing fades.

"I'm sorry, Bonn," Blanche says, plopping down next to me on a bleacher. "I haven't seen him either."

I sigh. "I feel stupid. Part of me got my hopes up that he'd be here."

Blanche opens her mouth to respond, stops.

Jimmy—Hazel's Jimmy—is coming our way with a determined and steadfast walk.

"Bonnelyn?" he starts.

"Hi, Jimmy," I say dryly.

"Would you like to dance?"

That question, it sets me on edge. Jimmy has always worshipped Hazel in a spineless way. But he's here. That means something. I sidestep Jimmy, spotting Hazel with her ridiculously big cone hat with long flowing veil. She spins, clutching her hat to keep it atop her annoyingly perfect blonde head. Rather, Roy spins her.

I tear off my eye patch.

"Bonn . . ." Blanche says.

I swallow, my stomach on fire, staring at Roy's satisfied expression, as he leads Hazel forward, backward, to the side.

"Bonn," Blanche repeats. "What are you 'bout to do?"

Hazel's big mouth is flung open in a smile, eyes locked on Roy.

I'm storming toward them. My breathing grows faster and faster, matching my pace. I grab the lace of Hazel's veil, ripping her hat off.

"Don't touch him!" I scream.

Hazel yelps in surprise. A few people 'round us gasp and cover their mouths. Hazel advances on me, hand raised before I can swing my own. She swipes at my head, but Buck jumps in, restraining her. The punch glasses he once held now litter the grass at his feet.

"Get off me!" Hazel screams at Buck. Her elbow connects with his gut, and he grimaces.

"Bonnelyn," Roy roars, an orange glow from the fire flickering on his face. "What the hell is wrong with you?"

I feel my own face burn—from anger, from embarrassment. "She's evil," I growl, pointing at Hazel, my outstretched arm shaking. "She's been feeding you, and everyone else in our school, one line after another 'bout me!"

"That's not true!" Hazel yells, and sneers back at me, struggling again to free herself from Buck's arms.

"Don't deny it, Hazel. You've been trying to get between Roy and me for months."

"You did a fine job of doing that yourself," Roy says to me, his brown eyes huge.

Blanche runs up, pulling me against her. She whispers into my ear, "Relax, Bonn." She turns to Roy. "You two need to talk. And not here."

Roy looks 'round at the openmouthed faces of our classmates. One of our teachers appears through the crowd. "Fine."

He turns on his heels, and Blanche pushes me after him. I stumble forward and smooth my ruffled hair beneath my handkerchief, trying to maintain whatever teeny, tiny amount of dignity I have left.

He leads me beneath the bleachers.

I hang my head, stare at my feet. The rush of adrenaline I felt only moments ago evaporates. "I'm sorry. I—"

"Acted like a complete crazy person." He tears devil horns off his head. "Jesus, Bonn. You attacked her."

I press my hands against my face, stretching my skin. "Hazel makes me so angry."

He throws his hands up before crossing his arms. "Why? She wasn't doing anything. You can't blame Hazel for all of this."

Only moments ago, I saw the way she smiled at him, and how he smiled back at her. I grit my teeth. Hazel knew what she was doing, and

Roy ate it up like his favorite dessert. Even Jimmy knows it, asking me to dance to finally take his own stand against her. But sayin' that now won't help; it'll only make me seem more childlike, guilty.

Roy shakes his head. "I don't know what to do, or say, or think anymore." He uncrosses his arms, his face turning sad. "This hasn't been easy on me, 'cause this is *you*. I've tried to rationalize things, maybe too much. I can deal with that speakeasy. But I keep coming back to the same thought: you kissed that jerk."

I step closer, touching his arm, my stomach tingling when he doesn't pull away. "I wish I could go back and change things. A lot of things."

"I wish you could, too, Bonn. But it doesn't work that way." He steps back, and my hand slips from his arm.

I could tell him how I got a tattoo to prove my commitment to us, but with how he's scrutinizing me, forever inking his name on my skin now seems rash, crazy. Crazy ain't going to win Roy over. Not after I attacked Hazel. All I can do is lower my head and count the beats of silence between us, while that stupid tattoo burns between my legs like the worst sunburn I've ever had.

When I look up, Roy licks his lips, swallows. "As much as I want *us* to exist, this"—he pulls out a stained, creased piece of paper from his pocket—"doesn't seem possible anymore. Too much has happened."

My doodle of us together, happy, old and gray.

I knead the back of my neck, squeeze 'til it hurts.

We stand there awkwardly, the seconds ticking by.

"I'm going to go," Roy mumbles, and steps 'round me.

I stare at the rows of shadows the bleachers cast and rub my arms. Behind me, the sound of his shoes against the gravel grows quieter. With each step, I grow panicked, frantic.

My heart pounds. My brain buzzes. A million thoughts run through my head, but none of them is how to fix this mess I made. All I know is that I can't let him walk away. If I do, I know this will be the last time he does.

Then it comes to me, what to say. Something I know Roy won't—can't—ignore. Not after years of sitting at our table, climbing the tree in our backyard, dodging the swing of my ma's hand after he let a cuss slip out, with a devilish grin on his face, identical to my brother's.

"My ma is sick!"

I feel slimy as soon as the words leave my lips. But it doesn't stop me from holding my breath, waiting, listening. The sound of his shoes against the gravel grows louder.

"What?"

I turn, facing Roy, but I'm unable to look at anything but his shoes. "My ma is sick," I whisper.

With the back of his hand, he nudges my chin up 'til our eyes meet. "Is she okay?"

"I don't know. Won't know 'til after her surgery." A tear slips down my cheek, and my breath hitches. "I've changed, and I'm sorry for all the bad that came with it. But we can find each other again. Please don't leave me, Roy. I need you. I'm sorry. I'm—"

"Shh." Roy pulls me against his chest, and I breathe in his familiar scent of Ivory soap. "I'm here, Bonnelyn. I'm not going anywhere."

I hold on tight, a sliver of a pleased smile cracking my lips.

19

ROY SQUEEZES MY HAND, MOST LIKELY TO CHECK ON ME. I'VE been staring at the hospital's waiting room wall for an indiscernible amount of time.

"This is taking too long," I say to him and my brother.

Buster's got his head propped on his hand, elbow on the chair's arm. He looks up. "Dr. Peterson said it'd take a while."

"I know." I breathe out. "But shouldn't they be done with Ma's surgery by now? Maybe we should call Billie and Aunt Marie so they don't worry."

"And tell 'em what?" Buster says. "I'm sure Billie is sleeping anyway."

"Yeah." I recross my legs. "I guess it can't be much longer."

Buster shrugs and grabs a newspaper atop a stack of magazines. But I know my brother is worried too. His muscles are too tense. His jaw is too rigid. I exhale again, but it does no good. My mind drifts to dangerous places, to an operating room in Europe, where my daddy died during the Great War.

I don't know much 'bout that day; Ma made sure of that. But I was home when the uniformed officer came to our front door. I was also secretly there when my aunt raced into town to comfort her. I sat slumped outside Ma's bedroom door, listening to her wail.

"I can't picture him that way," Ma cried. "Dirty, bleeding, helpless."

"Then don't," Aunt Marie said. "Remember him whole, with his wicked smile and his deep, lazy laugh."

Ma bawled louder after that.

I held back my tears, needing to listen. But how "The surgeons did all they could" and "Henry died during his sleep" became things I regretted hearing. For months, as a seven-year-old, I was afraid to sleep, for fear of not waking. I decided, long ago, that sometimes not knowing is better.

Now I'm ready to throw that theory out of the tiny hospital window into the cool Dallas night.

I squeeze Roy's hand back, so thankful he's here with me, so thankful he's on his way to forgiving me. But I need to stand, to do something, and I free my hand. That something includes pacing 'round the room. I stop to fix a crooked picture frame on the wall.

"Relax, Bonnelyn," my brother says. "Dr. Peterson and the surgeon said the operation should go without a hitch."

I cross the room and grab Buster's wrist, the one without the cast, to check his watch. "I'll wait five more minutes," I say. "Ten o'clock. Then I'm finding a nurse."

"Suit yourself."

I slump back into my chair, tap my foot, clench the armrests with both hands. "Anything good in there?" I ask Buster, referring to the newspaper.

He flips 'round the paper.

STOCK MARKET INVINCIBLE. "BUY, BUY, BUY!" EXPERTS ADVISE.

"Oh, this fella at—" I stop myself from finishing my thought 'bout how Mr. Champagne Cocktail mentioned the stock market the other week. I sheepishly glance at Roy from the corner of my eye.

He rubs his jaw. "You can say it, ya know: 'Doc's.' You're allowed to talk 'bout that place 'round me."

"I know. I'm sorry."

"In fact, I'd like to see this Doc's of yours for myself."

I smile.

"I wouldn't mind seeing that article 'bout the stock market, either," Roy adds.

A nurse with tired eyes rounds the corner into the waiting room. "Mr. Parker, Miss Parker," she says in an even voice. The smile disappears from my face. "You can follow me. Your mother is out of surgery."

"How is she?" Buster asks.

"Everything went just fine," the nurse says, still deadpan. "She's groggy and heavily medicated, so she'll be a bit confused. That's normal."

The word *normal* sticks with me. "Normal" should be my daddy whirling Ma 'cross the living room, dancing to music he hums into her ear. Or filling that last chair at the dinner table while Little Billie serves us more than canned beans.

Roy touches my arm. "Bonn."

I don't respond, still stuck in my head.

"Bonn," he repeats.

"Yeah? Sorry."

"I'll go call your aunt, then meet you in there, okay?"

"Thank you." I tuck my hair behind my ears before following the nurse down the brightly lit hall, the hospital eerily quiet this time of night, and into Ma's darkened room. Three sets of curtains create separate areas. With each one closed, I don't know who's inside or why they're here. That unknown has my skin crawling. The nurse pulls back the third curtain for us to walk through.

Billie and Buster take after our daddy, tall and lean. I have my ma's height. We're small-boned, small-chested, and she's too tiny in this giant hospital bed. A white sheet is pulled high, only her arms and head sticking out. Wires and tubes look like they're keeping her tied down, as if she's some prisoner of the hospital.

The nurse brings her finger to her lips, making a *Shh* sound, then points to the other curtains. I ignore her, saying, "Ma," and I take her hand, carefully avoiding a tube. Her eyelids flutter. A slow smile spreads 'cross her face before she mutters my name.

Behind me, Buster stands half in the little area, the curtain propped on his shoulder. I motion for him to come closer, and his movement shifts our ma's eyes to him. In the darkness, Buster's blond hair appears darker.

"Henry?" Ma says, her voice cracking.

A tear slips down my cheek. Buster stops midstride.

She struggles to lift her head. "Henry, is that you? Are you back?"

I cling to her hand, not wanting to let go, and stare at her pale, hopeful face. I open, close my mouth. I'm not going to tell this woman that her husband, my daddy, ain't here. I won't make her relive that moment when her world came crashing down 'round her. I look to Buster, pleading for him to do something, say something. But he's gone, the curtain settling back into place.

Confusion makes the creases along her forehead more pronounced. But then her features smooth and she smiles. "My Henry always finds his way back to me."

I raise her hand to my lips, kissing it, and leave wetness behind from my tears.

"Ma . . ." My lips quiver as I search for something to say. "Little Billie says hi."

"Sweet girl," Ma mumbles, her eyelids fluttering once more.

"Bonnelyn."

I whip my head toward the voice, a head poking through the curtain.

Doc Peterson gestures for me to join him.

I turn back to Ma, her eyes firmly closed. Gently, I release her hand and step slowly away from her bed.

"Let's go into the hall," the doctor says.

Buster is already there, both his hands and his forehead pressing against the wall.

He sees me. "I'm sorry," he says. "I couldn't—"

"It's okay," I respond, not sure if that's true, but not caring, and only wanting to hear what Doc Peterson has to say.

"Surgery went well," he begins. "We removed the breast."

I shudder, and Buster's skin pales.

"Is that all then?" I ask. "Is she better?"

"For now. We're fortunate we caught it early. But, if we need to, we could consider radiotherapy. It's fairly new. It's harsh. It's expensive. There are risks involved." I cover my mouth with my hands. "Why don't you two go home, get some sleep?"

"No, I want to stay. Buster, you go home. Someone needs to be there when Billie comes home in the morning."

"Are you sure?" he asks. His eyes tell me he wants to be anywhere but here.

I nod.

After Buster leaves, Doc Peterson squeezes my shoulder. "Take some days off from work, help your mother recover."

"No," I say. "I can't. I'll keep working."

I don't tell him it's 'cause we need the money to pay for this surgery and my ma's recovery. But he knows. He dips his head before he, too, leaves.

I go back to my ma, quietly pulling a chair up beside her bed. I bite my lip, watching her sleep, not allowing myself to cry again. Ma's always been so strong. She may not have liked how her life progressed—losing Daddy, raising us alone, struggling for money, and now this—but she faces it head-on, always.

Roy pokes his head through the curtain into the little room. "Hey," he whispers.

I force a smile. He lifts a spare chair, and I wait for the commotion I know will ensue, 'specially since it's dark. Roy bangs the legs against a table and scrapes 'em against the floor, the noise echoing in the quietness, 'til he settles next to me.

"Hi," I say to him. A genuine smile tugs at my lips. Roy wraps his arm 'round me, pulls me against him, and I feel safe, fortunate that we found each other again. "Thank you for being here."

"How could I not be, Bonn?"

"Plenty of reasons, but I'm glad you're here. You easily could have walked away from me."

"But I didn't." He kisses the side of my head. "I won't."

Those words . . . so simple, yet I could float away. And in that moment, I allow myself to float, to keep dreaming of Roy being beside me as we grow old and gray. "Marry me."

A sliver of space forms between us so he can see my face, his own face creased with confusion. "What?"

I cradle his hands in my lap. "You said before that when I'm ready, you'd marry me. I'm ready, Roy."

"Bonn—"

"I know we got some figuring out to do, and I've messed up big." I glance at my ma, back to Roy. "But there's so much uncertainty in this world, and if I've learned anything, it's that I'm certain I've loved you for as long as I can remember."

"What 'bout your dreams to finish school, get—"

"I still have those dreams, and then some. I want it all; you know that. We'll just reach it all together, after we're married. I don't know why I made a stink 'bout having everything perfect before we say 'I do.'"

There's silence between us, but unlike under the bleachers, electricity laces this conversation.

"Bonnelyn," Roy starts, and I hold my breath, "you're being unfair to me again." He pauses, and my heart may as well be in a vise. "I want to be the one asking." Something between a sob and a laugh comes out of my mouth as he lowers down to a kneel, and he says, "Will you marry me?"

"Yes!" I say, not caring how loud that word comes out, and fling myself into his arms. Framing his shadowed face with my hands, I kiss him, and it feels like layers of weight fall away.

"BEFORE WE GO TO DOC'S . . ." ROY LEADS ME FROM MY MA'S house, both of us decked out in our glad rags. Roy's even in a three-piece suit he borrowed from his daddy, who got it from his daddy.

"You ain't backing out, are ya?" I rub my neck. "I really think you're going to like Doc's. And I thought it'd be a nice way to celebrate our engage—"

"Relax, Bonn. I wanted to show you something first. Besides, I look too good to stay in."

I tilt my head, smiling, and my curiosity builds as we walk past the library, where we stop.

"Here we are." He motions.

"Our house?" I ask. I haven't been here in weeks, haven't even been able to walk past it.

Roy nods, and the simple gesture has me releasing a breath I didn't know I held.

She looks the same, the white of the porch and fence gleaming in the darkness. I go to say as much, but Roy says, "What I want to show you is inside."

Hand in hand, we walk up the broken pathway. Roy opens the door, flicks on the light, and I gasp. Before, I'd stripped the wallpaper, leaving behind an unfinished mess. Now a floral pattern in a soft yellow covers the walls. Crown molding gives the room an elegant style. All the trim is painted white, matching a built-in bookcase.

"You did all of this? You built that?" I raise my hand, taking his with mine, and demonstratively examine his hand. "But where are all your cuts and bruises?"

"Very funny." Roy steps inside, closes the door. "You like it?"

"I love it. I absolutely love it."

I love that he kept working, even when things weren't right with us. I love that he did this for me, for us.

He smiles. "I know things were weird between us, and I wasn't sure how to act or what to do. Instead of facing you, I avoided you, coming here. I worked, thought. And," he says, "I couldn't fathom how one"—he pauses—"mistake could unravel over ten years of you and me. Or the next eighty we've been planning."

I return his smile halfway through his ramble. "Roy Thornton, you are too good for me."

He laughs, and I lean into him. "Here, let me show you more," he says.

"There's more?" I ask, my stomach fluttering with excitement.

"There should always be more."

Together, we walk through the rooms. The tiny bathroom now has a sink and tub. The flooring in the kitchen has been mended and polished to be like new. Cabinetry needs to be refinished, but we can do that together. The two spare bedrooms still need paint on the walls, new trim work, and such. I adore seeing the rooms all the same, thinking of all the possibilities for what and who could one day fill these empty spaces.

Then we come to our bedroom. I'm nervous walking in, and my palms are sweaty. I don't know why; I've come in here before when Roy first showed me 'round.

The room's simple, the walls a soft blue. A mattress is on the floor. No furniture, yet. Soon I'll be bringing over mine.

"I was in here the other day," Roy says, behind me, his hands on my shoulders. He spins me to face him. "Just standing here, thinking."

"'Bout what?" I ask.

"You, us, the moment you became more than a silly crush."

I look up into his familiar eyes, practically jumping out of my skin for him to continue.

"Do you remember that day we were riding our bikes along the tracks?"

I laugh. "Which time?"

"When we were thirteen, and you fell off and skinned your knee?"

"The time I thought I could ride with no hands?"

"Yes, that time. You were doing good, 'til that rock came out of nowhere," he teases.

"I went right over my handlebars." I still remember how the perfectly circular scrape matched the setting sun.

He nods. "Afterward, I helped you home, pushing both our bikes, while you hobbled next to me, doing your best not to cry."

"I didn't."

"You didn't. Not 'til I cleaned your cut. But I saw something more than tears in your eyes as I bandaged your knee. You trusted me and needed me. I swore to myself that I'd never let you be hurt again. You were—are—someone I'd do anything to protect, no matter how life changes us as we grow older. That's why I came back; that's why I sat beside you; that's why I kept working on this house."

I hear all that. I do. But all I can think 'bout is how I want to kiss him.

I hold my breath when his hands gently frame my face. His chest rises and falls, slowly. Roy moistens his lips, and I ache inside. I ache for him, for the boy who will one day be my husband, who will forever protect me.

He moves closer, his forehead lightly pressing against mine. I feel his warm breath and smell his familiar scent of Ivory soap. His lips skim over my lips, his kiss soft, then hungrier.

Roy stops, meeting my eyes, recognizing my desire. It's easy. I'm breathless.

"Thank the Lord," he says, "that we're getting married next week."

I playfully fan myself. "Ain't that the truth?"

Roy slides a hand 'round my waist. "I've shown you mine; now you show me yours."

• • •

"I really do think you're really going to like Doc's," I say.

Roy's laughter drowns out the muffled sounds from the other side of the door. "You've told me that 'bout five times now, Bonn. You trying to brainwash me?"

I shake my head, but I can't resist one last comment. "This place means a lot to me. The music, the singing, the energy. It's like it invigorates me."

A smile stretches 'cross his face. "Go on, then. Show me."

I bounce on my toes, feeling seven and not seventeen, and swing the door open.

The upbeat jazz I've come to know and love is a tidal wave. I keep my eyes trained on Roy as he steps into the basement. The chandelier in the middle of the dance floor catches the red glow of the DOC'S sign and casts shimmers of color on his face. The poker tables, the dance floor, the bar, back to the tables—I watch him scan the room, that smile still on his face. But he also slips his hands into his pockets, as if he's a bit overwhelmed.

"All right!" Roy shouts.

I lean closer to hear him and nervously twist the hem of his jacket.

"All right," he says into my ear. "This place is a real eye-opener."

"In a good way?"

He smoothes his lapels. "That's yet to be determined."

That response is good enough for me. I release my grip, slide my hand down his arm, pulling his hands out of his pockets and intertwining our fingers. "Let me show you 'round."

I point out Raymond at the tables, before we hug the edges of the room to avoid the chaos of the dance floor.

"Mary," I say, coming to the bar, "I want you to meet someone."

"Oh, good, you're finally here," she says.

"Sorry. I wanted to make sure my ma got her meds and was asleep before—"

She turns to Roy. "You must be Saint Bonnelyn's very understanding and loyal boyfriend."

"Fiancé, actually," Roy says. "And you forgot 'very forgiving.'"

Mary chuckles. "How 'bout a drink to celebrate? Whiskey seemed just fine with you before, Saint Bonnelyn."

Roy raises an eyebrow at the fact I've had alcohol, but doesn't say a word. He also doesn't say no when Mary slides a glass of brown in front of him.

"You don't have to drink it, if you don't think you should," I whisper to him.

"When in Rome, do as the Romans do."

"Roy, you know that's not what I meant."

Roy flicks his gaze to Mary, back to me, as if I'm embarrassing him.

Mary raps her glass against the bar. "You two going to drink or exchange pleasantries?"

"Drink," Roy says. "You wanted me to experience your world, didn't you, Bonn?"

I sigh, trusting Roy.

We tap glasses, the sound of a trumpet eating up the *clink*, then sling back our brown.

Roy goes into a fit of coughing. I lick some spilled whiskey from the back of my hand and remember how it burned, the first time I swallowed it down.

"Want another?" Mary grins mischievously.

Roy pushes his glass toward her. "Why not?"

I sigh again, that trust waning. "Where's Blanche?" I ask Mary.

She points to the ceiling. "Taking her break with Buck."

"Say no more."

"More" comes out like a shout, Rosie having just sung her final note onstage. Roy grins at my outburst.

"Saint Bonnelyn," I hear, coming through the speakers. Rosie waves at me, motioning for me to hop to it and join her. "Come sing with me."

Mary gives me a go-ahead nod, and I lean over the bar toward Roy. "This will be a bit different than the choir music you've heard me sing."

It comes out as a question, being that I'm still unsure how Roy is handling his immersion in the speakeasy world—besides the whiskey; he's clearly okay with that.

He grabs my chin, his thumb rubbing against my cheek. "Thank you for finally sharing all of this with me, Bonn. If you're here, I'm here."

Trumpet and piano harmonies erupt into the room, cheers from the crowd accompanying the melody. The music and Roy's sentiment fill me with warmth as I scurry toward the stage. An overly friendly patron kisses my cheek, and I feel Roy's eyes on me.

Rosie pulls me up, midclap, and I realize Roy's eyes are really on the man who kissed me. I ignore the guilt that he's probably thinkin' 'bout Henry and fall into a rhythm with Rosie, both of us clapping, both tapping a foot, waiting for the instrumental opening to finish, while the dance floor is a frenzy of fox-trotting flappers and their men.

Roy sits at the bar, clapping, no longer consumed with the man, and I chuckle at him, partly in relief but also 'cause each slap of his hands is severely off the beat.

I moisten my lips, preparing to sing, when my attention is pulled to the door. In walk Blanche and Buck and, trailing a beat behind them . . . Clyde.

He doesn't waste a breath before looking at me, drinking me in, a moment I can't seem to pull myself from. Even if he didn't resemble a shorter version of Buck, I'd have recognized him.

It's his eyes. It's those same intense, captivating eyes I first saw in the alley.

Deep down, I have this desire to know what he saw, what he did, before he stepped into this room.

And before he stole my thoughts.

I swallow, realizing at the last moment that the song's chorus is beginning. I drop my gaze and sing, "*I've found a new baby, a sweet honey boy.*"

When I look back up, I train my eyes toward the bar. Roy is still clapping, and I remind myself how good it is that he's here and that we're working toward the life I've always wanted. I smile at Roy, and belt out, "*His new kind of lovin' has made me his slave.*"

Blanche appears behind Roy, working the bar, and Buck and Clyde saddle up to bar stools beside him. I can't help myself from sneaking a peek at Clyde. He's turned just like Roy, with his back to the bar, watching me perform.

I grasp the microphone with both hands. "*His sweet turtle-dovin' is all that I crave.*"

For the rest of the song, I engage with the dancers, gesturing and smiling and shimmying, and I fight the fear that if I were to glance again at the bar, my gaze would fall on Clyde before Roy.

When it's time to step away from the microphone and into the cheering crowd, I delay my return to the bar by gathering glasses from the poker tables. With my arms full, I use my shoulder to wipe a loose strand of hair from my face and slowly breathe out. That's when I see Roy and Clyde talking.

I don't know why it sets me on edge, like I've gone and done something wrong, but my palms grow sweaty against the glass surfaces. I duck beneath the bar's partition.

"Bonn!" Blanche shouts. "That was fantastic, as usual."

I smile, pausing a heartbeat before focusing on Roy. "Seriously, Bonn," he says. "That sure takes it up a notch from what you do on Sundays."

As I stare straight at Roy, an out-of-focus Clyde sits next to him, dimples I didn't notice before still recognizable on either side of a sly smile.

I don't acknowledge Clyde. It's stupid of me. There's no reason not to introduce myself. He's Buck's brother, not some random fella. Technically, we've already met, and in a life-and-death situation, no less. But instead of being sane and extending my hand and offering Clyde a friendly smile, I say, "I got to get these glasses clean," and turn on my heel.

With each step into the back room, past the bathtubs, to the sink, I mentally chastise myself for being so rude.

"Bonn?" Blanche says, behind me, and I jump, nearly dropping the glasses.

"Blanche, don't you sneak up on me like that."

She raises her hands. "Blanche ain't sneaking. I just wanted to come see how things are going with your ma, with Roy, and um, maybe see why you ran away like a bat out of hell. I was going to introduce you to Buck's brother, then *wham*, no more Bonn."

I concentrate more than needed on setting the glasses down next to the sink, flip on the water. "My ma is doing okay. Still waiting on an update from Doc Peterson. It's fine, though; she's obsessed with planning the wedding." I keep on talking, staring at the wall, barely taking a breath. "Roy is good—surprisingly, really good. He seems like a natural. Here at Doc's, I mean. And he's been treating me like a doll. Been working on the house . . ." I trail off, knowing I'm babbling.

"That all sounds nifty, Bonn," she says, and I startle again. Blanche is now standing beside me. "But that water's been running for a while and all those glasses are still dirty. So—and I'm no genius—I think something else is clogging up your pretty li'l brain. Does it have anything to do with how your eyes quit working and couldn't turn in Clyde's direction?"

"You ain't as dumb as you think you are."

Her hand flies to her hip, elbow bent. "Now, I never said I was a dumb

Dora. I only said I'm no genius." She chuckles at herself, then her laugh lines disappear. "Okay, so Clyde."

"So Clyde." I wring my hands together. I already let one non-Roy distract me, and I saw how good that turned out. "I think it'd be best if I kept my distance from him. I can't quite put my finger on it, but there's something 'bout Clyde, and with the wedding in a few days—"

"Bonn," she says, and taps me with her hip. I stumble to the side. She reaches for a glass, puts it under the faucet. "It's okay. Just keep your finger to yourself then."

I chuckle at her nonsensical response. "For someone so smart, you seem to have forgotten to use soap to clean those glasses."

She splashes me. "Go make sure your fiancé is enjoying himself. I doubt Clyde will still be here."

"You think he left already?"

She bobs her head. "Most likely. He doesn't have much reason to stay, now."

I cock my head at her, but she ushers me back into the main room. There's no Clyde—or Roy. I knit my brows, not able to stop the nerves churning inside of me, the worry that Roy could be having it out with Clyde somewhere. But why would he? This is my insecurity talking. Prewedding jitters.

I survey the room, peering 'round the dancers, and exhale, finding Roy at a poker table, Clyde nowhere in sight.

That's a good thing, I tell myself, and close the book on Clyde Barrow.

21

BUSTER USES HIS GOOD HAND TO FIDGET WITH HIS BOW TIE. I swat him.

"Stop that. You'll only mess it up."

"It's too tight." He smiles at me, crow's-feet appearing next to his eyes. "How come I'm the nervous one?"

"I'm good and nervous," I say, smoothing my hands down Ma's old wedding gown. I chew my bottom lip, looking at the church's double door I'm set to walk through, as soon as the music begins.

Marrying Roy was always in the plan, I suppose. But after almost losing him, after almost losing the only love I've ever known, "one day" simply became "now." It was desperate of me to use my ma's sickness to lure Roy back. It was compulsive of me to tell Roy I'm ready to marry him, while sitting at her bedside. Yet, here we are, no more distractions or roadblocks, and marrying Roy feels like a necessity to fixin' things, if I want a chance for those doodles that sat atop my bureau my whole life to come true. There's no way I'm letting some devil-may-care boy lure me away again.

It doesn't matter how Roy and I got to the point, just that we're here. I'm ready to become Mrs. Roy Thornton.

"Hey," Buster says, holding out his bandaged arm. "Help me out of this."

"You don't need the cast?"

"I'll be okay for today."

"Does that mean you'll be back at the plant soon?"

Buster laughs.

"What?" I didn't mean for the question to come out sounding so desperate. I slide the soft cast off his arm. "Of course I'll still help Ma out with money, but I'll have a duty to Roy now, too."

"I was thinkin' I may try my luck with duck."

My eyes widen. "You think you're going to support our family shooting duck? Buster, I can't believe—"

"Oh, Bonnelyn, you make it too easy. I'm only razzing you. Been having some thoughts recently 'bout getting a job as a broker."

"You'd know how to do that?"

"Have some faith in me, would ya? I've been studying up on stocks. Been keeping it to myself, didn't want to jinx it, but I made some connections already. Even got myself a snazzy suit for the interview." Buster pats our daddy's old jacket that he wears. The piano roars to life on the other side of the door. "I reckon it's time to get you hitched."

I swallow. "I reckon it is." Looping my arm through Buster's, I say, "Don't let me fall."

Buster squeezes my arm against his side. "Not like I could stop you, if you set your mind to falling."

As the doors open, I lower my head, slowly raising my gaze again, bit by bit. At the end of the aisle, there's Roy—hands behind his back, tall, handsome, a smile on his face. Pastor Frank stands beside him, his grin bigger than Roy's, larger than mine.

Buster starts walking first, taking me with him. With each step, the gown's heavy fabric shuffles 'round me. The high collar itches my neck, and I restrain myself from fidgeting with the buttons like my brother did with his bow tie.

The piano music is slow, steady. I think it's fitting for the life Roy and I will have together. No surprises. Roy's doodles coming to life: posing in front of the Eiffel Tower, riding horses with dogs running 'round our feet, holding hands by the sea's crashing waves. Maybe even a new drawing of me, up onstage, Roy in the front row.

I broaden my smile, finally meeting Roy's eyes. I see love there, the kind I hope to be long-lasting and enduring, and release the breath I've been holding.

Buster leads me past the few in attendance: my sister, my ma, my aunt, Blanche, and Buck. And on Roy's side, only his parents, sitting hand in hand.

A flash blinds me, and Blanche peeks out from behind her camera.

Roy stretches a hand toward Buster, shaking it, before Buster passes me to him. Roy's hands are clammy, and it puts me more at ease. So does the way his Adam's apple bobs, the same way it did when he first said he wanted to marry me, outside our one-day home.

"Thank you all for sharing in this day," Pastor Frank says, pure happiness in his voice. There's no "Dearly beloved," no formalities. Pastor Frank knows I wouldn't want any hullabaloo. He begins sharing a story of Roy and me as pups, and how he knew we'd end up holding hands at the front of his church.

Blanche coughs, my attention shifting to her. She gives me a thumbs-up, but a tight smile.

Now, of all times, ain't when I should be dissecting Blanche's brain instead of listening to Pastor Frank, but her gesture and that expression don't seem to match. Lately, she's been so supportive of me marrying Roy and, only moments ago, helped me into my gown, followed by a rather uncomfortable *First time with a man* pep talk. But part of me wonders if my best friend has simply been on her best behavior, trying to fix her mistake from when she wrote that note.

Blanche glances over her shoulder, back at the church doors. Buck nudges her, and she lips something to him.

"I didn't think so," Pastor Frank says, humor mixing with the glee in his voice.

Roy squeezes my hands. Heat rushes up my back as I quickly, guiltily return my focus to Roy, where it should've been all along.

Pastor Frank lays a hand on Roy's and my shoulders. "Let us proceed, now that we've unnecessarily established that no one objects to this matrimony."

At our pastor's remark, a chuckle or two comes from my right. An overwhelming urge wells up inside of me to have a silent conversation with Blanche 'bout why she looked over her shoulder at the exact moment Pastor Frank asked if anyone objected to Roy and me getting married.

Roy tightens his grip. His blond hair is slicked back today, a style he's never worn before. It appears darker, 'cause of whatever he's put in it. And, somehow, it makes him look more dangerous, 'specially with his square chin and prominent brows.

I lean closer to Roy as Pastor Frank presents our vows and asks me if I'll take Roy's hand in marriage.

"I do," I whisper.

Roy returns the sentiment, and then he's dipping me, his mouth landing on mine, even before Pastor Frank can pronounce us man and wife.

Little Billie squeals from the first pew, and our families clap at the fact that we're now Mr. and Mrs. Roy Thornton.

Roy grins, sweeps me into his arms, and carries me down the aisle. He doesn't put me down 'til we've gone a block over, him hugging me closer against the biting wind, and we've stepped through the door to my ma's house.

"Hey," I tease. "This doesn't count as carrying me over the threshold. I don't live here no more."

"Don't worry, Mrs. Thornton, I've got plans for you later."

Nerves jumble my belly at finally making Roy my Roy Toy, but I play the part, licking my lips, leaning closer. "'Bout time for those plans, don't you say?"

"Yes."

I laugh at the quickness and the firmness of his answer, and decide telling Roy 'bout my tattoo ain't so crazy anymore. "I've got something to show you."

"Do you now?"

I nod. "But ya can't see it yet. It's in a spot that's a bit . . . private."

"What is?"

"I may've gotten your name on me."

His eyes light up, and he reaches for me. "Where?"

I swat his hand away. "Now, Mr. Thornton, where's your patience?" But I realize I don't got a lick of it either. I pull Roy out of the doorway, hiding us from our family walking toward the house. Eyes trained on my husband, I gather my wedding gown, pulling it higher, higher, having to gather the dress 'cause of its volume.

I know the exact moment my dress is high enough. And I do believe Roy doesn't suck in air for a few seconds.

"Bonnelyn," he finally says, pauses, whistles. "I'm going to need a closer look at that. Much closer."

I drop my dress, biting my lip to hold in a laugh. "Not with everyone headed this way."

Roy moans, and I laugh freely, successfully leaving Roy wanting more for a second time.

Little Billie wraps her arms 'round us both, offering us her congratulations. From there, it's one hug after another, 'til both our families are packed into Ma's tiny house.

I let Blanche slip by without questioning her. It'd be poor form to ask her, in front of the husband I just propositioned, if she was expecting someone to burst through the chapel doors and shout, "Don't marry him!" And, as far as our silent conversations go, she doesn't take the bait when I cock my head at her.

My shoulders rise, fall with a steadying breath, and I join my family in the living room for an afternoon of food and, as the day progresses toward night, some secret hooch from Buck.

In the end, my aunt and the Thorntons have gone home—Roy's father stumbling out of the house—and I sit at a table with my wedding gown sprawled out 'round me like a moat, playing cards. Ma is wrapped in a shawl on the couch, laughing along with us young'uns, covering one yawn after another.

"Bonnelyn, honey . . ." Ma gestures down the hall.

I push back from the table, rustling Little Billie's hair as I pass her, and meet my ma in her bedroom.

She pats the bed beside her. "I have something to tell you, but I wanted to tell you privately, as not to steal any attention from your big day." I start to laugh, but her tone is serious, if not giddy. She grips my hands together in her lap. "Dr. Peterson said I've got a clean bill of health."

"No more cancer?"

"He's going to keep an eye on it, but he says I'm okay. *We're* okay. Once these stitches are out, I'll be back to work. And now, with Buster getting that job . . . I'm just feeling so relieved. Everything will go back to normal."

Happy tears form, and I squeeze my ma's hand.

"Which," she adds, "includes you going back to school, Bonnelyn."

School. I've been avoiding it while I've cared for my ma, and, ultimately, 'cause of Hazel and her gossip hags. But now I smile at the idea of Hazel seeing me prance down the hall with Roy's ring on my finger.

Ma kisses me good night before shooing me out of her room, encouraging me to enjoy the rest of my night.

Back in the living room, Roy's stack of poker chips is higher than anyone else's.

"Y'all," he says, his voice booming from the hooch, "this is getting embarrassing—for y'all."

I shush him.

Blanche objects, "That's only 'cause none of us know how to play. Your pile would look like mine against a real shark."

He shrugs. "Well, I reckon it's time for the real celebration to begin, anyway. Think you can get all of us into Doc's tonight?" Roy asks Buck.

Buck sips from his flask, passes it to me. "Yeah, I can make that happen."

I take a mouthful of brown, dulling the itchiness of the gown's fabric, and watch Little Billie straighten, all her tiredness gone.

"Billie, we need you to stay here," I say. Her pout isn't unexpected, but she doesn't put up a stink. Billie just gives Blanche a hug and disappears into her bedroom.

"Poor li'l thing," Blanche says, her eyes trailing Billie. Then she turns those eyes on me, excitement making the greenness of 'em brighter. "Your ma and I made you something. Well, it was more your ma than me. I can't sew a lick." She gives Buck a *Sorry* look, and he laughs. She pulls a box out from under the sofa. "I wanted to take you out yesterday to celebrate your last night as a free woman, but your ma didn't want you hungover on your wedding day. Go on, open it," she says.

Roy's hoot overpowers my awestruck gasp. I dangle the thin, white fabric, embellished with pearls and diamonds.

"Them gems ain't real," Blanche says with a wave. "But I reckon this is more fitting for dancing than that bulky gown you're wearing."

Truth be told, I can't wait to get the gown off. I love my ma for keeping her dress for me, and hope to pass it on to Billie and then my daughter one day, but, my Lord, it's heavy.

In no time, we're climbing out of Big Bertha and slipping through the apartment-side door into the physician's office. Raymond quickly greets us at the top of the stairs, a cheek kiss for me and a shoulder slap for Roy, then ushers our group down the stairs, not wanting us to linger on the main floor.

Being at Doc's after the wonderful day I've had couldn't seem more right. Rosie is onstage, belting out a tune. The dance floor is packed. Mary is running up and down the bar, serving drinks. I don't even feel bad that that snarky gal is manning it alone.

Blanche clearly doesn't, either. She's got Buck by the hand, dragging him out to dance. Roy takes my arm, leading me, and my mind flashes to weeks ago, when I daydreamed 'bout Roy swinging me 'round on this very dance floor.

He twists me toward him, and I slam into his chest. We burst into laughter, the sounds getting lost in the volume of Doc's. Apparently, I never fully imagined the extent of dancing with a very clumsy and slightly intoxicated Roy. But a smile never leaves my lips, and we don't stop dancing 'til our clothes are soaked through with perspiration.

"I didn't think I'd get you this sweaty 'til later," I say, and I mean it. I'm done saving my love; no more leaving Roy wanting more.

"Does that mean I'll finally get another—more intimate—look at that tattoo of yours?"

"And then some."

His jaw nearly hits the floor. "I'll drink to that, Mrs. Thornton."

• • •

I open my eyes once, twice, straining to keep 'em open the third time. Sleep clings to me, and I groan. As I roll over and see my husband, disappointment only makes me groan again. Even with my nerves at becoming Mrs. Thornton, yesterday had gone wonderfully—'til the whiskey flowed too smoothly.

Last night, there was no carrying me over the threshold. Supporting Roy's weight as he drunkenly stumbled into our house was more like it. My sexy dress wasn't crumpled on the floor 'cause Roy haphazardly threw it there in the heat of the moment. I tossed it to the ground after slipping into a long nightgown, covering up Roy's name.

My wedding night hadn't gone like it does for the lovey-dovey couples in my books or films.

I turn my back to Roy. He stirs, the mattress dipping as he moves closer. I pretend to be asleep. His fingertips brush against my neck, moving aside my hair. His lips touch my skin, gentle. Roy shifts, his hand moving to knead my stomach. Slowly, his palm drifts up 'til he cups my breast. He tightens his hold, and that's when I've had enough.

"No, Roy."

The bed shifts again. I turn onto my back. Roy is propped on his elbow. "What?"

"If you think this is the backdrop for my first time making love, you're sorely mistaken, 'specially after how you acted last night."

He runs a hand through his greasy hair, now sticking together in clumps. "I'm sorry. I guess I got caught up in everything. You looked so good in that dress."

"Stop. You got caught up in whiskey, not in me. The dancing part was fun. The many shots that followed, not as much." I sit up, pulling the covers with me. "Buck had to carry you out of there."

"I know. I'm sorry," he grumbles, but it almost sounds like it's more in annoyance than regret.

"Are you, Roy? Do you know how embarrassing that was for me?"

Roy runs a hand down my cheek. "Let me make it up to you."

I can forgive Roy for last night. Lord knows he's forgiven me for worse. But the fact his breath smells like a possum died of alcohol poisoning leads me to swing my legs off the mattress, which is still lying directly on the floor, and say, "No."

I storm away, not sure where I'm headed.

PART II

A BONNY LASS

22

BLANCHE SITS WITH HER LEGS CROSSED, A SLEW OF PHOTOS surrounding her. On Buck's coffee table, a shoebox is filled with even more.

I lean back against Buck's couch, unable to help the smile that creeps onto my face. "Blanche Caldwell."

"Mm-hmm," she says, creating another stack of photos.

"When did you become so sentimental?"

She holds up a photo. In it, my elbows are on the bar top, my feet on the ground, my back arched. Roy leans over me and my sparkly dress, our faces barely touching. We counted down from ten after that, bringing in 1928. That was nearly half a year ago, only weeks after we said "I do." An attempt to start the new year on a good note.

"When did you become such a vixen?" Blanche asks.

I snort. "Tell Roy that. He says we don't do it enough. He wasn't complaining that night, though." I wasn't, either. I slip off the couch, tug on my sweaty dress, and sit beside her on the floor. "Here, let me see some of those."

I thumb through the stack of photos from the school bonfire last year. A pirate, a court jester, and a sassy feline. Though the element that stands out most to me is not my costume but the apprehension disguised by my forced smile.

Blanche pushes another photo toward me. I'm walking down the aisle in my ma's wedding gown. My smile isn't what I'd call forced, but there's a similar apprehension, as if I knew the day—and Roy—would unravel.

When I went back to school, we held hands, I showed off my ring, and the satisfaction of working toward my dreams swelled inside of me, but the moment didn't gleam as much as I hoped it would. Maybe I'll get a do-over when school starts again in a few weeks.

I pick up another pile of pictures to distract myself from the lingering disappointment, and then another. Blanche stands in front of a Christmas tree with someone I can only assume is Buck's ma. Buck naps beside a picnic basket, the trees budding with signs of new life. I flip through one camera angle after another, with some shots way too close to poor Buck's face. There's Buck swinging from the rope at the river. And Blanche standing in Big Bertha, arms raised, head back, Buck at the wheel.

Happy . . . they look genuinely happy.

Blanche says something. My gaze falls on a picture of Clyde, and her voice becomes background noise. He's sitting on the edge of a shiny car, arms crossed, his own tattoo, too small to make out, peeking out from beneath his short-sleeve shirt. I can't help wondering 'bout the story behind it. I can't help wondering 'bout Clyde's story and the secrets he's hiding in his hazel eyes, squinting against the sun.

My cheeks flush. I've pulled the color of his eyes from a long-ago memory, not from this black-and-white photo.

"You've gotten close with Buck's family," I say. Not a statement but a question.

Blanche stops talking, begins again. "Sure, I'll answer that, being you ain't interested in the story I was trying to tell."

"Sorry," I say.

She waves me off, grabs the photo of Clyde. I hold on a second too long, snapping my hand back when I realize, and there my cheeks go, flushing more. Blanche stares at the photo and shakes her head, as if she's remembering something, and I widen my eyes at her—a silent *Tell me* that she doesn't see.

"I took this photo before one of his trips."

I wait—one, two, three seconds—as not to appear too eager. "To go where?"

She uses the photo to fan herself. "Ain't really my story to tell."

I laugh. "Since when has that stopped you?"

"Now I certainly won't be spilling the beans."

I roll my eyes. "Just to prove me wrong?"

"You got it. All I'll say," she continues, and I hide a grin, "is this car got Clyde into heaps of trouble. It was a rental, and the funny thing 'bout rentals is that you got to return 'em. Clyde didn't, so the joke was on him. Cops busted him, locked him up for a few days."

"Was he going to return it?"

"With Clyde, who knows? That boy's got sticky fingers."

"That ain't good." Not good at all. Says the girl who once rode shotgun in a stolen car. But I had no part in stealing it, and Buck told me the car was returned safe and sound. That is, after the scratches I put on her were buffed out.

"What's it matter to you, Bonn?"

That question stops me. It shouldn't matter to me. And it doesn't.

Blanche continues, "Thought you were keeping those fingers away from Clyde?"

"I am."

"Uh-huh. But I'd be careful letting your voice get high-pitched at the mention of Clyde's name when you're 'round Roy. This heat is enough to turn a fella rabid, and Roy don't need no help to foam at the mouth."

I get to my feet and, before I can stop myself, glance again at the photo of Clyde. His expression is proud, like he's 'bout to do something big.

Probably something hugely illegal. Maybe that's why I'm walking toward the door. The word *illegal* seems to go hand in hand with that boy, Blanche mentioning his antics as if she's describing the weather. "We should get downstairs," I say.

• • •

Down at Doc's, the door swings open—every hour at thirteen and thirty-three—letting in four more eager patrons. By midnight, we're at full capacity, and it's turned into one of those electric nights where a buzz fills the air. And people are generous with their money, have been for the past few months. My bank account is fattening, has been for the past few months, 'specially with Ma back working and her medical debts nearly paid off. Buster, on the other hand . . . He's struggling to get clients, but he even has clams trickling in. It's nice not to be the only one helping out our ma.

The door swings open once more, and in walks Roy. The clock reads half past twelve, and I reposition my weight.

Blanche pauses from her conversation with Mr. Champagne Cocktail to nudge me. "Looks like Mr. Bonnelyn Parker doesn't follow the rules of Doc's no more."

"Well, it appears Mr. Blanche Caldwell has no problem letting him in," I rebut.

"Did you know he was coming tonight?"

I catch Roy's eye, wave. "He had off from the plant, so he said he was going to work on the house all night. Reckon he needed a break, yet again. Or he decided our kitchen was better unfinished."

"Or he got thirsty."

Roy settles at a poker table.

"Or," Blanche amends, "he got the urge to gamble."

"But not say hi to his wife first."

She whispers into my ear, "The heat making you rabid, too?"

I playfully snap my teeth and her face lights up with amusement. I wish I were half as amused. I didn't put his name on my bank account so he could use our money so frivolously and so often at the poker table. Even if he says he's winning, I imagine there's a better use of his time.

I glance again at Roy, aggravated. And, as the night progresses, I only grow more so. Somehow he has a drink in his hand. I go up to perform onstage, and although Roy waggles his eyebrows toward me, then casts a glare at a man who whistles at me, that's the extent of our interaction.

I'm tempted to wrap my arms 'round his neck, a little more tightly than usual, and kiss his cheek, but he angrily slams down a hand of cards. I keep walking toward the bar. Between mixing drinks, I keep an eye on Roy. Each time, his hair is a bit more mussed, and the knot in my stomach pulls tighter. Blanche has called Roy hot and cold, but right now he only seems hotheaded.

"What can I get ya?" I ask a man with red hair. He's got a smart look.

Hat, cane, pocket watch, bow tie, fitted vest—he has it all. And I bet his clothing is tailored, too. That costs a pretty penny.

A burst of movement 'cross the room startles me, and I knock a glass onto its side. A man has his arms 'round Roy's neck, bending Roy at the waist, screaming at him. My hand flies to my mouth. With the music, their voices are lost; a chair falling onto its side is noiseless. It's like watching one man pummel another in a silent film, 'til Rosie stops singing and the instruments trail off. The roar of the brawl envelops the room.

"Roy!" I shout, adding my voice fruitlessly to the mix. Rushing from behind the bar, I seize shoulders, waists, arms to create a path through the crowd that blocks my vision from Roy.

Breathless, I break through and act on impulse to separate them, grabbing the other man's shirt, as if my five-feet-nothin' strength could do an ounce of good.

Roy's elbow juts out, and a flare of pain shoots into my jaw and ear. I don't realize 'til after it's happened, but I'm on the wet floor, face stinging. Blurred voices hang on top of me, asking if I'm okay.

I mumble a response, more concerned with Roy than my throbbing head. Buck has Roy's arms behind his back. Raymond has the other man pinned against the ground.

"Roy," I say, this time a whisper.

Blood trails from his lip. His shirt is torn. But the thing I observe most clearly is how he looks like a crazed animal, his head twitching toward the door.

Buck leads him in that direction, and I follow close behind. My thoughts are as twitchy as his movements: who and why and what on earth just happened?

He's never gotten into a fight at Doc's before, even with his smart mouth.

Once outside, Buck pulls open a car door. "I'll take you home, Roy."

"I'm going too," I say.

"No," Roy says.

I raise my chin and, for good measure, put one foot inside the car. "I'm going too."

"Best to listen to the lass," Buck says.

I climb in. Roy stares straight ahead and doesn't say a word as he settles beside me. I dig my fingertips into the seat's leather and steady my breathing, trying to ignore how the side of my face pulsates.

Besides the rumble of the car's engine, there ain't a lick of noise, and I watch Roy from the corner of my eye. He wrings his bloodstained hands, every once in a while dabbing his lip, and stares out the window as Dallas turns to Cement City.

Give him a few minutes, I tell myself, and probably what my ma would say to do. All I want to do, however, is pummel him with questions. I want to take his hand. I want to protect him.

"End of the road," Buck says, and pulls the parking brake into place outside our little house. He twists backwards, one arm over his seat. "You two going to be all right?"

Before I can answer, Roy is out of the car and striding into the house. My voice comes out exasperated at his behavior, at not thanking Buck. "Yeah. Thank you. Tell Blanche I'll talk to her in the morning."

When I go inside, a crashing noise comes from another room of the house. I sigh, grabbing a wet rag from the kitchen to clean Roy's lip. Then I hesitantly step into our bedroom. "What're you doing?"

Roy yanks open a dresser drawer; it nearly falls out. "What's it look like I'm doing?"

"It looks like you're packing a bag."

He doesn't bother to face me. "Then there's your answer."

Anger courses through me. I throw the rag at him with as much force as I can muster. The rag hits his back, leaving a wet splotch on his dirty shirt.

"What the hell, Bonnelyn," he says, his voice stilted by alcohol.

"Oh, no you don't. You don't get to have a drunken bar fight. You don't get to storm into the house, act like a lunatic, and then yell at me." I bite my lip, then very deliberately say the words, "What happened tonight?"

Roy freezes, a shirt in hand. He drops to his knees, his head falling against our bed. "I messed up."

I kneel beside him and touch his back. He doesn't flinch this time; his elbows just sink deeper into the bed. "How?"

"I wanted to blow off some steam. I've been working so hard, we've both been working so hard on the house, and nonstop at our jobs and . . ." He trails off.

"We have," I say.

"I thought the hand was in the bag. At the table, I mean. I was wrong. Jenkins had a better hand. Jenkins *always* has the better hand. This wasn't the first time I couldn't pay up. And he ain't okay with that."

The groan of our ancient fridge from the kitchen is all that passes between us for a few moments. "What are you sayin', Roy? I thought you've been winning. You *told* me you've been winning."

"Not enough. I owe him. And this bloody lip doesn't cover it." For the first time, he looks at me. There's fear in his eyes. "I got to go."

He stands, and my hand falls off his back.

"What?"

"I'm leaving. I have to."

"None of this is making sense. Where are you going?"

He bends to kiss my forehead. "Listen, Bonnelyn. Don't open the door for anyone you don't know. Don't leave this house."

"Roy," I say, my voice shrill, panicked. "You're scaring me. This is all insane."

He runs a hand through his hair, picks up his bag, then he's gone.

Roy's gone.

23

I SCAN THE STREET AND TREES, MY FINGERS DRUMMING AGAINST my knees, searching for Roy through Big Bertha's windows. Though I know it's hopeless, scanning for my runaway husband is a routine I've fallen into over the past ten days, no matter where I go. Now it doubles as a way to pass time while I wait for Blanche to return to her car. I peer again at Roy's parents' house. Blanche is walking back down their front path.

Once in the car, she shoves a bucket of brushes into the backseat, then a broom. Buck protests at the new additions to the backseat. She turns on me in the front seat. "God, that was embarrassing."

I don't care. "What did you find out?"

"A few things." She sighs and holds up her pointer finger. "First, Mrs. Thornton ain't interested in buying anything. But"—she holds up a second finger—"Mrs. Malone next door may want a broom, 'cause she was outside the other day whacking a stray cat and the broom looked like threads were holding it together. Or something. Third, Mrs. Thornton thinks it's so nice I've found something valuable to do with my time. Like I'd actually sell crap door to door for real. And, lastly, she hasn't seen or heard from Roy in days."

"So she knows he's missing?"

"No. I worded it carefully." Blanche puts the car into gear, pulls away from Roy's childhood house. "But she said she's been meaning to stop by to see you both."

I sigh. "Great."

Buck sighs too. "Ah, some air. Thank Jesus we're moving again. It's hot as Hades back here."

"Hey," Blanche says, and taps the underside of my chin. "We'll find him. This is Roy we're talking 'bout. Not Al Capone."

"I'm pretty sure Al Capone does his fair share of gambling," Buck chimes in.

I ignore him. I ignore the swirling, opposing feelings of fear and annoyance that Roy's disappearance has caused.

"Maybe it's time we go to the police," Blanche says.

Buck leans forward. "Nope. Not smart."

I rub my forehead. It's not smart. They'll ask questions, and they'll want to know where Roy was gambling. "Let me go back to Doc's. Maybe he'll see me and he'll come in."

"Roy?" Blanche asks.

"No, Jenkins. I don't know how much he's after, but I got money in the bank."

"Does Roy have access to that money?" Buck asks.

"Of course," I say, irritation slipping into my voice.

Buck whistles. I look over my shoulder, and his head is shaking slowly side to side. "Ain't good, Bonn. Think 'bout it. Why didn't he pay off Jenkins from your account to begin with? That lad dug himself too big a hole. Again, not smart."

"Shut your trap," Blanche says to Buck. Then to me: "Using yourself as bait to get to Jenkins is what's stupid. We'll keep looking, okay? I know you're probably sick of me by now, but I ain't leaving your side. Roy left to protect you, and you're doing a poor job of protecting yourself."

"That's why you lassies got me. I'm the muscle."

"Buck," Blanche barks, "you ain't helping, with all your backseat yapping."

He leans back, crosses his arms.

"Where haven't we looked?" she asks me.

I bite my lip, thinking. But the only image my brain produces is of Roy's face, his lip bloody, his hair stuck together in clumps. Besides, we've already checked the plant, the river, his parents' house, school, and Doc's. It's not like Roy goes much place else or has many friends to turn to. He's always been attached to my family and me and, reluctantly, to Blanche. His lack of connections hasn't stopped us from endlessly driving 'round Dallas, though. And Roy's on foot. He doesn't have a car. He didn't take his bike. My heart tells me he's still close by. He's got to be. But, right now, I also don't trust my heart. One second it's bursting with anger that he's run away, that he's left me. The next second, I'm pulsating with fear that the man I married is hurt, or worse.

I count to five to calm my racing heartbeat. "There's nowhere else to look," I say. "Can you take me home?"

"We've got another hour or so of daylight. Are ya sure?" Buck asks.

I keep my voice even. "Yes." I just want to be alone, to struggle with my thoughts in private.

Blanche steers Big Bertha into a U-turn. I allow my mind to go blank and stare at the nothingness outside the car's window.

"Slow 'er down."

Buck's urgent voice dissolves my daze, and I sit up straighter.

"What?" Blanche asks.

"Stop the car."

Blanche slams on Big Bertha's brakes. I lurch forward, both hands slapping against the dashboard.

"Up ahead," he says.

My eyes jump from spot to spot, the tenseness in Buck's voice making it hard for me to focus. I grip Blanche's arm, now seeing what Bucks sees. Seeing that the door to my house is ajar.

"The wind," Blanche says. "The wind must've pushed it open."

I don't need to be a mind reader to know that no one in the car believes that statement, Blanche included.

"There a phone 'round here?" Buck asks.

"The library," I stutter.

"Both of yous, stay here. I mean it, Blanche."

She must've started to rebut, but I don't hear it. I'm unable to break my gaze from the darkness between the door of my house and its frame. Could Jenkins lurk in that darkness? Could Roy, forgetting to shut the door in a drunken stupor?

Minutes pass and shadows fall 'round us. The sun drops, drops, drops 'til it's gone, taking some of the heat with it. The entirety of my house is dark now. The only movement comes from Buck, pacing outside Big Bertha, dabbing his forehead with a handkerchief every few steps.

Two pinpricks of light appear down Cemetery Road. The car stops beside ours. Out gets a man. Side by side, Buck and the other fella hold themselves in similar ways: feet wide apart, shoulders back, heads up.

"Clyde," I whisper.

"Yeah," Blanche says. "I had a feeling that's who Buck was callin'. Hmm, I wonder where he got that car."

"What do you mean by that?"

"Shh. I'm trying to hear them."

"Shouldn't be hard," I say. "Ever notice that Buck talks as loud as a megaphone?"

Blanche laughs. "Nothin' has been more true. But that boy has his reasons. Now, shh."

Two lights flick on.

Buck comes back to the car, flashlight in hand. "Blanche, no fightin' me on this. Either you don't get out of this car or yous go wait at Bonnelyn's ma's house."

"No," I say, beating Blanche to a response. "I've been avoiding my ma. Don't think she'd be too keen 'bout my black eye or the fact that my husband up and left me."

"Option one it is," he says, and twists his head in through the window to kiss Blanche. "Baby, you stay here."

Buck pulls back, taps on the door once, then strides away with Clyde. Beams of light dance ahead of them as they make their way to my house.

Blanche huffs. "The fact he told me not to go anywhere only makes me want to go somewhere. You'd think he'd know that by now."

"You two bicker like an old married couple."

I wait for her to say something disparaging 'bout marriage, but she only grins and says, "We do."

With her smile, a pang of sadness overcomes me. Roy and I should be fighting like an old married couple. We're the ones married. But no, he's God knows where, doing God knows what. While Clyde . . . I didn't expect Clyde to slip into my head at that moment.

But Clyde, he's here—in my head and in real life—helping me.

I clasp my hands together, my wedding band digging into my skin.

Blanche seems just as tense as me, but for different reasons. Her fingers grip the steering wheel, as if she's ready to scoop up Buck and get the hell out of here at the drop of a hat.

Every now and then, Clyde's and Buck's flashlights cast a glow through a window of the house, and Blanche and I hold our breath.

The wait is torture. Finally, two shadows appear on the front porch.

Blanche exhales.

Buck comes back to Blanche's window, leaning in. "No sign of anyone. Someone tore up the house, probably looking for some clams. Sorry, Bonn."

"I want to go see if anything is missing." Not that I have too much of value. Even my family earrings are more sentimental than anything.

"Tomorrow," Buck says. "I don't want you staying there tonight, and it's getting late."

I sigh. My gaze falls on Clyde, next to Buck, or at least what I can see of him. Standing straight, his face is above the car, but not his tattoo. "Thanks," I say absently, studying the initials USN beneath his short-sleeve shirt.

"Not a bother," Buck says. "But I do need a drink. How 'bout you, Clyde? Fancy joinin' us at the apartment?"

"All right," I hear, in that same captivating voice I remember from the alleyway. "But she's hot." He takes a hand out of his pocket and points toward the other car. "Got to take her back first."

I tense, Blanche shakes her head, and Buck laughs.

He laughs, at his brother stealing a car. As if he does it every day. Maybe he does. It's a feeling I can't shake, even after we get to Buck's apartment. The stifling heat doesn't help matters much. I take one sip after another of my beer, trying to cool my body and my nerves. 'Cause, sure, Clyde stole that car to come help me, but it's not like I asked it of him. He did it on his own accord, and fast. Within minutes of getting that call from Buck, there he was, so easily and readily breaking the law.

The Barrow boys are nothin' but trouble. Though I reckon I'm the reason why they put themselves in a precarious situation this time. I'm the reason Clyde stole a car.

Perhaps I'm nothin' but trouble, too.

I take a big gulp of my drink.

A knock sounds on the door and my stomach flutters. I swallow my beer. Blanche skips toward the door, grins at me over her shoulder. She yanks it open, and there stands a boy 'bout six inches taller than Clyde Barrow.

Roy's back.

24

THERE'S AN OLD NEWSPAPER ON THE COFFEE TABLE. BEFORE I know it, I have it rolled into a weapon. I race 'cross the room and whack Roy repeatedly, between sobs, each smack fueled by warring emotions.

He stands there, lets me.

Eventually, I stop. I drop my paper, rest my head against his chest, and will air back into my lungs. "Are you hurt?"

He wraps his arms 'round me. "From your spaghetti arms? I'll survive."

I push him away, look him over. Besides the gash on his lip, he looks fine. "I mean from the past *ten days* you've been gone, you ass."

"I'm fine, Bonn."

"Where on earth have you been?"

He sighs. "Can I come in? This hallway is suffocating."

"I'm going to suffocate you," Blanche says, back on the couch, "if you don't start answering her questions. You should be on your knees, groveling, right now."

"Pipe down," he says to her.

"No," I say to him. "You won't talk to her that way. Who do you think helped me look for you every day? Who do you think kept my spirits up while you were God knows where?"

Roy runs his hand through his hair. "Okay, okay, I'm sorry. I've just been on edge the past few days."

I stretch out my arm, blocking his way into the apartment. "*You've* been on edge? You run away, leave me holding the bag. You're lucky I wasn't home when Jenkins came by. He broke in, Roy. Made a mess of our house."

Roy's nostrils flare. "When?"

"I don't know. Today."

"That bastard." His jaw tenses. "I just paid him. If I ever see his face again—"

"You ain't gambling ever again, so there won't be a need to see his face ever again."

Roy licks his lips, looks like he's 'bout to say something, but then thinks wiser of it.

"Say"—Buck comes up beside me—"things are heated out here." He laughs at his joke. No one else does. "Come in, sit down. We'll all have a drink and get to the bottom of this."

"Bonn?" Roy says.

I roll my eyes and drop my arm from the doorframe. "Fine."

Buck is the true saint and makes small talk while he gets everyone something cold. Roy sits on a chair opposite the couch. He finishes his first drink in a matter of gulps. Buck, Blanche, and I line up on the sofa, ready to interrogate him. I start by pinning Roy with a glare, waiting for him to spill where the hell he's been. Now that I know he's okay, anger is all that's left.

Roy's knee bounces as he takes one sip after another of his new drink. "At first, I didn't know where to go," he begins. "I just knew I had to get out of Cement City. Town's too small. Wandered a bit in Dallas. Walked all night, actually, racking my brain on where I was going to get that kind of money." He takes another gulp of his drink.

"And?" I prod.

"I ended up with nothin' but cobwebs up here"—he taps his head—"sitting on the steps by the promenade."

"At school?"

He nods.

"We checked there," I say to myself.

"I wasn't outside long. I had a stroke of luck and Hazel came by—"

"Hazel Griffin?" I ask, as if there's another Hazel he'd be referring to. Blanche reaches out, pins my hand to my knee. It may stop me from slapping him 'cross the face, but it doesn't stop my tongue. "You were with Hazel—the manipulating, conniving Hazel Griffin who wants nothin' better than to steal you from me?"

He won't meet my eyes, but he says, "Relax, Bonnelyn."

I grit my teeth at his response and at the idea of him alone with Hazel, her cooing and dabbing his bloody lip. Blanche pushes down harder on my hand, her fingers just as tense.

"Hazel's working on a summer project for the newspaper, so she has a key to the school. She let me in and I hid out there."

"And that's it? She simply let you in?"

"I mean, no, she came by from time to time, brought me food, a change of clothes. She has an older bro—"

"I know." I don't want to hear 'bout her brother.

Thus far, Buck's kept his mouth shut, one leg crossed over the other. Now he leans forward, narrows his eyes at Roy. "How'd you get the money, lad?"

The money. The name Hazel Griffin was a whack to the face, and I didn't even think 'bout that part. "If you borrowed money from Hazel Griffin, I will never forgive you."

Roy freezes, his near-empty drink halfway to his scabbed lip. "I had a man who wanted nothin' more than to rearrange my face, and you're worried 'bout your ego?"

His words came out a touch slurred. Blanche's voice comes out dangerously low and slow. "Watch yourself, Roy."

Buck wraps his arm 'round my best friend. "I think you best explain, lad. Or I won't stop Blanche and Bonn when *they* rearrange your face. In fact, I'll hold you down myself."

Roy swallows. "All right, all right. Hazel's brother knows 'bout stocks from his classes at the university. He had a few ideas 'bout how to get rich quick thataway. I took a li'l from our bank account."

I narrow my eyes but don't say anything, once again warring with myself. I'm angry as a busted beehive, but I'm also relieved that money was there for him to use. This is Roy. Roy, my husband. I made a vow to him, and now that I'm in this mess, I got to keep this marriage together and honor that.

At my lack of verbal response, Roy shrugs. "It worked out. I didn't need much. I borrowed most of it from a, um, broker, on margin."

"That *um*—what'd that mean, Roy?" I ask.

"Look, Buster helped me out. He was happy to do it."

"You went to *my* brother?"

"It's fine, Bonn. Really."

"No, it ain't. What if you would've gotten him hurt somehow?"

Roy shakes his head. "That goon Jenkins doesn't even know Buster exists, and, like I said, Buster was happy I came to him. He's been having a hard time getting clients, being he's green 'round the gills. But we made a bundle, and fast. He's on the map now. He can contribute to your family again. You should thank me."

"Thank you?" I stand. "I'm staying here tonight. I think it's best you go home, alone. Now."

I keep my expression stern. Roy's in the need of some hard lovin', even if I am counting my blessings that he's close enough to touch.

When Roy delays, both Blanche and Buck stand up beside me.

Slowly, Roy also pushes to his feet. "I'll see you tomorrow?" he asks, and gently touches the fading bruise on my face.

"Yes," I say. I'll give him that. I need to give him that, 'cause I got to believe that we'll be fine in the light of a new day. Being with Roy is all I've ever really known.

• • •

Tomorrow comes, just as it always does, and I go home. What I ain't expecting is what I see. I let out a string of small gasps as I walk through the door. Buck gave me an idea of how badly Jenkins messed up my house. But now, as I scan the living room, not a pillow is out of place. In fact, those pillows are fluffed.

I continue into the kitchen—where for the past six months, the cabinets were unfinished and hardware was missing—and I find Roy, up on a ladder, tool-thingy in hand, putting on what appears to be the final knob.

"You did all of this last night?" I ask.

Roy startles, nearly falling off the ladder. He lets out a low laugh at his own clumsiness, then steps down to the floor. "And this morning. You're halfway to a smile. I missed that smile. Got to thinkin' what life would be like if I never saw it again."

His words are soft, like butter, but mine are sharp when I say, "You can't do that to me again, Roy. Leave me like that. You can't do that to us. I won't have it."

He steps closer, cups my face with his hands. "I won't. I promise. I'm sorry I put you through that, for you getting this"—he trails his thumb over my fading bruise—"and for how I acted last night. When I got there, Blanche had it out for me. My guard went up and it wasn't right of me."

That's all good and well, and I can forgive Roy's erratic behavior. I can even understand why he hid out. But the visual of him with Hazel Griffin is hard to swallow. I can picture her doe-like eyes oozing all sorts of sympathy all over him, and Roy eating it up like jam. However—and it's a big however—a demanding voice in my head says, *Let it go.* Me harping on Hazel will only cause added strain. Besides, he didn't seek Hazel out . . . the way I welcomed Henry's attention at Doc's. Or how I wonder what attention from Clyde Barrow would be like.

Clyde. I'm just now realizing he never showed last night, though I got to imagine that's for the best. Someone like Clyde Barrow probably steals hearts faster than cars.

"Bonn?" Roy says, and dips to my height. "Can you forgive me?"

I push aside the disappointment and focus on the here and now. "For better or for worse, right?"

"Better, then."

"Better," I repeat, needing to believe it.

25

I'VE A PEP TO MY STEP AS I PULL OPEN—NO, ROY BEATS ME TO IT, holding open the door to Southwest Dallas High School for me. It's our first day back, and I offer him a smile and a thank-you.

After Roy came home, the days and weeks that followed were light and fun, better. Roy and me were both on our best behavior, having more nights reminiscent of the one we had on New Year's Eve. We've been trying to put—and keep—the pieces snugly together, and my grip loosens on the fear that things are slipping away.

I reckon some of my pep is also 'cause we're entering a new school year, with a renewed focus on becoming a teacher and a news reporter.

The sense of stability I've always wanted is within our reach, 'specially with the house nearly complete. Only took us close to a year and a half, but just yesterday I lost track of time, simply staring at how the living room has been transformed, with its elegant wallpaper, polished floors, crown molding, and elaborate, ritzy draperies. All how I once imagined.

Each month we pay the mortgage, chipping away at what we owe the bank.

On a good month, we put money aside for a rainy day, and I like to imagine what important thing we'll use the money on. That trip to Paris, perhaps.

Roy takes my hand in his, leading me down the school hallway. I tilt my chin up, smiling whenever anyone takes notice of us: married, no longer at odds, onward and upward.

This was the moment I hoped for, six months ago.

Outside my classroom, Roy stops, pushes me back against the lockers.

He leans closer, closer, kissing my forehead. "See you after school."

"You tease," I whisper, receiving a wink in return, and walk into English.

I groan, as if on cue. I knew I'd see Hazel Griffin today, at some point, but first period of the day, and in my favorite subject, is a bit cruel.

Blanche's pep talk pops into my head: *If she gives you any lip 'bout cozying up with your Roy Toy, smack that tramp right in the kisser.* I smile to myself, imaging the sting of my palm meeting Hazel's rosy cheek.

"Somebody's in a good mood," Hazel says from her desk.

"Why Hazel," I start, and greet her with a fake grin, "if you keep going out of your way to talk to me, I'm going to think you want to be friends."

She wrinkles her nose. "That could get awkward, since Roy and I spent such intimate time together recently."

And there it is, I think, *just as Blanche predicted.*

Hazel holds up her pointer finger. "Although you had no problem sharing a man with Blanche." Hazel shrugs. "What do you think, ladies?"

Hazel's flock snickers.

My smile only grows, and I purposely use my left hand to tuck a strand of hair behind my ear, flashing my silver wedding band. "Yes, I've been meaning to thank you for helping my *husband*. He told me all 'bout it."

Some of Hazel's queen-bee resolve slips, showing in the tightness of her lips. "It was my *pleasure*." With that, she flips her hair and returns to her minions.

"Have a wonderful morning, Hazel," I say, knowing her practiced ears will still hear me.

I don't like the way she insinuated pleasure—with my husband—but if that's all she's got to throw at me, so be it. In fact, I do believe I've won a battle with Hazel Griffin, and, as the hours tick by, my winnings include not having to see her for the rest of the day, even though her insinuation does linger in my mind.

After the final bell, I meet Roy, waiting by our bikes. I kiss him, deepening the kiss with a frisky nip of his lower lip.

Roy touches his mouth. "Good afternoon to you, too."

"Hello." But that's all I say, for now. Soon, we're pedaling toward home.

I turn my head toward Roy, the wind tossing my hair into my face. "Hazel tried to stir things up with me today."

"Oh?" He raises an eyebrow.

"Yeah, it was kind of pathetic how she implied things happened between you two."

His feet stop, and he coasts forward on his bike. "You know Hazel likes to talk."

I do. I also know his reaction and his response don't quite add up, and I narrow my eyes. "Like I said, pathetic."

"Well," Roy says, pedaling again. "You won't have to worry 'bout her for long. Decided today that I'm going to drop out of school."

I twist my handlebars toward Roy, my bike swerving. "You *what*?" I don't like his flippant expression. "But it's the first day."

"Yep. Which means no more school paper, which means"—he flicks a finger at me as if he's 'bout to make some monumental point—"no more Hazel."

Dust kicks up 'round me as I plant my feet on the ground, nearly throwing myself over my bike. Roy stops soon after, adjusting on his seat to see why I've stopped.

"Okay, let's forget 'bout Hazel a second here." This is bigger than Hazel. "You're quitting school, the newspaper?"

"I do believe that's what I just said, Bonn." He smiles sweetly.

But no, that smile won't work on me this time. This ain't how things were supposed to go. "You said we'd finish school, Roy."

"Listen, Bonn—"

"You promised me you'd get a good-paying job as a reporter." My knuckles turn white on my handlebars. "And that I'd become a teacher." *That's* how things are supposed to be. "That's how things are supposed to go," I repeat out loud, needing for him to hear it.

"Things change, Bonn."

"Things change?" My voice raises another octave. "That's your response?"

"You've got that look in your eyes like you're 'bout to have a nervous breakdown. But this is a good thing." He holds up his hand to quiet me.

"The stock market is on the up, no longer a rich man's game. And we're going to ride it right to the top, easy money. We don't need me to be a reporter. Hell, if you wanted to quit school, you could. No need for you to waste your time."

"No . . . What . . . It's not . . . I don't want to drop out of school." I want the original plan. I want what I thought was *our* plan.

Roy shrugs. "Then don't. But I've supported you and the way you prance 'round on that stage. Least you can do is support me in this."

With that, he continues pedaling toward home.

• • •

Blanche twists her lips. "I don't know what to say, Bonn. Roy is horrible?"

I press my palms into my eyes, groan, flop my hands onto the bar top at Doc's. "He's messing everything up."

"Maybe he'll change his mind?"

"Doubtful. Roy's got a thick skull. Says he even wants to take out a loan so we've got more to play with." I shake my head. "And you know what makes it worse? He tried to act like dropping out of school was a good thing 'cause he wouldn't see Hazel anymore."

Blanche stops mixing a drink. "He brought up Hazel?"

"Yes." I twist my lips. "Sort of. I did first. But then," I add quickly, "he used her to make me feel better 'bout his decision. I don't like that."

"So what are you sayin', Bonn? You think Hazel gave him a helping hand in more ways than one?"

"God, Blanche. Can you be any more cavalier 'bout it?"

She slides Mr. Champagne Cocktail a drink, then looks at me. "Shoot, you really do."

I bite my lip, finally saying, "I don't know. My brain has been ticking through things. Remember at Buck's place, when I mentioned Hazel, Roy skirted 'round it with that bumbling apology? And Hazel spouting her mouth off doesn't mean much, 'cause, I mean, she spouts off 'bout everything. But then"—I shake my head—"Roy responded poorly when I brought her up today. And using her as an excuse . . . To me, that screams guilt."

She clucks. "Maybe."

"So I ain't being paranoid for no reason?" I slide a beer to a customer who walks up, knowing it's what he wants before he has to ask.

"I don't know, Bonn. You got your hand caught in the cookie jar, right?"

I cock my head at her.

"Your kiss with Henry."

I rub my eyes again. "I try not to think 'bout that. And we weren't married then."

"Try as you may, but you did. And cookie stealers are more likely to think that someone is trying to steal *their* cookies right back, 'cause they know how it's done." Blanche runs a hand down my arm. "A light touch here, a sexy glance there. 'Oh, your lip is bloody? Let me help you with that. Silly me, I'm too far away. Here, let me move closer. Wow, I never noticed the specks of brown in your—'"

Mr. Champagne Cocktail bursts into laugher, the sound covering how I holler Blanche's name.

"Blanche, sweetheart," he says, "you sure know how to string some words together."

"Seriously," I say, under my breath.

She waves her hand. "Nah. Bonn's the one good with words. I just know 'bout cheating, prior to Buck."

Mr. Champagne Cocktail snaps his fingers as if his luck has run out. "In that case, I'm going to stop wasting my time at the bar." He slides off his seat, and Blanche blows him a kiss.

"So now I'm legitimately worried," I say to her. "And depressed. What a combination."

"Where is Roy tonight? At the plant?"

"No, but he said he was going to stay away from the tables."

"Oh good. So he's at home reading a book?"

"You're lousy at this. You know Roy can't make it two pages before he drifts off. He said he wanted to talk to Buster more 'bout stocks. I'm sure he'll be dipping into our account again." I shake my head. "Money I work so hard for. But, as Roy says, I can stop working after he strikes it big. Not that I want to. Moron."

"Boy had a taste of luck and now he wants to slurp down the whole bowl. Little does he know, that'll just lead to a bellyache."

I stare at my best friend. "Where do you come up with this stuff?"

She slings her arm 'round my shoulders. "Honestly, I don't know. My mouth just opens and gibberish comes pouring out. But I do reckon you're being paranoid 'bout Hazel."

I scrunch my face, unconvinced. "I think you're tryin' to make me feel better."

"How 'bout this? It's a fact that Hazel will do whatever she can to get under your skin. Implying she got cozy with your husband is child's play to her."

I nod, exhale. "You're right. Okay, I'm focusing on that. I'm letting it drop."

I need to let it drop.

"Please don't break anything else," Mary jokes, but her concentration is on someone out on the floor. "Have you two seen that man before?"

"Who?" Blanche says.

Mary nods her head toward the tables. "There, at the table with Raymond. Raymond let him in, then asked Buck to switch with him at the door."

"Why?" Blanche says. I stare at the red-haired man. He does look vaguely familiar.

"Raymond wants to keep an eye on him. He's been in once or twice, asking lots of questions 'bout the place."

"Police?" Blanche asks.

"Nah. We'd be pinched by now if he was with the law. I think he's poaching us."

"Which means . . ." Blanche says.

"Bet ya he's opening another speakeasy in town, seeing how it's done." Mary rubs her lips together, thinking. "If only we could find his joint. I need to know what Doc's is up against, if their place is a threat to ours."

"We'll find it," I say, without missing a beat, and motion between Blanche and me.

"There you go again, volunteering." Blanche grins. "But you know I'm in."

"Good," Mary says.

Yes, this is good, a good distraction from Roy's upheaval of my plans. I ain't 'bout to let Doc's be taken from me, too.

26

"I'D REALLY PREFER IF YOU LASSIES WAITED HERE."

"Nope," Blanche says to Buck. "Can't shake us now. Besides, this was our idea. You're the one taggin' along."

"*My* idea," I say from the backseat. I take a puff of my cigarette and blow it out slowly, an earlier argument with Roy still swirling 'round me like the smoke. I tried to get him to reconsider going back to school after winter break, but he'll hear nothin' of it. In fact, he's been working less, playing the stock market more. I don't like it. It's too fickle—not like holding down a job, not like finishing school to get an even better job.

At least he's not playing cards, hasn't even stepped foot in Doc's in months. It saves us from fighting 'bout that, though we haven't been doing much talking, in general, almost as if we're living in different worlds. I haven't even told him we're tracking down Red Head, as Blanche refers to our poacher.

Buck shifts uncomfortably in the driver's seat of Big Bertha and glances 'cross the street at the darkened grocery store. I don't bother sayin' anything more; they can quarrel all they want 'bout if Blanche and I are going inside the Supper Club or not.

My door ain't locked.

After Red Head left Doc's the other month, Raymond followed him home. Once we knew where he lived, trailing him a few times wasn't hard. It didn't take long for Blanche, Buck, and I to find his hole. From there, we only came late at night, letting the days pass in between visits, as not to raise suspicion, waiting for the perfect time to make our move. Our trio has been nothin' but thorough as we scrutinized the joint and how it works, paying people off for information.

The Supper Club doesn't have the same rules as Doc's, where we stagger letting people in. Doc's is also in the heart of Dallas. This here club is off the beaten track. Just an hour ago, the grocery store went dark. People started slipping into its alley not long after. Same thing has happened every night we've come.

Buck taps his finger on the steering wheel. "Going to ask one more person the password."

Blanche sighs. "We already know it. Monday is 'escargots,' Tuesday is 'duck confit,' Wednesday is 'ratatouille' . . ."

I roll my eyes at the ridiculousness of the passwords, as if anyone 'round here could afford these fancy French foods.

"Thursday is—"

"I know," Buck says. "Just want to make sure. We ain't kind to people who show up off schedule, ya know. Can't assume this place is any different if ya futz the password. And it's Saturday . . . They could mix things up tonight."

He scratches his temple with some rolled-up bills.

Blanche huffs. "We don't got time for this, and I don't like those other gals working my shift while I'm sitting in Big Bertha."

Buck goes to respond, but I'm already shrugging off my coat, snatching the bribe money from Buck's hand, and climbing out of the car. I saunter toward a couple approaching the grocery store and flick my cigarette to the ground.

"Excuse me," I say, startling the woman. She gasps, covering her mouth. After an eyeful of me, equally gussied up, she lets out a soft giggle.

The man tips his hat toward me. I close the distance between us, pressing my lips against his ear. "Filet mignon?" At the same time, I press the money into his hand.

When I pull back, his lady wears a scowl like she's 'bout to leave a handprint 'cross my face, but the man is clearly amused, smirking. He nods, and I'm gone, practically skipping back to Big Bertha and leaning in Buck's open window.

"Filet mignon," I repeat.

"Oh, really?" Blanche says sarcastically.

Buck narrows his eyes in a playful manner. "Let's go."

"Good." Blanche pulls on a brunette wig. "'Cause Mary ain't happy we're missing so much work."

"She won't be happy if we get caught, either, and bring unwanted attention to Doc's."

I shake my head at their bickering, and Blanche throws another wig at me.

Wigs on—a mustache for Buck—the three of us casually walk down the darkened road and turn into the alley for the first time.

"I'm regretting not asking Clyde to come," Buck says to himself.

I startle at Clyde's name, having not heard it for so long.

"You get that boy into enough trouble," Blanche retorts.

Taking careful steps 'round the potholes, so reminiscent of the alley where I first saw Clyde, there are two things I wonder: what trouble Buck has gotten his brother into recently, and why I'd feel safer if Clyde were here.

Pushing the thoughts away, I wrinkle my nose at the alley's foul smell and rub my arms, trying to chase away winter's chill. We find the door, barely visible from the road, at the back of the alley.

Buck hesitates, then whispers, "Shit, what if there's a special knock?"

Blanche rolls her eyes, steps up, and raps the door three times. A little square in the door slides open, and in a true-to-form Blanche Caldwell sultry tone, she recites the password.

The square slides closed, and I scour the alleyway. Going into Doc's is one thing—it's *my* illegal establishment—but walking into someone else's lion's den to snoop 'round gives me a prick of heebie-jeebies.

The door silently opens. We've been accepted, so far.

Blanche goes first, past the muscular doorman, with Buck second, me last—just in case they get any ideas of letting only us gals in.

There's nothin' but shadows in the room we enter, and I glean that it's similar to the back entrance to the diner I used to work at—crates, shelving, and boxes. But this room has a trapdoor, with light seeping up through its cracks. It's the only form of light in the room, giving us no choice but to walk toward it.

"Looks like we're going down," Buck whispers.

He pulls open the trapdoor, and when Blanche and I stand there like dolled-up mannequins, he descends the ladder first.

Blanche goes next, grumbling 'bout how this place marginalizes women and their shoes by making them climb down a pencil-thin ladder. I awkwardly lower myself through the hole, never having been one for athletics. My arms shake as I descend each rung.

The three of us squeeze into a room barely big enough for two, with a lone door inches away. Music pulsates through it.

"Let's do this," Buck says, now grinning, and double-checks that his mustache is in place.

A Rosie-like voice hits us as we walk in. A glowing THE SUPPER CLUB sign hangs behind her. Scanning, I see poker tables, a dance area, the bar.

"It's almost identical," I say.

"Only bigger," Blanche says. "A lot bigger."

"Twice the size," Buck adds.

"But they don't serve food," Blanche says matter-of-factly.

"Baby, neither do we."

"Sure," she counters. "But we don't put it in our name."

Buck and I can't deny that; Blanche's logic makes sense, for once. We fumble through the too-crowded dance floor to the bar and order drinks. Chewing on my straw, I peer over my glass, taking in the room, but mostly watching the girl onstage. With Christmas not far away, she's got on a Santa hat.

I lean toward Blanche and talk into her ear. "Rosie is better."

Blanche nods. "So are you. You see Red Head?"

"Nah," Buck says. "But that's fine. We got what we need, now that we've seen the inside. Our location is better. We're more exclusive. And as Bonn here said"—he winks at me—"the entertainment ain't as good. Mary won't be happy, but she won't be piss mad either. This place ain't a real threat."

I exhale a breath I hadn't even known I was holding. With Roy turning my life upside down, I needed this. I needed Doc's not to be in jeopardy.

"Well," Blanche says, "we might as well make the most of the night." She grabs Buck's hands, tapping her feet like she wants to dance. He laughs.

"You two have fun," I say. "I'll keep the bar company."

Blanche pats my butt, and I climb onto a recently vacated stool, watching them go off to the dance floor. The familiarity of the speakeasy puts me more at ease. I order another drink and begin to watch the people. Among the flailing limbs, I spot Blanche in her red dress and fake dark hair.

She once said she was jealous that Roy and I were each other's firsts. With how she smiles now, I reckon none of that matters to her anymore. She may've found Buck after going through a laundry list of men, but it's like Buck and Blanche were always meant to be. Like Roy and me. Right?

Roy—he's obviously on my brain, 'cause I spot a fella who looks eerily similar, striding toward the bar. I sip my drink, swallowing slowly as his eyes pass over me. Every fiber in my body tightens. The square chin, prominent brows, slicked-back blond hair . . . That ain't a Roy replica; that's Roy himself.

I force the drink down my throat. It burns. I cough and massage my neck, my eyes glued on Roy. He pushes through the crowd, his torso twisted to one side, one arm trailing behind him.

Anger flares inside of me, adding to the burn. What the hell is he doing here? Roy promised me he'd stop gambling after he got himself into trouble, but here he is, walking away from the poker tables. I stare at him, willing him to acknowledge me so I can catch him in the act. Brunette disguise or not, there's no way Roy won't recognize my glare—he's seen it plenty lately. I shake my head, sipping through my straw, waiting, almost anticipating more sharp words with him. But his eyes pass over me.

He creeps nearer and nearer to the bar, finally breaking through the crowd, and behind Roy, fingers intertwined with his, a blonde girl leans forward to whisper something to him.

I choke on my drink. The smile that crosses Roy's face is a punch to my gut. That smile steals my resolve, and I turn my body, putting my back to him, protecting myself from seeing any more. Staring at the bar,

I grasp my drink with shaky hands, cursing myself for losing my will to confront Roy, cursing myself for ever trusting him.

Roy squeezes up to the bar, next to me, and flicks his hand toward the bartender to catch his attention. Breath neither enters nor leaves my lungs. The closeness of Roy—with another girl—freezes every part of my anatomy, including my brain. He bumps into me, and the rigidness of my body sloshes the drink in my glass, spilling it.

"Oh, sorry." Roy passes me a napkin, our bodies entirely too close. I feel his breath on my face, reminding me to breathe, and our eyes meet.

"Bonnelyn?"

I stutter something incoherent.

Over the next few seconds, his face transforms, the paleness of his skin turns pink, his nostrils flare. "Did you follow me? In a disguise?"

"No," I manage, now hating myself for sounding so weak. But I ain't weak. And Roy is the one whose voice should be trembling. Not mine.

The blonde girl wraps her body 'round Roy, peering to see me. A deep sound rumbles in my throat. "Baby, who's this?" she says.

That does it. Seeing the possessiveness in her eyes, the anger in Roy's—both reactions snap my wits back into place. I think of Hazel. I think of myself, sans my dark wig. I think of this tramp. Ignoring her, I focus on Roy, and I ain't going to let him treat me like this. "Clearly, you have a thing for blondes, *baby*."

His tramp gives me a *Huh* expression. I rip off my fake hair, pin her with the coldest glare I can muster. "I'm his wife. Who might *you* be?"

Roy grabs my elbow, drags me toward the room's outskirts.

"What the hell are you doing here, Bonnelyn?"

"Me?" I shout. "I could ask you the same. Though I think it's quite obvious."

"I ain't doing nothin'."

I bunch my dress in either hand, fighting for composure. "I find that hard to believe."

He shrugs. "Fine, I ain't doing nothin' you haven't already done."

"What's that supposed to mean?" I ask, and mimic his shrug, exaggerating it.

"That you've made it easy."

"*I* made it easy?"

"Yes, *you*." Roy's lips curl into something resembling a smug, vindictive smile. "You're the one who dragged me into this world of sin. You're the one who got caught first." He crosses his arms, as if he's just made a monumental point.

He hasn't. I throw up my hands, let them slap against my thighs. Though I should be slapping him 'cross his conceited face. "This isn't a tit-for-tat situation, Roy. You don't get a free pass to cheat 'cause of something stupid I did over a year ago—something I apologized for; something you said you forgave me for. Something that happened *before* we were married."

Roy doesn't say a thing, his arms still tightly crossed, so I say, "You know what, I always thought you were oblivious to how other girls fancied you." Hazel's ongoing attempts to steal Roy flash through my mind. "But now I'm thinkin' you knew, and you liked the attention." I shake my head, furious, disgusted. "You were only pretending to be a good guy."

"Look at yourself." He takes a step closer, and I retreat a step, my back hitting the brick wall. "You're up onstage, wearing practically nothin', getting pure joy out of the way men drool over you. I've seen it with my own two eyes. And I don't like it one bit, *Saint* Bonnelyn."

I swallow. His words are hurtful; this whole situation is hurtful. But I force myself to keep it together, raising my voice. "I like who I am. But you"—I wave my hand in his general direction—"are a disgrace, Roy, coming here *behind my back* to gamble and do God knows what with other women!"

My shout catches the attention of those 'round us. Roy leans close, and I smell the alcohol on his breath. "Like I said, you make it easy."

"No, Roy. None of this is *my* fault." I hate how my voice hitches, giving away that my heart is pounding from both anger and pain. I raise my chin. "Now, get out of my face."

Roy falters, taking a step away. He turns back, eyes narrowing, lips parting.

I'm ready for whatever he's 'bout to say. I'm ready to tell him how he's stomped all over our dreams. Then he closes his mouth, leaves, nothin' more than a coward.

Part of me still wants to sling those words at his back, but instead, a cry bubbles up my throat.

My knees give way. Blanche is there to catch me.

• • •

Blanche paces 'cross the living room. "I'll kill him."

I take a sip of hot chocolate. The heat soaks into my hands and soothes my throat. I wish I could lose myself in Buck's couch, just disappear into it.

"You're obviously staying here tonight," she adds.

"Just give me the word, Bonn," Buck says. "I'll beat that moron senseless."

"Thanks, but it wouldn't do any good." I squeeze my hands, my skin growing hotter. "I'm okay."

Blanche growls. "The hell you are. How could he do something like that to you?"

Buck shakes his head. "I've only known the lad a short time. And I'll tell ya what—that kid is different now than that first night he came into Doc's."

"Maybe I broke him," I say, and put down my mug, afraid I'll spill it. He's been distant, focused on himself more than us. His anger's been quick to spike; he's been quick to give me the cold shoulder. "Is he this way 'cause of me?"

Blanche takes my hand. "You may've introduced Roy to this world, but you certainly didn't put that blonde on his arm."

"I keep thinkin' 'bout Henry's wife, when she caught us together. Then there I was, the wife that caught her husband with a pretty li'l thing. Poetic justice, no?"

"That ain't poetic, Bonn. That's life being cruel."

"Whatever it is, it feels like everything is falling apart. First Roy drops out of school, then he goes behind my back . . ."

"Maybe all that's falling apart is Roy-related," Blanche says. "Would that be such a bad thing?"

"I don't know." My skin itches. "I guess I need to figure that out."

"Give yourself a few days. Let the dust settle, Bonn."

"No." Roy may've lashed out at the club, but that's his style. Strike first, coddle later. “It needs to be now, not later. Besides, we’re supposed to have dinner with his parents tomorrow.”

“Charming,” Blanche says sarcastically.

As she drives me home, my foot taps like a jackrabbit, ticking down the seconds ’til I confront my husband. My anger has led to nothin’ but uncertainty, and I’ve still no idea what to do with Roy. Hold on to him, hold on to what I know? Or walk away, into the unknown?

Only moments before seeing him at the Supper Club with another girl, I was musing ’bout Roy and me being meant to be. I’ve been so focused on holding on to my dreams, convincing myself that Roy belonged in them, even if it felt like I was the only one still working toward them. Did I pull the wool over my own eyes?

I blow out a slow breath, and realize that I’m lost.

“Do you want me to come inside with you?” Blanche asks.

I shake my head.

Blanche blindly digs through the bag on her lap as she drives. “Okay, here.” She hands me a key. “This is to Buck’s apartment. Let yourself in if you need to, anytime of night, it doesn’t matter.”

I nod, wordlessly thanking her. We turn onto Cemetery Road. Roy’s and my house is dark. Not even the porch light is on. I get out of Big Bertha, the slam of the door sounding too loud for this time of night. I wave at Blanche and try my best to smile reassuringly as I scurry up the path to the house. Key ready, I slip quickly into our too-quiet house, uncertainty giving me the fuel I’ll need to yank Roy out of bed and grill him for answers: How often? How far? With who? What next? What now? Why bother?

I ain’t sure if hearing Roy utter that information will make me more or less sure of what I want, but I need to know. I go straight to our bedroom, flick on the light.

“Wake up, R—”

The bed is empty, untouched. My pace and my breath quicken as I go from room to room, finding each one vacant. Royless.

Hand over my mouth, I drag my feet back to the bedroom, plop down on the bed, the weight of my emotions pulling me down like an anchor.

I kick off my shoes, and one hits our bureau. I notice a drawer ajar. I instantly know something is off, wrong. As I pull open the drawer, my eyebrows scrunch. All his union suits are gone, even the sleeveless ones. My hand falls off the drawer's knob. He only wears those in the summer months.

In a frenzy, I yank out the rest of Roy's drawers, the final drawer crashing to the floor, only a ratty old belt that no longer fits him falling out.

In a matter of steps, I stand in front of our closet, heaving in air. I crack it open and release a sob. Half the closet is bare. His slacks, his button-down shirts, his flight jacket, they're all gone. Sinking to the ground, I hug my knees and rock back and forth. But no, I can't—I won't—allow myself to cry.

The idle purr of Big Bertha's engine seeps through the walls of my empty home. I listen to the comforting sound for what feels like forever, 'til the car's gears click into place and the engine slowly fades away.

27

THE BANGING ON MY DOOR IS INCESSANT. I KNOW WHO IT is. It's been the same person for the past week. Not Roy, but Roy's daddy, with his ma right beside him.

And for the past week, ever since missing dinner at their house, I've hidden out of sight in the hallway, peeking 'round the corner 'til they gave up and left.

I curse. This time, the damn pounding won't stop, and I'm afraid my ma will hear, a few houses down. I swallow my pride and open the door.

"Where is he?" Mr. Thornton slurs. The shape of a bottle is noticeable beneath his heavy blazer.

I want to throw up my hands. I don't have the slightest clue, didn't look for him this time.

Instead, I recite the simple words I've practiced in my head but haven't yet said aloud: "Roy left me."

Mrs. Thornton lets out a wail, her scarf shielding her face as she turns into her husband. He demands more answers from me.

"I don't have any," I deadpan.

And, frankly, they're lucky I don't say what I'm really thinkin': their son is a cheating, lying, alcoholic bastard—exactly the reason why I cut him off, if he goes sniffing 'round the bank.

I'll save them from that description, though, and I know why. Guilt. Roy's ma blames me for his leaving.

Roy's daddy says his son's been acting foolish from the moment he bought me this damned house.

I reckon a portion of what they're sayin' is the truth. Ever since Roy bought me this house, pushing his dreams on me before I was ready for them—or him—I've started questioning things. Did we have enough passion? Would being Mrs. Roy Thornton hinder my dreams? Was something missing with Roy that made Henry, then Clyde Barrow, slip into my mind so readily?

So I stomach the accusations from Roy's parents 'til Mr. Thornton yanks on his mustache in frustration, whips out his bottle in plain sight, and eventually leads a hysterical Mrs. Thornton away from my doorstep.

After facing Roy's family, I know it's time to face my own.

• • •

Buster paces 'cross our living room. "I'll kill him."

My ma sits quietly in her favorite chair, knitting. I glance at her before saying to my brother, "You sound like Blanche."

"Fine. Blanche and I will kill him. That bastard did more than only lie to *you*."

I raise an eyebrow, wondering what reason Roy told Buster 'bout his skipping town, but Billie chimes in, "I know how to use a shotgun now."

I force a smile, and I work up the courage—and the resolution—to say, "I'm not going back to school after winter break." I eye my ma and quickly add, "For now." But I know that addition is for me—a promise that I will go back. I may've lost my husband, but I can't lose that piece of myself. "With Roy gone, and with seeing everyone at school . . . I just can't—"

Ma shushes me. She puts down her needles. She gets out of her chair. She wraps her arms 'round me. Her actions and her silence speak volumes. She doesn't tell me that Roy will find me again, or that everything will be okay. Or that taking time off from school is a bad idea. Ma only comforts me the best way a ma knows how.

Things are different for me, after that moment.

I stop thinkin' I'll walk into the house and find Roy with a big gesture and an even bigger apology. Once I accept that, it's easier to accept that Roy only continued from my childhood into my almost-adulthood 'cause he was safe, familiar, undisturbed.

Our Mason jar of doodles goes into the very back of our half-empty closet. Roy's name remains on my upper thigh. There, always there.

I no longer go to the library; the idea of reading someone else's romantic happy ending has lost its appeal.

Instead, I throw myself into Doc's, relishing every moment onstage, where I feel whole.

When the clock strikes twelve on New Year's Eve, I swallow the last of one drink and pour another, loathing the happy couples 'round me in Doc's who kiss and clink glasses and cheer.

1928 is gone, and my heart has gone with it. In between sips, I swear off all men, vocally, to anyone who will listen, while knowing deep inside I still crave finding and having an enduring, endless love. I spend the first half of 1929 that way: in between sips, drowning my sorrows in bottled hell.

Whiskey is today's drink of choice, while I watch a representative from the bank suffer through the summer heat to put up a FOR SALE sign in my front yard. My senses may be dull, but I saw this coming. I couldn't afford the payments with my tips, and I wasn't willing to watch my bank account dwindle for a house that never truly became a home.

What's worse, when this house sells to a young, perky couple with nothin' but stars in their eyes, I won't see a single clam. That's something else to hate Roy for: never putting my name on the mortgage. And now I'll move back into a tiny room with my thirteen-year-old sister.

It's amazing how life passes: one hour at a time, yet each day bleeds into the next. At the kitchen table, one morning, I eye the newspaper 'cross the table, curious of today's showtimes. Recently, I spend my days sitting in the dark at picture houses. *The Night of Love. Framed. Afraid to Love. Marriage. The Primrose Path.* There's something peaceful 'bout silent films, 'bout imagining the music that could accompany each scene.

Buster shakes his head. "I can feel you staring at me to get those times. Give me a second, would ya?"

My brother's response cracks a slight smile on my face. "What ya reading, anyway?"

He flips the paper 'round for me to see the headline.

WALL STREET RECOVERS FROM PANIC AFTER STOCKS CRASH.

"I thought the stock market was booming?"

"Has been. Ya see that vacuum I bought Ma?" Buster turns the page. "That drop was just a false alarm, 'cause stock prices plummeted the other day."

"Why?"

He shrugs, but says, "Bunch of people got spooked and sold their shares, but then, that afternoon, this fancy New York City banker insisted that banks were still lending, and he invested a huge chunk of his own money. Some of his banker friends did, too. People started to relax a bit." He gives the newspaper a shake, settling into his new page. "Now things are recovering, prices are going back up. It was crazy, though; a bunch of Wall Street folks committed suicide when they first heard the news."

"God, that's lousy, and depressing." Depressing ain't what I need right now. "You ain't scared that this type of thing is going to happen again?"

"I reckon if the big-dog brokers say the market is safe, then it must be, right?"

"I don't know." And I'm happy my money is no longer in the game.

"Regardless, I want to chat with some of my clients and assure 'em all is well. You working tonight? Bet ya a couple of 'em will be at Doc's, but it's hard as hell to get in there."

"I'll tell Buck to keep an eye out for you."

He smiles, then flips a few pages of his newspaper to yank out today's showtimes for me.

• • •

By the time Doc's is at full capacity, I've watched Buster talk to two clients, and now he's eyeing up Mr. Champagne Cocktail at the bar.

I admire that 'bout my brother, picking himself up after Kenney Rogers crushed his dreams between two slabs of cement. Took him some time—too much time, in my opinion. But here he is, with a full client roster, and in the midst of a very animated conversation with Mr. Champagne Cocktail.

Buster moved on. He's making something of himself, just as our daddy hoped for us.

On the way to the back room, carrying an armful of glasses, I give Buster an awkward thumbs-up and make the decision: I'm going back to school. I'm still going to stand in front of a classroom.

I need to keep that promise to myself, even if I am a year behind in getting my diploma. Being older than my classmates will give 'em something else to gawk at me for. But at least Hazel's smirk won't be among 'em, her having graduated.

Blanche follows me into the back room. "I saw that."

"Saw what?"

She mimics the thumbs-up I gave Buster. "That positivity. I thought you forgot how to be that way."

"Funny," I say dryly.

"No, but seriously, it's good to see you a little more upbeat. I know the past few months have been"—she makes a clicking noise—"rough."

I press my lips together, thinking. "A year . . . It's been nearly a year since Roy up and left," I say, more so to myself, that length of time fully sinking in. "And ya know what? That's long enough."

A hint of a smile creeps onto Blanche's face. "Yeah?"

I let out a breath, flick on the faucet. "Yeah. I'm going to make some changes, get myself back on track, starting with school. Tomorrow." It feels good to say it out loud, even if it reminds me 'bout what I've lost: someone to come home to after a long day of teaching. "You know what's sad, though?"

Blanche strokes my hair. "What's that?"

I turn my back to her, begin washing the glasses. "I was so high and mighty when you were talking 'bout that tooth analogy and Roy and me."

"My *what* analogy?"

I roll my eyes. "You were sayin' how you wish your relationship with Buck was like mine with Roy: my first and only boyfriend. Like my first and only tooth, since we're not sharks and we only get one set of 'em."

"I'm confused."

I roll my eyes again. "Imagine that." I set aside a clean glass. "In the end, you were all happy 'cause you said that Buck is your adult tooth and all the other boys you've been with were your baby teeth—the ones you're supposed to lose."

She laughs. "Okay, now that makes sense. Blanche is pretty smart."

Suds drip onto my feet. "I want an adult tooth."

I want someone to share my dreams with, a hand to hold as I take my first steps onto a sandy beach.

"Does this mean you're done swearing off men?" Blanche asks with a sheepish grin. "I believe your exact words were how they're the devil and they can all burn in hell."

I pick up another dirty glass. "Perhaps. I don't want to be some damsel who needs a man, but—"

Blanche holds up her hand. "Trust me, a damsel couldn't have survived like you have. You, Bonnelyn, being the A student that you'll, uh, be once again, are simply graduating from distress to happiness. And I'm a strong believer that necking aids in happiness. It's proven, scientifically."

I laugh. "I'd like to see those reports."

"It's good to hear you laugh, Bonn."

"Yeah," I say.

"Hey, I've been thinkin'." She doesn't give me a chance to object, 'cause when Blanche thinks, it's never good. "Your birthday is coming up. Nineteen. As in, the very last year before twenty. I think that deserves a li'l hoopla."

"That makes me nervous."

"No. No nerves; just fun. We could be one of those *crazies*."

I stare at her blankly.

"You know, when people do crazy things for fun. That one man sat on top of a flagpole for days."

I shake my head.

She twists her lips. "Did you hear how that other man strapped himself to the wing of a plane?"

"Right," I say. "Let's use the spare plane I've got lying 'round out back."

Blanche tips a fake hat to acknowledge my sarcasm. "Something less outlandish?"

"Um, yeah," I say. "But listen, Blanche, I don't think I'm up for anything *crazy*."

She taps her lower lip with her finger. "Of course. I need to think like Bonnelyn, not Alvin 'Shipwreck' Kelly."

"Who?"

She sighs, feigning exasperation. "The fella who sat on the flagpole."

I snort. "You ain't going to stop 'til you think of something, are ya?"

She grins, showing her teeth. "Nope."

"Fine." I knead the back of my neck with my wet hand, trying to also think like Bonnelyn. Which, frankly, is plain ol' pathetic. Now that I think 'bout it, *fun* is exactly what I need. I've spent the past year wallowing 'bout one thing or another. And, my God, I reckon I've grown tired of myself. I need a renewed pep in my step.

"A dance marathon," I suggest, and smile at the idea of letting the beat take over my body. Just moving. Not thinkin'.

"Yes," Blanche says enthusiastically, and claps her hands together once. "That'd be perfect. You know what? Let me talk to Mary. I bet we could do one this weekend. I think the record is three weeks."

"You'd last three hours, tops."

"Challenge accepted," Blanche says with a curt nod. "Okay, I need to find Mary, then get back to the bar. It'll be hard to pull this together so fast, but I can do it." She walks to the door that leads back into the main room of Doc's, then stops, her face devious. "Great idea, Bonn. This is going to be your best birthday yet. I'll pick you up. And as far as your dance partner . . . I know the perfect adult tooth for you."

She winks, and his name passes between Blanche and me in a heartbeat.

Clyde Barrow.

28

CLYDE BARROW? THE CRIMINAL. THAT AIN'T WHO I NEED TO GET my life back on track. I chew my bottom lip, glancing at Buck's apartment door for what feels like the millionth time.

Beside me on the couch, Blanche lowers her magazine. "Whatever is going on in your pretty head is probably juicer than the goop I'm reading in here." She taps the cover of *Photoplay*. "So tell me, why is meeting Clyde so scary when he's been hitching your breath for years?"

"He hasn't been . . ."

Blanche raises her eyebrows, and even I know that's a fib. I can't deny Clyde's got an allure to him. Problem is, I don't think it's the right kind.

Instead, I say, "He's older than me. He's been arrested, probably more times than I care to know. He doesn't go to church or school or—"

Blanche narrows her eyes. "Would ya look at that? You've gone and described Buck."

I cringe.

"My ears are ringin'," Buck says, coming into the living room. "You lassies talking 'bout me?"

Blanche sets her magazine on the coffee table, props up her feet. "Bonn was just mentioning some of your better qualities."

"Is that so?" Buck laughs, stops behind the couch, and wraps his arms 'round Blanche. He leans in and kisses her neck. "Bonnelyn is blushing," he says to her. He tilts his head toward me. "I assure ya, Clyde's a good lad. Like yours truly." He snorts. "But if ya break his heart, you're going to have to answer to me."

There's a knock at the door. I jump, my hand flying to my chest.

Blanche's feet clunk to the floor. "And here he is now." She skips to the door.

I wish I put on plaid today, then I'd blend right into the couch. Then Clyde's gaze would pass over me. Then I wouldn't wonder, once more, what those eyes have seen. Then I'll find a boy unlike Roy and Henry and Clyde, to start anew with.

But no. Clyde strides in and sets his sights on me. Just like that.

My mouth goes dry. I swallow roughly and study the deep red of my nails.

"Bonnelyn," Blanche says.

She tugs my arm, and I stumble to get my feet under me. My stomach is fluttering—and I hate that it's fluttering. 'Til now, Clyde's only existed in my head, where he was a safe distance away, where he ought to stay. But now he's standing in front of me, his hand stretched out, waiting for me to lay mine in his.

I won't be rude. I offer my hand. His skin is clammy, despite the redness of his cheeks from being outside.

"The name is Clyde," he says. "Clyde Barrow. I've been wanting to *officially* meet you for some time now."

"Bonnelyn," I respond.

My gaze slides to his eyes. And, in those deep, hazel eyes, I could lose myself. I could forget that I am Bonnelyn Parker from some no-name town. That, right there, scares the dickens out of me. I try to pull back, but his grip is firm.

"Bonnelyn," he repeats. "Well, that name ain't pretty enough for the likes of you. I reckon *Bonnie* suits you better."

Bonnie.

He nods, seeming satisfied. Then Clyde bends, smiling up at me as he presses his chilled lips to my hand. "Hi, Bonnie."

"Hi," I say, weakly.

I breathe him in, recognizing the scent of gasoline. He's younger than I imagined, no more than nineteen or twenty, but he's matured, like a man should be. It's an impression I get, not only from his dark, slicked-back hair but also how he walked in here, like he knew where he was going. He doesn't wear a suit like Buck. His baggier trousers and plain white tee give him a look all his own. A handsome, carefree one.

"Why're you staring at her like that?" Blanche asks Clyde.

My hand is still in his hand, the spot he kissed still feeling cold from his lips.

"I'm trying to catch the breath Bonnie took away," he says.

Buck laughs boisterously and smacks his brother on the back. "Clyde fancies himself a poet."

Or somebody who's had plenty of time feeding lines to girls.

"Well, don't scare Bonn off," Blanche says, stealing my hand from Clyde's. "We're going to get our dresses and faces on. You two boys, behave yourselves."

Blanche pulls me 'cross the living room, and I take another peek at Clyde, when he's not looking. He runs a hand over his dark hair, dimples framing a wide grin. His eyes jump to me again, and somehow that smile grows larger. Somehow, the butterflies in my stomach flutter faster.

Blanche presses the bathroom door closed behind us. She turns to me with a serious expression. "Sorry 'bout how intense Clyde was. You're not going to run away, are you? I don't think you'll fit through the window. Even if you did, we're three stories up."

"I'm fine," I say, just as serious, and casually sit atop the toilet lid. But, inside, I feel upside down, attracted to someone who ain't good for me—a road I've stumbled down before.

"You're lying," Blanche says with a hand on her hip. "But look, I ain't asking you to marry him, just dance with him. And I'll be there the whole time. It'd mean a lot—to him, I mean. That boy's been waiting to meet you for ages."

My head perks up.

"And you've been wanting to meet him, too!"

"Shh," I say. "Keep your voice down. That ain't true." But could it be, even if only a little?

She laughs louder.

"Blanche," I say between my teeth.

"Okay, okay," she whispers. "But how 'bout getting to know him before ya write him off? You ended up liking Buck just fine. Now"—she holds up two dresses for herself—"red or black?"

"Black," I say, wanting to be the only one in red tonight—a thought that almost has me changing my mind and having Blanche put her other dress on.

Over the next hour, we primp and ready ourselves for the night ahead. Clyde's and Buck's voices float through the wall, here and there. Sometimes their voices sound serious, and other times as if their ages have regressed ten years.

"They better not break anything," Blanche says, and rolls her eyes. "I just bought that new coffee table."

"Do you live here now?" I ask, realizing I should already know this, as her best friend.

"In the bathroom?"

I shake my head at her.

"Yeah, I mean, you know I've been staying here most nights, but now I help Buck with the rent and all. My pa's got a new girl, who hasn't taken a liking to me. Besides, I'd rather live here." She shrugs and reaches for her bright red lipstick.

I lightly touch her arm. "You sure you're okay?"

"I mean, what can I do? Pa's always been more interested in his law firm than in me. Makes sense a new girl would eat up more of his time. Honestly, I doubt he'd notice if I disappeared for real. Only reason why he wanted me to start paying my own way or find a man is so that he could wipe his hands free of me." She pauses. "Like mother, like father?"

"That's not true, Blanche."

"It is." She studies herself in the mirror with an unreadable expression. "But it's something I accepted awhile ago." She turns to me. "But enough 'bout my pa and his women. Let's get our dancing shoes on."

I bite my lip. Blanche can be hard to read. But she wiggles her fingers, and I hand Blanche her pair, slipping on my own.

"Well, look at us," Blanche says. "We're the most bonny lasses this world has ever seen."

When we stroll out into the living room, it's clear the boys believe it, too. Buck whistles, and Clyde's lips part ever so slightly.

I fidget with my crochet hat, making sure it's straight though I just checked it in the mirror.

"You lassies look great," Buck says enthusiastically, then sweeps Blanche up in his arms. She squeals and yells at him not to muss her hair.

Clyde and I stand opposite each other, awkwardly. I scratch my collarbone, pull on my stud earring.

"You look nice," Clyde says.

"Thank you. You look nice, too."

He smoothes his plain white tee and, like before, I notice the three letters inked on his upper arm. USN. "I reckon I'm a bit underdressed. These juice joints ain't my thing."

"Oh?" I respond, distracted by what those letters could mean.

"Too many people all in one spot." He shudders, as if someone runs a feather down his spine.

I may not agree with him—I love the energy and crowd at Doc's—but I smile at his animated reaction.

Blanche skips back to us. "We better hurry. Mary wanted to start the dance marathon promptly at five."

We descend the steps to Doc's, and anticipation for the music's upbeat tempo courses through me. Blanche flings open the door, and my jaw drops at the amount of people who've showed up, and at such short notice.

"How did everyone get in here without causing a scene?" I ask, leaning close to Blanche so she can hear me over the roar of the crowd, a crowd that's got all of Clyde's weight on his heels.

"Didn't you see the sign out front, for a free health exam?"

I laugh. "Mary thinks of everything."

She spots us, waves us in, then hops up onstage in front of a band. "Ladies and gentlemen, welcome to Doc's very first dance marathon."

I quickly count at least thirty couples, everyone throwing their hands up and cheering.

Mary shushes them. "Before we begin . . ." She makes another *Shh* sound. "Before we begin, let's go over the rules. You'll be dancing in pairs. You're required to remain in motion—that means, pick up one foot," she says, demonstrating with her own feet, "and then the other. Shuffling is fine, but if you stop, or if a knee touches the ground, you're out. Every forty-five minutes, I'll sound the horn and you'll get fifteen minutes to rest. Everyone understand?"

The crowd hoots and hollers.

Mary laughs. "Well, okay then. Ladies and gentlemen, I only have one more question for you: How long can you last?" She swings her arm up and the band springs to life.

The sound of "When the Saints Go Marching In" fills the too-crowded basement. I can't help the huge smile that spreads 'cross my face. Mary searches for me, catches my eye, and lips, "Happy birthday."

"Dance!" Blanche says to me, already holding on to Buck.

Everything is happening so fast that I feel a bit light-headed. I turn and find Clyde, with his thumbs dangling from his trousers' belt loops.

"I also ain't much of a dancer," he says with a lopsided grin.

"You don't like crowds. Or dancing. Why'd you agree to come?" I shout over the music, the laughter, the idle chatter. 'Round us, people already swing and twirl. In my mind, the answer I want to hear prickles the back of my neck.

"I had to meet you!" he shouts back.

A couple bumps me and I stumble to the side. Clyde grabs my arm to steady me. His touch and his response send shivers down my arms.

"I don't happen upon many girls who can handle a gun like you," Clyde adds.

This surprises me, and I laugh. "What?"

"You impressed me. Fearless." He extends his other hand, nodding for me to take it. "I'll warn you, though—you take my hand again and I may not be able to let you go."

I stare at his hand like it's foreign, hesitating. Truly, I don't know the first thing 'bout the one and only Clyde Champion Barrow, besides his questionable past. And, really, this boy should remain a mystery from my past. But—I press my lips together—I like how he sees me.

Fearless.

Quick, as not to change my mind, I place my hand in Clyde's, willing to let him swing me 'round the dance floor.

"I'm going to need your help here." He tightens his hold of me. "I'm afraid I have two left feet."

His modesty stirs something inside of me, and I raise Clyde's arm to spin underneath and toward him. I stop against his chest. One hand embraces mine. The other drops to my lower back, and I suck in my belly, acutely aware of his fingertips holding me against him firmly.

I am just a lonesome trav'ler through this big, wide world of sin.

The upbeat Dixieland lyrics surround us, a contrast to how Clyde and I are moving, swaying back and forth, completely out of sync with the music, my palm flat on his chest.

Come and join me in my journey, 'cause it's time that we begin.

"Bonnie," Clyde says in his raspy tone, and hearing that name again hitches my breath. "Red is a good color on you."

My cheeks grow hot, hotter as our eyes meet. I drop my gaze. "We ain't dancing like everybody else. . . ." The others are twisting, twirling, fully engrossed in the energetic spirit of the dance marathon.

Clyde smirks, even as his heart pounds under my hand. "I told ya I ain't much of a dancer." He leans closer and adds, "Do you want to get out of here?"

"And do what?" I ask, trying to force my voice louder than the noise, louder than my own heart pounding in my ears.

Clyde grins at my response. I don't know what he's so happy 'bout; I didn't say yes. Yet, I didn't say no, either. He backpedals toward the exit of Doc's. My hand begins to slide from his, and I feel the roughness of his calloused fingertips, before he regrips, not letting go.

And we'll be there for that judgment, when the saints go marching in.

He knocks into dancing couples, but simply sidesteps, adjusting his path, his eyes not leaving me. I look over my shoulder, searching for Blanche.

Sorry, Clyde, I could say. *Can't go. Blanche insists I stay.*

'Cept Buck swings Blanche 'round and she has an ear-to-ear smile on her face, not wasting a second on me. It's not as if she'd help me anyway. That she-devil would most likely usher me out the door with Clyde.

I decide it can't hurt to slip away for a few minutes, though it's not lost on me how I joked Blanche wouldn't make it three hours and here I am, not lasting three minutes.

We stumble up the stairs, onto the sidewalk. The cooler dusk air jars my senses, and I clutch my sequined neckline. My breath comes quicker, and I ask, "Where're we going? I don't want to be long."

"You'll see, Bonnie."

"Clyde . . ." I look up, down Elm Street and steal back my hand. "I don't know."

He bobs his head and rubs his bare arms, as if he's searching for the right thing to say.

But I don't need the right thing; I need answers. Fearless or not, I can't go running down the street hand in hand with a boy who knots my stomach with uncertainty. Not after Henry. Not after Roy.

I need to know more. "Your tattoo." I hesitantly touch the same spot on my upper arm. "What do those letters mean?"

Clyde takes a deep breath, traces the USN, a solemn expression on his face. "I'm afraid it's not a good memory."

I picture the three letters on my own skin and say, "You don't have to tell me."

As I avert my eyes, then look back, Clyde slowly nods.

"It seems I do, Bonnie. 'United States Navy,' that's what it stands for."

The navy? I blink, remembering the naval officer who knocked on our door all those years ago, derailing our whole lives. "You served?" I manage to ask.

"Wanted to." He rubs his mouth. "Got this here tattoo, rented a car, drove for hours, got turned away."

I step closer to Clyde, letting a couple pass us more easily on the sidewalk. "They wouldn't let you enlist?"

"A medical rejection. I had malaria as a boy. Almost took my life, but"—he taps his right ear—"ended up only taking a bit of my hearing."

I wrap my arms 'round myself, as much for warmth as to keep from touching him. "I didn't know. I'm sorry."

Clyde sucks on a tooth, and I'm even more sorry I'm making him relive an unhappy memory. "Shouted real good. Punched a wall. Neither did me any good. So I left, kept driving after that," he says. "Nowhere in particular. Just knew I needed to put miles between me and that moment."

I cock my head to the side. "You got arrested, didn't you, for not returning that car?"

Clyde laughs, and I startle at the noise. "Buck told ya 'bout that, did he?"

I shake my head. "I saw that photo Blanche took of you"—*the one where you looked so proud, capturing the moments before you set out to enlist*—"but Buck did tell me 'bout stealing those turkeys to give your ma Thanksgiving dinner."

Clyde's dimples appear. "Reckon you know all my secrets, Bonnie." He pauses. "'Cept for where I want to take you right now. We got to hurry, though."

I twist my lips. It's not that I ain't curious where; it's that Clyde's all shiny. Even in his casual tee and pants, he's polished, practiced. Ain't that exactly the type of boy I should be taking a wide berth 'round? I heard, one time, how the most poisonous of animals ain't the dull ones but the ones that catch your eye.

"Bonnie, you know what I learned from both those experiences?" Clyde touches his tattoo.

"What's that?"

"Sometimes ya got to take what you want."

My lips start to curl into a smile, liking the boldness of the sentiment, even if I ain't sure what he means. I'm jolted forward with Clyde's sudden strides, trailing behind him, my hand in his.

"WELL, AIN'T THIS COZY," CLYDE WHISPERS, THE SOUNDLESS opening credits casting a light glow on his face. He rocks his shoulders against his plush, red seat, getting comfortable. "Glad you could join me."

I bite back a smile, flipping my ticket stub for *Broadway Melody* forward and back. The chilled air still labors in my lungs from racing down the street to the Melba Theater. "You think you're something, don't you?"

Clyde crosses his ankles. "Not sure I know what you mean, Bonnie."

I cross my arms. "Ironic, how you already had two tickets."

He shrugs. "Like I said, dancing ain't my thing."

"But films are?"

"Nope." He prolongs the word into two parts. "Not really. But you like 'em."

At a loss for how to reply, I scratch my non-itchy nose. Eventually, I say, "How do you know that?"

He smirks. "Blanche showed me a photograph."

"Funny," I whisper.

He points to the front of the theater, lowers his voice further. "It's starting."

I'm left staring at his silhouette as the opening chorus drowns out any lingering conversations in the room. This boy is definitely shiny. Confident. Smooth. Like now, leaned back in his seat, arms relaxed on either armrest, not a dark hair out of place, grinning.

Lord help me, I'm grinning too. I slouch into my seat, also getting comfortable, ready to enjoy the vaudeville sister act of Anita Page and Bessie Love. I won't tell Clyde I saw this film last week. Then, I sat alone, wishing someone filled the seat beside me.

My eyes flick to the screen, where I recognize New York City's skyline, then back to Clyde. The lines of his cheekbones cast shadows on his cheeks. A scar on his temple, similar to one Roy has, catches the dim light.

I sit up straighter. That half-inch blemish is sobering.

I was with Roy when that branch scratched his face. His scar was harmless, a mistake. Clyde's could be from anything. A brawl. Some petty theft. One of those moments where he felt the need to take what he wanted.

Though it didn't do me much good to marry a man I knew my whole life. Does knowing Clyde's nothin' but trouble make it better—going in eyes open? Even if what I know 'bout him only dusts the bottom of the barrel?

On-screen, the actors' voices boom. That's what should be capturing my attention. Yet, it's not. I strain to study Clyde from the corner of my eye, wondering if I'm foolish for each moment I spend with him.

Clyde doesn't turn his head. He doesn't angle toward me, yet his lips move. "I like music."

"Huh?" I say to him.

Clyde twists, his hazel eyes glistening from the screen's hue. "I ain't much for dancing or films, but I like music."

He begins to return his focus to Queenie Mahoney on-screen, but I stop him with my question. "What kind of music?"

"Strummin'."

"You play the guitar?" I ask loudly. The man in the row behind us shushes me. I don't care. The idea of Clyde playing music, something that makes me feel alive, has me sitting even straighter in my seat.

Clyde nods. "With a few words thrown in."

I wouldn't have pegged Clyde as someone to cradle a guitar in his lap.

"Well, don't go looking so stunned, or whatever that face is, Bonnie."

Buck said Clyde fancies himself a poet, and now I want nothin' more than to hear him sing. God knows I've already witnessed how clever his words can be. "Will you play for me?"

He twists his lips.

"Clyde," I press.

His response sounds like Lazy and Exasperated went and had a baby when he says, "All right."

We're shushed again, and I turn my attention to the screen, where it doesn't stay long. The idea of Clyde playing music is too intriguing. I'd guess his singing voice is even lower than his usual voice. I see the song's melody, slow, steady. I wonder how well he can carry a tune. A few long minutes pass before I give in and ask, "I'd like you to play for me, now."

Judging by the quickness of his snort, I'd wager the reaction slipped out before Clyde could stop it. He studies me a heartbeat longer. "All right."

The response is bookended by his adorable dimples.

• • •

Clyde says he doesn't live far, yet, in a matter of blocks Dallas flip-flops from affluent to penniless. Wood fills windows instead of glass. Debris clogs the gutters. Graffiti covers beaten-down fences.

Cement City may be humble, but it's a pocket full of good. Here, I'm wary of what folks are hiding in their pockets. I squint through the setting sun, pleading with it to stay in the sky a little longer, and scan the street for any unseemly characters.

A man 'cross the road fits the bill. He whistles provocatively, and my stomach tightens.

"Don't mind Old Jed," Clyde assures me. He raises his voice. "Whistlin' hasn't gotten him nowhere in years."

Old Jed grumbles, and I sidle closer to Clyde, nearly bumping him with my elbow, my arms tightly crossed. Each rhythmic *click-clack* of my Mary Janes sets me more on edge, sounding like a plea for me to go back.

I'm 'bout to listen. I'm hard-pressed to believe I got caught up in what Clyde's singing would be like. Now I'm traipsing 'round town with a boy I hardly know, 'bout to step foot into his home.

By myself.

With no one knowing where I am.

Go back, go back, go back.

Clyde's pace slows, the demands of my heels slowing, 'til all is quiet.

"Well," he says, "here we are."

I chew on my lip, finally asking, "A service station?"

"Home sweet home." Clyde's voice is dry, deadpan. "Guitar's inside," he says, as if reminding me why I'm here.

Wishing for more is a feeling I'm quite familiar with, a kick to my butt that gets my feet moving. I follow Clyde, navigating a boneyard of cars, and we enter through a side door. The scent of cinnamon wraps 'round me in the darkened room.

"Let me just get the . . . ," Clyde says. A dim light flickers on a moment later, and the corners of a narrow room take form. "Ain't much."

There's a touch of shame to his voice again, but I can't reckon as to why. I ain't in any position to judge the fact his home is tacked onto the back of a service station. And really, it's quite homely, with the touch of a woman: fresh-picked flowers, framed photographs, a shawl thrown over the back of a chair, and stacks of books on the fireplace's mantel. The apartment is neat and tidy, even if the room is miniature size.

Clyde takes a large, demonstrative step forward, now standing in front of a worn, brown couch. "Welcome to my room."

I join him, my hand dropping to a folded blanket and pillow. My response comes out whispered. "You sleep on the couch?"

"Yeah, I don't need much in life, and I'm in and out of town so much and all."

Doing what? I want to ask, but Clyde's already saying, "This is my parents' place."

I glance toward the hall, a new wave of nerves coursing through me that I'm 'bout to meet them.

"They're down by the tracks. They're there every Saturday 'round this time."

"I see." I bite my bottom lip. I don't see, but I'm relieved they ain't home.

He runs a hand over the slight stubble on his chin and cheeks, and I scan the room further to distract myself. My gaze stops on the spine of a poetry book, then his guitar.

"You going to make good on your word and play for me?"

Clyde settles himself on the couch, then the instrument on his knee. He pats the spot beside him, pauses with his fingers ready to strum. I sit and fold my hands in my lap, watching as he clears his throat, swallows, clears his throat again. Clyde's head tilts down, and he looks up at me from under his lashes.

"I started this here song a while ago, but she ain't done," he says. "Was hoping you'd help me finish her."

"Me?"

His fingertips slide down the strings once, letting the soft sound vibrate 'round us. "You'll see."

He goes back for more, a dark melody forming with each stroke, and moistens his lips. Clyde says, more than sings, "*Death is a five-letter word, with a five-finger clutch.*"

His head stays down, his jaw relaxed, eyes closed. "*It cornered him, pitting him against the bigger man . . . By the throat, edging closer, nearing Death's final touch.*"

The rhythm quickens, the beat an unexpected surprise.

"*Then there she was, light in the dark, defying Death's plan . . . She stared it down, held on tight, fired off a shot all her own . . . Ohh*"—he draws out the word, as if taunting Death—"*Oh, oh, oh, death for the boy has been postponed.*"

Clyde's fingers shift to a higher pitch on the guitar. He smirks and sings from the corner of his mouth, "*'Cause lean closer, listen close . . . How the story ends, no one knows . . . But one thing's clear, you'll see . . . Bonnie and Clyde, meant to be, alive and free.*"

That last line, that last note hangs between us.

I forget how to breathe.

"That's all I got for now," Clyde says softly. "Thought maybe we could do the next verse together."

"Together?" I wring my hands, staring into the eyes of Clyde Barrow, the criminal, the charmer, the . . . boy who wrote me a doggone song to show me how he cares.

"Yeah, Bonnie. You and me. What do you say?"

"YOU RAN AWAY?" BLANCHE'S MOUTH HANGS OPEN.

Beside her, I tap my heels off the base of the bar, gripping the mahogany ledge with my fingertips. "No, I walked away and got a bus home."

"Same thing." The sound of Blanche's heels against the bar add to mine; only her bouncing is more energetic. "So, let me get this straight. That lad wrote you a song . . . with verses and everything . . . before you ever really met?"

"Well, one verse. But that's *so far.*" I take a long, deep breath. "He asked me to finish it with him."

"And that's when you ran away?"

"I didn't . . ." I rub my face. "Fine, maybe my pace was brisk, but before I left I said I'd think 'bout him and me."

As Bonnie and Clyde, meant to be, alive and free.

Blanche's head bobs. "You told him you had to think about it?"

I nod.

"See, that's where you two are different. Clyde wasn't thinkin' with his head."

"Blanche," I say, my legs no longer swinging, "don't be crude."

"Bonnelyn Parker, I was referring to his heart. If Clyde was using his noggin, he'd have realized it was too soon to put an *and* between your names. But I'm personally glad he sang you that song."

"I know, I know, you've been wanting us together all along."

"Well, yes." Blanche bumps my shoulder with hers. "But part of me was curious why someone like Clyde Barrow has pined for you for *so* long when he's only known you through occasional glances. I mean, you're foxy and all, but it makes sense now. He thinks you saved his life."

I frown. "Glad that's all cleared up for you." I can't say I didn't question what made Clyde gooey-eyed for me, but it stings when your best friend was temple-tapping too.

Saving his life, though . . . That's loaded, heavy. And the way he depicted us, alive and free—why wouldn't we be?

I've never stood behind bars. I kick my feet. Guess I came close, if that raid were real, since this place is illegal. Question is . . . is being here, is going on alcohol runs and riding in stolen cars more or less illegal than how Clyde breaks the law? I ain't even sure I know the full extent of how he has, but could it be the same? Could our intentions?

I subtly shake my head. Doesn't matter. I'm more than a life of crime, with dreams for myself. Now I shift my weight, sliding my hands beneath my dangling legs, the bar smooth under my palms. Reckon Clyde could have dreams; he dreamed once, after all. Before it was ripped away. What's he hope for now? A boy who thinks with his heart must have something new to hold on to.

Something more than simply me, the girl who stared down Death, who took matters into her own hands.

I smile.

"All right," Blanche says. "Don't keep Blanche in the dark. Bad enough you kept me waiting all day to tell me 'bout last night."

I shrug. "Shouldn't have skipped school."

She stares me down, her eyebrows raised for added effect. "Well? Yes or no to Clyde? What's the verdict?"

"Don't have one," I say. Besides how I like his perception of me. It's my perception of him that's wishy-washy.

Blanche bangs her heels against the bar. "Is it the whole *no church, no school* thing? Or more than that?" Her mouth forms an O, drawing out a similar sound. "Is it his elephant ears?"

"Look alive, ladies," Mary says, coming in from Doc's back room, her arms full of bottles. "First patrons should be arriving in three, two, one . . ."

Four men burst through the door and, on cue, Rosie's voice booms from the stage. All at once, Doc's comes to life with music and laughter. Blanche and I hop down from where we're perched on the bar top, Blanche complaining that her gams are too tired from dancing to stand.

No surprise, Mr. Champagne Cocktail sidles up to the bar. Blanche gets to fixin' him his drink. The night gets busy, the door swinging open to let more people in, again and again, right on schedule.

"Blanche," I say, looking up from where I kneel, putting some new bottles beneath the bar.

"Yes'm."

"Elephant ears?" I prod as I stand.

She laughs. "Forgot I said that. So, those, they're huge, ain't they? Like two car doors on either side of Clyde's head."

I roll my eyes. "Don't be silly. His ears are fine."

"If you like 'em big. Though what ain't big is that boy's height. No sirree. Sure glad Buck got different genes."

I narrow my eyes. "Clyde ain't short, Blanche. He's taller than me."

"There!" Blanche smiles smugly. "You did it again. It's curious you're defending a fella you ain't interested in."

"What's curious is, A, how you're picking out the flaws of a boy you *want* me to fancy, and B"—I allow my irritation toward Blanche to get a bit catty, wanting to get under her skin—"how you've been with Buck all this time, yet he still hasn't told you his *real* name."

Now Blanche is the one to narrow her eyes. But considering she doesn't fire back at me, I don't know if I'm the one she's irritated with.

I let her stew, pouring a tumbler of whiskey to busy myself so my mind doesn't drift back to Clyde. I take a small mouthful before turning my attention to Mr. Champagne Cocktail. "How those stocks of yours doing? Buster make you rich yet?"

He takes a sip of his drink, runs his tongue over his lips. "That dip in the market left many scared; I'm no exception. The weekend showed some promise, even if there were some happenings yesterday that got people panicking again. I've got all my money in her, save what's in my pocket, and I intend to use it so pretty girls can serve me drinks. Best distraction, if you ask me." He winks.

I shake my head at his flattery and raise my glass. "To your prosperity."

We clink, but he doesn't lower his glass, keeping it pressed against mine.

"What're your dreams, sweet Bonnelyn?"

His question catches me off guard. Teaching, sure. But I clear my throat, the last few years running through my head, days where my dreams involving Roy, involving companionship, took a dip—a big one—and never recovered. I still want that. My daddy would want me to have that partner in life.

The door to Doc's opens, and a prick of excitement stirs in my belly as I watch a boy who has perfect-sized ears—and perfect timing—walk in.

"Guess you could say I'm figuring out my dreams. But," I say slowly, "they may've recently been given another chance." I pause, my gaze flicking to Clyde. "If I let 'em."

Mr. Champagne Cocktail clinks his glass against mine again. "I'll drink to that."

Clyde walks up to the bar, but there're no seats. He stands there awkwardly, behind Mr. Champagne Cocktail, hands in his pockets, and it may be the cutest thing I've ever seen.

I meet his nervousness with spunk, shouting over the room's volume, "Doc's two days in a row?"

"It's more so that I want to see you two days in a row."

Well damn. Mr. Champagne Cocktail chuckles as he turns and puts a hand on Clyde's shoulder. "I think this seat will do you more good than me."

"How sweet," Blanche says, as Clyde taps his knuckles on the stool, not sitting. "You wanted to visit your future sister-in-law?"

It takes a second, but a smile cracks Clyde's lips. "Actually, I wanted to see if Bonnie has a break coming up."

Blanche takes a bottle from my hand, freeing me to go. I almost don't let it go, not sure I'm ready to step out from behind the bar, to have nothin' in between Clyde and me. Then he can touch me, prickling my skin with intrigue.

But I ain't a believer in accidental happenings. After all those nights of sitting outside the Supper Club, I caught Roy cheating the one time I ventured inside. And now Clyde has walked into Doc's at the exact moment I toasted to second chances.

"I'll cover for you with Mary," Blanche says to me, "if Clyde tells me what Buck's real name is."

He looks back and forth between Blanche and me, clearly confused, but also amused. "You must be skunked if you think I'll double-cross Buck." He points to the ceiling—I'm assuming at Buck's apartment. "He'll pull out that Colt on me. But I'll give you a hint, which should cover Bonnie for a few minutes. Six letters."

Blanche's forehead creases. "You'll be lucky if that gets you sixty seconds. You better hurry, Bonn."

She pushes me toward the bar's partition, and I duck under it, grabbing my coat as I go.

No words pass between us as Clyde and I go up the stairs, through the doctor's office, stopping at the door. Clyde helps me into my jacket, his fingertips trailing over my neck and leaving behind a trail of goose bumps. I break the silence with a soft, "Thank you."

It's a cool autumn night, and, outside, the air feels good against my flushed cheeks. Up and down the block, the streetlights cast halos of light. Clyde extends his arm for me to loop mine through, and as we walk from one halo to the next, I jump from thought to thought, finally landing on, "The song you sang me was beautiful."

"You mean *our* song?"

My cheeks flush. I hesitate. "About that . . ."

"I'm coming on strong, ain't I?"

"Yeah," I say, honestly.

Clyde laughs, a real deep-bellied laugh. "Blanche was right. I hate when that happens."

A smile cracks my lips. "Me too."

"Here's the thing, Bonnie—I've been waiting awhile to meet you." His free hand touches the arm I have looped through his. But then, as if he thinks better of it, he stuffs his hand in his pocket. "I came to the church the day you got married."

I gasp and remember Blanche's glance at the church doors in the middle of the ceremony.

"I couldn't stop my feet from bringing me there, after seeing you at

Doc's the week before. But I couldn't interfere with your happiness, if you truly were happy with that other fella. But when he left that first time—"

"When you helped Buck search my house."

"Yeah. Well, I saw him—your husband—walking up the stairs to Buck's place. It took all my strength not to stop him and give him a piece of my mind, and maybe even a black eye for ruining my chance to finally meet you. Then, after that fool left the second time, I was itching to see you. But Blanche said it wasn't a good time, that you'd push away any man who came knocking."

"She was right."

He stops us, and his body leans forward, toward me. "What 'bout now?"

Glow from the streetlights light up his face—a face so vulnerable, so honest—and I push aside my fear that I could be hurt again. Doesn't stick, though; those thoughts come back like a boomerang. I let out a breath and say, "Roy took a lot from me, and I'm just now getting my feet under me."

"I don't want to stand in your way, Bonnie. I want to stand by your side."

Another smile cracks my lips.

"Was that too much?" he asks, turning his face away. But all it does is make his adorable dimple easier to see. He turns back. "Listen, I'm heading out of town for a few days. Reckon that should be enough time for you to get back on your feet, no?"

I laugh, not expecting I would, so freely, or that my shoulders would sag at the mention of Clyde leaving town. "Where are you going?" I ask, before I can think better of it.

"This copper, fella named Jacobs, has it out for me. He doesn't have a warrant or anything, but he's always bringing me in to see if he can trip me up, get me cuffed. When he sets his sights on me, it's best if I get away for a bit."

"Clyde." I scrape my sole against the sidewalk. "Why'd you tell me that?"

"Bonnie." He tries for a smile, though his voice is serious. "I ain't ashamed of my past. It's made me who I am; it's brought me to this exact moment in my life, standing here with you."

I look beyond his adoration—I have to, or else I'll get swept away in a direction that may not be good for me—and I focus on what's important, asking, "But what 'bout your future? Don't you want more for yourself?"

"'Course I do." My gaze drops to his hand, which is subtly clenching and unclenching at his side. "But the name Clyde Barrow ain't carrying much prestige. I've been handcuffed ever since my first arrest. Makes it harder to go after what I want."

"What is it you want?"

Clyde chuckles. "Believe that's the fourth question you've asked me in a row." He gently touches the underside of my chin when I open my mouth, and says, "I want to be alive and free. With you."

"So I've heard," I whisper. "But, Clyde, I need to be with somebody who—"

"Someone more straight and narrow?"

I nod, staring at him, waiting for his next words. I hadn't realized, 'til this very moment, how badly I want a clean-shaven version of Clyde Barrow.

"All right," he says. "Starting over. A job, my own car—"

"Not just taking what you want."

"Yeah. It won't be easy, and not nearly as fun." He smirks. "But I can try for that. If it means you'll be my gal."

My smile starts slow, but soon stretches 'cross my face.

"Is that a yes?" Clyde asks.

"It's a yes to supper, if you ask."

"Bonnie." His voice is like a feather teasing my skin. "Would you be a doll and have supper with me when I get back?"

"Why, Clyde, I thought you'd never ask."

• • •

The next morning, Clyde's hypnotic voice still streams through my head. Ever so softly, there's a second voice, in my ma's tone, telling me that daydreaming 'bout a boy who evades the police ain't a good thing.

I skirt through the kitchen, avoiding my actual ma, and as I bike toward school, a sly smile spreads 'cross my face at how she doesn't know *I* evaded the police the first time I laid eyes on Clyde Barrow.

The difference was—and my shoulders tense as I cross the tracks into

Dallas—the police didn't know me from Jane. But Clyde . . . they've got an eye out for him, always do.

I hear it before seeing it, the roar of too many people downtown, and I jerk to attention at the unusual crowd. The bike's momentum carries me 'round the corner onto Elm Street. My brows scrunch. A blur of men in long dark coats and hats crowd the sidewalks, the streets. Shouting. Jostling for space.

Pedaling closer, I decipher their angry voices.

Wall Street.

Crash.

Their expressions are panicked, their fists are balled. I search the crowd for a familiar face, for my brother, for Mr. Champagne Cocktail, Blanche, or Buck. But I don't see anyone I recognize.

In a mob this large, it doesn't take long to pick up more tidbits of conversations and piece together why people are rioting in the streets. Yesterday, the market went into free fall, leading to the highest decline ever. Today, the market has just opened, yet the ticker is already falling behind, too many people selling their shares at once. One man proclaims, "Nothin' those fancy New York City bankers can do to save the day this time."

My mouth drops open, and I push my bike through the crowd, soon realizing it's easier to leave it propped against a nearby shop. Banging and screaming pulls my attention to a new ruckus. I use a nearby man's shoulder to prop myself higher, not caring I don't know him. Men are pounding on the bank's door. Inside, the bank tellers, their movements frantic, are trying to keep it closed.

Like part of a breaking wave, I stumble forward with those 'round me. The doors to the bank are thrown open, people rushing inside. I move with the men, nearly whisked off my feet, my heart beating erratically, 'til I'm at the door, then inside the lobby, having no other choice.

Outside, a gun is fired, followed by a string of gasps, profanities, screaming—some belonging to me. I grip the coats 'round me; otherwise, I know I'll lose my footing and be trampled.

Through the bodies, I catch glimpses of hands grasping the bars of the teller windows, shaking them. Even behind their metal cages, the bankers take steps back, heads rocking from side to side, palms up.

I yank on the coat beside me. "What's happening?" I scream to him.

A crashing sound.

I duck and use my arms to protect my head as shards of glass rain down. The room darkens. Steps away, another crash, another hanging light being smashed. The lobby grows even darker, louder.

"What's happening?" I ask the man again. He looks over me before down at me. "It's gone," he says, and then his voice is directed at anyone, his panicked face jolting from side to side. "All of our money is gone. Bank used *our* money to invest. Lost it all."

I tighten my grasp on the man's sleeve. "What?"

31

THAT NIGHT, WE STILL OPEN DOC'S, PATRONS STILL COME IN, but it isn't a typical night for us. It's as if the lights are dimmed, the music softened, the electricity in the air tapered. Mr. Champagne Cocktail isn't at his usual seat or pulling his normal antics on the dance floor. Not as many drinks are poured. Tips are lower.

I go home with less in my pocket—a lot less. In the morning, I go to class, but my thoughts are anywhere but here. They're stuck on yesterday, on how the crowd swarmed the bank's vault, banging their fists, doing nothin' but bruising their skin. That vault was practically empty. That was when I learned our money, everybody's, was spent "on margin." Roy used that phrase before, but I didn't know what it truly meant. I didn't know two little words could mean so much, or that the bank was allowed to use my money for their own gains, losing it all when the market collapsed.

Still, I have to check, see it again firsthand, not understanding how my money could be gone when I wasn't even playing the game. As I ride by the bank on the way home, my heart's in my stomach. The windows are boarded up, the door chained shut.

The crash didn't play favorites. It took the same amount from me that it took from Mr. Champagne Cocktail. He doesn't come in that night, either. Or the next.

Now I'm sitting at my desk, for show, my hands folded in my lap, my pencil untouched on my notebook. My teacher drones on, her own enthusiasm lackluster.

At the end of the day, it's time for the inevitable. The lower amount of money from Doc's ain't enough to get by on. But it was supposed to be. Doc's was supposed to keep me in school, and now it can't.

Frankly, that makes me mad. Madder still when I think I should be standing in front of this classroom by now, but 'cause of Roy, I'm a year behind, still sitting at this desk. And now I need to be out there, first in line, trying to find a second job. I can't sit here any longer. Not with nothin' in the bank. Not when jobs are going to be even harder to come by. I've no other choice but to sign away the last inklings of my dreams. For real this time. Permanently. With no hopes of coming back. I was kidding myself that my life would allow me to get my degree.

The door to the school's office opens soundlessly. My footsteps, as I approach the desk, seem too quiet. Everything 'bout this moment feels like my time spent at Southwest Dallas High School will soon be forgotten: the talent shows, my victory in the spelling bee, the poem I wrote that my teacher tacked to the blackboard.

At one time, those were notches in my belt on my path to becoming somebody. But none of those matter anymore, not when my desire to be more than poor dangles broken, like those damn lights in the bank. It was hard losing Roy, but I hadn't truly lost myself, 'til now.

I slide my disenrollment papers 'cross the desk, Bonnelyn Elizabeth Parker signed at the bottom, and the clerk accepts it. Just like that. She won't question me; she probably saw this coming after I took that long break. She won't frown at me; I'm over the legal dropout age. So few of my classmates graduate—now even less. I can't be the only one who'll trade in lessons for hours at some remedial job, if anyone is even hiring. I need to be up early, knocking on doors, before they are all gobbled up.

I thank her—for what, I don't know—and leave the tiny room. I don't want to think anymore 'bout what I just did. I don't want to think 'bout Buster once again being out of a job, or the possibility of my ma losing hers if people go back to making their own clothes to save money. My feet simply move, carrying me out of the building, a chill running down my spine.

"Bonnie?"

That name: only spoken by one person. Despite the darkness of my mood, my heart flutters.

Clyde leans against a tree at the bottom of the school's steps, arms and ankles crossed. He'd appear casual if it weren't for the concern etched 'cross his face.

"Clyde," I whisper, but in my mind, it's as if I scream. Maybe it's 'cause his presence speaks volumes. "You're back already?"

"Never left. Spent the last couple of days trying to find myself that job."

He never left. With each step down the stairs, I let that sink in.

"But then Blanche told me what you were up to. . . ."

"That girl's got a big mouth," I say.

He fidgets, uncrossing his arms, patting his palms against his thighs. "Should I not . . ."

"No." I stop in front of him. Clyde Barrow is all nerves, and I'd be lying if I said butterflies aren't taking flight in my stomach. We're inches apart, but I want to move closer. It'd take only a slight roll onto my toes to be in perfect alignment. "I'm glad you're here."

He pushes off the tree, steps closer. "How you doing?"

"I've been robbed." I drop my school bag to the ground. "That's what it feels like."

I could elaborate, 'bout how I'm not simply referring to my bank account, but Clyde is nodding.

"Never told you why I wanted to enlist, did I?" I raise a brow, and he says, "Wish I could say it was 'cause of duty, but I'd be lying. I spent too much time sitting 'round, wasting my day, or running away, trying to stay a step ahead of the law. But I wanted to make good, be somebody, and for the name Clyde Barrow to end in a handshake instead of a door in my face. So, when the navy turned me away, I felt like the floor fell out from under me. All my plans went to hell."

I nod, biting my lip. He gets it, maybe better than anyone.

"Remember this feeling, Bonnie." He takes a moment, swallows. "I reckon decisions are only going to get harder from here on out."

"That ain't what I want to hear."

Clyde intertwines his fingers with mine, looking down as if he's asking if I'm okay with the gesture.

I squeeze his hand.

"I'll make ya a deal," he says. "You keep clawing your way to what ya want, and I'll keep trying to do the same."

"But what is it that you want? You didn't quite answer that one the other day."

He swings our arms between us. Back and forth. Slow. "A stretch of land to farm. Been trying to find some for my family. Land is hard to buy, even harder to keep nowadays, but . . ." He shrugs, trails off.

"No, tell me."

"I want a simple life, away from the rules and the people telling me that I'm doing wrong."

"Maybe if you stop doing wrong, you'll stop hearing it." My voice comes out teasing, needing to help ease the tension in both our shoulders.

He smiles, his chest rising with a soft laugh.

I return his smile—not something I thought would happen today. But then I sigh, thinkin' of my Mason jar. Not what's in it but what I etched on it. Clyde and I aren't so different, both wanting more than the odds we were born with.

Clyde nudges my chin, brings my head up. "Hey, let's see that smile again. When one door closes, another one opens, right?" He smiles slyly. "But, on the chance it don't, you can always pry it open."

My face is mock-serious, or at least that's the look I'm going for. "It's that mentality that landed you behind bars in the first place."

Clyde chuckles. "You may be right, Bonnie."

"I take it you didn't have much luck finding a job?"

He rubs his nose. "Lots of those doors being slammed in my face."

"What 'bout Doc's? I know it ain't your thing, but . . ."

"This crash hasn't been kind to the doctor either. You know that." Clyde touches his ear. "And he's already done so much for me. I won't ask any more from him. I'll keep knocking on other doors, though. For you, Bonnie."

There I go, smiling again, eyes glued on Clyde. With his lazy smirk, he watches me right back, his eyes dancing over my face as if he's memorizing each plane, each curve, each freckle.

Love comes in at the eye.

A William Butler Yeats poem jumps to the forefront of my mind, and I'm happy Clyde stands across from me, that he came here for me.

"Well, what's going on here?" A looming figure appears beside us. A head taller than Clyde. Square chin. Prominent brows. Light, shaggy hair.

"Roy?" Disbelief and confusion pummel me like a rainstorm.

"Hello, *Bonnie*."

I glance 'round, as if answers are hanging in the air. But it's the same setting as always: a few trees, a few classmates, a laundry service and shoe store 'cross the street. "What are you doing here?"

Clyde angles himself in front of me.

Roy's once handsome eyes penetrate into me. "Him? You went from me to this lowlife?"

My mind races to keep up, not knowing how Roy recognizes Clyde, 'til I remember them sitting side by side, both watching me sing.

"I don't think who Bonnie spends her time with concerns you anymore," Clyde says, his tone even, dangerously even.

Before I can pin Roy with another question, he's got his hands on Clyde's chest. I stumble backwards, toppling onto the grass on my bottom. Their shoving throws them onto the promenade, against the school's steps. Roy lands on top of Clyde. His fist connects with Clyde's cheek.

"Stop!" I scurry back to my feet, standing over them, and try to pull Roy off Clyde.

He knocks me away as if I were nothin' more than a gnat, and I clutch the railing to keep from tumbling down the stairs.

I wipe the hair free from my face, backpedaling 'til I'm off the steps, disbelief still clouding my head. Roy's here. But why? Why's he back? Where's he been?

Though the most important question right now is how I'm going to get Roy off Clyde. I call for help. Again and again. Only a few of my classmates remain, all keeping a safe distance away on the promenade, backing farther away when the fight moves to level ground.

"Stay away from her," Clyde says, between his teeth.

"She's *my* wife."

"Could've fooled me."

Roy growls, lunging at Clyde. Clyde twists, grabbing Roy's coattails and throwing him to the ground. No hesitation, Roy is back on his feet, using the back of his hand to wipe blood from his lip. They circle each other, collide, arms intertwining like two bears in a fight.

"Enough!" I cry.

Neither of them pays me any mind. I run both hands through my hair, frantically look . . . scream . . . for help. No one 'round us does a thing. My heart leaps when I see two men jogging toward us. The sheen of their buttons and an emblem on their hats catches the afternoon light. I squint, cursing, realizing too late it's the police responding to my calls.

"Clyde," I whisper, panicked. "It's the law."

I've been a dumb Dora, screaming my head off when the police station is only a few blocks away.

Clyde's head pops up, the skin 'round his eye already blue. His grip on Roy loosens. Roy punches him again, connecting with Clyde's jaw. With my own fists, I pound on Roy's back, my voice turning to sobs. "Stop it, Roy. You'll hurt him."

Two hands yank me back. The policeman releases me, grabs Roy. The other officer has Clyde's arms behind his back before I can blink.

"Are you okay, miss?" the officer asks me.

"Yes," I say, and once again wipe my hair from my face. I run my hands down my coat. "This man," I say, and point to Roy, "attacked us."

The officer tightens his grip on Roy. The other policeman releases Clyde, who immediately backs toward the grass.

Roy spares me the slightest of glances. It ain't remorse I see. It's calculation, as if Roy knows more 'bout Clyde than he's let on.

"It ain't me you want," he says.

No. Every inch of me tenses.

"This here is Clyde Barrow."

"Clyde Barrow?" parrots the officer who released him. He yanks a weapon from his belt.

Clyde merely holds up his hands.

"Well, I'll be damned," the officer says. "Jacobs has been looking for you for quite some time." He turns to his partner. "It's always the women that lure 'em out of hiding."

"No." I quicken my steps toward Clyde.

"Stay where you are, miss," the officer says to me.

I stop, though every part of me wants to latch on to Clyde's hand again.

Run, I think.

Run, Clyde.

But he doesn't. He stands there, his eyes on me, as the policeman cuffs him.

32

UNDER MY COVERS, I STARE THROUGH THE DARKNESS, THE memory of the police hauling away Clyde stuck in my mind. He didn't resist. He stayed, those hazel eyes trained on me. Yet—I roll onto my side, a sliver of the morning light seeping above the covers—Buck told me how Clyde put up a fight when he was arrested for stealing turkeys.

That arrest has stuck with him, Clyde said as much, but it can't be why that officer has it out for him. It's got to be bigger than that.

And all these thoughts and unknowns equate to me staying in bed, feeling up and down 'bout Clyde, when I should be out looking for a job. Ain't that why I gave up school?

Buster's sudden voice fills the house—an outburst. I slowly get out of bed, find Billie still sound asleep, Duke Dog curled in a ball at the bottom of her bed. I stretch my arms 'cross my body, feeling a tug of pain where my tailbone met the ground.

My feet bare, I pad into the living room to investigate. Buster runs his hand through his hair. The radio is angled toward him, the volume low.

"Buster, what's wrong?"

An agonized-sounding growl escapes from my brother. "Do you even have to ask?" He heaves a sigh. "I got to stop listening, but I can't. So many people are now in debt 'cause of me, 'cause the 'powers that be' "—he mimes quotations in the air 'round the phrase—"told me the market was a sure thing."

Our beat-up couch cushion sinks, angling me toward my brother as I sit beside him.

"I'd paint a pretty picture, sayin' how investing was the key to wealth. Hate your factory job? No problem. Invest, and it'll save you from your miserable lot."

He slams his fist down, and I cover his hand with my own. But I'm angry, too—more than angry. Sullen. Roy went to Buster. He begged Buster for that pretty picture. Somehow, I'm the one left with all the broken pieces, when Roy's been God knows where, doing God knows what. Is it wrong that I took pleasure in seeing Roy hauled away by the police yesterday?

"Buster, what are you—what are we—going to do now?"

His fist tightens. "Shit, I don't know."

A new worry surfaces, one beyond concerns for my own future. "Are you in danger? Are your clients going to come after you?"

"They'd be stupid to come anywhere near me. Most of my clients borrowed money from the bank to invest." He gets up, starts pacing, eyes falling on the radio every few steps. "They come after me, they better come with a pocketful of cash to pay back the bank. I reckon their pockets are empty."

I hear a knock on the door, and we both startle. My heart rate quickens at the possibility that it's Clyde, or Blanche. Blanche said she'd let me know as soon as she heard anything 'bout Clyde from Buck.

"Sorry," I say to Buster, and motion toward the door.

He nods, his attention returning to the radio.

As I touch the doorknob, I realize I'm still in my nightgown, but it doesn't stop me from throwing open the door. My heart ticks even faster—but it's 'cause Roy stands before me, in the same clothes as yesterday. "What the hell do you want?"

"Bonn, can I come in?"

"No," I say. The cool air sends goose bumps up my arms, down my legs. I cross my arms, hiding how the cold affects my breasts beneath my nightgown. "I already know what you're going to say: 'Oh, I'm so sorry for gambling, for getting caught with a girl, for those horribly mean things I said to you. I'm even more sorry for leaving you for a goddamn *year*.' "

I leave out how my blood is also pumping 'cause he ratted out Clyde. I want to keep this 'bout us.

Roy sighs, scratches the scruff on his jawline. "But it's true. I am sorry. You've got to believe me."

"You've got a funny way of showing it, ambushing me yesterday like that."

Buster's footsteps stomp up behind me. I lay a hand on his arm, stopping him from storming past me.

"Buster," Roy says, "tell your sister she has to believe me."

My brother's expression screams *Not a chance*, but he calmly says, "I think Bonnelyn can make decisions for herself."

I smile at my brother before turning back to Roy. "I can talk for myself, too, but I reckon you've got it all wrong. Here's what you *should* be sayin': 'I know there's no explanation good enough for lying and cheating, for abandoning you, for putting you in a position where you had to walk away from what you want. So, I'm going to leave, for good this time.'"

"Yes. Yes to all of that, 'cept the part 'bout me leaving again." He keeps his tired eyes down as he says, "This is the first place I came after the police let me go, the only place I wanted to go. I left last year 'cause pride clouded my judgment and made me say things I didn't mean. Then I was scared you wouldn't forgive me. I didn't want to come back 'til I could give you the world. But the market took everything from me, and then some." He looks up, sincerity in his eyes. "In that moment, I realized I could lose everything, but not you. I can't lose you, Bonnelyn."

I uncross my arms and widen the door's opening. "So you're done gambling? You're done drinking, and cheating, and lying?"

Roy steps forward. "Yes. Yes, to all of it."

"You're ready to give me the world?"

"Of course. I'll do anything, Bonnelyn."

"Good," I say. I open the door farther.

"Bonn?" my brother says.

I wave off Buster. "'Cause, Roy, whatever sweet girl you're with next doesn't deserve to be with the Roy Thornton I was foolish enough to marry."

Using all my body weight, I slam the door closed in Roy's face.

Behind me, Buster whispers, "Damn."

I stand there, collecting my thoughts. I spent the past year wallowing over Roy, and for what? I loved Roy the boy. As a man and a husband, he leaves much to be desired. He only came back, pockets empty, 'cause he doesn't know what else to do. He doesn't love me. He loves the *idea* of me.

Like how I once loved the idea of him. I know this now. Hell, I convinced myself I needed Roy. But I don't. I slammed that door, and Roy's return only punctuates how my heart is pulling me toward starting over with Clyde.

"Buster, watch the window. Let me know when Roy's gone."

I rush to my bedroom to put on clothes, any clothes. Billie sits up in bed, rubbing her eyes. I kiss her forehead, feeling euphoric. She gives me a funny look, probably being that I'm springing 'round the room.

"He's gone!" Buster says from the other room.

I slide on a hat to hide my disheveled hair and race out the door, grabbing my bike.

With each cycle of my legs, I feel liberated. Clyde's lyrics may've been 'bout how I saved him, but if I wrote my own, it'd be how people come into your life when you need 'em most, and save you back. You save each other, like a partnership. Nothin' one-sided 'bout it.

I hop off my bike at the police station and lean against a fence 'cross the street. Clyde waited for me outside my school, and I'm going to wait for him now. Taking one deep breath after another, I tap my foot. If Roy was released not long ago, I reckon Clyde should be next. He's got to be next.

But my shadow gets smaller and smaller, 'til I'm standing on it, and people taking their lunch breaks crowd the sidewalk. I lean left and right, maintaining a clear sight of the station's door, and begin to second-guess that Clyde will be emerging. That officer, Jacobs, had been looking for him. What if they keep him?

Clyde walks out of the door, and I straighten, question forgotten. As if he was hoping I'd be waiting, his eyes—one blackened—immediately find mine from the other side of the street. I'm 'cross that street in a matter of seconds, cars be damned, and stop at the base of the station's stairs.

Clyde strolls down, the laziest of smiles on his face. "My goodness, ain't you a sight for sore eyes."

"I wish I could say the same for you."

He hoots with laugher and tugs on his dirty shirt, then his wrinkled trousers. "I got nothin' to hide from ya."

That sentiment seeps deep into my bones, thinkin' of the two-faced jerks from my past and how Roy is a real-life Jekyll and Hyde. I gently touch Clyde's bruised cheek. "Are you hurt?"

"From the pigs inside? Nah. In fact, I woke with a smile on my face, happy I was there when Roy came back for you."

My insides warm, and I impishly smack his chest. "Why didn't you run from the police, you fool? I know 'bout your 'heat rule.'"

Clyde wraps his arm 'round my shoulders and leads me back toward my bike. "That rule don't apply to you, won't ever. I wasn't going anywhere 'til I knew you wouldn't be left alone with Roy."

The seriousness in Clyde's voice stops me from smiling. That he stayed for me is exactly what I wanted to hear, needed to hear. But there's more I need to hear. "Clyde, I have to know why, specifically, they were looking for you."

Precious seconds pass while Clyde leads us out of the street, seconds when my confidence at coming here for Clyde deflates. He squares my shoulders to his, looks me straight in the eye. "I've looted some places 'round town, like the lumberyard. But—"

"But why?" That kind of theft shakes me more than cars. Automobiles are a luxury 'round here. Those people are doing all right for themselves. And Clyde gives 'em back when he's done. "Why, Clyde?"

"Land costs a pretty penny, Bonnie." He scratches his jawline. "I help my pa at the service station, but it's not adding up. To put money away, I skim from businesses, ones that have sold out to the Man. Big corporations own over half of our country's industry now. At least that's what Buck says. He knows 'bout this stuff more than me. All I know is I'm hurtin' for money more than them. They'll be fine. One month where their books don't balance. My family, though—they deserve a different type of life, away from here." He pauses, as if he's debating his next words, then says, "You serve illegal drinks. I took a little from the rich. Is it really all that different?"

Yes, I want to scream. But it's not. We both did it for our families. We both did it to become more. And Clyde says he'll stop. He'll stop, without asking me to do the same.

"No," I say, and my desire to be with Clyde overpowers my doubts. The distance between us seems inconsequential now. I walk into his chest, and his arms close 'round me. "Will they leave you alone now?"

Clyde sighs. "One can hope, 'cause big things await us, Bonnie."

"Oh, yeah? Like what?" I say into his chest, concentrating on the positive, not on Clyde being a target tomorrow, the next day, the next week.

"Anything." He kisses the side of my head. "Anything awaits us."

Clyde's response is whimsical. It ain't realistic, not with all I've worked for lying broken at my feet, but he makes me want to believe that anything is possible.

"Jobs?" I ask.

"I got something else in mind. The job hunt can wait one more day."

I ain't sure of that. I quit school to find a job. But it's so tempting to get caught up in the whimsical with Clyde.

He kisses the side of my head again. "How 'bout we have that supper?"

I pull back. "It's lunchtime."

"It's going to take a few hours to get to the Gulf," Clyde says matter-of-factly. "You've always wanted to go to the water, haven't you?"

I grin. "Yeah?"

"Okay, well, let's go."

"Right now?"

"There's no time like the present, Bonnie."

I roll onto my toes, fully anticipating the trip with Clyde, along with all those other unnamed things that await us. But, before this moment passes us by, I say, "You're exactly right. There is no time like the present."

With Clyde's shirt bunched within my hands, I pull him toward me. Slow, our kiss starts slow, then Clyde winds his hand 'round the nape of my neck, and I melt into him. When we part, breathless, remaining inches apart, the space between my legs still tingles.

• • •

Air whips at my hair, tossing it carelessly into my face, behind my shoulders, into Blanche's face. She raises her arms above her head, lets out a holler—so reminiscent of the photo of her, with Buck driving.

"How much longer?" Blanche yells into the wind.

Buck shakes his head. "Four hours and fifty-five minutes."

Blanche slumps down in the backseat of Big Bertha. I settle next to her, my teeth chattering, and meet Clyde's lazy smile in the rearview mirror.

"We've only been on the road for five minutes?" she says.

I laugh, but I also think, *Take your time*. This is the very first time, in my nineteen years of being on this earth, I've gone beyond Cement City and Dallas.

And I have Clyde to thank for that, even if Blanche made it possible with her car. Had to figure she'd insist on going on the trip as well.

I try to absorb as much of the passing landscapes, the cityscapes, the neighborhoods, the open road as I can, happy Blanche also insisted on having the top down, despite the chill in the air.

Buck's and Clyde's voices drift back to me, arguing over the best route to take. Clyde holds up a map, pointing to his preferred path. I smirk, enjoying the scenery and the boys' bickering. Though, after last night's lack of sleep, worrying over Clyde in jail, along with the weight of facing life again after we return, it doesn't take long before my eyes grow heavy.

When I wake, my head is on Blanche's shoulder and we've stopped. I lift my head and Blanche dabs her sleeve.

"Thank goodness you're up. You've been drooling on me like that dog of yours."

I wipe my chin, pull my collar higher to shield more of my neck from the too-cold air. "What're we doing?"

"Just filling up the tank."

"Where's Clyde?"

"Inside, getting some grub."

I spot him through the service station window. Buck is chattin' it up with the gasoline attendant. "Buck can yap with anyone, can't he?"

Blanche nods. "Probably talking business. His family owns a service station back in Dallas."

"They *own* it?"

"Yeah, fooled me. I saw dollar signs when I learned that. But it ain't like that. They're making enough to get by. Buck told me they lived under their wagon when they first moved to Dallas."

"Why'd they come to Dallas?"

"They were farmers."

"Oh," I say, not needing more of an explanation. I know the war led to a rise in farming, all those mouths to feed in Europe. But with the war over, those countries didn't need our farms anymore. Lots of families here had to pack up and head toward cities to afford putting food on their own tables. Ironic, really. "Well, Clyde's got a hankering to move back. He told me he's been looking for land."

"Yeah." The humor vanishes from her voice. "Dallas has some bad memories for their family."

"What do you mean?"

Buck's whistle announces his return, and Blanche clamps her mouth shut.

"All ready to go," Buck says, and hops into the driver's seat. Blanche leans forward in her seat, wrapping her arms 'round Buck's neck. "Where's Clyde?" he asks us. "The lad tire of ya already, Bonn?"

I narrow my eyes, earning a boisterous laugh out of Buck.

Clyde returns, and we're on our way. In less than an hour, we've left behind any type of civilization, and Big Bertha bounces down a rocky dirt road. Blanche and I exchange *This car better not get a flat* looks. On either side of us, wildflowers form a path in one direction: toward the sea. Though, ahead of us, a dune, speckled with sea grass, blocks any glimpse of the waves.

"We're here!" Buck proclaims.

Blanche squeals and ushers the boys out of the car so we can put the roof up and change into something more suitable for the Gulf—not that either of us will go in the freezing water.

The boys scoff at Blanche's silly desire to wear bathing suits, and I don't blame them.

We emerge, beach shoes on our feet, stockings to our knees, shorts—cut higher than I'd like—covered by a one-piece top. Skintight, all of it. I pull my jacket tighter against the cold as the boys whistle, no longer scoffing.

Blanche shimmies her shoulders, not bothering to button her coat, then jumps into Buck's arms, wrapping her legs 'round him and nearly whacking him upside the head with her parasol. Buck carries her up the dune, laughing at her antics.

Clyde holds out his hand. "Truth be told, I wish it was warmer so you didn't have to wear that coat."

I blush but swag my hips a bit more than usual as I walk toward Clyde. He takes my hand, and we trek up the sand mound together, the sun setting on our backs.

This is exactly how I wanted seeing the Gulf for the first time to be: seagulls chirping in disjointed melodies, my feet sinking into the sand, and sea grass swaying gently in the breeze, whispering to us.

The dune makes me work for each step, 'til there it is.

Freeze.

I want to commit every moment of this to memory. Me. Clyde. The sea. I knew it'd be vast—Ishmael said as much in *Moby-Dick*—but, my God, I feel like the blueness could swallow me from a hundred feet away. What I didn't know, and what I want to remember forever, is the security Clyde's hand brings me. Somehow, it makes the Gulf—hell, maybe even the world—more approachable.

"Let's go," Clyde says with a grin.

Buck is already running toward the water, Blanche still in his arms, her parasol and coat left behind in the sand. He bounds into the water, pants and all, his laughter deep and mischievous. Blanche screams at him, trying to shimmy up him like a tree while Buck dips, the waves catching her butt.

"You'd be smart not to try that with me," I warn Clyde.

"I know better than to cross my lady." Dimples appear. "Come on." He tugs my arm and we slip down the other side of the dune's bank, the sand giving way 'til we reach the bottom.

I tilt my head back and breathe in the salt air. "I feel so insignificant."

Clyde pulls me closer. "Not to me."

It's one of his cheesy lines, but it still makes me swoon, and it's something else I'm eager to stow away to always remember.

I squeeze Clyde's hand. "I ain't sure I'll be able to go back to reality after this trip."

He stretches out our arms as we pass on opposite sides of a large piece of driftwood. "I always believed it's best to take life one day at a time. There ain't ever any promise of a tomorrow."

I sigh. "Well, if tomorrow comes, I'm going to need to find myself another job to get by. Doc's is slow, got nothin' in the bank—"

Clyde brings us back together, the driftwood behind us. "Then we'll make the most of it tomorrow. We both will."

"I'm . . . I'm okay with that."

I spent enough time planning out my life, worrying too much 'bout having it all figured out. But I'll make it work, taking it as it comes. I'll still be there to help my ma. Little by little, I'll rebuild again. The waves crash beside us, coming inches from our feet, receding at a slower pace. I smile.

We find ourselves stretched out on the sand, blankets wrapped 'round us, the sun fading behind the dunes, the waves becoming lost in the darkness. With a fire crackling at our feet, we pass 'round that dinner Clyde promised me, along with some brown.

"I've an idea!" Blanche announces.

I pause, the bottle nearly touching my lips. "Uh-oh," I say, my voice a higher pitch than usual from the giggle juice.

Blanche snatches the bottle from me. "Let's play a game." She looks over the fire, focusing on each of us. Once satisfied with our accepting expressions, she goes on, "It's called Sip or Swear It. Someone says a statement. If it's something you've done, naughty friends, you sip." She holds up the bottle. "If not, you have to swear on your mama's grave you haven't."

I put both hands to my cheeks, my lips squishing.

"Bonnelyn looks nervous," Buck says.

Clyde chuckles, but he shifts uncomfortably, too.

"I'll go first," Buck says. "Sip if you've ever snuck out of your parents' house."

"Child's play," Blanche says, and swipes the brown.

"Give me that back." Buck takes a mouthful. "Someone had to lead, as an example for Clyde."

"Exactly," Clyde says, and snatches the bottle next.

I sit there, unmoving.

"Ya got to swear it, Bonn," Blanche says. "Say, 'I swear on my mama's grave that I've never snuck out of the house.' "

I do.

"Louder," she says.

I raise my voice.

"Louder! Make me believe it."

I scream, then add, "But, in my defense, I've snuck *in* plenty of times."

"Semantics," Blanche says. "How 'bout this: sip if you've ever"—her brows dance—"in a church."

No one moves to claim the bottle, 'cept Blanche.

"Baby," Buck says, and shakes his head at her, "I do believe you're going to hell."

"I'll save you a place," she says back, and climbs into his lap, leaving her blanket behind. Buck envelops her in his. "Bonn, it's your turn."

I lick my lips, try to think of something wicked I've done. Determined, and driven by the warmth from the hooch, I rack my brain, my lips pursing as something comes to me. I wiggle my fingers for the bottle and Blanche hands it over. "Sip if you've ever seen Blanche Iva Caldwell's boobs."

I throw back a gulp.

Buck doesn't say a thing, just holds out his hand, reaching 'round an openmouthed Blanche in his lap.

Blanche shrugs. "I reckon I've seen 'em plenty of times." Buck messily pours whiskey into her mouth.

Clyde waves his hand, gesturing toward himself. "Sorry, Buck, but your girl wasn't exactly discreet when she was changing in the car."

Blanche bursts into laughter and holds the blanket tight 'round Buck as he tries to shimmy out from under her. Clyde jumps up from the sand, palms out, but he's laughing like a goon.

"Aw," Blanche says, giggles again. "Would you look at that? My bubs bring us all together, make us a gang."

"Oh, we're a gang now?" Buck says.

"Yes," I say. Clyde settles next to me again, and I lean into him, the fire flickering in front of us. "I like that. We're the Barrow Gang."

33

MY HAND DANGLING OVER THE COUCH'S EDGE FEELS EMPTY, vacant. I struggle to open my eyes. My first fear is that someone came for Clyde, nailed him to one of his crimes. But his pillow and blanket are stacked neatly on the floor of Blanche and Buck's apartment, and I relax back into the couch.

"Did I wake you?" I hear.

A smile pulls at my lips even before I turn my head. There he is, the signs of sleep still in his hair, perched on the armchair, pulling on his second boot. A little sand from the Gulf has slipped out of his shoes.

"Tell me that clock ain't right and we've only been back for two hours." I push to a sit and yawn. "What are you doing up?"

Clyde shrugs. "It's tomorrow, ain't it? I'm going to make good on my promise to ya."

This boy is something, off again to find a job, to do right by me. But I laugh, saying, "I don't know if the birds are even awake."

A mischievous look 'crosses his face. "How 'bout I go find out?"

After a soft kiss on my forehead, he's out the door, pounding the pavement, and I sink back into the couch. I should be out there, too. I pull my blanket up to my chin. But, right now, I can't help wanting reality to wait a few more hours, like as soon as I start looking for that job, I'm officially replacing my teaching dreams.

The door flies open.

"Bonnie!" Clyde calls, breathless, as if he just took three flights of stairs two steps at a time.

He says a bunch more. All my tired brain deciphers is how I need to hurry. Lassies are swarming, whatever that means.

Clyde barely gives me the opportunity to use the restroom, swish some water 'round my mouth, and throw a coat over my shoulders before we're out the door.

"Where're we going?" I grip the stair's railing, happy that Clyde's pace has slowed, but he only tells me again to hurry.

He whisks me onto Elm Street and points. "See all 'em down there?"

I squint. "Yeah?"

"Those lassies are outside Marco's Café."

"Okay?"

"Marco's has got a spot open for a waitress."

Clyde drags me again, my mind still playing catch-up. There's got to be twenty, no, at least thirty women crowding the entrance to the café, all of 'em hollering 'bout being picked for the job.

I laugh. "How do you reckon I'll be the one to get it?"

He half turns toward me, winks, pulls me faster.

"How is there even a job up for grabs?" I ask, between ragged breaths.

Clyde taps his noggin. "Marco's being smart, gonna stay open twenty-four hours a day, hoping to become the spot where everyone goes for gossip 'bout our damned country. He needs one more lassie to add to his rotation."

My stomach hitches with excitement. Marco's Café is in the heart of Dallas. That means one thing: it pays well, much more than my old diner did. I'd be stupid to pass this up.

Within steps, we're at the back of the crowd, the very overwhelming crowd of women, all with their claws out. The door to the café opens and out walks Marco—or a man I assume to be Marco. The volume of pitched voices rises. He points to a woman, asks her if she's ever waitressed before. He waves her off, points to another. Women jockey for Marco's attention. Elbows jab. Hats fall.

I bite my lip. Going up on my tiptoes does nothin', and it ain't looking good for me, way back here. I shoot Clyde a panicked look.

"Get up on my shoulders," he yells over the roar.

"What? No. I'll crush you."

"Please, you could fit in my pocket."

"If you had a bigger pocket."

His eyes shine with amusement, but also earnestness, as he motions to the frenzy of women in front of us. "It's now or never, Bonnie. What did I say before, 'bout sometimes having to pry open that door of opportunity? Uncle Sam certainly won't do it for you."

I groan. That's for damn sure. Clyde drops to one knee, and I climb onto his shoulders. We wobble—once, twice—'til he's steady on his feet. I fling my arms into the air, waving my hands. My coat slips off my shoulders and Clyde tightens his grips on my thighs.

I feel like a loon, but I also feel good, determined, as adrenaline courses through my body. I match the other women's screams for attention, and then it happens: Marco points directly at me, up here on Clyde's shoulders, taller than the rest.

• • •

Blanche spoons some cheese grits into her mouth, making a very satisfied-sounding moan.

On my feet, I glance 'round, shushing her. A man and woman at the adjacent table lift their brows, though the husband's expression differs from his wife's. His is nonchastising.

"These here grits are to die for." Blanche licks her spoon, and I refrain from peeking again at the man. "Much more suitable to Blanche's standards than your old diner's."

I refill her coffee, my head bobbing. "Pay's much better, too."

Blanche drops a sugar cube into her coffee, eyeing me. "Does that mean you're going to get off my couch soon? Can't blame you for not wanting to share a room with Billie no more, but I've lost track of how many nights you've stayed with us."

Nine, starting the night we got back from the Gulf.

Three nights with Clyde on the floor, me on the couch, arm dangling over the edge, not wanting to let go of his hand.

Six nights with Clyde on the couch, me in his arms, holding me against him, the warmth of his breath caressing the back of my neck, heating my entire body.

I don't plan on stopping now. "Now we're even, after you stayed at my ma's house all those nights."

Blanche presses her lips together. "I wasn't doing any funny business on your couch."

I laugh. "Well, I don't got enough for my own place. And Clyde's had no luck finding another job."

Blanche's eyebrow arches. "You ain't going to deny necking with him?"

I hold up my pointer finger, telling her to give me a second, and slip away, leaving Blanche with her mouth hanging open. I go from table to table, refilling coffee, checking on orders, pleased the morning rush has been busy. Between here and Doc's, I'm busy enough to help Ma pay our bills. I'm thankful she's still at the factory, and with only a slight dip in her hours. With Buster striking out at finding something new, my tips wouldn't be enough by themselves.

Blanche's booth is in the corner, always giving her a clear view of me. I chuckle to myself—even more when I walk back toward her and her stern face.

"Well?" she says.

Wiping my hands down my apron, I say, "This is me, not denying that"—I lower my voice—"necking."

Blanche's face lights up. "Petting, too?"

"I ain't going to answer that."

Blanche's interest finds its way back to her bowl, and I think to myself, *Petting, too.* But no more than that. I finger my wedding band, not certain why I keep this thing on. Another reminder, to go along with my tattoo, perhaps? Maybe I'll toss aside the silver band once I finally make something of myself. Not as a teacher. I ain't trying for that right now. Not only has life stood in the way but also that wound feels too fresh, too painful to push on right now. So I'm doing as Clyde suggested, taking every day as it comes but keeping my sights set on the big things that await us. "Anything," he said. *Anything* could await us.

"Wouldn't it be amazing," I say to Blanche, "to make it big, to see your name in lights one day? Clyde and I could do it together. He'll play. I'll sing."

Blanche smirks, a spoonful of grits halfway to her mouth. "I reckon Clyde's more likely to see his name in black and white than in lights."

"Nope." I let the end of the word pop. "Not anymore. He's given that all up."

"So I've seen." She taps her spoon on the edge of her bowl. "Actually, I wouldn't mind if Buck did, too."

I let out an exaggerated gasp. "I thought the fact he's been arrested was scandalous and delicious?"

"Clyde's idea of a quiet life on the farm don't seem half bad. Buck in overalls, nothin' underneath, sounds mighty scandalous and delicious to me."

I glance over my shoulder. A few people are doing that thing where they nonchalantly raise their chins to look 'round, for me. "I worry 'bout that."

"Buck in overalls?"

"No, farming. It ain't an easy way to make a living." Though I could see myself in that life with Clyde. Really, any life with Clyde.

Blanche shrugs. "Not sure there's an easy way for anybody nowadays." She points to her empty bowl. "Can I get more of this?"

I leave to put in Blanche's order and begin my loop of the room, beginning with the round tables by the windows.

In between *What can I get ya?* and *Would ya like me to top you off?*, I keep an ear to the gossip, still mostly 'bout what's being called Black Tuesday, the day the market fell apart. Most say it started falling apart with the opening bell. Like madmen, people were shouting, "Sell! Sell! Sell!" It's no surprise over sixteen million shares switched hands. One woman, caught up in the drama, claims it took fifteen thousand miles of paper to record it all. When another woman starts yapping 'bout the investors who jumped from windows, I turn away, and the table in the corner catches my eye.

Clyde and Buck have joined Blanche.

I smile, anticipating Clyde's smooth voice as he greets me.

He'll pull me into his lap, and I'll have to playfully squirm and say, "Let me go. I'm on the clock."

The whole time, though, I'll want to find that spot, just south of his shoulder, that God may've made for the sole purpose of me resting my head.

Clyde runs a hand along his hairline, and that's when I'm snapped from my fantasy. His face is etched with concern. I rush over to my friends. "What's going on?" I ask Clyde.

"Bonnie." His eyes ain't as vibrant as usual. "I'm sorry, but I got to go. We just came in to borrow Blanche's car."

Blanche's expression is just as concerned as Clyde's. I turn back to him. "Why? Are you okay?"

"Just a situation at home," Buck answers for Clyde.

"Someone tell me what's going on."

"I will," Clyde says, and half stands to sidestep from the booth. "Later. What time are you done today?"

"Now," I say, lying, and untie my apron. "I'm done now. I'll tell Marco I ain't feeling well."

Clyde studies me, and I hate that I can't tell what he's thinkin'. Finally, he says, "All right. Let's go."

The four of us pack into Big Bertha, boys in the front, girls in the back. I manage to hold my questions as Dallas passes us by, becoming less populated as we head toward Cement City, not toward the Barrow home. Finally, I whisper to Blanche, "Where're we going?"

She leans closer. "I reckon it's better you know what's going on. Remember that train accident a few years back?"

I strain my memory. "You mean," I whisper, "when that little girl was hit?"

Blanche nods yes, then toward the Barrow brothers. "I started to tell you before, how Dallas has some bad memories for their family . . ."

I don't need her to say more. I also remember how, at the time of the accident, the little girl was the same age as Billie, eight. My heart drops. The situation was, and still is—as Clyde stares out the windshield, motionless—devastating.

Neither of the Barrow brothers has said a word since we left the café. We turn down a dirt road lined with trees, parallel with the tracks, and my chest tightens as I realize we're going to the spot where their little sister was killed.

I gasp, hoping it wasn't audible, hoping I ain't right: today's the anniversary of that little girl's death. Blanche squeezes my hand. When Buck slows the car, I stare at my knees, afraid to see what awaits us.

"You can stay in the car if you want," Blanche whispers.

She reaches for the door handle, and I slowly look up, find a gray-haired man and woman sitting alone, with their backs to us, at the edge of the tracks. The setting is serene: the sounds of the rushing river on the other side of the tracks, splotches of wildflowers lingering into the colder months, the man's arm 'round the woman.

But all those things somehow make this worse, that something so beautiful could be the setting for something so tragic.

Three car doors close, one after another. A crash of thunder follows, and I notice the darkening skies. Blanche slips her hand into Buck's, but they move only a few paces from Big Bertha. Clyde walks on alone. I bite my lip, not knowing how to act.

Clyde's and my relationship is new. Does he like to deal with his emotions alone? Or is he the type of person who wants me there for support? He hesitated before he said I could come along. Why?

I stop torturing myself and get out of the car. But I stop next to Blanche, not following Clyde. He now sits beside his mother.

"She's down here every weekend," Buck says in a low voice, his sad eyes trained on his family. "But it's always harder to get her to leave on this particular day, and with a storm coming . . . Clyde's the only one who can ever get through to her."

"I'm so sorry, Buck."

He presses his lips together, nods. We stand there in silence, the darkness becoming more prominent with each passing minute. Finally, Clyde and his parents stand, and his ma hugs him, her shoulders shaking. It's almost as if his daddy needs to be in constant contact with her, shifting with every motion she makes, as they begin walking down the road, away from us and toward an old, beat-up car.

Buck exhales. "We'll give 'em a few minutes."

'Til what? I think. Blanche heads back to Big Bertha, and I follow, unsure what's going on. In the front seat, they exchange quiet voices. I feel out of place in the back of Big Bertha, out of place having witnessed something so private in Clyde's and Buck's lives.

When Buck begins driving, I'm happy to be moving, to be doing something. But that relief turns to a jumble of uncomfortable nerves at the sight of the Barrows' service station. My mouth goes dry at the thought of walking through their door, as if I'm invading something too personal.

"Cumie makes the best food," Blanche says.

Buck pulls the parking brake, rubs his hands together. "Ya can say that again. Ma's got the golden touch."

The shift in their tones, mannerisms, is jarring.

"You'll see, Bonn."

"Okay." The word comes out prolonged, a question mark attached to the end.

My feet are heavy as I follow them to the apartment. Thunder rumbles in the distance, the sky dark. 'Cross the street, Old Jed sits on his stoop and, honest to God, part of me would be more eager to spend time with him than to go inside the Barrows' solemn home—if Clyde ain't happy to see me there.

The scent of cinnamon greets me, and I breathe in the comforting fragrance. Embers are fighting to take hold in the fireplace. Everything is neat and tidy, same as I remember it from before. Mr. Barrow sits in an armchair, reading the paper. He glances up and smiles, before wetting his thumb and noisily turning the page, giving it a firm shake to set the new page in place.

It's as if I've walked into another world, even more so when I trail Blanche and Buck to the kitchen. Mrs. Barrow, short and plump, flutters from the stove to the sink to the counter.

"'ey, Ma!" Buck calls.

She turns, her hands finding her apron.

"Oh, Blanche," Mrs. Barrow says, and rushes over to envelop her in a hug. She then turns to me. "And you must be Bonnie."

I've a face full of breast before I know it, and I stutter out a muffled greeting.

She pulls back, eyes bright, even brighter smile. "Tweed kettle and grilled tomatoes, how's that sound?" she asks.

No one objects—I don't even know what it is—and Mrs. Barrow claps her hands together.

Clyde strides in through a back door, arms full of tomatoes, a few large raindrops staining his shirt. Nerves speckle my stomach, unsure how he'll react when he sees me.

"Oh, good!" Mrs. Barrow inspects the tomatoes he plops onto the counter. "Reckon this will be the last batch we get before winter comes. Now out, out." She ushers us from her kitchen.

I'm the first one to stumble into the living room, and I'm inclined to keep walking right out the door, into the rain.

Clyde grabs my arm and whispers, "I was hoping they'd bring you, despite everything. How you holdin' up?"

"Me?" Truly baffled, I study his face for any sign of the pain I saw down by the river. "I should be asking you that. But you look okay. Everyone seems fine."

He aimlessly plucks a chord on his guitar, which leans against the couch. "Situation is a wee bit strange, huh?"

"Yes, a wee bit."

"Come on," he says, and leads me out the side door, the rain pummeling the tin awning above us. Clyde slides his hands 'cross my belly, propping his chin on my shoulder. "That, inside," he goes on, "is how my ma copes, one extreme to the other. She grieves at the tracks. But when she's within those four walls, it's as if she pretends her life is different. Like if she scrubs a little harder, cooks fish that's perfectly pink, fluffs the pillows just so, it'll make our family whole again."

"Oh, Clyde." I face him, wrapping my arms 'round his narrow waist, at a loss for words. His heart thumps under my ear, and it's one of the best sounds I've ever heard. Strong. Resilient. Fearless.

"I'm afraid I don't believe it, though. We're born whole, then life takes a little more from ya each day, each experience, each loss. It ain't something you can get back."

"But it's okay, I think . . . to pretend." I tilt my head to see his face, not disagreeing with him, but understanding that's how his ma gets by. At seeing the slight curl of his lips, I smile coyly. This boy sees through my words. He knows I ain't only referring to his ma. Here I am, spending my days in between daydreams and Clyde's arms.

"There's nothin' wrong with pretending while you mend, Bonnie. But my ma's been doing it for years now. Breaks my heart. Why I'm going to get her out of here."

I sigh and rest my head again, staring out into the rain. "You're a good man, Clyde Barrow, and here I am, tying your hands behind your back."

"That ain't true."

"But it is." Guilt forces my eyes closed. "The work's not coming, and you're barely putting anything away for that land. You ain't even going out to look for it. All 'cause of me."

"Hey, Bonnie?"

The rain may sound angry 'round us, but when I look up, Clyde's got an understanding look in his eyes, and I talk first. "Clyde, I'm starting to think that you had it right all along." I'm starting to fully realize what Blanche said forever ago, 'bout life needing elbow grease, 'cause right now I've got a B version of Doc's and I'm working a dead-end waitress job. That ain't how I pictured myself thriving. But Clyde has it worse—doesn't have a real job at all, no way to save for what he wants. A thought comes to me, and I say it aloud. "Life will do what it wants with you, huh? Eat you up, spit you out. Comes a point when you got to push back, make things happen for yourself."

"I don't like hearing ya say it, Bonnie." But he nods, keeps nodding. "It ain't fair, though."

"It's not," I say into his chest.

He puts space between us, 'til I see his out-of-place smirk. "So you are in agreement, then, that I should meet your ma as soon as possible?"

"Huh?"

"It's not fair you met my family but I haven't met yours. So I'm going to make that happen."

I laugh, and, honestly, this has been one of the most backwards afternoons of my life.

"So, tomorrow then?" he asks.

"Sure," I say, and throw up my arms. "Seems I'm agreeing to everything nowadays."

Clyde laughs. I do, too. But I also swallow, nervous 'bout two things: basically telling Clyde he's free to run amok, and how my ma will react to me bringing home a convicted felon—on a Sunday, no less.

34

IT'S BEEN FORTY-SEVEN, -EIGHT, -NINE SECONDS OF SILENCE 'round our dinner table. Clyde sits in Daddy's old seat, which probably ain't winning him any points, 'specially since the last boy who sat there was Roy.

I chew my chicken more thoroughly than need be, willing Billie to say something. But for once, the cat has my sister's tongue. At least Buster has stopped glancing at his shotgun, which he specifically spiffed up earlier and conveniently left leaning against a cabinet. The only one who's fine with Clyde being here is old Duke Dog, snoring at Billie's feet.

Clyde doesn't seem to mind my family's cold shoulder. He's a proper gentleman, complimenting my ma on her lemon chicken and asking Billie 'bout school. With Buster, I told Clyde to mind his own, unsure of a safe topic for him to talk 'bout with my brother. Clyde's done good. Still, I'm seconds away from leaping out of my chair and turning on the radio for background noise.

Ma clears her throat.

"So, Clyde, do you have any hobbies?"

He wipes his mouth with his napkin, and I pray to God an illegal activity doesn't come out when he pulls that napkin away.

"I like to tinker with cars. My family owns the Star Service Station over on Eagle Ford Road, so I get my hands dirty now and again."

Tension eases from my shoulders. "Clyde also reads quite a bit of poetry."

"Is that so?" Ma says, her voice even.

"Yes," I answer for him. "William Butler Yeats."

"My ma and I like to read it together," Clyde says.

"And he plays the guitar."

"Oh?" my ma says, but she doesn't direct the question at Clyde. "Anything else you'd like to tell me 'bout Clyde, Bonnelyn?"

Billie chuckles, and my cheeks flush. Ma's pointed look doesn't help matters, either, probably questioning how much time I'm spending with this boy, 'specially with me not biking home 'til after the sun comes up, to bathe and change clothes.

Clyde jumps in, saying, "I taught myself to play the guitar a few years ago. I'm not very good and can't read the music, but for me, it's all 'bout how the music vibrates through my bones. It's beautiful, makes me feel alive."

Ma nods, softly chewing her chicken, and I let out a small breath.

"Your daughter and I actually started a song together, but we have a few more verses to go."

"Do you now?"

I subtly shake my head at him, a plea not to elaborate on the song, even if my ma is finally showing interest. I'm rather confident she won't want to hear 'bout how I saved him from a hooligan trying to kill him while he was bootlegging liquor.

"Your daughter's been a great inspiration," Clyde says, with an impish grin.

"Growing up, I used to sing in the church choir," Ma says in a gentler tone, and sets down her fork.

I smile; the first glimpse of the real Emma Parker is shining through.

"Say, that must be where Bonnelyn gets her voice."

Ma chuckles. "I'm flattered."

Billie says, "She's going to be famous one day. Did Bonnelyn tell you how she wanted to be an actress when she was little?"

" 'Til," I say, "I realized I wasn't any good. I'm plenty fine with simply going to films."

"Yeah, best to stick with singing, Bonn," Buster says, rocking back on the chair's back legs.

"Don't listen to your brother," Ma says, and motions for Buster to lean his chair forward. "You never know what the future will bring, sweetie."

I don't, but I'm relieved to know that, after winning over my family, Clyde will be part of that future, without us having to go behind my ma's back.

Someone knocks on the door, and Duke Dog shoots to his feet, barking incessantly.

"It's probably Blanche," I say, talking over the noise. "You know how nosy she is; probably wanted to see if Clyde would crash and burn."

As I walk to the door, Clyde says to my family, "I ain't much for fire."

I smile to myself, and pull open the door. "Blanche Cald—"

"Good evening, ma'am," an older fella says in a flat voice. He tips his hat, covering his overgrown brows. A shiny emblem catches my eye as he returns his hat to his head.

"Yes?" I throw my weight to one side, keeping a hold on the door. If he's here for Roy, this conversation won't take long.

"I'm Officer Jacobs."

And, just like that, my heart could dislodge from my chest.

"I have reason to believe that Clyde Barrow is inside your residence. And this here"—he holds up a paper—"is a warrant for his arrest."

I bite the inside of my cheek, my brain rushing to think of something to say. I land on, "Who?"

"Clyde Barrow, the man who was arrested a few weeks ago with your husband. That name doesn't ring a bell?"

I swallow. "Not a lick."

"Mrs. Thornton . . ."

I grimace at the use of Roy's surname.

"It'll be unfortunate if I have to arrest you for obstructing justice."

Officer Jacobs drops his hand to his cuffs. Mine tightens on the door. "Don't come to my house and threaten me. Now, if that's all—"

He exhales, then shouts, "You hear that, Clyde Barrow? We know you hit up Buell Lumber. Someone came forward. Claimed they saw ya. I've got enough to put you away now, and if you don't show yourself, I'm going to haul this young lady down to the station for questioning."

I move to shut the door, but Jacobs slides his foot into the doorway.

I'm left counting the beats of silence, willing Clyde to keep his butt in my daddy's chair, hoping I'm a better actress than I think, and praying for the stalemate to be over, for the officer to give up and leave. But footsteps grow louder behind me, and I curse under my breath. Eyes trained on the officer, I keep my feet where they are.

Two hands touch my shoulders, gently moving me aside, and I want to cry out for Clyde not to hand himself over. But he will; he already proved that once.

Clyde holds out his arms, and my eyes blur as I watch him get cuffed for a second time. The officer yanks him forward and Clyde resists, straining to turn to see me.

"I ain't leaving you, Bonnie. I'll be back for you."

The officer snorts. "Not for a long time."

Inside, I'm screaming with every ounce I've got for that pig to take his hands off Clyde. He saves me. I save him. That's how this is supposed to work.

I take a step forward, stop. I know getting myself arrested will do neither of us any good. I need to be strong for Clyde—for myself—to give us a chance. So I raise my chin and say, "I ain't going anywhere."

35

AFTER A FEW WEEKS OF VISITING CLYDE, I KNOW THE ROUTINE. Get the bus at ten. Check in at McLennan County Jail's front desk. Let an overweight, underloved guard frisk me with lingering, probing hands. Then wait in the cold, sterile, cement-walled room 'til the clock strikes eleven and the inmates all file in.

I shift uncomfortably in the hard chair and eye the other visitors. Some try to quiet their young children. Others look worn down, as if a strong breeze could knock 'em over.

I've chatted with a few of 'em. Many of their men fell apart after the crash, either committing robbery after losing their money or simply having too much time to find trouble after losing their jobs. Unemployment is up, along with aggression. Both are the highest ever.

Of course, there's the other half of the men, like Clyde—and his cellmate, says his wife—who were on a path to these cells long before the stock market took a nosedive.

The old Bonnelyn wouldn't be okay with a man stealing to give himself a leg up, but Bonnie, she's a different story. Clyde picked me up when I was at my lowest point, ironically giving me what I've desired all my life: love and stability. Just not in the way I expected. I couldn't ever feel poor with Clyde by my side.

I've had plenty of time to come to that conclusion, plenty of time to think 'bout a life without Clyde. And I'm still here, staring down the barrel of his five-year sentence, 'cause of the thefts he committed over the past few years. After he was sentenced, my ma said, "It's time to let him go. Clyde ain't the right boy for you."

But I told her, "We thought Roy was, and look how he turned out. With Clyde, I know *exactly* what I'm getting, and that's a man who'll always be good to me."

That's stability. Clyde's words, and more so his actions, prove to me that we can have the kind of love that's long-lasting and enduring.

The doors to the visitation room click open, and I sit up straighter, eager to see my man. A parade of inmates walks through, in their white prison garb, followed by armed guards. Clyde's cellmate settles at a table 'cross the room, visiting with his wife, Olive. Nice girl.

Scruff hides Clyde's face, but it can't hide his happiness when he sees me. My stomach flutters with excitement and desire, but also with apprehension, as I scan his body for signs of the other inmates and those damn guards roughing him up. In prison, Clyde's smaller size makes him the runt of the litter.

His limp is improving. But a new gash cuts 'cross his forearm. There's always something new.

He sits opposite me, and I stretch my hands over the table, stopping an inch from his skin, yearning to touch him. I tried that once, and a guard wagged his gun at me a second later.

"How are you?" I ask him.

One, then two dimples show. "Better, now that you're here."

I smile, too. "You say that every time I come."

"It's true today, will be true the next time you're here."

"I hate to think 'bout you here another day."

"Bonnie, it'd be okay if you didn't come. You shouldn't be spending your days off at a place like this."

"Nonsense." But I think 'bout his sentence and nearly shudder at what all that time could do to both of us. Clyde stuck in here. Me, stuck in my static life, waiting for it to begin again with him.

He moves his hands closer to mine as we talk, as each precious minute passes us by. When the guard yells that time is up, it takes all my strength not to leap 'cross the table and cling to Clyde's neck.

"No," I say, breathless. "It's too hard to leave you."

Clyde licks his lips. "I'll be okay, Bonnie."

"Will you?" I ask. Will Clyde's carefree demeanor survive five years in this place?

He stands, offering me a single nod. It's clear, even in his baggy clothing, that he's lost a few pounds. I bite my lip, stifling a cry, as Clyde shuffles back through the door with the other inmates.

Later, at Doc's, it's no surprise that Clyde is all I can think 'bout. Five years—five years without him, besides a couple measly minutes, and only on the days where work ain't standing in the way. I shake my head. That's not okay. So much wasted time, when we could be creating verse after verse in our song.

Our song. In between mixing drinks, I do my best to write down the lyrics on a napkin, needing to see the words, to imagine the melody, to reread the lyrics again and again.

Blanche banters with a new patron, but I don't have the heart to get to know the random faces that replace our regulars. Regulars are a thing of the past, no one having enough money to let off steam more than once in a while.

I should be happy the dance floor is half filled tonight, that, despite all those empty pockets, people still come to drown their doubts in our bathtub gin, but I keep thinkin' how Clyde once wanted something so badly he had it inked on his body. Yet it was ripped away from him, unfairly, against his control.

And me, I'll have three letters forever etched on my skin, now nothin' more than a reminder of a dream that chipped into pieces. I thought I'd lost it all. Then Clyde helped me find myself again. He opened my eyes to a different kind of life, a blank page to fill, a song to finish. I can't let the possibility of that happiness be taken from me.

And that's what's happening. The world today ain't giving Clyde and me a fighting chance. It's backing me against a wall: I can not see Clyde for five years, let those four walls confine him, break him, change him.

Or I can take matters into my own hands.

Isn't that what I told Clyde, that there comes a point when you got to push back, make things happen for yourself?

I thumb the napkin, brushing over the words *Bonnie and Clyde, meant to be, alive and free.*

I'd gladly turn the guards' guns on them, demanding they let Clyde go, if I could end that five years right this second. I can feel that gun in my hand. I'd do it. I'd do it for Clyde—and me.

I bite my lip. Even if I got him out, our lives wouldn't be the same. The name Clyde Barrow would be equivalent to "fugitive." But I'd still be saving him, even if he'd have to lie low. Lower than before.

It'd be a new way of living. Together. That's what's important.

Pressing my lips together, I release a *Hmm* from deep in my throat. An idea forms. I peer 'cross the room, note how Buck is manning the poker tables.

"Blanche!" I shout over Rosie's singing. "I'll be right back."

"Where you going?"

"Just need a minute." I snatch my bag from beneath the bar.

I push through the sweaty bodies and cigarette smoke, also pushing away any thoughts that I could be losing my mind, and make my way to Buck's apartment. Pulling out the key that Blanche gave me, I let myself inside.

It's dark, eerie. But it's probably only eerie 'cause I'm sneaking 'round like a lovesick fool. Honestly, I don't doubt that Blanche and Buck would support the crazy plan bouncing 'round my head, but the fewer people involved, the less that could go wrong.

I risk turning on a light and begin to scrutinize Buck's apartment, opening drawers, peeking beneath cushions, scouring closets. With a smile, I find what I'm looking for, beneath his mattress: a pistol.

It's heavy in my hand, it feels heavier than the gun I fired in that alleyway. Maybe it's the implications behind the gun's purpose.

I won't be firing at a wall this time.

• • •

My palms are sweaty. My heart thumps so loud I hear it in my ears. I was unable to sleep last night, telling myself again and again that my crazy plan will work, and, today, tiredness weighs me down. Still, I urge my legs faster toward the jail's entrance, afraid that, if I slow, I'll lose my nerve. I'll start thinkin' 'bout what'll happen if things go sour. I could end up in a cell, more fragile than Clyde. Clyde's sentence could get doubled. The wrong kind of shots might be fired.

Hell, I realize how loose my plan actually is. But I can't turn back now.

Stopping in front of a prison guard, I hand over my bag to a second one, spread my legs, extend my arms to the sides.

The first man palms my waist, his fingers firmly pressing into my dress. He slides his hands lower, bending as he goes. The top of his head brushes against my breasts. His hands wrap 'round my outer thighs and I gasp, my heart skipping a beat. I force breath back into my lungs and say, "You go any farther inside my legs and I'll report you for lewd behavior."

He chuckles to himself, as if it's a game, then moves his hands lower, down the outsides of my legs, 'round my ankles. I will my pulse to slow as he runs a hand along my neckline, taking care when examining my breastbone. His hot breath hits my face as he drags his fingers through my hair, way too close for comfort.

Finally, he's done. Disgusted, I yank my bag from the second guard, who is now finished with his search, and head toward the visiting room. When I'm sure no one is watching me, I slip inside the restroom and kick open the doors to empty stalls. With my skirt hiked up, I tear the tape from my inner thigh, from right over Roy's name, and carefully remove Buck's pistol.

In the mirror, I watch my chest rise, fall. I've done it; I've smuggled a gun into the prison. A new wave of panic hits me, centered on the fact that, after I do this, after I pass it to Clyde, I could be sending him to his death. He could get caught—I rub my mouth—but he could also escape. I remind myself of a simple truth: we can be together, now, not five years from now.

When life closes one door, another opens, or you can pry it open. Right?

The chance of being with Clyde *now* is worth it all.

I take one final look at myself in the mirror—lips thin, cheeks rosy, eyes vibrant—and I'm ready. In the visitation room, I slink into a seat at the table farthest from the guards and lay my bag on its side, the opening facing the wall. I subtly glance at Olive, who is also waiting for her man.

When Clyde comes into the room, I fluff my hair, smiling pleasantly. "How are you?" I ask him in a sugary voice.

As if he's gauging my odd behavior, his response comes out slower than usual. "Better, now that you're here."

"I've decided that I ain't coming no more."

Clyde's head twitches, like he heard me wrong.

I smile at his reaction. Before he can truly be let down, I extend a shaky hand and tap the inside of my bag, momentarily revealing the gun.

"Bonnie," Clyde says between his teeth.

"Yes?"

He presses his hand so hard, so long, against the table that his fingertips turn white. His eyes scan the room, though his head remains still. "I reckon you're a better actress than you give yourself credit for."

"Why, thank you," I say.

"And mighty proud of yourself." He chuckles. "My God, Bonnie, what am I going to do with you?"

I shrug. "Someone once told me that big things await us." I lower my voice. "But not in here."

He glances again at the bag, and my smugness begins to wane, nerves setting back in. It's almost time.

Clyde must notice the change in my demeanor, and he shifts in his chair, clearly uncomfortable with not knowing my plan.

I rack my brain for a way to fill the void in our conversation, so we don't raise suspicion, but then the commotion begins.

Olive has her man, William, in an embrace. The guards yell at them. She only holds on tighter. Guns raised, the guards stomp 'cross the room toward them.

I shove my hand into my bag, thrust the gun toward Clyde. The scraping sound it makes against the table seems like the loudest thing I've ever heard, despite the uproar in the room.

He fumbles with the gun—the first time I've ever seen him panic—but quickly recovers, bending to put the gun under his pant leg.

When he straightens, heaven help me, there's amusement in his eyes. "Bonnie Parker, you're going to be the death of me."

"Me? I thought I was the one who defies Death's plans?" I ask, referencing a line in our song.

The guards yell, at last gaining order, and they demand that all inmates vacate the room.

“Tonight,” Clyde whispers. “By the river.”

I subtly nod. I have to clasp my hands together to stop from touching him; I'm hungry to feel the softness of his lips. As he walks away, a deep sadness comes over me, my body feeling heavy at the realization that the last time I did feel his touch was when he moved me aside to surrender to the officer.

That won't be—can't be—the last time.

36

PALM FACING UP, I EXTEND MY HAND, AND WAIT.

Blanche twists her lips, one hand on the doorframe of her apartment. "You expect me to give you Big Bertha's keys without knowing why?"

"Yes," I say, trying to hide my annoyance and worry and fear. "I will tell you all 'bout it after I get back."

"Which will be when?"

"By the morning." I let out a controlled breath. "Blanche, come on. This is important."

"But then—"

"Listen, Buck will be very happy when I return. Give me your keys for him."

"You mean Freddy?"

I shake my head in confusion, irritation. "What?"

"I'm calling him Freddy 'til he tells me his real name."

"Your daddy's name?" I squeeze my eyes closed, searching for more patience, continuing before Blanche can respond. "Please, this is important. I need your keys."

She sighs. "Fine. You know, *you're* becoming the dramatic one."

"Mm-hmm," I say, and snatch the keys she dangles in front of me.

Once in Big Bertha, my foot itches to press the pedal to the ground. I arrive faster than the bus normally takes, much faster, then loop 'round to the back of the prison grounds. An old dirt road lies beyond the fenced exercise yard and a row of trees, parallel with the river.

I park, hidden by the trees, but, second-guessing myself, I drive more—then a little more—searching for the best cover. I reverse one, two, three trees.

Get it together, Bonnie.

I cut Big Bertha's lights and engine and force my hands into my lap.

The breath I let out is slow, almost as slow as the setting sun. I'm not sure what time Clyde plans to make his escape. But I'm here.

I roll down the window, shiver, and promptly put the window back up. 'Cept, I realize I can't hear as well, and what if Clyde calls my name? The glass goes down again and I peer out into the darkness.

Just as promptly, the trees play with my eyes, branches becoming limbs, the trunks becoming Clyde's torso. Worse yet, my mind wanders again, to dangerous places, places where Clyde gets caught, his jail sentence gets longer, or—I shudder—he finally succumbs to Death's plan.

No. I pull the napkin from my pocket and squint, barely making out our song in the darkness, but needing to hear Clyde's voice: *Death is a five-letter word, with a five-finger clutch . . . It cornered him, pitting him against the bigger man . . . By the throat, edging closer, nearing Death's final touch . . . Then there she was, light in the dark, defying Death's plan . . . She stared it down, held on tight, fired off a shot all her own . . . Ohh, oh, oh, oh, death for the boy has been postponed.*

Those words, those positive words, are what I need right now, even if only in my head. They remind me how I've never truly told Clyde how I feel 'bout him. Studying the cadence, the sequence of rhymes, the rhythm of Clyde's lyrics, I flip over the napkin.

The first line comes to me in an instant.

Dreams can be forgiving, with second chances to strive.

I scribble it down, now unable to see the ink on the napkin. I place my finger on the last mark of the pen, so I know where to write again, and compose the next line in my head, making it personal, using *she*, the way Clyde used *he*.

But only if—she says from the heart—dreams are big enough.

No. I clear my mind, rejiggering the sentiment, pulling from how I felt right before I'd met Clyde.

But only if—she says from the heart—all is truly lost.

Yes. The next words fall into place, as I imagine myself at that breaking point.

Love has failed, hope is gone, feeling no need to survive.

I pause and imagine the guitar's beats. This is where the rhythm quickens; this is where it all changed for me.

Then there he was, after all this time, saving her, no matter the cost . . . He looked into her eyes, held on tight, told her he'd never let go . . . Ohh—I draw out the word in my head—*oh, oh, oh, hope for her future has been restored.*

I put down my pen. I smile, despite how my heart aches for Clyde. It's too dark to read the lyrics back to myself, and I hold 'em against my chest. That helps.

This is going to work. It has to.

But, with each passing minute, I fall victim to thoughts of everything that could go wrong. I light one cigarette after another and jump at every delicate sound outside the car.

It's not Clyde. It's never Clyde.

My fingers tap faster. My knee bobs up and down.

This ain't going to work. Too much time has passed. He's been caught. The confidence I've forced into existence wanes. That limp, those bruises . . . they'll be child's play compared to how Clyde is punished 'cause of my foolish, love-struck plan.

I hear a burst of noise—the clattering of a chain-link fence. Then voices, two male voices. I try to swallow, but my mouth is too dry, and my mind buzzes with activity. Prime the engine? Shout Clyde's name? Hope it's him?

It's got to be him, and every second I'm doing nothin' is another second Clyde can be caught. I flick the headlights, hold my breath, and pray it's Clyde's eyes that see the burst of light.

It's sickly quiet. My chest burns for air. Two figures creep 'round a tree, and I exhale.

Clyde. I know it's him.

A sob escapes me. I'm running toward him before I even knew I left the car. Jumping on him, I wrap both my legs 'round him, nuzzling into his neck. Cinnamon and nicotine. That scent somehow still remains, after all this time locked in a cell. Or maybe it's my mind once again willing what I want into existence.

Clyde holds me with one hand, strokes my hair with the other, whispering my name into my ear. I was worried he wouldn't survive, but it's not 'til this moment that I truly grasp the danger he's put himself in, that *I've* put him in, by giving him that gun.

When he puts me down, we're back at the car, and Clyde gently raises my chin, kisses me. My knees go weak. I want more kisses, an endless amount of them, but another man stands beside us. I wipe the tears from my eyes, happy my plan worked, and hold out my hand toward him. "You must be Olive's William."

"In the flesh. But let's do our introductions in the car, yeah?"

Clyde laughs, already jogging to the front of Big Bertha to prime the engine.

Soon we're driving away from the prison, driving toward freedom.

William whoops in the backseat. "Holy shit, man. We did it."

I squeeze my hands together so tightly—from nerves, from excitement—that my knuckles ache.

"How on earth did you fellas escape?" I ask.

"You tell her," William says to Clyde. "It was your brilliant idea."

"Not without risk to you, Will."

"Ain't that the truth." There's humor in William's voice.

Clyde reaches over from the driver's seat, frees my hand from my own tight grip. "We've got you to thank, Bonnie. Will and I had a good laugh over how you conjured this whole plan, involving his girl."

"I'm mighty thankful, too," William says. "Even though those guards gave me a good whop on the back of my head when Olive clung to me like a baby monkey."

"Sorry 'bout that," I say.

"No bother. I got a thick head."

"Now *that's* the truth," Clyde says. "When they came 'round for roll call, those guards turned white when they saw me holding the gun to Will's thick head."

My jaw drops. "You did what?"

"I had to make 'em think I was going to shoot him."

"Risky, right?" William says from the backseat. "Wasn't sure they'd give two shits 'bout me. But Clyde here was acting like a raving lunatic, his spit flying everywhere. He made me look like a saint."

"Eventually, they had to open our cell to save Will from me."

"Clyde and I jumped the guards."

"No," I say in disbelief. "But what if—"

"It worked, Bonnie. We're fine. I took a guard hostage and Will helped me round up all the guards. Put 'em into our cell."

From William's voice, I can tell he's grinning when he says, "It's easy to escape when there's no one to stop ya."

I sit there a moment, part of me in shock that they pulled it off. I lift Clyde's hand to my lips, kiss him, noticing the bruises on his knuckles. I hate to think how they got there.

"Buck's going to be so excited to see you," I say. "I mean, I know you might have to lie low for a bit."

Clyde doesn't respond.

"You hear me?" I say, not remembering which ear is his bad one.

"Man," William says behind me. "I ain't looking forward to this conversation with Olive, either."

I twist to see William better. "What do you mean by that?"

"Bonnie," Clyde starts. "Listen. Will and I agreed we'd give ourselves an hour to say good-bye."

Good-bye? No.

"For now," Clyde says. "They're going to be looking for us, and we got to get out of the state, let our trail grow cold."

"So . . . what?" I say, my voice hitching. I pull free from Clyde's grasp. "You're going to leave me?"

That's not how this was supposed to go. How did I not fully think that through?

William's arm shoots into the front seat, pointing. "There. Second house on the right."

Clyde slows the car. They get out and exchange a few words, a pat on the shoulder, before Clyde eases back into Big Bertha.

It may be childish, but I won't look at him. I can't look at him.

"I'm not choosing this, Bonnie . . . to hide out."

"How long?"

"A few months, maybe. Got to see how much interest they take in us."

I half turn. "Okay. So take me with you."

"No, Bonnie. I can't do that. It's too risky. But I'll be back for you. Trust me. I ain't letting you go." He blows out a low whistle. "Still can't believe you put yourself at such risk for me."

I wait a beat, swallowing the fact we're not going to be together. Not yet. Then I face him fully and say, "For us. I risked it all for us. This is what we do, right? We save each other, trust each other." I lick my lips. "I ain't happy 'bout you leaving, but I know you'll be back." From my pocket, I pull out the napkin and hold it out to him. "I wrote you something."

"What's this?"

"Read it, silly. It's our second verse."

He angles the napkin toward the streetlight. "Bonnie, your handwriting is atrocious. Wouldn't ever be able to read this."

I playfully smack him. "I wrote it in the dark, while waiting for you."

"Read it to me?"

As I recite each word, it's as if Clyde goes through the emotions with me, 'til his hand is lost in my hair. "It's true. I won't let go. I'll fight for us 'til the very last breath I take. That was beautiful, Bonnie. Truly."

"So were your words. Here," I say, and flip over the napkin. "Did I get the first verse right? I wrote *those* in the light, but I had to pull 'em from memory."

"I'm sure you remembered 'em perfectly."

"Will you sing me our chorus?"

And there's that lazy smile I've come to know and love. He clears his throat dramatically, and I laugh. Setting our verses aside, I climb into his lap, both of us snug in the driver's seat, to feel the rise and fall of his chest as he sings, "*'Cause lean closer, listen close . . . How the story ends, no one knows . . . But one thing's clear, you'll see . . . Bonnie and Clyde, meant to be, alive and free.*"

Like before, that last line, that last note, hangs between us. And in my heart, I know nothin' has ever been more true.

We're Bonnie and Clyde.

AUTHOR'S NOTE

First, thank you for riding shotgun as I told my version of Bonnie's origin story. It was a blast to bring to life and I hope you enjoyed experiencing Bonnie's immersion into the speakeasy world and later into the arms of Clyde Champion Barrow.

But how much of what you read is real? A lot, though I don't claim to be a historian. A lot is from my imagination, too. Much of the imagined elements are because there are varying accounts of Bonnie's and Clyde's lives and their run-ins with the law. I took what I could find and ran with it.

The name Bonnelyn is an example of something I crafted. Even before I wrote a single word, I imagined Clyde to be the one to coin the name Bonnie. Then I went searching for a name that could truly show her evolution from a church-going gal to the image we all have of Bonnie as an infamous outlaw. Bonnelyn has a nice wholesome ring to it, wouldn't you say?

Bonnie was the middle child. Buster was her older brother, Billie her little sister. Emma, a seamstress, was her mother's real name. Their dog was even named Duke. They lived in Cement City. Her daddy, Henry, did die when Bonnie was young, but he wasn't in the war. He was a bricklayer. Not much about Bonnie's childhood or background is known, but I tried to pull as much as I could. She was a good student. She married Roy Thornton (though she did so at sixteen). He did leave her multiple times (even more times than I depicted in this story) and turned out to be a pretty bad dude. In real life, Bonnie also dropped out of school. Was it because of the stock market crash? Probably not. But since the market crashed during the timeframe of my story, I wanted to show a plausible way in which the crash could have affected Bonnie and her motivations.

Bonnie and Clyde both came from poverty and wanted more for themselves.

Bonnie's love of films and music, performing in school pageants and talent shows, working at Marco's Café, her tattoo, sneaking Clyde a gun in jail . . . also all true, although I took creative liberties with specific details.

Clyde, he's a mixture of real and make-believe as well. He had an older brother, Buck, but I didn't include their five other siblings. Clyde didn't have a little sister who was struck by a train.

But he was from a poor farming family who later owned the Star Service Station on Eagle Ford Road in West Dallas. Clyde did have aspirations to find farmland again for his family. One of his first arrests was for stealing turkeys for the holidays. It's also based on real life that he got himself in trouble for not returning a rental car and for robbing Buell Lumber, along with many other businesses. Clyde did get a *USN* tattoo, tried to enlist in the navy, and received a medical rejection because of a childhood illness, possibly malaria. It's also true that, although Clyde's hearing was damaged, he had an ear and knack for the guitar.

And he sure did fall for Bonnie instantaneously.

If you kept cursing me for making you wait for Bonnie to officially meet Clyde, that's because they didn't do so until Bonnie was nineteen. I hope it was worth the wait. There are various accounts of how this happened, so I had my own fun with it, borrowing a favorite pastime of the Roaring Twenties: dance marathons. There was simply no way I could write a book set in the 1920s and not put us in the middle of a foxtrot. Bonnie's speakeasy life, in general, is one I fabricated, including shifting the release year of Fats Waller's song "Ain't Misbehavin'" from 1929 to 1927. I read accounts of Bonnie and Clyde going to juice joints, but your guess is as good as mine if she ever served drinks in one or crooned onstage.

Blanche is a real member of the Barrow Gang, but I gave her some extra love in my book. She didn't meet Buck until 1929, after he'd been divorced twice and had a few kids, details I chose to leave out. However, Blanche's voice is one of the first that spoke to me and because, in real life, she had a large role (although it turned out to be a reluctant one) in Bonnie and Clyde's life of crime, I wanted her to be heavily involved in Bonnie's fictional life leading up to their crime spree. Bonnie and Blanche weren't childhood best friends, but I think their depicted relationship works well in the story, and I had such a good time writing their banter and made-up history.

There's a lot more I could mention. Emma didn't have cancer and Buck was never stabbed (to my knowledge). Clyde really was a short dude with big ears. Their song lyrics are all mine. But I want to keep this (relatively) short; you did just read a novel, after all. If there's anything I didn't include here that you're curious about being fact or fiction, please feel free to ask. You can find me at jennilwalsh.com.